DERRICK
Murder 01

MW01126412

Copyright

Version 1.0
Copyright © 2014 Julien Rapp
All rights reserved

This book is a work of fiction. Characters, names, places, and events are the products of the author's imagination or used fictitiously to tell an entertaining story. Any resemblance to any actual people, living or dead, business establishments, events, or locations is purely coincidental.

Chapter 1

A tall man with a light tan, wearing white slacks and a dark blue polo shirt shielded his eyes from the sun with his hand as he stared off into the distance. "And Etsuo Kagawa slices one off to the left and into the mouth of a great white."

"Your humor grows tiresome Mr. Packard," Mr. Kagawa shot back as he pulled another ball from his bag. He was in his late fifties and several pounds overweight. He had short salt and pepper hair, and his face showed more than a few lines of stress.

"Sorry, Mr. Kagawa. But if you are going to build a golf resort of your own, you should learn how to play the game, and how the banter on the course works."

"Banter Mr. Packard?"

"Business Mr. Kagawa. And out here you need to learn how to play both."

A third man, Mr. Sando, stepped over to them. "And you definitely should not be playing at a thousand a hole." He and Mr. Packard laughed as they walked over to their golf carts.

A stern looking man in his early fifties, with pure white, short-cropped hair strolled up toward Mr. Kagawa. His skin was light with a pink tinge, and he was wearing a starched, tan, button-up shirt. He bowed slightly as he walked past. "Perhaps the fourteenth hole will be luckier for you."

Mr. Kagawa dropped his driver into the bag and followed the others on toward the green.

Paul Covington, a childhood friend of Derrick Dreadlow, and now a friend of Derrick's new friends in Hawaii, was staring at his computer screen in the study of his New York apartment. He reached for a mint in the candy dish by his laptop and sat back. He grinned as he popped it into his mouth. "Professor Quon Li my friend. Christmas is coming early for you this year."

Late that evening, a green glass and bronze banker's desk lamp was the only light on in the office of Mr. Etsuo Kagawa. He stared aimlessly at his tidy teak desktop, then sat back and nervously adjusted his light blue tie as he talked on the phone. "I have given it a great deal of thought. And my answer is the same as last time."

"I am sorry you feel that way, Mr. Kagawa."

"I assure you sir, that it was a most generous offer," Mr. Kagawa said as he turned and gazed out his office window. The sky was clear. Two bright stars twinkled off to the west as the moon sank lower. "But I... we... cannot accept it."

"This is our final offer, Mr. Kagawa. Perhaps you would like a few more hours to reconsider your position."

Mr. Kagawa pulled a handkerchief from his pocket and wiped beads of sweat from his brow. He slipped it back into his pocket. "No. No, I... I have made my decision." He sat up and straightened out his shoulders as he spoke firmly. "We are not going to continue to do business with you and your associates."

"We will be in touch, Mr. Kagawa."

"But I just said..." The line went silent.

Mr. Kagawa slowly placed the phone back on his desk. He took a deep breath as he sat there in silence. His gaze drifted out his door into the dark and empty office where his secretary would sit during business hours. He stood up, stepped over to the window, and gazed out at the lights of the city below. His mind was racing. He had probably just made the second worst mistake of his life. However, he knew he had to draw a line. He had no choice. He would lose his hotel if he didn't. Everything he had worked for, fought for.

Kagawa stepped back to his desk. He pulled out his handkerchief again and wiped more beads of sweat from his brow. He dropped it onto the desk then picked up the phone and dialed a number.

A woman's voice answered. "Hello."

He turned to the window. "I need to speak to Mr. Fukuhara, please. It is extremely urgent."

"One moment please." He stood there as he watched the light of a plane glide effortlessly across the sky.

"This is Mr. Fukuhara."

Mr. Kagawa turned back to his desk. "Good evening Taka. It is me."

"You delivered our answer Etsuo?"

"Yes."

"What was his response?"

"He said that he would be in touch."

"But you told him no?"

"I did."

They both fell silent.

Chapter 2

It was a quiet Sunday morning in Honolulu. The sky was a clear azure blue. A gentle breeze blew in from the northeast, and the temperature was a comfortable seventy-six. Derrick Dreadlow reached over and turned off the stove. The aroma of freshly squeezed oranges filled the air mixing with homemade Dreadlow huevos and a fresh pot of coffee.

"You have been busy this morning haven't you?" Haruku Kobayashi said as she entered the kitchen in her condo with his goddaughters Kattie and Becky. The girls yawned as they pulled out chairs and sat down at the table.

Derrick beamed as he prepared a plate for everyone. It was the first day of his vacation do-over. The first two weeks were derailed by multiple deaths and an attempt at saving the country from a major international incident. OK. Maybe it was only two deaths. No one knew for sure. But keeping the entire incident out of the press was the primary goal assigned to Derrick and his team. And that they had accomplished. They solved the case and kept it quiet.

Now, his biggest worry this morning was not to overcook the eggs. He and his goddaughters were all looking forward to time together, swimming, fishing, and seeing the sights of Oahu. It was the stuff that typical tourists to the islands do. And today was a special day for the girls. Derrick had promised them a combined party for both their birthdays. However, he had not had the time to work on it, let alone set it up. Fortunately, Haruku, his friend, as well as his partner's sister, came to the rescue as usual. She and her family had an afternoon and evening all planned. They would arrive at her parents' house at 1:00 in the afternoon for fun and of course, food.

It was a slow start to their day. Haruku and the girls were still dressed in robes and slippers as they sat around the table.

"This smells wonderful," Haruku said as Derrick set plates of huevos in front of everyone. "Just how early did you get up this morning?"

"Around 5:30."

"Did you go for a swim?" she asked.

"And I squeezed in a workout downstairs in your gym."

"Uncle Derrick? Why do you swim in a pool when you have a big ocean right across the street?" Kattie asked as she reached for her juice.

"I can count the laps better." He looked up as the doorbell rang.

"I'll get it, Derrick. Are you expecting anyone?" Haruku asked as she got up from the table.

"I'm on vacation," he said as he put the pan on the counter by the sink. "So it could be anyone."

"That's not funny."

"You're not going to work today are you Uncle Derrick?" Becky asked as she picked up her fork and poked at the black beans covered in salsa.

"No," he said as he set bowls of fruit down in front of the girls. He reached out and hugged both of them. "Nothing in the world is going to take me from my favorite goddaughters today."

"Do we have jelly?" Becky asked.

"Jelly on huevos?"

"She puts jelly on everything," Kattie said.

"I'll go take a look." He opened the door and looked inside.

"Mommy?" the girls called out.

"Huh?" Derrick banged his head as he stood up and turned around.

Becky and Kattie jumped up off their chairs and ran over to Nancy.

Derrick closed the door. "Hi. What brings you to the islands? The gorgeous weather?"

"Derrick Dreadlow," Nancy said in a deep, stern voice. "We need to talk. Now!" It wasn't her usual soft congenial tone. It was the one reserved for when she was really ticked off. Derrick could see her body tense as she spoke.

"Ok…"

"Can I get you some coffee?" Haruku asked.

Nancy ignored her. "John can watch the girls while we go out into the other room." She turned to Haruku. "And you come with us, missy."

That can't be good Derrick thought as he glanced over at Haruku. She shrugged and raised her hand's palms up as they followed Nancy into the other room.

"Was France not to your liking?" Derrick asked as they filed out of the kitchen.

Nancy turned to Derrick. Her eyes narrowed. Her nostrils flared. "I've come to take the girls home Derrick."

His mouth dropped open. "Home?" He stared at Nancy as she turned red. "Why?"

"Why?" She shoved a large envelope marked urgent into his chest. "This is why!"

Haruku stepped closer to Derrick as he opened the envelope. He expected something inside to bite him as he slipped his fingers in and pulled out several photos. He wished it had been over that quickly.

Haruku reached up and covered her mouth as she gasped at the top image. "Oh my god!"

Nancy pointed to the photos. "What is this all about?"

Derrick looked up at Nancy. "Where did these come from?"

"They were delivered to our hotel room as we were getting dressed yesterday morning." Nancy pointed to the photos again. "What are these Derrick?" She shifted

4

on her feet and pointed to Haruku. She shook her fist with one finger sticking out a mere inch from Haruku's face. "And why is this woman taking care of my children!"

"This isn't…" Haruku stammered. She tried to take a step back, but the coffee table was behind her.

"What? Are you going to stand there and lie to me? Are you going to tell me that isn't you passed out on the floor in that… that… whatever it is you're wearing?"

Derrick flipped through a couple more photos. They were all of Haruku drinking and fighting with other women at the club. And one where she was beating on the bouncer Amosa.

"That was…" Haruku tried to get the words out as she stood there wide-eyed, her mouth open gasping for air. Her eyes watered and her body shook as she turned to Derrick then back to Nancy.

Derrick turned to Haruku then back to Nancy. "This isn't quite what it appears to--"

Nancy reached over and yanked the photos out of his hands. She pulled out the last photo and shoved it in his face. "And what the hell is this?"

He leaned back to look at the photo. Oh shit, he thought as he stared at the photo.

"Oh god," Haruku gasped again.

Dawn broke over the horizon. The long shadows from the rising sun stretched out across the sleeping city. A silver and blue helicopter landed on top of a building overlooking a park on Flower Road.

The city of Kobe was still quiet at this early hour. The helicopter idled as a man in his late twenties stepped out. He wore a black sports coat, black slacks, and a black turtleneck sweater. He was in stark contrast to the two other men in light gray suits, white shirts, and light blue ties, escorting him across the rooftop. They passed through a doorway leading to an inside elevator. They all stepped in. One of the men in gray pressed a button on the express elevator down to the first floor. From there, the young man stepped out of the building alone and walked across the street to a bench in the park. He sat down beside an elderly gentleman with sparse gray hair. The old man was feeding the pigeons from a paper bag.

They sat in silence for several minutes. Finally, the old man reached into the bag again and pulled out a small black lacquer slide box with a samurai warrior in a striking pose on top. He slid the box open. Inside was a tiny USB drive. He closed it and handed it to the younger man. The younger man slipped it into his pocket as he stood up. He turned and nodded politely, then walked back to the tall building across the street.

"I, I can explain…" Haruku began. Her eyes were red as she tried to wipe away the tears.

"I'm sure you can missy." She pointed to the photo that Derrick was staring at. "But I don't give a damn." It showed Derrick carrying Haruku out of the club in his arms. With Pele leading the way. "But I'm more interested in how you explain this." She shoved the photo into Derrick's chest.

"Whoever sent these…" Derrick began.

"I hope you're not going to try to tell me these are some Photoshop frame up," Nancy said.

"I was just going to say that…"

Haruku put her hand on his arm to stop him. She turned to Nancy. She took a deep breath. "They are real. God, I wish I could say that they weren't. I don't know how you got these. But that was the old me. I've changed."

Nancy pointed to date stamps down in the corner. "Then you've changed a hell of a lot in just the past couple of months."

Haruku stood up straight and stared Nancy in the eye. "Yes. I have. And Derrick and Pele… my whole family has helped me. I'm not proud of what I did back then, but I can't… I will not deny it. But I am changing. Changing back to what I was before."

Nancy turned to Derrick. "I can't believe that you knowingly let this woman watch my children. How could you?"

Derrick held up the photos. "I wouldn't have let this woman take care of the girls. But this isn't Haruku. Not really. And certainly not now. Haruku is a kind and generous…"

"What? Are you sleeping with her to get her to take care of the…" She stopped. Embarrassed by what was coming out of her mouth. She didn't know Haruku. But she knew Derrick. She was married to him for several years. And he wouldn't even think of such a thing. "Sorry. That was out of line."

"We are friends. Good friends." He stood firm and stared unblinkingly into Nancy's eyes. "And I wouldn't hesitate to let Haruku watch my own daughter."

Nancy stood there for a moment. "And what makes you such an expert?"

"She would never do anything that might endanger the girls. I am sure of that."

Nancy grabbed the photos out of his hands and flipped through them. She pulled out two more and held them up in front of Derrick and Haruku. "What about these? How do you explain these?"

Derrick and Haruku looked at them.

"These were taken in just the past two weeks!"

Derrick looked down at them. "Well, I don't know…"

Haruku sighed with a sense of relief. "This is my friend Akamu."

"He looks like he is leaving this condo at," Nancy reached over and turned the photo. "At 6:00 in the morning." She shoved it back at them. "Did he stay the night? Were the girls here?"

Haruku took a small step toward Nancy. "No. He didn't spend the night. He came by to get the title to my Miata."

Derrick looked over at her. "The title to your Miata?"

"And what about that one?" Nancy asked pointing to the other photo in Derrick's hands. "The girls are just a few feet away, and this guy is giving you an envelope full of money."

Haruku took the photo. A woman was standing mostly off the edge of the picture. "My grandmother was with us. Whoever took the picture didn't get her in it. And yes that was an envelope with money in it. It was over five thousand dollars in hundreds if you want to know."

Nancy and Derrick looked at her.

"Akamu sold my Miata for me. He was giving me my money. After his commission."

"You sold your Miata?" Derrick asked.

"Yes."

"But your grandmother said you loved that car?"

6

Haruku looked up into Derrick's eyes. "That was the old me." She reached out and took the photos. "That car was the old me. The me that I am trying to get away from."

Derrick turned to Nancy. "Haruku isn't Mother Teresa. I know that. But she isn't the devil either. She made some mistakes, but she is working hard to change that."

"And you honestly believe that?" Nancy asked holding up the photos.

Haruku looked over at Nancy. "I have been in AA for several weeks now. And I am seeing a psychologist. Derrick knows that. I told him." Haruku turned to Derrick. "I am trying to change. I am."

He reached out and placed his hand on her arm. "I know. Pele knows. Your family knows."

"Well I don't," Nancy said. "I'm on the other side of the planet thinking that my girls are in good hands and I get this at my door."

"I don't know who took them, or why, or why they sent them to you," Haruku said. "Or who was watching me at 6:00 in the morning."

Derrick took the photos and stuffed them back into the envelope. "I have a damn good idea."

"I don't care. I'm still taking the girls home with me." She turned toward the kitchen. "John. It's time to get the girls ready to go."

John stepped out of the kitchen with Kattie and Becky.

"But mommy? What about our party today?" Becky asked.

"What party?" John asked as he knelt down by them.

"We're having a birthday party for the girls at my parent's house this afternoon and evening," Haruku said.

John looked over at Derrick then up at Nancy.

"Are you in trouble Uncle Derrick?" Kattie asked as she looked up at him.

"It seems that way, Kattie."

"Does this mean we are leaving Hawaii?" Becky asked as she looked over at her sister.

"I think so," Kattie said. "Mommy is mad at Uncle Derrick for some reason."

"You could at least let the girls come to their party before leaving," Derrick said as Nancy took their hands. "You can come too."

"I… I'll think about it," she said as she led them back to their room to pack.

"Some of our things are still at Uncle Derrick's house," Becky said.

Nancy reached down and placed her hand on Becky's shoulder. "Your father will go pick them up later. Now let's go get you dressed."

Derrick turned to John. John shrugged. "That was a shock for her to see those photos. I've got to admit, it was for me too."

"But you can't think that I'd…"

John shook his head. He glanced over at Haruku then back at Derrick. "I don't know what to think. In the past, I'd say your judgment of people was spot on. But after Lynn… I just don't know what to think."

"I met her at one of your parties." He realized how stupid and childish that must have sounded as soon as it left his mouth.

A few minutes later John left with Nancy and the girls.

Haruku turned to Derrick and started to cry. "I am so sorry Derrick. I've just made another big mess out of things."

He reached out and pulled her close. She sobbed in his chest as he held her tight. "This isn't your fault Haruku."

"I would never do anything to hurt the girls. Or you." She sobbed as he held her. "You have to know that."

Derrick reached out and ran his hands gently along her back "I know Haruku. I know. I believe you." He gripped her firmly as he took a half step back and stared down into her watery hazel eyes. "None of this is your fault Haruku."

She slid her arms up his chest as she gazed up at him. "Yes, it is. If I never…"

He slid his arms around her as he pulled her up against him. "You went through a rough patch. I don't know what it was all about. Maybe someday you'll tell me." He could feel her quiver as he held her. "Not as a cop but as a friend." She sobbed. "Anyway. I don't believe that was the real you. The real you is a good person. I believe that."

She pushed back slightly and gazed up at him. "Do you really believe that?"

He reached up and brushed away her tears with his finger. "Yes. I do." He inhaled slowly as they stood there staring at each other. "I trust you Haruku. I'd trust you with my life. And more important, I would trust you with the lives of Kattie and Becky. I did trust you. I still do."

"Thank you."

Chapter 3

The young man in the black sports jacket and sweater handed his boarding pass to the female attendant at the gate. He readjusted his backpack on his shoulder as she ran the pass through the scanner. She nodded as she handed it back to him. In Japanese, she said, "Enjoy your flight, sir." He nodded and walked down the ramp to the waiting plane.

Pele Kobayashi pulled up behind the patrol car and parked her RAV.

Officer Barnes glanced up at their surfboards strapped on top. "Sorry to call you out," he said as she and Kengi stepped out.

Kengi Nakamura was a member of the Tokyo Metropolitan Police. He was a friend of Derrick and had met Pele while attending an Interpol conference in Honolulu the week before. He decided to spend a little more time in Hawaii on vacation. They were both still wearing wetsuits as they walked over to Officer Barnes.

"No problem Barnes," Pele replied.

"I'm sorry to call you out on your first day off in a while Detective. But I thought you would want to see this," He led them toward a blue car in the Ewa Villages Golf Course parking lot. He pointed to the right front tire. It was low. Almost flat. "Someone reported it to security. They thought maybe it was a guest and would come out to find a flat tire."

Pele nodded as she stepped around the car.

"Security tried to page the owner. They didn't get a response. They called to have it towed away, and it showed up on your list."

Pele turned to Officer Barnes. "Is this Judy's car?"

He nodded. "It's the stolen blue Civic on your list of cars to look out for. What do you want me to do with it?"

Pele walked back over to her RAV and pulled out her phone. "Quon. Sorry to wake you, but I need you over at the Ewa Golf Course right away. And bring your kit." She turned back to Officer Barnes. "I want a truck out here to take it back to the station for further analysis after Quon is done here."

Kengi turned to Pele. "Is this just another day in paradise?"

"Everyone else comes here for a vacation. I guess we need to go somewhere else. Even for just a day off."

Derrick slipped his cell into his pocket as he and Haruku finished cleaning up the kitchen.

"You are a busy guy this morning," she said as she rinsed off a dish and set it aside to drain.

"The first call was Pele. She's out with Quon. They found another stolen car. With a part missing."

"And?"

"Another car was stolen early this morning. We don't know yet if it is one of this cluster or not yet."

Haruku glanced over at him. "Was that other call from John?"

Derrick nodded as he put the box of cereal back in the cupboard. "Yeah."

"Did he say anything about the girls and the party?"

Derrick picked up a towel and a wet dish. "He said Nancy was still thinking about it."

Haruku shook her head as she stared down into the soapy sink. "If you'd never met me the girls would still be here."

Derrick stepped over to her side. He reached out and slid his hand up her arm as he gazed into her eyes. "I don't want to hear any more talk like that Haruku. If I'd never met you, I would never have had the time I did with the girls." He took a deep breath. "Or I'd be unemployed." He gave her a one-arm hug and pulled her in close. "So don't think for a minute that I'm not glad that I met you."

"Thank you." She reached out and slid her hand up his chest. "Oh, my…" They looked at his red Hawaiian shirt. It was all covered with soapy water. They both laughed. "I'm so sorry Derrick."

"No worries. The label said it was wash and wear."

"Yes. But I don't think they meant at the same time." She reached for another towel and wiped off the bubbles.

"I've got to go out for a bit Haruku. I've got to go meet Bink, and then go meet John at the condo for the rest of the girl's things."

"All right. I'll finish up here."

"Will you be here when I get back?"

Haruku glanced over at the clock on the microwave. "I don't know. Should I go get the party ready or not?"

Derrick looked over at the clock as he put the dish in the cupboard and the towel on the counter. "Yes. I'd rather have my friends mad at me than the girls disappointed."

"Then meet me at the house when you're done."

Chapter 4

"Did you find anything?" Pele asked as she and Kengi watched Quon and Xin go over the blue Honda Civic with a fine toothcomb. Xin was an intern for the forensics department at the HPD and a student of Quon's at the University of Hawaii. He was also the brother of Quon's girlfriend, Fei Chen.

"We have three sets of prints. We will run them back at the station. And we have fiber and soil samples from the carpet and the tires," Quon said.

"And one more thing Professor."

9

Quon and the others turned to him. "What is that Xin?"

"The air-conditioning compressor is missing."

"Bingo Bango," Pele said.

Everyone turned to her.

She cleared her throat. "Derrick says that. Sometimes."

"So this is one of your missing parts cases?" Kengi asked.

"It looks like it," Pele said. She turned to Quon. "Call me when you get the prints and any other useful information."

Quon put the evidence bag into the box. "Oh. That reminds me. Another car was stolen early this morning."

"I knew I should have checked my email when I got up."

"You mean instead of actually taking a day off?" Kengi asked.

"And you don't check yours every day when you are at home?"

Kengi shrugged. "Before I get out of bed."

Pele turned back to Quon. "What was it?"

"A 2002 Ford Taurus."

"Red," Xin added.

"OK." Pele looked around. No cameras were pointing at this part of the parking lot. She turned to Officer Barnes. "Go around and pull footage from any cameras in the area to see if we can spot who left the car here."

"How far back should I go?"

"As far back as when it was stolen, or you have footage that might show us who dropped it off here."

Barnes nodded. "What about the tow truck?"

Pele pointed to a truck just coming around the corner. Barnes nodded. "OK. I'm on the video."

Quon turned to Xin.

Xin nodded. "I know. Set up the station and get the popcorn."

Quon nodded. "I will add this data point to my statistical magic for Derrick."

"And plug in the Taurus," Pele added.

"But we do not know that it is one of these?"

"Let's assume it is for now."

"That could skew the data."

"OK. Then run it both ways."

"I will get on it as soon as we get back to the lab."

"Thanks, Quon," Pele said. "If you could wait here until they load the truck then go back to the garage with it."

"And you?" Quon asked.

Pele glanced down at her wetsuit. "I think we'll go change and meet you at the station." She waved for Kengi to follow her back to her car.

"I guess surfing is off for today?" Kengi asked.

"I'm sorry Kengi. But with Derrick on vacation, and us being tied up with that conference last week…"

"Not to mention the dead men and the missing drone."

"Yes. But I'd like to get these solved if I could. You understand."

Kengi nodded. "You know, the sad thing is that I do."

They both laughed as they headed back to her RAV. Pele unlocked her car. "I have been promising to take Derrick surfing ever since he got here and that was almost six months ago."

Kengi opened his door. "So you're saying I shouldn't hold my breath if I'm only here for the week."

"I'm sorry Kengi."

Kengi slid in and closed the door. "At least I got to try on the wetsuit."

Pele started up her RAV. "That's farther than Derrick got."

Chapter 5

Nancy was sitting on the edge of the bed in her hotel room with Kattie and Becky. John was sitting on a chair by the sliding door to the lanai.

"So no one ever left you at home alone?" Nancy asked. "Not even at night?"

"Oh no," Becky said. "Haruku was always there with us. And kuku. That is what she called her grandmother."

"Anyone else?" Nancy asked.

"There was Ailani and Father Bishop. We would go fishing with them," Kattie added. "Ahulani was there with us. Sometimes Haruku had some things she said she had to do."

John looked over at Nancy. "It might have been her, appointments."

Nancy looked over at him then back at the girls. "Anyone else?"

Becky sat back and thought for a moment. "Bink would come by sometimes in the evening with Uncle Derrick. He was funny. We'd all play games."

"And he liked the brownies we made," Kattie added.

"You made brownies?" Nancy asked.

"Aunt Haruku taught us how to do a lot of things," Kattie said. "Like snorkeling, tai chi, Japanese, Italian, Hawaiian, and some of the history of Hawaii."

Becky nodded as she sat there. "Aunt Haruku is very smart."

"Aunt Haruku?" Nancy asked.

"That's what Ailani said we should call her," Becky said.

John looked down at his watch. "I've got to go meet Derrick soon. What should I tell him about this afternoon?"

The girls turned to Nancy. "We want to go to our party," Kattie said. "E'olu olu'oe."

"What?" Nancy asked.

"It means please," Kattie said.

"Please mommy?" Becky asked. "We'll be good."

Nancy reached out and gave them a big hug. She sighed. "It's not you that concerns me."

Derrick opened the garage doors where he stored his growing collection of cars. As the last door went up, he and Bink stepped inside. Bink Whitcomb was an old friend. He was a Chief Inspector for the police in London. He was also a colleague of Derrick's when working Interpol cases.

"You weren't kidding when you said you made a few additions to your collection," Bink said as he looked around.

"Somehow I don't see Lady Westfield in the pickup or the Studebaker," Derrick said as they entered the first garage of the three.

"I can just get a rental like I had planned Derrick."

"Nonsense Bink. I'm sure we can find something that will be fun for you and stylish enough for her."

Bink was taller, and twenty or so pounds heavier than Derrick. He glanced over at the Mercedes 230 SL. "A bit small for me."

Derrick laughed. "I barely fit in it myself, but she is fun to drive." They walked to the next garage. "Here we have the classics, the Mustang and the T-Bird."

"The Mustang would be fun," Bink said. "At least for me."

"What about the Thunderbird?"

Bink stepped over to it. "She might enjoy that."

"I also have a '54 Mercury Monterey now. Basic black exterior and red interior. Or I also have this reddish…"

"My god man."

Derrick followed Bink over to his '54 Eldorado. "Marta calls it the pimpmobile."

"It's so… so red. Inside and out," Bink said.

"It has white rear quarter panels." Derrick pointed to the lower rear fender. "And whitewall tires."

Bink laughed. "I can just see Lady Westfield if I pick her up at the airport in this."

Derrick nodded to the last garage. "I think I have something more to her liking. And you will enjoy it yourself. You've just got to pick a color."

"Pick a color?" Bink asked as he followed Derrick into the last garage.

"Yeah. I've got a set of these." Derrick waved his hand at his Mercedes line.

"Three 280 SE 3.5 Cabriolets. They are works of art Derrick."

"You have your choice of dark green, astro silver, or deep blue." Derrick walked halfway into the garage. "Or I have another 230 SL and an R107 SL."

Bink stepped up to the deep blue 280. He reached out and ran his hand over the medium brown colored leather seats. "Now this would do nicely."

Derrick pulled a key off a ring of keys and tossed it to Bink. "Enjoy the islands, my friend."

Twenty minutes later Derrick was standing in the hallway of his condo with John. A suitcase was standing on the floor between them.

"I don't know," John said. "She hasn't decided what to do yet. She is really pissed. But I think her blood pressure is almost back to normal."

Derrick nodded. "Can't say I blame her I guess."

John looked over at Derrick. "For what it's worth Derrick… I think the girls were in good hands. Haruku seems to be… well… better than what those photos show. And I know a thing or two about people as well."

Derrick let his hands fall by his side as he shifted on his feet. "Thanks, John. I know this hasn't been easy for either of you."

"But I've got to ask Derrick. Who would stoop to something like this? They must really have it in for you."

Derrick made a fist and tapped it against the wall. "Not just me."

"I don't know how you, and people like you do your jobs." John turned toward the door as he pulled his keys out of his pocket. He turned back to Derrick. "Nothing is sacred to some of these people is it?" He shook his head. "To drag your family and friends in is just low."

"It usually doesn't come to that."

"Kind of a code?" John asked.

Derrick forced a smile. "Something like that." He glanced down at the suitcase. "But the world is changing."

John reached out and shook Derrick's hand. "I guess it's good that you and people like you carry on. Or where else would the rest of us be?" He reached down and picked up the suitcase.

Derrick stepped over to the door and opened it a crack. "You've got the address. We'll all be at the house. Ready to party." He turned to John. "You know. In case Nancy decides to let the girls come."

John waved and headed down the hallway toward the elevators.

Chapter 6

Derrick got into his E350 and started west along Beretania Street. He slowed down as he passed the police station just a couple of blocks from his condo. Pele's RAV was parked out front with two surfboards still strapped on top. He pulled into the parking lot and got out. Quon's Tucson was also there.

Derrick scanned the basement lab as he stepped off the elevator. It was dark except for the back corner. "Working on your day off?" he asked strolling up to Quon's work area.

Quon, Pele, and Kengi looked over.

"You should talk," Pele said looking at his shorts and red Hawaiian shirt.

"What are you doing here?" Kengi asked. "Aren't you on vacation?"

Derrick laughed as he looked around at them. Everyone was in shorts, sandals, and polo style shirts. "I should ask the same of you."

"Yeah," Pele added. "I thought you were going fishing with the girls this morning."

"There was a slight change of plan." He didn't want to get into what happened.

"Don't you have a party to get set up?" Pele asked.

Derrick hesitated. "I was just on my way to help out when I saw your cars out front."

"We found the blue Civic," Pele said. "With a part missing. And earlier this morning a 2002 red Taurus was stolen."

Derrick nodded. "The age could fit the profile."

"Quon is running the numbers with and without the new theft to see if there is a pattern."

"Good. Where did you find the blue Civic? In the southeast corner?" Derrick asked as he walked up to the workbench.

"The Ewa Village Golf Course."

"That fits," Derrick said. "What about the yellow Civic?"

"Nothing yet."

"I wager that when we find it, the compressor is missing," Derrick said. "Where is the car now?"

"In the garage," Quon said.

"So what have we got?" Derrick asked.

Quon turned back to his laptop. "We have three sets of prints. And we already know one belongs to Judy. We're still running the other two."

"Xin is running soil samples from the tires and carpets," Pele said.

"And I've got some fibers. Clothing most likely," Quon said.

"How is your analysis coming?" Derrick asked.

Quon looked up. "The search for a pattern where none exists?"

"That would be the one," Derrick said.

"Nothing useful yet. But I have added this car to it now."

Derrick sat down on a stool. "I want you to try something else along with it."

"With or without the Taurus?"

"Since you've already got both going, do both."

"So what is your new idea?" Pele asked.

"It came to me when I was showing Bink my car collection this morning."

She grinned. "You show him the pimpmobile?"

"What is the pimpmobile?" Kengi asked.

"You will have to show it to him before he leaves," Quon said.

"Back to my thought," Derrick said. "I'd like you to add to your mix, every registered car on the island that matches the cars make, model, and year, of the ones on our stolen parts list."

"That could be a lot of cars," Pele said.

"Then I want you to create a map showing their locations. Overlay the shops and schools that Pele and Soto have been working on that might be involved." Derrick glanced over at Pele and grinned. "In their spare time."

"Anything else?" Quon asked.

Derrick sat there for a moment. "Yes. Factor in any students or employees at these schools and shops that have records for stolen cars and minor theft."

"That is a lot of information to crunch," Quon said.

"And…" Derrick sat back for a moment. "Set up rings at say five, ten, and fifteen miles out from each hit."

"That could take a while," Quon said.

"Yes," Derrick said. "But isn't this the age of big data? Let's see what we can glean from it." He stood up and started to walk away. "Let me know when you have something." He paused as he rubbed his chin. "One more thing Pele."

"What's that?"

"Let's make sure that every patrol out there is looking for this red Taurus. The sooner we find it, the sooner we know if it is a part of this parts theft ring."

"We can get the word out to the press."

"No. I don't want to alert the perps that we are on to them. If it is them." He started toward the elevators again. "See you all later."

"Where are you going?" Kengi asked.

"I'm on vacation."

"Nice of you to drop in," Pele yelled out.

"My pleasure." Derrick waved as he walked over to the elevators.

Cooking pots filled the stove. Colorful plastic bowls and decorative ceramic pots filled the table and countertops. Haruku was busy on a cutting board in the kitchen of her parent's home cooking alongside her mother and grandmother.

"We are making an awful lot of food here," Haruku said as she paused and looked around.

"It will get eaten eventually," Kailani said as she closed another Tupperware bowl and opened the refrigerator. It was full. "We may have to start filling the one out on the lanai."

"So we don't know if Kattie and Becky are coming or not?" her grandmother Ahulani asked as she prepared manapua.

"We can call Nancy if you think it will help," Kailani offered.

"No thanks." Haruku shook her head. "I don't know what to do." She reached up and wiped her forehead with the back of her hand. "I guess we'll just wait and see what Derrick says when he gets here."

"Tomas will be here soon to start the grill. Guests start coming in three hours." Kailani turned to Haruku. "Are you sure we should not cancel this?"

Haruku turned to face them. "OK. I screwed up again. I'm sorry. But Derrick said to go ahead and hope that they come."

The doorbell rang. Kailani picked up a towel and wiped off her hands. "That will be the people setting up the games for the girls. I'll show them to the back." She turned to Haruku. "Well don't just stand there feeling sorry for yourself. We've still got a lot of work to do."

"I know mom."

Ahulani turned to Haruku as Kailani left the kitchen. She reached out for her hand. "Things will work out dear. I am sure Derrick understands."

She took in a deep breath then let out a long, slow sigh. "I don't know why kuku."

Pele and Kengi were walking through the crowd of people gathered at the International Market Place on Kalakaua Avenue. She gazed around at the stalls selling trinkets, jewelry, shirts, and chances to find valuable pearls in an oyster.

"This is quite a place," Kengi said as he watched a woman jump up and down after picking an oyster with a big pearl inside.

"At the end of next year it will be all gone," she said.

Kengi turned to her. "Gone?"

She snorted as she shook her head. "Progress. A new expensive mall. Like we need another one of those."

"How long has this been here?" he asked as they wandered around between the vendors with the other tourists.

"Since the 1950s." She took a deep breath. "Another piece of history gone." She stopped for a moment. "I come here at night sometimes just to watch the people. Average people from all around the world. People that have often saved up for years just to take a once in a lifetime trip to paradise."

"It must have been exciting growing up here," Kengi said as he gazed at the other tourists milling about, or darting in and out of little stalls selling T-shirts. There were all kinds of art, trinkets of metal, and baskets ringing the edge. Nothing terribly expensive. But priceless souvenirs of a trip to a tropical island that most people only see in travel brochures or the photos from friends of friends.

"I can't imagine living anywhere else," Pele said as she glanced down at her watch. "I should probably head to my parent's house. I said I'd try to get there early to help set up. Would you like to come along? You are coming to the party anyway, this way you won't have to drive around looking for a place to park."

"It would be my pleasure," Kengi said. "What time will Derrick be arriving with his goddaughters?"

"Around 1:00 or so. He was taking them fishing with his friends Ailani and Father Bishop. But I don't know what they are doing now."

Ailani looked up from his eReader. "You're late."

Derrick sat down between Ailani and Father Bishop. "It's just one of those days." He opened his bag and passed out coffees. A large white hot chocolate Frappuccino for Ailani. A Green Tea for Father Bishop. And a Mocha Frappuccino Light for himself.

Ailani turned to Derrick and smelled the aroma. "Something new?"

"Haruku and Pele have both been after me to cut back on coffee and eat healthier. This is my compromise."

"Where are the girls?" Father Bishop asked.

"Where's the Danish?" Ailani asked.

Derrick took a sip of his coffee. "The Danish were long gone by the time I got there."

"Pity," Ailani said.

Derrick glanced over at the park. "I'm late for everything aren't I?"

Ailani nodded. "The show is over. The women and their dogs are long gone too."

"You look troubled my son," Father Bishop said as he took a sip of his tea.

"Nancy showed up at Haruku's place this morning."

"All the way from Paris?"

Ailani sat back and watched a sailboat motor into the marina. "That can't be good."

Derrick took a long drink. "It wasn't."

They all watched as an older man played with his dog over in the park while he told the events of the morning.

"Now that just isn't the same," Ailani said as he turned from the park to check his fishing line.

"No," Derrick agreed.

"Is the girl's party still on then?" Father Bishop asked.

"Yep," Derrick said as he watched a cloud drift slowly across the sky.

"Will the girls be there?" Ailani asked.

Derrick took a sip of his coffee. "Dunno." He reached into his pocket and pulled out his cell. "Vibrate." He flipped it open. "Dreadlow here." He finished his coffee as he listened. "OK. On my way."

"Going back to work?" Ailani asked as he put trash in the bag.

"Duty calls." Derrick stood up.

"Isn't that what got you into this mess?" Father Bishop asked.

Ailani handed Derrick the bag of trash. He nodded at the can down the street. "It's on your way."

Chapter 7

Derrick pulled into the strip mall parking lot. A short, roundish man in a Grateful Dead T-shirt and black slacks approached as he got out of his car.

"Hey Derrick, I didn't expect to see you out here this morning."

"I didn't expect you either Soto. I thought this was your day off?"

"And you're on vacation. Go figure."

"So what have we got?"

Detective Soto ran his hand over his remaining short-cropped reddish blond hair. "It must be your lucky day. It's the car you have been waiting for. Joyce and Xin are going through it now before we take it back to the garage."

"Great work Soto."

They stepped over to the yellow Honda Civic. "Is the compressor missing?"

"Yep."

"Just like you predicted," Xin said.

Derrick grinned. "I love it when a theory starts to come together."

"I have already called Quon and asked him to add the new data into his scenarios," Xin said.

Derrick turned to Soto. "I don't suppose we've found that Taurus yet?"

He grinned. "We've got to save something for tomorrow."

Derrick stood in front of the door in his khaki shorts, brown sandals, and a bright red Hawaiian shirt. He reached out and rang the doorbell again as he glanced down at his cell. It was just after noon. The door opened.

"Hello, Derrick. Come in," Eito said as he stepped back.

"Hello, Eito. Taking the day off from the store?"

"Yes. The advantage of owning it and being semi-retired. Everyone is out back." He closed the door and led the way.

Derrick glanced at the photos lining the hallway. "I guess I never noticed these before."

They paused for a moment as Derrick examined the photos of Pele and Haruku growing up. In several, they were together and laughing. Some were sports photos and graduations. Tomas, then Tomas and his wife, Tomas and his wife with their children. Pele and Haruku, each alone.

"Life goes by too fast," Eito said as they resumed their walk to the backyard. "Any word about the girls?"

Derrick shook his head. "Their plane leaves in two hours."

"Do you think Nancy will let them come?"

"She's worried about the girls."

Eito nodded. "Having daughters is harder than boys."

"You should know. Two beautiful daughters."

"Two beautiful girls in paradise. Tourists looking for a good time. Young sailors and airmen away from home."

Derrick paused for a moment. "Damn. I never thought of it that way before. How do you cope?"

"I had them study martial arts since they were young. And learn how to shoot." He slid the back door open.

"That explains why Haruku is showing my goddaughters the basics."

"Good things to know."

Derrick looked around as he stepped out onto the lanai. Kailani and Ahulani were busy putting the finishing touches on the party. A castle and trampoline sat at the edge of the yard. Floats were lying by the pool. Some food was already out but still covered in plastic.

"Hi, Derrick."

He turned. Haruku was standing there in a long red dress with yellow swirls, sandals, and holding two pitchers of juice. "Any word from Nancy?"

"No."

Fei and Quon stepped out carrying plastic cups, plates, and utensils. "Hi Derrick," Quon said.

"Any word on the girls yet?" Fei asked as she and Quon put everything at the end of the table.

Derrick shook his head. "Anything new on our car case?"

"Do you always talk shop?" Fei asked.

Derrick shrugged. "Keeps my mind off other things."

"We identified the other two sets of prints in the blue civic," Quon said.

"And?"

"Judy's mother and a friend of hers from work."

"What about the yellow Civic?"

"Same. Owner's and friends."

"Any luck with the soil samples or fibers?"

Quon took a sip of his juice. "Joyce is on fibers and Xin is still analyzing the soil. We should know something later tonight or early tomorrow."

Pele pulled up into her parent's driveway. As she and Kengi got out, a deep blue Mercedes 280 SE parked across the street.

The door opened, and a man stepped out. He turned to Pele and Kengi and waved. "Aloha!"

Pele waved back. "Aloha."

"Bink and his wife are early," Kengi said.

"Your parents have a fantastic view from here," Bink said as he stepped around the car and opened the door for his wife.

"You must be Lady Westfield." Pele held out her hand as Bink, and his wife joined them walking up the driveway.

"Please. Just Mildred." She had a warm smile and a touch of blond in her short gray hair.

Bink waved his hand as if displaying his wife. "And as you can see from her bright yellow and orange silk dress she has gone native."

"Welcome to our islands," Pele said. "I hope you're having a good time."

"Positively stunning Pele. I am so glad I came. We've always talked about it. And now we've done it." She turned to Bink. "And we may come back again. It is so lovely here."

"And the skies are blue. Not various shades of gray," he added.

Stepping out into the main terminal, the young man in the black sports jacket and turtleneck sweater scanned the area.

"Aloha. Welcome to Honolulu International Airport," announced a soft voice over the PA system. "The baggage claim area is located…"

Excitement and anticipation permeated the air as brightly dressed tourists, business people, and residents hopping from one island to another, rushed around with only the thoughts of what they had to do concerning them. The young man, like them, had only his thoughts of what he had to do as well.

He turned and slipped into a restroom. A few minutes later, he came out wearing dark blue pants, a blue Hawaiian shirt, and mirrored sunglasses. He mixed into a crowd and followed them out of the terminal.

Outside the terminal, he waited a few minutes then boarded a city bus heading for Honolulu. He searched around for an empty seat near the back, but close to the door.

Several minutes later, the bus made a stop. Several people stepped off. A young woman in dark slacks, a T-shirt with a picture of a heavy metal band on it, and carrying a package sat down next to him. He stared straight ahead as the bus resumed its course. She ignored him.

Several stops later, the woman got off. Without the package.

As the bus entered the downtown area of Honolulu, it came to another stop. The young man slung his backpack over his shoulder and reached over for the package. He followed several other people off the bus and disappeared into the crowd.

Derrick was standing off to the side of the pool with Pele and Quon as everyone else mingled, chatted, and drank fresh mango pineapple juice.

"So you think it was Trang that sent the photos?" Quon asked.

"I've seen him following my sister around. I just thought it was part of his perverted investigation," Pele said as her face turned red. "When I get my hands on that little…"

Derrick reached out and put his hand on her shoulder. "Let's not play into his hand."

Pele clenched her fists. "Are you going to let him get away with this?" The juice in her plastic cup ran out over the top as she squeezed. She stepped back. "Oh shit."

"You should tell the captain," Quon said.

Pele looked over at him as she changed hands holding her cup and shook the juice from her hand. "What? Like running to the teacher?"

Derrick grinned. "Hardly. However, I'll deal with him when the time is right. For now, maybe we should all be watching our backs. Who knows what else he might be capable of?"

The only light in the basement lab still came from the corner where Quon worked. Xin was staring at his computer screen going through soil samples as Joyce went through fiber samples on the next workstation.

"This is interesting," Xin said lost in his own world.

Joyce blinked and rubbed her eyes. "What's that?"

He sat back. "Come have a look."

She stood up, stretched, then joined him. She shrugged as she stared at the screen. "What am I looking at?"

Bink joined Derrick by the grill as Tomas went inside for some sauce. "Do you think Nancy will let the girls come? I know she isn't particularly keen on us police types, to begin with."

Derrick poked at a hamburger with a long metal fork with a wooden handle. "She is really pissed this time. And rightfully so. If I had gotten those photos of my kids… well, let's just say she is handling it better than I might have." He reached for a spatula and took off a burger, dropping it into a bun and handing it to Tomas's older daughter Danielle. "Enjoying your break from college?"

She smiled. "What break? Dad has me working in the office." She walked over to the pool and sat down.

"Ah, the passing of youth." Derrick turned back to the grill. "So, how does Mildred like the resort?"

"I think we may be back next year."

"And the car?"

"How early do I need to get my reservation in if we come back?"

Derrick was standing back behind a palm tree pretending to look out at the ocean. "Good work you two. Why don't you get out of there and enjoy the rest of the day."

"When do you want to go over it?" Xin asked.

"Can you meet me tomorrow morning at 6 AM?"

"Here in the lab?"

"Yes." He hung up and slipped his cell back into his pocket.

Derrick refilled his glass and one for Haruku. He handed it to her then slipped his cell out of his pocket to check the time. It was now 01:15. All the guests were there. Todd had brought his wife and children. Tomas's wife and children were there.

Soto and Kali brought two of their grandchildren who were visiting. Tomas had even invited some of the people from the stores that had children.

"Maybe they are just running late," Haruku said as she slipped her arm through his.

"Maybe."

They heard something inside and turned to the empty doorway.

The door slid open. Ahulani and Father Bishop stepped out to the lanai. "Guess who we found," Ahulani said as she and the Father stepped aside.

"Uncle Derrick! Aunt Haruku!" Becky and Kattie came running out of the house and over to them. They were wearing brightly colored dresses they had picked out while shopping with Haruku. They knelt down and gave the girls a big hug. "We missed you," Becky said as she threw her arms around Derrick. He looked up as Nancy and John stepped out onto the lanai.

"Why don't you go talk to them," Haruku said. "I'll introduce the girls to everyone they haven't met yet."

"OK." They stood up. Derrick walked cautiously toward them. John nodded. Nancy just stood there watching the girls and Haruku.

John walked past Derrick toward the pitchers of juice. "You owe me one."

Derrick nodded slightly as he continued.

"Aloha. You must be John. I am Tomas. The older brother of Pele and Haruku." He reached out to shake John's hand.

"Aloha," John replied.

"Let me get you a drink and introduce you to everyone."

"Thank you, Tomas."

Derrick stepped up beside Nancy. "I'm glad you decided to let the girls come to the party."

"It's all they were talking about."

Father Bishop stepped over and handed Nancy a drink. "We're so glad you could make it. Kattie and Becky have been a delight to know. So much energy at that age. And so many questions." He turned and stepped over to Ailani and Ahulani.

"Thank you, Father," Nancy replied. She turned to Derrick. "All they were talking about was Uncle Derrick this, Aunt Haruku that, Ailani…" She turned back to the girls. "You've all made quite an impression on them."

"A good one I hope. They knew nothing about…"

"If I hadn't received those photos… I would never have suspected…"

"People can change," Derrick said. "Well, some people. Given a chance, and under the right circumstances."

Nancy bit her bottom lip as she thought. "It amazes me, how you can be so optimistic about people, with all that you deal with day in and day out." She turned to Haruku. "And people that will attack those around you."

"I can assure you…" Derrick crushed his empty plastic cup. "He will be dealt with in due course."

"It was a hard decision to come here."

"I know," Derrick said. "Given our past. And your reasons for…"

She turned to him. "My reasons for leaving you?"

Derrick stared down at his empty, crushed cup.

Kattie, Becky, and the other children were taking turns running in and out of the castle and chasing each other around the backyard.

Bink and his wife walked over to them. "Nancy," Bink began. "I'd like to introduce you to my wife. Mildred."

Lady Westfield held out her hand. "It is a pleasure to finally meet you after all these years Nancy."

Nancy nodded as she held out her hand. "It is a pleasure to meet you as well Mildred. I have heard so much about you."

Derrick was refilling glasses at the picnic table. Kali walked over to Nancy as she watched Kattie and Becky playing with the other children. "Once the islands have you they never let go."

Nancy turned to her. "Well that certainly seems to be the case with Derrick. And now my daughters."

"Not you?"

Nancy watched as the girls ran over to Haruku. John was off to the side talking and laughing with Tomas and Todd. "Not now."

"Maybe you just need to give it a chance?"

"I had my chance. I chose a different island." She watched as the girls dragged Haruku over to Derrick. They were all sitting down on the grass together eating something.

Ailani and Father Bishop strolled over to Nancy. "Sharp girls," Ailani said. "We have a birthday gift for them. I hope you don't mind."

"What kind of gift?" Nancy asked.

"A couple of eReaders. With some ebooks they might enjoy. You can check the content first. And I haven't activated the Wi-Fi. I'll let that up to you."

"That's very generous of you both."

He turned to watch them. "They remind me of my own daughter, and granddaughter when they were young."

"Well thank you. I am sure they will enjoy it. They are like sponges for knowledge."

"And good at fishing too," Father Bishop added.

Ailani's eyes danced as he watched them.

"Does your daughter live here in the islands?" Nancy asked.

"Yes. She's a doctor."

Nancy nodded as she glanced over at Father Bishop.

"I have hundreds of children." He glanced around the backyard. "Maybe even thousands." He paused. "Figuratively of course."

"Will you be staying in the islands long?" Ailani asked.

Nancy shook her head. "Not long."

"Pity. They grow on you if you give them a chance."

"So I've heard."

Ailani and Father Bishop wandered over to Ahulani and Eito.

Derrick walked over to Nancy as he watched the girls running around with some of the other children. "Look. I have decided to retire from police work."

Nancy turned to him.

"I've given this a great deal of thought this past couple of weeks. And if that's what it takes."

Nancy stood there as she watched him.

"It's what you've always wanted," he continued.

"Yes, it is." She looked over at the girls talking with Haruku and her grandmother as they drank some juice.

"They seem to be enjoying themselves," Derrick said.

"Maybe I was wrong."

Derrick laughed. "You? Wrong?"

She cracked a slight smile. "Just don't let it get out. But I can make a mistake once in a while." She looked over at him. "Every decade or so. You can't retire."

Derrick took a deep breath. "The price of keeping this job is getting too high." He turned to her. "I can even move back to New York."

"Oh no." She shook her head as she pushed her hand out. "Oh no. I'm not going to be the one that ruined your life."

"Ruined? I'm just exploring new possibilities."

"And what would these new possibilities be? What would you do? Fish? Work on your cars?"

Derrick shrugged as he looked over at Kattie and Becky. "Isn't that what you've been hoping as you kept buying them?"

Haruku looked over at them and waved. Then turned back to the girls.

Nancy turned to him and put her hand on his. "No. Maybe."

"No?"

"You can't quit. It is who you are. I can't change that. No one can change that." She turned to watch Haruku. "Haruku can't even change that."

"What's your point?"

Nancy kept her eyes on Haruku as she played with the girls. "She accepts you for who you are. No questions asked. She seems to be able to adapt in ways that... I couldn't."

"But what about her past?"

She turned to him. "You have always looked for the good in people."

"I don't always find it."

She looked up into his eyes. "But you give them the opportunity to find it in themselves. If they don't..." She turned back to Haruku and the girls. "It's not for lack of opportunity on your part. It is their failure." She scanned the people in the backyard. "If the girls stayed..."

Derrick watched the girls. "No Haruku?" He glanced down at his feet as he ran his sandal over the grass. "That is... if the girls stayed..."

Nancy looked around the crowd of people gathered there. "In a few short months, you have touched the lives of many people from all walks of life. I'd say her chances are better than average of making it."

Derrick cleared his throat. "And what are the chances of the girls finishing their month here? Without Haruku?"

Nancy laughed. "I'm afraid that letting them stay here without Haruku, would be like telling them to wait an hour for me in an ice cream shop. Without eating anything." She grinned. "Not gonna happen." Her smile melted away as she turned to Haruku. "I don't know. Maybe you two balance each other." Her expression became stern and hardened as she turned and looked up at Derrick. "However... if I get another photo or a phone call..."

"I piss off a lot of people. And now some of them know who you are."

"And apparently where to find me."

He took a sip of his juice. "And I can't guarantee that I won't be called in on another case."

"Deep down I know that. I don't like it. It scares me. Don't tell me." Nancy said with a sigh. "Just promise me one thing."

Derrick looked into her eyes. "Name it."

"You get the asshole that did this."

"Oh, I will. You can count on that." He didn't want to tell her that he suspected it was a fellow cop. That would make things even worse. And right now he was back in the plus column with points in her eyes. Maybe only one or two points. But it was something.

Haruku looked over at them nervously. Then quickly turned back to the girls.

Nancy took a sip of her juice. "I know that you'll be called in on another case."

Derrick took a sip of his juice. "Probably."

"And I know that you won't be able to say no."

"Possibly."

She looked at him.

He shrugged. "Probably."

She turned back to Haruku. "And she knows it too. And I'm sure she'll be there to cover for you."

"Probably."

Nancy laughed. "More than probably. And she will watch over the girls."

"This is hard for you isn't it?"

"You have no idea."

"Yes, I do." He finished his juice. "So why are you doing it?"

"Look at them. They love you. They miss you not being around."

"I love them like they are my own." He reached for her plastic cup. "Get you another?"

She nodded as she scanned the backyard again. Everyone was enjoying the evening. "You have a lot of good friends here Derrick. The islands agree with you."

He reached out and held his palm up. "What can I say? It's paradise." He noticed her staring at Haruku again. "Do you trust her now?"

She turned back to him. She placed her hand on his arm as she looked up into his eyes. "I trust you."

Derrick's shoulders slumped as he leaned over and kissed her on her cheek. Everyone was watching and knew what that kiss meant.

Ailani turned to Father Bishop and Ahulani. They nodded as Ailani began... "I took off for a weekend last month just to try and recall the whole year."

Father Bishop and Ahulani joined in. "All of the faces and all of the places, Wonderin where they all disappeared..."

Danielle turned to her father. "Oh god. Not again."

Tomas grinned. "A Jimmy Buffet classic." He raised his drink as he, Haruku, and several others joined in.

"Ran into a chum, with a bottle of rum, and we wound up drinkin all night."

Nancy scanned the backyard. "What's going on Derrick?"

"This happened once before at a barbecue I gave out on the beach a while back."

"You? You held a party out on the beach?"

"Just a small thing. Maybe twenty people. And Tomas has promised to teach me the fine art of the luau someday."

She looked over at him. "You are definitely not the Derrick Dreadlow I used to know."

"I hope that's a compliment."

She grinned as she held out her glass. "It is." They joined in. "I think about Paris when I'm high on red wine, I wish I could jump on a plane. So many nights I just dream of the ocean, God I wish I was sailin again."

John looked over at Nancy. Haruku was dancing around with Kattie and Becky. Everyone had joined in by now. Even the older children seemed to know the words.

Nancy paused for a moment. "Your friends are crazy Derrick."

"I think it's the sea air."

Her eyes sparkled as she looked at him. "And it definitely suits you." She sighed. "It was good that you left the Big Apple and came to paradise."

"Even paradise has its dark side."

"So I'm finding out."

"But on the whole, it's a great place to live."

Soto and Kali jumped in behind Derrick and Nancy. "With all of my running, and all of my cunning, If I couldn't laugh I just would go insane. If we couldn't laugh, we just would go insane. If we weren't all crazy, we would go insane."

As the sun sank lower on the horizon, a Cantius 41 cruiser with its running lights on, slowly backed away from the dock. A couple of minutes later, the man at the helm was guiding his boat out of the La Marina Sailing Club. A woman was preparing dinner in the galley as two children sat in the upper salon playing cards and watching the sunset.

He took a deep breath as he glanced down at the screens on the control panel and steered slowly out to sea. A night out away from everything, everyone, would be just what he needed to clear his head and think about what to do next.

"We can stay!" Kattie and Becky were shouting as they ran up to Derrick and Haruku.

Haruku knelt down and gave them a big hug. "This is wonderful girls."

Derrick glanced over at John and Nancy. Nancy nodded slightly. Derrick nodded and knelt down with the girls as they threw their arms around him.

"This calls for something special," Pele said as several people gathered around.

"What did you have in mind?" Derrick asked as he looked up at her.

"How about a day at the beach tomorrow? No work." She looked around.

"It's a Monday."

"And we worked most of the weekend."

"I've got surgery," Fei said.

"I have got more orals," Quon said.

Soto shrugged, "I've got to be in tomorrow. Something about stolen cars..."

Pele looked at Kengi, Bink, and Mildred. Bink leaned back and raised his hands in the air. "We're on vacation. What do you say, dear?"

"Splendid idea."

"I'm up for it," Kengi said. "Where are we going?"

The Cantius 41 cruiser cleared the marina and headed out to sea. Clear skies and gentle waves stretched out ahead. The aroma of dinner cooking drifted up from the galley.

Derrick walked over to Nancy and John. "Thank you. For the second chance."

Nancy looked over at the girls as they danced around Haruku. "Just one more thing Derrick. And this is really important."

"Name it."

She turned to him. "They need to be home on the Sunday flight we have already booked for 7 AM. And you need to get to the airport early."

"I will. They will. Guaranteed," Derrick, said with a wide grin.

Nancy beamed as she knelt down. Kattie and Becky ran over to her.

John turned to him. "We are going on a three-day vacation with the girls. It is the only trip we'll have with them this summer before they start school."

Derrick nodded. "No worries."

John took a sip of his drink. "If they aren't there in time…" He glanced down at Nancy as she tasted something Becky was feeding her. "I won't be able to cover for you."

Derrick nodded as he looked over at Nancy. She glanced up at him. "Understood."

Chapter 8

"Let's make a quick stop at my condo before we hit the station," Derrick said as he turned up to the front door and parked.

"Need something?" Pele asked as they got out.

"Just some shirts and my electric toothbrush. I miss it." He held the door open for her. "Like an old friend you just can't live without."

"Uh huh."

Derrick checked the time on his cell as the elevator door closed.

"We've still got time," Pele said. "Kengi is packing the RAV."

"Haruku is packing the Cherokee."

"And the trailer?" she asked.

"I have it all loaded and parked out on the street. She just packs a few things and the girls."

"And we all meet right out front as soon as we finish down here."

Derrick glanced up at the floor numbers. "That's the plan."

The elevator stopped, and the door opened. "Quon and Xin said they'd make it quick. Quon has exams at nine." Pele stopped as they crossed the lab back to Quon's corner.

Derrick stopped and turned to her. "What?"

She glanced around. "Derrick…"

"Yeah?"

"When you take the girls back to New York…"

His eyebrows furrowed momentarily. "Uh huh?"

"Is Haruku going with you?"

"I hadn't planned on that. I've already imposed on your sister enough. Plus I was going to take care of a few things while I was back there."

"Are you going to be checking into the stuff on Lynn's case?"

"Like the safe-deposit box? With agent Norton?"

She looked down at her hands as she rubbed them together. "Yes."

"And possibly with Eddie looking into Lonnie?"

She looked down while fidgeting with her fingers. "I was wondering if I could… you know…"

"It's not an official case as far as the HPD is concerned, so I'm doing it on my own time and…"

"I'll take time off and pay my own way."

He shrugged. "OK. I'm sure Kattie would like that. Remind me to send you the flight info."

"Thank you, Derrick."

"No worries. I know Kattie would like to spend more time asking you about being a policewoman."

"You're not afraid of what Nancy will say?"

"I think it's too late for that."

It was a quiet, upscale neighborhood a few miles from Telegraph Hill. Street after street of tight row homes with no front yards to speak of, and tiny patches of grass or gardens between the homes and the garages, that in turn, backed against an alley. Mr. Fukuhara was in his small wood-paneled study working at his computer. There was a soft sound of breaking glass. He looked up, shook his head, and went back to work.

A few minutes later he sat back to reread his email. He nodded and reached for the send key when the door to his study opened. He looked up. "Who are--"

There was a single muffled pop. The door to the study closed.

Quon looked up from his computer as Derrick and Pele approached.

"Hey, Quon. I hope you didn't come in too early. I don't want you falling asleep during your exams," Derrick said as he and Pele pulled up a couple of stools and sat down.

"No. I am running on adrenalin at this point. Just a few more days and I will be finished."

"Good morning Lieutenant," Xin said as he came around the corner.

"Hi there Xin. So what have you boys and girl been up to?" Derrick looked around. "Where is Joyce?"

"She stayed late to get this ready, so we let her sleep in," Quon said.

Quon pointed to the large plastic screen he had set up on a cart by his desk. It was one he had invented, and Derrick had been using from time to time.

"I see you have another one of your screens," Derrick said.

"Several," Quon said with a grin. "The captain and the chief each have one as well. And I have over two hundred orders from the web. I am using a 3D printer to manufacture them on demand." Quon brought up a window with a map of the island. Red dots and black dots popped up across the island.

"What are we looking at?" Pele asked.

Derrick grinned. "Statistical magic."

"What?"

Quon pointed to the screen. "The red dots are the location where the cars in your case were stolen. The black dots represent where they were retrieved."

Pele pointed at the screen. "Red all across the island. Black, down in the southwest corner."

"Exactly," Quon said as he pressed another key. Seventeen blue dots came up on the screen.

"What are the blue dots?" Derrick asked as they all looked at the locations on the screen. "They seem to cover the western half of the southern part of the island."

"Yes," Quon said as he sat back. "The Kapolei and Ewa Beach area to be more precise." He pressed a key on the computer. "These blue dots represent the locations, schools, and businesses that are potential shop places where our suspects could be. Assuming they are not operating out of a home garage."

"That cuts the list Soto, and I have been working down considerably," Pele said.

Derrick nodded. "Let's go with the assumption it is a school or business. At least for now."

"That's still a lot of locations for a stakeout operation on an occasional, random series of crimes. I doubt the captain would approve the manpower for that," Pele said.

"Probably not," Quon said as he leaned forward. He pressed another button. Green dots came up over five of the smaller blue dots.

"What do these mean?" Derrick asked.

Quon nodded to Xin.

"Thank you, Professor. I did a soil analysis from both the blue and yellow Civics." He brought up a soil map of the island on another screen. "As you can see, in the area where Judy lives, Oxisols are common. And in the area where we found the yellow Civic, Andisols are common."

Derrick nodded. "I remember these guys."

Quon turned to Derrick. "I called Judy to see when she last cleaned her car. Her parents live in an area where Mollisols are common. She had said the day before it was stolen she had it washed, waxed, and vacuumed."

Xin grinned. "I found a lot of Mollisols in the carpet on the driver's side. If it had been vacuumed, she should get a refund."

"Gotta love those Mollisols," Derrick said.

"It may also mean that just one person stole the car," Pele added.

Derrick sat back and rubbed his chin. "Not necessarily."

"What do you mean?"

"Someone had to drive them around to find the right car."

Pele nodded. "And maybe followed them away from the scene of the theft." She whipped out her notebook. "I'll have them check for any cars that may be following the stolen car."

"Or truck," Derrick added. He turned back to Xin. "Sorry. You were saying?"

"Now," Xin went on, "the area where we found the cars, these five green locations are in areas rich in Mollisols."

Derrick stared at the map on the screen. "And that narrows our focus."

"If we had more data from the other stolen cars, we could come up with a higher probability," Xin said.

"Well if we get more stolen cars with parts missing we'll have more data," Pele said.

Derrick gave a quick snort. "Let's go with what we've got and try to stop any more cars from being stolen."

"How are we going to catch them?" Quon asked.

Derrick rubbed his chin as he sat there. "OK. Maybe one more car gets stolen."

"The Taurus," Pele said.

"If that car has a part missing I want it in here for a complete search." Derrick sat back. "But while we're waiting… let's see what surveillance footage is still available at these locations for the dates of the stolen Civics and see what turns up. And get the names of teachers, students in auto shops at the schools, and employees at these businesses."

"How are we going to do that without setting off alarms for the perps?" she asked.

"Pose as a tool salesperson."

"I'll get right on it," Pele said.

Derrick turned to her. "And our day off at the beach?"

Pele turned to Xin. "You heard him. Videotapes. I'll call Soto on our way about the sales angle." She turned back to Derrick. "See? I delegated. You should try it more."

Haruku scanned the coastline intently as they drove along the Farrington Highway west of Waialua. "Let's stop here Derrick. This should do nicely."

He peered out the window. "Looks nice. Sandy beach, a few palm trees. Clear skies. Not crowded."

"And restrooms," Ahulani added as Becky sat fidgeting in her car seat.

"Yes," Haruku said. "Plus good waves close in for you to take your first surfing lesson. And bigger breaks further out where you can practice your tow-in runs on the jet skis."

"Are you sure you want to place your life in my hands?" Derrick asked.

She reached over and slid her hand on his arm. "Absolutely."

"We can help teach you how to surf," Kattie said as Derrick pulled the Jeep into the parking lot and parked over at the northern end. Pele followed with Kengi, Bink, and Mildred in the RAV.

"This looks like a splendid spot," Bink said as he helped Haruku unstrap the four surfboards on the top rack.

"Are you becoming a surfing expert now dear?" Mildred asked as she unloaded a cooler.

"I am a trained observer, my love."

"Uh huh."

"And I am sure that Haruku knows the best spots on the island."

"Now that I believe."

Haruku nodded toward the waves further out. "This morning the waves are pretty calm. But in the winter when there is a storm off the coast it gets really gnarly."

Pele removed the two surfboards she had on top. When they had finished, Derrick and Kengi unloaded the jet skis.

"Where are we?" Kattie asked as they set up their beach camp for the day.

"The Mokuleia Beach area," Pele said.

"Is it a good place to surf?" Becky asked as she looked out at the gentle waves.

"It is today," Haruku said as she knelt down next to her. "The winds and the waves are calm right now. Perfect for you to help teach your Uncle Derrick how to surf. In the fall and winter, it can be very dangerous. But even now don't go out alone. There can be rip currents. Always have a surfing buddy. And a friend on shore if you can. Just in case."

"In case of what?"

"In case of a shark attack," Kattie said as she turned and grabbed her sister.

Becky put her hands up over her mouth. "Are there really sharks out there?"

Haruku gave her a big hug. "Not today sweetheart."

"Will the kahunas protect us?"

"Of course."

"The big waves seem to be way out there," Bink said as he set up their beach umbrellas.

"We'll stick closer in for now," Haruku said. "Let Kattie and Becky get used to a little different water than Waikiki."

"Not just them," Derrick said. "Someone still owes me a lesson."

"Me too," Kengi added.

There were only a few people in the open-air restaurant by the beach. It was the almost quiet time after the breakfast rush, but not quite time for lunch. In those fleeting moments, the staff cleaned up and got ready at the same time.

Mr. Watanabe poured his third cup of coffee. "I wish I'd never heard of this Blue Line thing, Tomas." He picked up a spoon. "It was a mistake. A terrible mistake." His hand shook as he picked up his coffee. "Big mistake."

Tomas took a sip of his coffee as he watched the people on the beach stroll by. "The idea was good. Sound. It could've worked. It still might. You guys just wanted to rush things, and it blew up in your faces." He set his cup down. "I warned you Daichi. I warned all of you."

Mr. Watanabe poured more sugar into his coffee and stirred. "Did Frank say when this deal will be done?"

"Pull yourself together."

"Did he?"

Tomas took another sip. "He said things are being restructured and should be ready for us to sign after the holiday."

Mr. Watanabe took a deep breath as he picked up his coffee again. "And not a day too soon."

"You guys should have listened to me."

"It is a little late for that now isn't it?"

Tomas shook his head. "Well unless we can hold it together, we could all be out millions."

Watanabe finished his coffee. "Big mistake."

"Catch the wave Uncle Derrick," Kattie yelled out. "Like this!"

Kattie turned to watch as a wave came in. She jumped up and rode the wave.

"That was a perfect take off," Haruku yelled out even though Kattie was now long gone.

"She seems to have this down pat," Derrick said.

"You're still doing your takeoff in two moves. You need to learn to do it in one. What's happening is that you're losing time and speed. And sometimes your board gets hung up on the lip."

"You don't want to learn a bad habit that you'll just have to unlearn later," Pele added.

"I can show him," Becky said as she turned to look for a good wave.

"OK," Haruku said. "Now watch her hands, Derrick. See how she positions her hands as she sets up for the wave. Position your hands by your chest. Then push up, chest up. And never get up on your knees."

"So much balance," Kengi said.

"It's in the mind as well as the body," Haruku said. "Now, after that, use gravity to your advantage. With your hands in position like this, use the big toe of your back foot to spring off."

"Support all of your body weight with your arms and shoulders," Pele said. "Use all that workout time down in your gym to your advantage."

Haruku nodded. "You want your front foot to end up in position a split second after the back foot. It will help you stay balanced and ready to turn."

"You can do it, Uncle Derrick," Becky yelled out. "Just watch me!"

"She's got it down perfect," Haruku said as they watched her execute a perfect takeoff.

"She could be a champion if she lived here," Pele said.

"They both could," Haruku added.

Derrick took a deep breath. "OK. Here goes nothing." He looked for a wave, got ready, went through the steps, then just as he was rising... his left foot slipped to far forward, and he flipped.

"Ouch," Kengi said.

"Your turn," Pele said. "Show him how it's done."

After three hours of lessons, Kattie and Becky were still surfing circles around Derrick and Kengi, but they were getting the hang of it and having fun. Bink was hopeless and continued with the body surfing style of a whale.

Mildred kept Ahulani company under the shade of the large umbrellas as Kattie and Becky slid onto the beach on their last wave. They dragged their boards up to where Mildred and Ahulani were sitting under the umbrellas enjoying the view.

"Hungry?" Ahulani asked.

"Yes," they said together.

"I can't believe it took me six months before I tried this," Derrick said as they all walked through the surf up to the beach.

"You didn't try it here when you came on vacation all those years ago?" Kengi asked.

Derrick laughed. "I had other things on my mind back then."

After a short break for lunch, they were all at the edge of the water again.

Haruku gazed out across the surf in her wetsuit as she held her board. Derrick was checking over his jet ski. Kengi was sitting on his waiting for Derrick to take a run out over the water. "Take me out there," she said pointing at breakers about three hundred yards out.

Derrick looked up. "Out there?"

"Yes. I know the waves are small this time of year. But it will give you some practice."

Pele stepped up beside her with her board and turned to Kengi. "You ready?"

Bink walked over. "You're not going out there are you?"

"The waves are tiny today," Pele said as she turned to Haruku.

"Almost like glass," Haruku said as she nodded.

"I don't know where you two buy glass," Bink said, "but that looks rough out there to me."

Derrick looked out as he adjusted his goggles. "You two do this for fun?"

"The fun comes in the winter," Pele said. "This is just a warm-up."

Kengi looked over at Derrick. "We asked for an ocean adventure."

"I was thinking more along the lines of--"

Everyone turned as the sound of an explosion echoed across the ocean.

"Blimey. I think that boat just blew up!" Bink said as he held his hand up over his eyes.

Smoke and flames were pouring out from a cabin cruiser out just past the breakers. Haruku shoved her board at Bink and jumped on the back of Derrick's jet ski. "Let's go."

Pele shoved her board at Bink as she jumped on the back of Kengi's jet ski. She turned to Bink. "Go call 911!"

"Are you going out there?" he yelled out as Derrick and Kengi fired up their jet skis.

"We're both certified lifeguards," Haruku called out as Derrick and Kengi started to turn. "Now go!"

Bink turned and ran as best he could through the surf carrying the two boards as the others raced out toward the burning boat. "Call 911!" He could see that his wife was already on the phone as Ahulani sat there holding Kattie and Becky. He turned as he stepped backward out of the water. The boat already appeared to be listing badly.

Nancy was staring out the window. They were at thirty-seven thousand feet, and it was pitch black out. She turned to John as he read a book. "Do you think we've made the right choice John?"

"Leaving the girls with Derrick and Haruku while we go back to France?"

"No. The other choice."

John took a deep breath. "Yes. It will probably never come to that. But yes. I think we did."

"I guess this will be a test won't it." She turned to look back out into the night sky.

"It's not like we have any other options now." He went back to reading his book.

"No. We don't."

Derrick and Kengi approached the listing and crippled cruiser. There were no longer flames coming out the side, but something inside was still smoldering. There was a gurgling sound then it rolled completely upside down and began sinking lower into the water. The fire was out. Derrick went to the right as Kengi went to the left. They slowed down, scanning the wreckage for any sign of survivors.

"There are no bodies!" Haruku yelled out as she stood up behind Derrick while holding onto his shoulders for balance. Pele was in the same position behind Kengi. "Pele! We've got to go under!"

Pele nodded. "I know."

"You've got to do what?" Derrick asked as he slowed and turned in a small circle. Haruku grabbed his arms tight. "You and Kengi wait for us!"

Before he knew what was happening Haruku and Pele, both took deep breaths, then dove under the sinking boat.

Kengi looked over at Derrick. "What should we do?"

"They know what they're doing. This time we follow what they say." Derrick stood up and searched the water. "Let's just be ready when they come back up," Derrick yelled out.

Kengi nodded as they both made small circles around the sinking boat searching for any sign of Haruku or Pele. Or anyone else in the water.

Under the surface, Pele went for the bow as Haruku went aft. Pele tried the hatch but it wouldn't budge, so she went aft to join Haruku. She didn't see her sister anywhere as she swam further into the boat. The pilot cockpit looked empty. As she scanned the interior, her lungs began to burn. She needed more air. As she turned to swim back to the surface, she felt a hand reach out and pull her up into an air pocket. Haruku was taking in deep breaths as she pointed to what looked like the forward stateroom.

They could see feet dangling in the water. Pele nodded as she took in several deep breaths. "Ready?" Haruku asked. Pele nodded again. They dove back under and made their way forward. Two children were floating in the water. The boy was trying to hold his head, and a young girl's above water in a small air pocket.

"We've got you," Haruku said as she took in a few deep breaths. "Take as deep a breath as you can and hold it for as long as you can."

The boy gasped.

"How many on board?" Pele asked.

He raised four fingers.

She looked around but saw no one else.

The boy's face dropped into the water. "I'm losing him!" Haruku yelled. She turned him over and gave him a couple of deep breaths to fill his lungs.

"I've got the girl. A shallow pulse." Pele said. "We've got to get them out of here."

Haruku nodded. They took several long deep breaths and dove back under. Haruku led the way through the forward cabin, then down through the galley area and out past the pilot cockpit.

As they made their way out, Pele saw blood and body parts in the galley area. She glanced over at the girl in her arm. She wasn't moving. There was no time to stop and check it out. She followed Haruku out and back up to the surface.

The water around the boat bubbled and churned as the bottom of the hull, now the top of the boat, slowly slipped completely under the surface.

"Where are they!" Kengi yelled out. "I don't see anyone!"

Derrick stood up again and scanned the surface for any sign that Haruku and Pele were coming back up. With or without survivors. "I don't see anything in the water yet." He could feel his heart pounding as they searched. Should they dive in? Or wait like Haruku had told them. They were lifeguards trained in this kind of thing. But still… they probably hadn't done anything this extreme in many years. If ever.

"Where did the boat go?" Becky asked as she and her sister clutched Ahulani's hands.

Bink dropped the surfboards on the beach then raced back out into the water as far as he could while still being able to stand in the surf. Mildred was still on the phone giving directions. She turned to Ahulani. "You and the girls look for all the towels and blankets you can find. When they get back, there will probably be people in shock and worse."

Ahulani nodded and led the girls back to the Cherokee and RAV.

"And get any first aid kits you can find," Mildred called out. "Yes. I am still here," she said on the phone. "No, I don't see the boat now. I think it just sank."

"Over there!" Derrick pointed then turned his jet ski toward the stern. Haruku and Pele popped up on the surface each clutching a child. Kengi reached for the girl as Derrick grabbed the boy from Haruku.

"Anyone else down there?" Derrick asked.

Haruku nodded. "Yes. Two more."

"Maybe one alive," Pele called out. "One is in a lot of pieces. That person must have taken the brunt of whatever exploded."

"I've got to get the other one." Haruku took several deep breaths and dove back under.

Pele looked up at Derrick. "Get them back to shore." She took a few deep breaths and followed Haruku down as the boat sank lower. The hull was now two meters below the surface.

"I'll take them back," Kengi said as he drove closer to Derrick. "You stay here and help them." Derrick brought his ski next to Kengi. Both children were now unconscious.

Derrick strapped the boy behind Kengi. Kengi positioned the girl in front of him as he got ready to leave.

"You sure you can do this?" Derrick asked.

"One of us has to stay here and help Pele and Haruku."

Haruku and Pele swam under the sinking boat and entered the pilot cockpit again. They found a small air pocket and took in quick deep breaths.

Pele nodded to her right. "I'll check forward. You check aft. We meet back here in thirty seconds. If we don't find anyone we've got to get out or we will go down with the ship."

Haruku nodded as they each took one more breath and dove back under.

Derrick watched Kengi for a moment to make sure he would get back safely then slipped into the water. He took a few deep breaths and dove as fast as he could. The boat was now about four meters below the surface. He swam under the boat and looked in the pilot cockpit. He couldn't see anyone. He swam a little to his left for a better look through the windows. The boat was sinking faster now. He guessed eight to ten meters.

He knew that in a few more minutes the boat would be too deep for any of them without diving gear.

Pele made her way back to the galley. She saw Haruku pulling a man out from the aft cabin. She swam over and helped her. The boat was sinking faster now. They had no time to search for an air pocket. It was now or never. They made their way back down to the pilot's cockpit. It was now the lowest point in the flipped over boat, but also the only way out.

Derrick swam back around to the stern just as Haruku and Pele emerged from the cockpit. Each of them was clutching the arm of a man. He grabbed the man's shirt as they all pulled the man back up to the surface.

As they got to the surface, Kengi and a small fishing boat were there waiting for them. Two men were leaning over the side. "We'll get him back to shore," the captain yelled down to them. They pulled the man on board. Pele climbed up on the boat with him.

Derrick turned to Haruku as they were treading water by the boat. "Was that everyone?"

She nodded as she took in a deep breath. "Everyone alive."

Pele leaned over the edge as the captain of the fishing boat fired up its engines. She turned to them. "I'll meet you all at the hospital."

"OK," Derrick called out as he and Haruku got back on the jet ski and headed back to shore with Kengi right behind them. He could see Mildred and Bink working on the children as an ambulance pulled into the parking lot.

He turned as they bounced along the tops of the waves. "You OK Haruku?"

"I'm fine." She wrapped her arms around him and held on tight. "How about you?"

When they got back to shore, they ran over to where the paramedics were treating the children.

"How are they?" Haruku asked.

"Unconscious," Mildred said as they stood there watching the children loaded into the back of the ambulance.

Bink turned to Derrick as the ambulance pulled out of the parking lot. "Why don't you and Haruku follow them in Pele's RAV? Kengi and I will clean up here while Mildred and Ahulani watch the girls. Then we'll take them home in your Jeep."

"Thanks."

"I've got some dry clothes in the bag here. We can change at the hospital," Haruku said as they climbed in the RAV. Derrick raced out of the parking lot with lights flashing and the siren wailing.

Chapter 9

Four hours later, Derrick, Pele, Kengi, Bink, and Haruku were sitting in the waiting room of a hospital in Pearl City. The three victims were airlifted to a bigger hospital for more intense care. Mildred and Ahulani had taken the girls back to Eito's house.

"Any idea what might have caused the explosion," Derrick asked as they all sat there.

"The damage appeared to be in the galley," Pele said.

"Cooking fire?" Derrick asked. "Propane leak?"

Haruku shook her head. "I wouldn't think so."

He turned to her. "Why's that?"

"That was a Canitus," she replied.

"Meaning?"

"There are no gas appliances in the galley," Pele said. "Unless they added it themselves."

"Just the engines," Haruku added.

"You two know your boats," Bink said with a nod.

"A lot of people would come into the stores and resorts bragging about them," Pele said.

"And you think the explosion occurred in the galley," Derrick asked.

"There was a big hole there. It's where the water poured in," Pele said. "It had to be a decent sized explosion too."

"Excuse me a sec." She pulled her cell out of her pocket. "Kobayashi here."

Derrick turned to the others. "Maybe we should take a closer look."

"It's at the bottom of the ocean," Bink said.

Derrick sat back and nodded. "There's that."

"That was Soto," Pele said as she slipped her phone back into her pocket. "They've got the red Taurus. Xin and Joyce are on their way to join him."

"Any missing parts?" Derrick asked.

"Soto said the hood was ajar, so he popped it open." She grinned. "Looks like some ignition parts are missing."

"Where was it found?"

"Ewa Beach area."

"Bingo bango," Derrick said as he glanced down the hall. "Here comes the doctor."

The doctor stopped in front of Derrick as he stood up to meet him. "Are you family or friends?"

Pele stood up beside Derrick as they both pulled out their badges. "I'm Lieutenant Dreadlow. This is my partner, Detective Kobayashi. We were at the scene of the incident."

"How are they?" Pele asked.

"They are all still unconscious. The man suffered a severe blow to the head. He is in a coma."

"Will they be OK?" Haruku asked.

The doctor shook his head. "I can't say for the man. The boy and the girl are in intensive care. But they appear to be in better shape. We will just have to wait and see."

"Brain damage?" Derrick asked.

The doctor shrugged slightly. "We won't know until they wake up."

"When do you think that might be?"

"I have no idea." The doctor looked over at Derrick. "I would like to notify their families."

"I'd like to know who they are so we can," Derrick said. "There were no IDs on the bodies, and the boat sank too fast to retrieve anything but the victims."

"They may be from the same family," Pele said. "The wife didn't make it."

The doctor nodded. "I see." He looked around at them. "Well, it will be tomorrow at the earliest before we know more about their conditions. For now, we just wait. Now if you will excuse me..." He turned and walked away.

Derrick nodded. He turned to Pele. "I want someone here when they wake up. We need to know who they are." He rubbed his chin as he stood there thinking. "And I'd like to know if this was just an accident." He turned back to Pele. "Check with all the marinas on the island. See if anyone has reported a boat or family missing. Let's get a dive team out there."

Pele nodded. "I'll check with the Coast Guard. I'm sure they will want some kind of investigation as well. Maybe we can go out together."

"Good. And..." Derrick trailed off as he thought for a moment.

"And?" Pele asked.

"Let's get Quon out there with us. Ask him if he has any toys that could help us at least identify the boat. That will give us something to work with."

"Like a little toy sub?" Kengi asked.

Derrick laughed. "Something like that."

"I'll call the captain and see if he can pull some strings and get a Coast Guard ship to take us back in the morning," Pele said. "In the meantime, I'll see if Quon can get anything off the man's prints."

Quon opened the door to the office of Compound Q. Workmen were busy running cables to the back of the building. Quon followed the wires to a back room.

Phil Adams looked up. "Hey there Quon. Get done early today?"

Quon nodded. "I will be glad when this is over."

Phil laughed. "Your Ph.D., or this installation?"

Quon dropped his backpack down on a chair by the door. "Both."

Phil climbed out of the raised floor. "Well, we've finished the security connections on all the doors and windows." He leaned over and dusted off his pants. "The security cameras, visual and IR are all installed across the Q."

"You and your men are making great progress," Quon said.

"You will have two security stations. A perimeter position at the guardhouse by the front gate. And a master control center back here."

Quon looked over at the racks where all the computers and video displays would soon be installed. "It seems like a bit of overkill."

Phil laughed. "Paul said you would need it as you get your company up and going. Best to do it right the first time around."

"When will Paul be back?" Quon asked.

"Couple of days. Maybe sooner. He said to tell you he has a surprise for you."

"Really? What kind of…" Quon pulled his cell out of his pocket. "Quon Li." He turned around and took a step away. "Hi Pele."

Phil looked over at him.

"I'm on my way." Quon hung up. "I've got to go."

Phil nodded. "Nature of the job. We'll be here when you get back."

"How are those people?" Kattie asked as Derrick helped Haruku set out dinner.

"They are all sleeping," Derrick said.

"Will they wake up?" Becky asked as she played with her fork. "They looked very bad when Kengi and Bink carried them out of the water."

Derrick sat down between Kattie and Becky. He reached out and took their hands in his. "The doctor said it is too early to tell. They need rest."

Kattie looked up at Haruku. "Are you and Aunt Pele heroes now for diving in the water and saving them?"

Haruku blushed as she poured water into everyone's glass. "No."

"The TV says you are," Becky said with a big grin.

"Have you done this before?" Derrick asked.

"Rescue people? Yes." She shook her head. "From a sinking boat? No. That was my first time."

Derrick nodded. "Me too. I'm mostly a land person."

"Were you scared?" Kattie asked as she looked up at Derrick and Haruku.

"Yes," Haruku said.

"The boat was sinking. Haruku and Pele had to act very fast to get those people out safely," Derrick added.

"I want to be just like you two when I grow up," Kattie said as she poked her fork into a slice of cucumber.

"Let's not tell your mother that when she calls," Derrick said in a low voice.

"I think I would be too scared to do that," Becky said.

Haruku turned to her. "Mildred told me you were a big help on the beach helping those children."

"I kept them wrapped in blankets."

"And that was a vital thing to do," Derrick added as he reached over and put his hand on her shoulder. "And brave." He turned to Kattie. "And Bink said you ran out to help get the children up onto the beach. That was very brave too."

"Bink needed my help. Kengi said he had to get back out to you."

"Well taking your surfboard out to put the children on was excellent thinking," Haruku said.

"I am seven now you know."

"Well not many seven-year-olds would think of that," Derrick said.

"Aunt Haruku is a good teacher."

Kengi opened the door by the hotel lobby waterfall. "Are your days always this exciting?" he asked as they stepped out of the hotel where he was staying and into the warm evening air.

Pele brushed her hair aside. "Fortunately no. What about you? I imagine a big city like Tokyo has a lot happening."

"Yes. But no ocean rescues. At least not for me. I didn't know you were a lifeguard too."

"Haruku was a lifeguard in high school and college. I sort of followed in her footsteps. She was better at it than me."

"You two were sensational out there."

"No." She looked around at the people on the street. "We were lucky today. Pure dumb luck. Another minute and we'd be at the bottom too. If Derrick hadn't been there to help, I'm not sure we could have gotten that man to the surface."

He stopped and turned to her. "So where would you like to go for dinner tonight. My treat."

After dinner and dishes, Derrick was sitting at the table with his laptop on while playing a game of mousetrap with Haruku and the girls.

Becky reached over and picked up Derrick's piece. "You are always the first one out of the game Uncle Derrick."

"I guess it's a good thing I'm not a mouse."

"You're silly Uncle Derrick."

Kattie rolled the dice. "Do you think I could ever become a policewoman like Pele?"

Derrick peered over the top of his laptop. "You can do anything you set your mind to Kattie. Just don't tell your mother I said that."

Kattie moved her piece then slid the dice to Haruku. "Your turn Aunt Haruku."

Haruku picked up the dice and shook them in her hand. "Anything new?" she asked as she looked over at Derrick.

He sighed as he sat back. "No. Nothing on the prints yet." He glanced down at the computer screen. "No boat reported missing. No people reported missing. Yet."

Haruku rolled the dice and moved her piece along the board. "What does that mean?"

He shrugged. "Could just mean he doesn't have a Hawaiian driver's license. Or they were tourists just passing through. Or it could mean it's a family that went out for a few days sailing around the islands. We've expanded our search to the other islands as well. Could mean a lot of things."

"Are we going to go visit Mr. Lipshitz this week?" Becky asked as she reached for the dice.

"Fran did invite us," Kattie said.

"Yeah. I think we can squeeze it in," Derrick said. "I'm sure he would enjoy seeing you again."

"When is his birthday?" Becky asked.

Derrick sat there for a moment. "I don't know. He never told me."

Pele and Kengi left the hotel restaurant and strolled along the concrete walkway toward the beach. The sun had set. The partial orb of the waxing crescent moon hung low over the ocean on its journey across the sky.

Pele reached out and held onto Kengi's arm to balance herself as she slipped her shoes off and stepped into the soft sand. It was still warm. He followed her out onto the sand. She stopped and looked down at his polished black shoes. "You might want to take those off," she said watching the foamy water sink into the sand just an inch from his feet. "Saltwater will ruin them."

He bent over and removed his shoes and socks. A moment later, he caught up with her and stepped between her and the surf. She laughed as she glanced down at his rolled up pants.

"What?" he asked as they strolled through the surf.

"Have you ever heard the story of Nā-maka-o-Kaha'i?"

He shook his head. "No. What is it about?"

"Nā-maka-o-Kaha'i was the older sister of Pele, the goddess of fire. They fought over a man, and Nā-maka-o-Kaha'i banished Pele from their home on Kuaihelani."

"And?" he asked as a surge swept up over their feet.

"She might reach out and grab you, pulling you back into the sea."

He laughed. "Because your name is Pele?"

A bigger wave came up as she reached out and pulled him further up onto the beach. Just out of the oceans reach.

Derrick reached over as his cell rang. "Dreadlow."

"Hi, Dread. Just can't seem to take a day off can you?"

"Hi to you too Captain."

"Be at the Coast Guard Station on Sand Island at 04:30 tomorrow morning. I've got them to send out a cutter with you, Pele, Kengi, and Quon on board."

Derrick glanced over at the clock on the wall. It was 08:30. "Can't seem to take an evening off can you?"

"What can I say. You're a bad influence."

"Thanks." Derrick hung up and set the phone down.

"Was that about the boat?" Haruku asked.

"Yeah. The captain got us a cutter to take us back out. I have to be at the dock at 04 hundred."

"Is that early?" Kattie asked.

Derrick snickered as he reached over and tickled her. "Let's just say you'll still be fast asleep." He looked down at a map he had spread out on the table by his laptop. "I wonder just how deep the water is. Maybe we can dive down before they try to raise it."

"I doubt it," Haruku said.

Derrick looked up at her. "What makes you say that?"

She reached for a piece of paper and picked out a few of Becky's crayons. She started to draw a diagram. She finished and slid it across the table to Derrick.

"What am I looking at?" he asked as he turned it around.

She leaned over and pointed. "This green part is the land. The black, remnants of the volcano. Notice how it slips under the water at a gentle slope then drops off sharply out here?"

"Yes," he said as she traced out the land with the tip of her finger. "Maybe we'll get lucky, and the boat will be here in the shallow part."

"It won't be."

"Why not?"

"You see these waves here?" She pointed to high waves cresting out from the shore.

"Yes."

"This is the breaker. In a normal wave, the waves break because the surface water is moving faster than the water below it. Now where we were, the waves moved from deep water to shallow water in a very short distance. The wave energy is forced up, and you get the waves people like to surf and take pictures of. The breakers."

Derrick nodded. "The science of surfing."

"What you don't know can kill you." She pointed at the diagram again. "Now surfers go out past it to what is called the takeoff zone."

"Where we were going to go before the accident."

"Yes. The people on that boat were out past that."

Derrick reached out to the diagram and pointed to a spot. "Out here past the drop-off."

"Yes. We were out on the eastern edge of the Kaieiewaho Channel."

"What is that?" Derrick asked.

"It's the channel between Oahu and Kauai. At its deepest point, it is over ten thousand feet deep."

Derrick turned to his map. "Well let's hope the boat isn't out there."

The light in the lounge was dim. Soft music played in the background. It was a calm evening as Pele looked out over the water. She couldn't remember the last time she had been on anything even closely resembling a date. Not that this was a date. Not really. It was... what?

The server left their Blue Hawaiian drinks then slipped away to another table. A big glow of light, reflecting off the water skimmed along the horizon. A cruise ship was approaching the harbor.

"I can see why you have never left," Kengi said as he reached for his drink. Two other just emptied glasses sat on the edge of the table. "It is paradise here."

She sighed as she reached for her drink. "It's my home. I belong here."

"And police work is your calling?"

She took a sniff, then a sip of her drink. "Ever since I can remember."

"You've never thought of anything else?" he set his glass down as he looked across the table at her. "Maybe a model or something?" He smiled. "You could you know. Be a model."

Her eyes sparkled as she laughed and thought back years ago. "I did work at our stores when I was a child. Then at our resorts when I was in high school and college."

"What did you do at the resorts?"

"I filled in here and there." She ran her finger around the top of her glass. "You know, lifeguard. Surfing instructor for tourists, tour guide..."

"No hula dancing?" he grinned as he watched the fire from the Tiki torches danced in her eyes.

She laughed. "I did do that."

"Really. What happened?"

"One night, my second night, I saw this man slipping his hand into a woman's purse and taking out her wallet. I jumped off the stage, threw him down on the table into a salad and tied him up with a lei."

"I'll bet the guests found that entertaining," Kengi said.

"The next day my father put me on security. In a back room watching video cameras."

"So not much future as an entertainer?"

Pele laughed as she shook her head. "Zip." She reached for her drink. "What about you? Did you ever want to do anything different?"

He sat back and looked out over the dark waters. "My life was how you say… pre-determined. I follow in the footsteps of my ancestors."

She leaned forward and put her elbows on the table and her face in her hands. She rarely had a drink, and now she was on her second of the evening. "And if your fate wasn't pre-determined?"

He shuddered and grimaced. "When I was growing up, I wanted to be a rock star. With my own band. Can you imagine that?"

She sat back. "Really? What instrument do you play?"

He grinned. "That was one of my problems. I don't play any."

"Are you a good singer?"

"Let's just say, people might pay me to stop."

She laughed again as she reached for her drink. "Well, at least we found our true calling early before doing any permanent damage to ourselves."

"Haruku is very smart," Kattie said as Derrick tucked her in.

"Yes, she is," he replied as he watched Haruku tuck in Becky.

"Do you have to go to work tomorrow?" Kattie asked.

He nodded. "For a while. But I'll try to get back here as soon as I can."

"What are we going to do tomorrow?" Becky asked.

Haruku reached over and slipped a stuffed dolphin under the covers next to her. "Why don't we call Uncle Derrick after breakfast and see where he is. Then we will decide."

"OK."

A few minutes later, Derrick and Haruku walked out into the living room.

"You should get some sleep if you have to get up in a few hours," she said as she followed him over to the lanai. He glanced out over Waikiki and the dark expanse of the Pacific beyond. She stepped up beside him and slipped her arm around his. "You have a long day ahead."

"Some vacation. I thought this part would be easier." He turned and started back across the room. He stopped in front of one of the pencil sketches hanging on the wall. It was a drawing of a woman struggling just above the rocky bottom of the ocean. Her face filled with terror. "The impact zone?"

She stepped up next to him and stared at the sketch. "Yes."

He could feel her warmth radiating from her body as she stood by him. He stared down at the lower right corner of the sketch. In the turbulent bubbles of the crashing wave, he could just barely make out two initials. *HK.* "Did you do this?"

She glanced down at the corner. "Yes."

He took a step back to take in the entire sketch. "You are quite good." She stepped back next to him. "A bit scary… but very real."

She stood there silently.

"Maybe I shouldn't ask. But was this by chance someone you knew?"

"Akela Sanders." She raised her hands up to her mouth and clasped them together. "She was my best friend. We often went surfing together."

"What happened?"

"One day, she called me and wanted to go surfing. She said the waves were cooking. I said I couldn't. I had an exam that afternoon and needed to study. Finals. So she went with some other friends."

Derrick glanced over at Haruku. Her eyes were watery. "You don't have to…"

"The waves were gnarly that day. They shouldn't have stayed out. But… the thrill got the better of them."

"She got caught…"

"She thought she was on the last wave of a set. But they said the next set came in so fast. She lost her balance in the impact zone. Then the next set came in and just…"

He reached out and pulled her close.

"We were supposed to leave the next week for a competition in Tahiti."

"I'm so sorry Haruku." He put his arms around her as she shook and sobbed on his chest. "I didn't know."

"I should have been there for her."

Pele reached out and took Kengi's hand. "I'll see you in the morning?"

"I am the one who should be seeing you home. Not the other way around."

"You are a guest in my city," she replied.

Kengi nodded. "Thank you. For showing me your city."

"My pleasure," she said with an uplifting tone in her voice.

"What time should I meet you in the morning?"

"How about 3:30."

He nodded slightly. "Then 3:30 it is."

"Good night Kengi."

He reached out and gently touched her hand. "Good night Pele."

She lingered for a brief moment, then turned and walked out of the lobby. As she started down the street, she pulled out her cell and scrolled down to a number.

"Hi. This is Eddie. I can't take your call right now. You know the drill."

"Hi, Eddie. It's Pele. I need you to do me a favor. But don't mention it to Derrick. Not yet…"

Chapter 10

The sun was rising behind them as Derrick stood out on the port side deck of the Coast Guard Sentinel-class Cutter with a cup of coffee in his hand. Because this wasn't a rescue mission, the captain wasn't pushing the ship to its full capacity. The twin 4300KW MTU engines were purring along at a mere 18 knots.

Quon stepped up next to him and took a sip of his coffee.

"You all set?" Derrick asked.

"If they can find the boat I will deploy my video sub, and we will take a look," Quon said as Pele and Kengi joined them.

"Look for a name on the stern first. That will at least give us a starting point," Derrick said.

"OK," Quon said.

"How hard do you think it will be to find it?"

"There are strong currents over there. And depending on just how far out the boat is… it could be deep."

Derrick took another sip. "Haruku said we were out past the breaks, so it's probably too deep for us to dive."

Quon nodded. "I hope I can send my submersible down while the salvage crew works."

Derrick turned to Pele. "When will the salvage ship be ready?"

"They are already in the area and searching."

He nodded. "I want to know the ship's name as soon as we can get it. From anybody."

Pele took a sip of her tea. "There are still no reports of an overdue ship or a family missing."

"Any missing people?"

"A couple of teens that don't fit the descriptions of our victims," she said.

"Any word on the survivors?"

She shook her head. "They are still unconscious." She pulled some papers out of her backpack. "I did print off some specs from the web for the boat we think it is."

"Let's go in where it isn't so windy and take a look." Derrick led the way back inside.

"Oh Derrick," Quon began. "I checked the computer last night after my orals and entered the new data into our stolen car search."

Derrick set his coffee down on the table. "How is that coming? Your orals I mean."

"Good. I think."

"So we will be calling you Doctor Li soon?" Pele asked.

Quon blushed.

"Are you going to stay with the police force after this?" Kengi asked.

"I hope so. At least part-time."

Derrick looked up from the map and the photos he and Pele had spread out across the table. "Part-time?" He reached for his coffee. "You going to spend more time teaching?"

"I have that and some other things I am working on."

"Like what?" Pele asked.

Quon grinned. "I will show you when it's ready."

Half an ocean away, Detectives Chuck Patterson and Stan Pusch entered a home near the top of a hill in San Francisco and looked around.

"He's back in the study," the officer called out as he peered out into the hallway.

"Nice place," Pusch said as they made their way down the hall. "Great view from up here."

"Must be nice to be rich," Patterson said as they walked down the hall.

"I'd like to try it someday."

"You got a rich relative I don't know about?"

"My wife buys a lottery ticket every Saturday."

"That's your plan?"

Pusch shrugged. "Gotta have a dream."

"Do we know anything about this guy yet?"

"Besides the fact that he's dead?"

"Yeah. Besides that."

"His name was Taka Fukuhara." Pusch looked down at his notes. "Owns a couple of hotels in the city. Married. A neighbor said the wife is away visiting their daughter in Miami."

"Like I said. Must be nice."

"You buy a lottery ticket this week? It's up to four hundred million."

"No one else in the house at the time?" Patterson asked.

Pusch shook his head. "Perp entered through a door at the back of the home. Broke a glass in the door."

Patterson poked around as the techs dusted for prints on every surface and photographed the scene. "Nothing disturbed anywhere else in the house?"

"No."

Patterson walked over to the desk.

The ME looked up at him then went back to work. The body was leaning back in the chair. "Bullet between the eyes. Nothing was taken."

"A hit?" Pusch asked.

"Be my guess." Patterson scanned the room again. "But why?" He glanced down at the computer. "Have the techs look at this. I want to know what he was working on when he died. I want to know about his family and his business associates. And ask the neighbors if anyone saw or heard anything." He turned to the ME. "Any guesses yet on TOD?"

The ME shrugged. "I need to get him back to the lab. But a quick guess, it could be two days. Give or take."

"Let's get something a little more definitive."

Derrick's cell rang as he stood out on the deck. They were rounding Ka'ena Point and would soon be at the site of the sinking. He noticed the waves were quite a bit higher today. That would make recovery more difficult.

"Dreadlow here."

He turned as Pele stepped out onto the deck.

"Judy. Thank you for returning my call."

"Have you found my car Lieutenant?"

"Yes, we have. Our forensics people are just about finished going over it."

"I am afraid to ask. But how is it? Did they damage it?"

"They did take a part off. Your air-conditioning unit is gone. But other than that it appears to be in good shape."

"When can I have it back?"

"I'll have someone contact you when you can pick it up. It might be a couple of more days."

"Thank you, Lieutenant."

"You're welcome." He hung up and slipped his phone in back into his pocket as he turned to Pele.

"Was that about the civic?" Pele asked.

"Yeah. I told her we found her car. Minus a part." He looked out over the water.

"That may get us a couple of points with the chief."

Derrick grinned. "Yeah." He nodded toward the upper deck. "Anything new yet?"

"The captain said the salvage ship has found what they think is the boat that went down."

"They think?"

She shrugged. "The sea claims a lot of boats."

A seagull swooped down over the bow as they plowed ahead. "That's not reassuring."

Quon and Kengi joined them on deck. "The boat is 95 feet down, on the edge of a cliff that drops off another 300 feet," Quon said.

"Wouldn't allow for much dive time," Derrick said.

"I will get my sub ready," Quon said.

"The salvage people start their retrieval yet?" Derrick asked.

"They are working on it now," Kengi said. "A race before it goes over the edge."

The salvage crew was getting ready to bring up the sunken boat. Derrick and the others were standing on the aft deck watching a video monitor as Quon's sub went deeper and deeper.

"Over there." Pele pointed down at the lower right corner.

Quon maneuvered his joystick and centered the image on the screen as his sub continued to descend. "The depth is about one hundred and ten feet."

"The salvage crew said the strong current is pushing it toward the edge of the cliff," Pele added.

Derrick nodded. "Quon. Can you bring it around to the stern?"

Quon maneuvered the sub. They watched as the salvage ship's divers set the last large strap in place to raise the boat.

"We probably don't want to get in their way," Pele said as Quon maneuvered the sub past the divers. "They are trying to get this finished before it goes over the edge."

"I see something," Kengi said as he leaned in closer. "Is that an 'A'?"

Quon moved in closer and refocused the camera. "I see an 'A.'"

Pele knelt down and leaned in. "A, Z, A…"

"M, I?" Derrick continued.

"A, Z, A, M, I," Quon said.

Pele stood up and pulled her smartphone out of her pocket. "Azami." She entered it into her search.

Everyone else continued looking at the video screen as Quon brought the sub to the port side. There was a gaping hole in the side along the waterline.

"That would do it," Derrick said.

"I've got a hit," Pele said. "It is registered to a Mr. Kagawa. Honolulu. It is out of the La Marina Sailing Club." Pele looked over at Derrick. "It's in Honolulu over on the Keehi Lagoon."

"OK," Derrick said as he turned from the video monitor. "Let's try to get in touch with this Mr. Kagawa and his family. See if they are our victims." He turned to one of the Coast Guard officers standing nearby. "Do you know where they will be taking the boat after they retrieve it?"

"I would imagine their yard. It is over by the La Marina Sailing Club," the officer said.

Derrick turned to Pele. "OK. Let's have a forensics team there with the Coast Guard people. I want to know if this was an accident or something else."

Pele nodded. "I'm on it."

Derrick glanced down at the time on his cell. It was already almost noon. He flipped it open and scrolled down his list of numbers. He turned to look out over the water as the others hovered around the monitor.

"Hi, Fran. Derrick here."

"How long do you think it will take them to raise the boat?" Kengi asked to no one in particular as they watched the divers working from Quon's sub.

"I don't know," Quon replied.

One of the Coast Guard officers walked up to them "We've got to head back and drop you off now. We've got another mission."

Quon looked up. "OK. I will bring my sub back up right away."

Derrick was scrolling up through his phone list and called another number. "Hi, Haruku. Sorry. Things are running a bit late. But we've made progress, and it looks like we're getting ready to head back to Honolulu now."

"What time do you think you will be home?"

"I don't know. I'll call you when we get closer."

Chapter 11

Derrick and his friends were down in the galley as the ship raced back to Honolulu. He glanced out the window. They were making good time on the return trip. The captain was pushing the 28-knot max of the engines.

Pele had her dark blue backpack on the end of the table, her laptop open, and on.

"So, what else can we find on this Azami?" Derrick asked as he turned back to Pele.

"Looks like Mr. Kagawa has owned it for the last four years. He's not a US citizen."

"How long has he been in the country?"

"I can't tell from this. But at least four years," Pele said.

Kengi pulled his cell out of his pocket. "I will see what, if anything, we have on him back in Japan."

Derrick nodded then turned back to Pele. "Do we have an address?"

"Yes." She looked back down at her laptop. "I just got a chat from the captain. He said that he called the hospital. They are all still unconscious."

Derrick stood up and paced around the table. "All right. When we get back to Honolulu, you and I will go home and change. Then we will go out to this address and see who is there."

She looked up at him. "And who isn't?"

"What can I do?" Kengi asked.

"You are supposed to be on vacation," Pele said. "Why don't you do some touristy stuff and I'll call you when we finish at the Kagawa home."

Derrick turned to him. "Savor the moment while you can."

Haruku slipped her cell into her purse and looked across the kitchen table at Kattie and Becky.

"Uncle Derrick is still busy?" Kattie asked.

Haruku nodded. "Yes. But, he will be done later this afternoon. And, he called Fran. We will visit Mr. Lipshitz when he is done. Then have a picnic on the beach. So, what shall we make to take along?"

Becky jumped up off her chair. "Brownies!"

"OK. Why don't you two get ready while I clean up here? We'll go surfing, practice our Italian, then come back and make a batch of brownies."

"Eccellente," Kattie yelled as they jumped off their chairs and ran out of the kitchen.

"No running in the house girls."

"Continue on Keahole Street. Veer right onto Hawaii-Kai. Your destination is on the right."

Derrick glanced down at the GPS system in his E350. "Mute voice." He glanced around the neighborhood as he slowed down. "A lot of condos here."

Pele nodded. "A lot of expensive condos. But you can still find some just under a million."

"What a bargain." A car pulled out as he slowed down. "We can slip in before the gate closes."

"You're not worried about scratching your drug auction E350?"

"I'm fast." He pressed gently on the accelerator and slipped in just as the gate narrowed the gap. "What's the mountain in the back there?"

"Koko Crater," she replied as Derrick slipped into a parking space and turned off the engine. "It has a botanical garden in part of it."

They walked up the steps to the second-floor unit and knocked on the door.

"I hear a TV inside," Pele said. "Someone must be home."

"Or it's on to make people think someone is home."

The door opened. An older oriental woman in dark blue jeans and a yellow shirt opened the door.

They held out their badges. "I'm Lieutenant Dreadlow. This is my partner, Detective Kobayashi. We're with the HPD."

She looked at them in their custom Italian cut suits. "You don't look like police."

Derrick nodded as they slipped their badges into their pockets. "We are looking for Mr. or Mrs. Kagawa."

"I am Mrs. Kagawa. My husband is not here."

Pele turned to Derrick then back to Mrs. Kagawa as she pulled her small black notebook out of her pocket. "Are your children with him?"

She gazed down at her hands as she shook her head. "Oh no. They left us years ago. Our daughter went back to Japan. Our son is a doctor in San Diego."

"May we come in Mrs. Kagawa?"

She took a step back as they entered the condo. It was spacious and had a wide view of the marina and Koko Crater. "Has something happened to my husband?" She closed the door and led them to a couch in the living room.

Derrick looked down at the docks lined up behind each condo.

"Do you own a boat?" Pele asked.

"A boat?" Mrs. Kagawa asked as she sat down.

"A cruiser named the Azami?" Derrick asked.

"Yes. It is my name."

"Do you like going out on it?" Pele asked.

She shook her head. "No. My husband is the sailor. He thought if he named the boat after me I would like it."

"But you didn't."

"No."

"Did your husband ever keep it docked out back here? In this marina?"

"Yes. When he first bought it. Then he moved it. He said he didn't want me to worry about it."

"That was thoughtful of him," Pele said as she glanced over at Derrick.

"When was the last time you saw your husband?" Derrick asked.

She sat there for a moment. "A couple of days ago I guess."

"Does he often not come home?" Pele asked.

She turned to Pele. "He has a very stressful job at the hotel. Sometimes he spends the night there. Sometimes he stays on the boat."

"What does he do?" Derrick asked. "Is he the manager or something?"

She shook her head. "He owns it."

Pele scribbled more notes into her notebook.

Mrs. Kagawa looked over at them. "Has something happened?"

Derrick sat back and took a deep breath. "There has been an accident Mrs. Kagawa."

She sat there for a moment then raised her hands to her mouth. "My husband. Is he…"

Derrick leaned forward. "He is in the hospital. He is in a coma. We would have notified you earlier, but we just identified him."

Pele finished writing some notes then looked up at Mrs. Kagawa. "Do you have any friends with small children?"

Mrs. Kagawa turned to her with a puzzled look. "I don't understand."

"Your husband wasn't the only one on the boat at the time of the accident," Derrick said.

"What do you mean? Who else was there?"

"That's what we are trying to determine," Derrick said. "Do you have any idea who may have been out on the boat with him?"

She sat there and looked down at her hands in her lap. She shook her head slowly. "No. I have no idea."

Down in one of the small conference rooms of the police lab, a tech was staring at a video screen. He hit the pause button, then looked up and scanned the room. "Xin!"

"Yes," Xin replied as he walked over to the workstation.

"I may have something here…"

Xin sat in the chair next to him. "Show me what you have."

"I guess it's time to go back home," Derrick said as he accelerated up the on-ramp to the H-1 freeway.

"And just where is that today?" Pele glanced over at him. "You're not exactly dressed for a visit to the rescue center and a picnic on the beach."

"I've got a change of clothes at…"

"My sister's place. It's OK. It makes sense. It saves time."

"What are you going to do?"

She looked over at him. "Follow these leads by myself. What else? My partner is on vacation."

"And Kengi?"

She turned and stared out the windshield. "Oh. I forgot about him."

Derrick laughed. "I'm sure he'll be glad to hear about that."

"You are one to talk." Her smartphone went off. "Kobayashi here." She sat there listening. "Uh huh." She shot a quick glance over at Derrick. "Are you sure?" She hung up and slipped her phone back into her pocket. "We need to go back to the station for a few minutes."

"Why?"

"Xin says he has something for us?"

Derrick took the off-ramp then got back on the highway heading in the opposite direction.

"So how are you and Kengi…?"

She turned and gazed out the side window. "He's nice. Interesting."

He glanced over at her. "Nice and interesting. Good start. You two do anything special?"

She shrugged. "Just dinner. Walking along the beach. Talking."

"Walking along the beach is nice."

She sat there silently, lost in thought.

"Tell you what Pele. Find out where this hotel for Kagawa is. Get some names, the manager, night manager, see if Kengi has anything back from Japan…" Derrick tapped the steering wheel with his thumbs as he sat there. "And check missing persons again. See if anyone has reported a woman and two kids missing. Then spend some time with Kengi. Tomorrow morning we'll go poking around some more. Together."

"What about Kattie and Becky?"

"Haruku has surfing and language lessons for them in the mornings. Why mess with a routine that's working? I'll call her when I leave the station."

"By then you should know if you are free the rest of the day?"

Derrick accelerated past a delivery truck slowing down to exit the highway. "Hmmm."

Pele turned to him. "Hmmm. What?"

"Let's try to pinpoint when this guy was last seen by someone who cared."

"What's that supposed to mean?"

Derrick pushed back in his seat and rubbed his chin. "Mrs. Kagawa didn't even ask us what hospital he was at."

Derrick and Pele were down in the small conference room in the lab where workstations were set up to go over the video footage. Xin and several other techs and officers were going through surveillance footage.

"What have you got for us, Xin?" Derrick asked as they walked up behind him.

Xin hit a couple of buttons on the computer. The image of a pickup filled the large screen at the front of the room. "We went back through the footage where we found the stolen car, and we discovered this truck always right behind it." Xin turned to Derrick. "We thought it might just be a coincidence. But then we tracked it through eleven more cameras over fifteen miles. Too many to be a coincidence."

"Have you got the plates and registration yet?" Derrick asked.

"Yes." Xin handed him a printout. "It is registered to Mr. Richardson in Kapolei."

"Great job," Derrick said as he handed the printout to Pele. "Find out everything you can on this guy. Work, family, priors if he has any…"

"And you?" Pele asked as she took the sheet.

"I've got a date with a parrot."

"How are those kids we rescued?" Kattie asked as Derrick turned off Highway 93 on their way to Fran's house to visit Mr. Lipshitz.

Derrick glanced up in the mirror at her. "They are still asleep Kattie."

"Is that good? Does that mean they are getting better?"

"Some sleep is good. Too much…"

"Are they going to die?" Kattie asked.

He glanced over at Haruku.

She turned to Kattie. "We will just have to wait and see what happens, dear."

Becky raised her hands up. "We are the four kahunas. We can make them better. Right?"

Haruku grinned. "We can always try Becky."

"Do you think Mr. Lipshitz will remember us?" she asked as Derrick turned onto Fran's driveway.

"He is a very smart bird Becky."

"He's riding out to greet us now." Haruku pointed to the parrot sitting on the back of a golden retriever puppy bounding out to greet them.

"A new member of the brood?" Derrick asked as they all piled out to say hello.

Fran nodded. "Yes. Kupa'a and Mr. Lipshitz hit it off right away. Now they are inseparable."

"Kapow?" Becky asked as she stepped back. Kupa'a's way of greeting appeared to be a wet lick across the face.

"Koo pah ah," Fran repeated slowly. "It means loyal in Hawaiian."

"He's big," she said as she reached back out to pet him. "Hi, Kupa'a."

"He'll get a lot bigger."

Mr. Lipshitz twisted his head as he sat on the back of the dog. "Hello, Becky. Becky want a cookie?"

"He remembers me, Uncle Derrick."

Kengi pulled a chair up to the side of Pele's desk and dropped a bag down by her computer.

She looked up from the screen. "I thought you were out playing tourist?"

"The thought of you in here working on such a beautiful day just didn't seem right."

"Well thank you for the thought, but it is my job."

He opened the bag and pulled out two burgers, fries, and chocolate milkshakes. "But even working policewomen need lunch. Which I guess you haven't had yet?"

She sat back and stretched. "I haven't."

"Then bon Appéti."

She unwrapped her burger. "This isn't what I normally have for lunch."

"Then you will have to show me what you do? What are you working on?"

"Another case we have involving a car theft ring."

"He is so smart," Becky said as she and Kattie played a game of find the peanut under the shell with Mr. Lipshitz.

"It's my turn to move the shells around," Kattie said as she hid the peanut under one then tried to move them around as fast as she could. Mr. Lipshitz watched as the girls giggled and laughed. Kupa'a barked and ran around in circles.

"OK, Mr. Lipshitz. Where is the nut?" Kattie asked.

"You can't find it this time can you?" Becky asked as she sat there and folded her arms across her chest. "We got you."

The parrot looked over at her. "Becky want a cookie?"

She pulled a piece of vanilla wafer out of her pocket and held it up. "Find the nut Mr. Lipshitz."

He stepped over to the shells and walked around them. Then he began pecking at the second one. Kattie reached over and picked up the shell. "How does he do that?"

Becky handed him the wafer. "He is a very smart bird."

"So how is Melissa these days?" Fran asked as they all sat around the table watching Mr. Lipshitz.

Derrick shrugged. "I haven't seen her in a while."

"I'll bet she is busy with that expansion of the clinic," Fran said as she reached out to calm the dog down and get him to sit quietly at her feet.

"I suppose."

Haruku looked over at Derrick.

Fran scratched the dog's ear as he slid his head onto her lap. "That has got to be costing a lot. The new equipment is a small fortune too."

"I guess business has been good."

Fran sighed thoughtfully. "It wasn't always that way. Her husband would always complain that she poured his money into that place as fast as he earned it."

"Did they argue about it?" Haruku asked.

Fran laughed. "That and having kids." The dog got up and left. "Then one day he was gone." Fran looked at Derrick and Haruku. "Rumor was, he ran off with another woman."

"Did they get divorced?" Haruku asked.

"She said--" Derrick began.

Fran shrugged. "I assume so. She never brought him up again. We knew it was a sore subject for her." Fran laughed. "She never liked to fail at anything."

Derrick nodded. "She mentioned that once or twice."

Fran sat back as Mr. Lipshitz found another peanut. "She built a big garage or barn after he left. Said she was going to get some horses. But then she got so busy with the clinic she never did get around to that. Just collected junk in it."

Derrick sat there thinking.

Haruku looked over at him. "Are you all right Derrick?"

He turned to her and smiled. "Yeah. Sure."

Mr. Lipshitz walked across the table and stopped in front of him. "Derrick want a cookie?"

Derrick reached into his pocket and pulled out a little wafer. "Tell me Mr. Lipshitz. When is your birthday?"

"Yes," Becky said. "We want to have a party for you."

He twisted his head as he looked up at Derrick. "Derick want a cookie?"

Derrick gave him the wafer. He made a mess as he took it in his claw and chomped down on it. "Maybe we'll just give him a date." He looked over at Becky and Kattie. "What would be a good date?"

"My birthday," Becky said.

"No. Mine," Kattie said.

Derrick gave Mr. Lipshitz another wafer. "How about…"

"June 25th," Haruku said. "Right in between."

Becky looked over at Kattie. They both nodded.

Derrick sat back. "OK then. Mr. Lipshitz. Your birthday is on June 25th."

"How old is he?" Becky asked.

"I think he is thirty-five," Derrick said. "Give or take."

"How old do they get?" Kattie asked.

"African Grays can live to be quite old," Fran said. "Anywhere from fifty to ninety."

Becky turned to Kattie. "Wow. That's even way older than Uncle Derrick."

"Gee thanks."

Pele glanced around the restaurant as Kengi took a call. After spending the afternoon working, she let him talk her into an evening of fun touristy stuff. First, a walk along the Waikiki shops. And now, dinner at one of the restaurants with a view of the beach and the ocean. For living here all her life, she hadn't spent much time going to the different restaurants that Waikiki had to offer. But she had been here before. No wonder so many people come here for vacation she thought as she reached for her iced tea.

"All right. Call me if you find anything somewhere else." Kengi hung up and slipped his cell into the pocket of his new pair of khaki shorts. "Sorry," he said as he gazed across the table at Pele. "You look beautiful. I like your dress. It is very colorful. Like spring in a rainforest."

"And how many springs have you seen in a rain forest?"

"None. But I can picture it in my mind."

Pele looked down at her plate as she blushed. "Thank you Kengi." She looked back up at him. "I haven't worn this in quite a while."

He beamed. "You should wear it more often. It brings out the green in your eyes."

She blushed as she set down her tea. "Was that your friends in Tokyo?"

"Yes. We have nothing on Mr. Etsuo Kagawa in Tokyo. They are expanding the search to other cities now." He picked up his fork as he stared down at his fish. "I think it is a little overcooked."

"You have no one to blame but yourself."

"I should have removed it when you told me to."

"I've been here before. I know how fast that grill cooks through."

Kengi scanned the restaurant. "I guess they don't want people standing up there hogging the grill all night."

Pele grinned. "Bad for business if they take too long."

"Did you like the brownies we made for the picnic?" Becky asked.

"I loved them," Derrick said as he tucked them in. "Now it's late. I didn't plan on a sunset picnic, so you two get to sleep." He got up and walked to the door. "Good night girls."

"Good night Uncle Derrick, Aunt Haruku," they said together.

"Good night girls. Now get to sleep." She reached for Derrick and whispered. "I'll go out in the other room."

"Will you have breakfast with us in the morning Uncle Derrick?" Becky asked.

"I'm afraid I will be at work for a few hours."

"Will you be checking on those kids?" Kattie asked.

"Yes."

"I hope they are OK," Kattie said.

"Me too," Becky added.

"We all do." He turned the light off and closed the door.

Haruku looked up from the couch as he stepped out into the living room. "What time will you be home tomorrow?"

He sat down beside her. "I'll try to make it for lunch?"

She reached out and took his hand. "Don't worry about them. We'll be busy."

He looked over into her dark eyes. "I'm not worried."

"You should get some sleep too. You were up early this morning."

He squeezed her hand. "I guess so."

Pele and Kengi stopped in front of her condo building.

"At least I got to walk you home tonight," Kengi said as he looked up at the tall building.

"I'd ask you up for tea or something," Pele began. "But I've got to meet Derrick early at the station."

He nodded.

"So he can spend the afternoon with the girls."

"I understand."

"Why don't you call me in the morning? Maybe we can have lunch again."

"I would like that very much."

He reached out for her hand and kissed it. "Until tomorrow then."

"Until tomorrow." She turned and walked up the steps. She smiled as she shot a quick glance back, then through the door.

He smiled as he stood there watching until she was gone. Then he turned for the long walk back to his hotel.

It was dark as Paul Covington stopped his car just off the H-2. He glanced down at his smartphone. "Yeah, Phil. I've got you on GPS."

"What is up there?"

Paul lowered the window and scanned the area. "Looks like some kind of a construction supply place."

"Big box or mom and pop?"

"Mom and pop. But successful from the looks of it."

"Think they'd like a partner? Or maybe they'd like to retire?"

Paul laughed as he raised the window back up. "I'll let you know."

"What shall I tell Quon?" Phil asked.

"You leave that to me. I'll let him know when the time is right." Paul disconnected and dialed another number. "Hey, sis. It's me. I need you to find out anything you can on a business."

"You going to see Derrick this trip?"

"I'll save that for when you come back. You got a pencil handy?"

"Pencils are so last century."

Chapter 12

Derrick reached for the towel hanging over the hand rest as he turned off the treadmill. He looked up at the TV as he wiped sweat from his forehead.

'...so there is nothing more important to me than the future of Hawaii. For those of us, that call these beautiful islands our home, for our children, and also for those that come to these islands to enjoy what paradise has to offer. It is important for all of us to protect this beautiful land and water that we have been blessed with.' The image pulled back from State Senator Richard Aneko to the swaying palm trees, the blue skies, and Diamond Head in the background. 'I look forward to your support that I may carry on the important work that lies ahead of us. Thank you all.' The image hung on the waves rolling onto the beach and parents playing with their children. 'This message has been approved by me, your friend and voice in the Senate, Richard Aneko.'

Derrick stepped over to the weight machine and adjusted the weights. "I guess he talks a good talk."

Pele walked up to her desk and dropped her backpack by a bag. She opened it up and looked inside. "We haven't done this in a while." She pulled out a breakfast burrito and a large mango tea.

"Too long," Derrick said as he looked up from his computer.

She glanced over at his screen as she pulled her laptop out of her backpack. "What have you got there?"

Derrick sat back as he took a bite of his burrito.

"Who is Jack..." She leaned over for a better look. "Is that Melissa's ex-husband?"

"Maybe."

She turned on her laptop as she sat down and opened her burrito. "Maybe?"

"I'm not sure if he is an ex or what."

"What makes you say that?" She took a bite then opened her tea.

"I'm not sure…"

"You think she's seeing him again and that's why she doesn't return your calls?"

He shook his head as he took a sip of coffee. "It's not that."

She sat back and grinned. "You don't take rejection well do you?"

"It's just something Fran said yesterday when we were visiting Mr. Lipshitz."

"And how is our star witness?"

"He's great. He seemed happy to see us. The girls love him."

"How can you tell if a parrot is happy to see you?"

Derrick shrugged. "He flies over to you and says hello. Then asks you by name if you want a cookie?"

"OK. So what's with this Jack guy?"

Derrick picked up his burrito. "I can't find him. Anywhere." He took a bite.

"Really? Well, I found some things on Richardson this morning before I came in."

He took a sip of his coffee. "Anything useful?"

She raised her burrito to her mouth. "He's clean. Not even a parking ticket. But…"

"I like the sound of that." Derrick took another bite.

"He's got two sons." She took a bite and chewed for a moment. "Sixteen and eighteen. Both in high school." She sat back. "They live in the Ewa corner of the island."

"Does the school have an auto shop?"

"It does."

"And the teacher?"

"He's clean too."

"What about the boys?"

"Curt and Fred. Curt, the older one, has a record. Minor stuff. Theft, vandalism."

"Bingo bango?"

"I was going to call the teacher in to have a chat later today. Do you want to be there?"

Derrick took a deep breath as he reached for his coffee. "Yes."

"And the girls?"

"Let's get this closed up so I can go on a real vacation."

"What about the Amazi?"

"Could just be an accident?"

"We can only hope." Pele took a bite of her burrito.

Quon was sitting in his dining room with Paul Covington. Paul was a longtime friend of Derrick's who helped out on an earlier case and took an interest in Quon's work. And, a real estate purchase he had recently made. It was Paul's men working on the updates to the Q.

"This is some fascinating stuff Quon," Paul said as he reached for his cup of coffee. "Your little workshop here and at the garage are incredible." He took a drink then set his cup back down. "But I have something really fantastic to show you."

"Why not do it at the office?" Quon asked.

Paul looked over at him. "Because this *is* about the office. Compound Q." He reached for another piece of toast. "And, I didn't want to go over it with you in front of others."

"Even Phil?" Quon asked as he looked at maps and plans spread out across the table.

"Phil is my top man. But I wanted you to grasp the significance of this in a more... secluded spot."

"So just what are we looking at? This looks huge compared to what I bought."

Paul sat back and laughed. "It's not huge. But what you got is way bigger than you thought. And you own it. However, many pieces are owned by other people now, even though technically the titles belong to the Q."

"How is that possible?"

"A government snafu. The old Compound M was mothballed. Shelved and forgotten. But the titles are quite clear and explicit as to what is included."

"But this is over a thousand acres!"

Paul nodded. "Yes. Fifteen thousand to be in the ballpark. And not all contiguous."

"But," Quon stared down at the map. "Some looks like open space." He pointed to a couple of spots. "There are some businesses on some of this. Some are quite narrow. Too narrow to be of any use. Unless..." Quon looked at Paul. "Tunnels?"

"Be my guess. Open spaces, businesses..." Paul looked down at the map. "Houses and tunnels."

"Are we going to evict all these people?"

"Oh no. That would raise too many suspicions." Paul pointed to a few spots he marked in red. "But we might want to purchase some of them... strategically. And others as they may come onto the market under normal circumstances."

Quon looked over at him. "We?"

Paul chuckled softly. "When I say we, I mean you."

"I do not understand all this." Quon sat back and reached for his coffee. "Just what are you trying to tell me here Paul? And not that I do not appreciate it, but why the interest in my work and my plans?"

Paul sat back. "OK, Quon. I like you. I respect you. And I think your work has great potential. So do others that I work with."

"What others?"

"Your designs for surveillance, for retrieving forensic evidence, for quantum computing and encryption... need I go on?"

"Yes," Quon said. "Where is all this going?"

"We, I, believe in you Quon. I don't want to see you waste years trying to get your vision off the ground. Your expertise is needed now. Today. So I am prepared to help jumpstart you."

"Jumpstart?"

"I want to see you get your labs up and running as soon as possible. I want to see you get your ideas out there in the real world. They will make a difference. Believe me."

"And what is in it for you? The '*we*' you mentioned a minute ago?"

"We want to begin taking delivery of your... products... as soon as possible. We want to see you focusing on your creativity. And... we are willing to pay."

Quon set his coffee down without drinking any. "Derrick knows you. And seems to trust you. But who are you? Really?"

Paul glanced down at the floor as he nodded. "Fair question." He looked back up at Quon. "I work as a contractor for a special branch of the U.S. government."

"CIA?"

"They only wish they had our anonymity."

"NSA?"

"Front page news."

"Then who?"

"I can't say yet. But…" Paul leaned forward. "You say the word and a whole new world will open up to you my friend."

Quon shook his head slowly. "No. First I want to meet with this boss of yours." He turned to Paul. His gazed fixed as questions raced through his mind. "How do I know if I want to be a part of this world?"

Paul sat back. "The world is a dangerous place, Quon. You know it. I can tell by the work you are interested in. And I know that you want to make a difference."

"Everyone knows that."

"Not that I'm knocking the HPD. But you are wasting your talents there. You are bigger than that. And I'm sure you can still help them out from time to time."

Quon sat there thinking.

"Many people have talents and vision. Not as good as you mind you. But few are doing anything about it. And fewer know how. But I can see that you are a man of ideas and action."

Quon sat there staring across the table at Paul. "Can you set up a meeting with this person?"

"You saw the work we can do. And you got a glimpse of what we're up against."

Quon took a deep breath. He wasn't sure what to say. Or do.

"We're losing Quon. We're losing to other governments. And to criminal organizations that are light years ahead of us in technology and funding. We need to make strategic investments to regain lost ground. And you my friend are one of those sound investments."

"I don't know," Quon said. "This is all so…"

"You can be a key player in our country's future Quon."

Quon rose from his chair and stared down at the maps and plans on the wall. "I want to meet this person first."

Paul got up and refilled his coffee. "OK. Then I will get you your meeting."

Derrick looked across the hotel coffee shop table as he stirred a little sugar into this coffee. Young couples with kids, and big families with lots of kids were sitting around having breakfast. Not early risers he thought as it was almost nine. But young couples probably have late nights, and it is hard to get kids up in the morning. He turned to the man sitting across the table from them. He was middle-aged, a few inches shorter than Derrick, and very lean. His facial expressions were those of a tired older man. "How long have you been the night manager at this hotel for Mr. Kagawa?"

The man sat back and thought for a moment. "It will be four years in September. I've been here at the hotel for almost ten years."

"As night manager, are you usually here this late in the morning Mr. Walters?"

"No. But we had two big tour groups come in from Tokyo just before my shift ended. I stayed to help get them situated."

"Do you know Japanese?" Pele asked.

"Yes." He looked down at his half-empty coffee. "My father was in the air force. I grew up in Japan."

Pele nodded as she made a note. "Is that why Mr. Kagawa hired you?"

He looked up and nodded. "It helped that I knew the culture. And the food they like. I started in the kitchen."

"When was the last time you saw Mr. Kagawa?" Derrick asked.

"Friday night."

Pele looked up from her notebook. "What time was that Mr. Walters?"

He shrugged, "I'd say 10:30. Maybe a little later."

"Does he often work late?"

He shrugged again as he raised his hands and held up his palms. "I guess. Our shifts aren't set in stone. Especially management and the owner. And he often likes to stay late."

Derrick sat back. "Are we talking work? Or something else?"

Mr. Walters grew quiet as he looked around. "I don't know what he does in his office. I never go in."

"Do you ever see anyone else go in?"

"My office is a little room in the back behind the reception area. I don't go up to the top floor."

"I see." Derrick pulled a card from his pocket. "Well Mr. Walters, should anything else come to mind, give us a call."

He took the card as he got up. "Sure thing Lieutenant." He stuffed it into his pocket and rushed out of the coffee shop.

Derrick and Pele got up. He dropped a ten and a five on the table. "Shall we see if the day manager is more forthcoming on Mr. Kagawa's extraneous work habits?"

The day manager, Mr. Ishida, sat back in his tall-backed leather chair. "I last saw him Saturday morning."

"Did he say anything to you before he left?" Derrick asked.

"No. But he looked troubled."

"How so?" Pele asked.

"He didn't say anything. He just walked right past me."

"And that's not normal?" Derrick asked.

Mr. Ishida shook his head. "No. He was usually a pleasant man. Not what you Americans would call jovial, but respectful of others. He always took an interest in his guests and employees."

"Any employees in particular?" Derrick continued.

Mr. Ishida stared at him from across his large wooden desk. "No." He straightened out a pen off to the side. "Never."

Derrick and Pele shared a quick glance. She jotted down another note.

"I think he was having an affair with one of his employees," Pele said as they waited for their car outside the lobby.

"Based on?"

"Woman's intuition."

"My coply tingle is in agreement with your intuition. I wonder who it is."

Derrick walked around to the driver's side of his E350 as the valet got out and handed him the keys. He glanced down at the young man's badge as he gave him a ten spot. "Say, Randy."

"Yes, sir."

Pele opened her door and stood there listening.

"Have you seen Mr. Kagawa around much?"

He shrugged as he stuffed the ten into his pocket. "I'd see him. He would say hello once in a while."

"Was he usually alone?"

Randy wiggled his eyebrows and laughed softly. "Not usually."

"His wife with him?"

Randy grinned. "I don't think so."

"What makes you say that?"

Randy looked around and leaned closer. "He spent a lot of time with Mrs. Onaga."

"Did she have a husband?" Pele asked.

"Separated I think."

"Any idea where we can find this Mrs. Onaga?" Derrick asked.

"She works in the restaurant. She's a waitress."

Derrick glanced over at Pele. "Do you happen to know what shift?"

"Day. Usually now. But I haven't seen her in a couple of days. She could be at home with a sick kid."

"Does that happen a lot?" Pele asked.

Randy grinned. "You could say that."

Derrick and Pele shared a quick glance. Derrick turned back to Randy. "Did Mrs. Onaga have a first name?"

"Katsua."

Derrick nodded as he opened his door. "Randy?"

"Yes, sir?"

"Do you know how many children Mrs. Onaga has?"

Randy stood there for a moment. "I think I heard her mention having a boy and a girl."

"Know how old they are?"

He shrugged. "Sorry. I never saw them. Never asked. She was Mr. Kagawa's girl you know."

Derrick snickered. "I think I'm beginning to."

Haruku and Ahulani put more suntan lotion on Becky and Kattie.

"You two look like you grew up on the waves," Ahulani said as she closed the tube and dropped it back into her bag.

"It's a lot of fun," Kattie said. "But I wish Uncle Derrick could be here with us."

"He said to meet him back at home at noon," Haruku said as she brushed sand off the blanket.

"Where are we going after that?" Becky asked.

"How would you like to see China town. We'll stop and try some different kinds of food," Haruku said. "Fei will try to join us."

"Do you know Chinese?" Kattie asked.

"No. But Fei does."

"I thought you knew everything," Becky said.

"Hardly."

Derrick and Pele walked up to their desks and turned on their computers. "What time does this shop teacher get here?" Derrick asked. "What's his name again?"

"Martin. Chuck Martin. Noon. His lunch break."

Derrick's phone began to ring as he logged in.

"Haruku saw that," Pele said with a grin. "You should be on your way home."

He glanced at the time on his cell. "Crap. I should've called her." He reached for the phone on his desk. "But she doesn't usually call me on this phone. Dreadlow."

"I heard you were in the building. Come over and see me. And bring your partner with you."

"We'll be there in a minute." Derrick hung up and put his laptop into lock mode.

"Who was that?" Pele asked.

"The captain wants to see us."

"If it's about the car case," Derrick began as he closed the door to Captain Henderson's office. "We just made a significant step forward."

The captain looked up as he waved for them to sit down. "I am glad to hear that. But it's not why I called you in here."

"You have another case for us?" Pele asked. "Derrick is still supposed to be on vacation you know."

Captain Henderson laughed. "Yes. Thank you for reminding me, Detective." He reached for four envelopes and slid them across the table.

Derrick looked down at them. "What are these?"

Captain Henderson sat back. "Invitations."

"To what?" Pele asked as she picked up one with her name on it.

"A big party. At the Ala Moana."

"Really," Derrick said. "And what's the occasion? A pat on the back for us?"

"When?" Pele asked.

"Saturday night. The 30th." Captain Henderson leaned forward and slid his hands together on the desk. "It's casual, Hawaiian theme. Hawaii: Gateway to the 21st Century. Anyone who's anyone from politicians, top business leaders, dignitaries, and entertainers will be there."

"Why us?" Derrick asked. "We providing undercover security?"

"It could be the work you two did over the past couple of weeks." Captain Henderson glanced over at him. "You seem to get noticed by people in high places. Dread."

"I don't plan it that way," Derrick said as he looked at the names on the other two invitations.

"They must have heard that Bink and Kengi are still on the island," Captain Henderson said.

Derrick glanced up at him. "And your invitation? Sir?"

He nodded to the opened invitation off to the side. "I'll be there. In all my years on the force, I was never invited to anything like this." He smiled. "And bring a date." He leaned forward again. "And... not each other. This isn't a stakeout. It's a social event."

Officer Marsha Kendal walked up to them as they stepped out of the captain's office. "Chuck Martin is here."

Derrick looked up from the invitations in his hand. "Who?"

"He's the shop teacher at the high school. Where is he?" Pele asked.

"Room 4."

Pele nodded. "Thank you, Marsha."

"We appreciate your coming in," Pele said after making introductions. "We just have a few questions to ask you about some of the cars that the students work on at school."

Chuck looked up at them, arms on the table, palms up. "Fire away."

"Where do the students get the cars they work on?" Pele asked.

"I have a few old clunkers around, and I let them work on their own cars, or cars of friends to get real-world experience. No crime in that is there?"

"None," Derrick said.

"Did anyone work on a 2002 Taurus lately?" Pele asked.

Chuck sat there for a moment. "Yes. Curt Richardson. He was working an ignition problem on a friend's car. He had a bit of trouble with it as I recall."

Pele shot a glance over at Derrick. He nodded slightly.

"Where do they get the parts they use on the cars?" Pele asked.

He shrugged. "Supply stores, junkyards, hell the internet I suppose."

"So you don't know where?" Derrick asked.

Chuck shrugged. "I don't check receipts if that's what you're asking."

Derrick turned to Pele as they all left the room. "Get a warrant for Curt's home. And I want some fiber and DNA samples to check against what we found in the stolen cars."

"Do you want to be there when we go in?"

Derrick nodded. "Let's try to do it in the morning."

"After breakfast, but before the girls finish with their surf lessons?" Pele grinned.

"I just want to be sure we have all our ducks lined up before we move in."

"Uh huh."

Derrick poured a cup of coffee as he and Pele stopped in the breakroom.

"You should be going home now, not pouring another cup of coffee."

Derrick stood there looking down at the half-filled cup. "Force of habit." He poured it down the sink. "You going to go with Kengi? To that party?"

She looked out the window as she made a cup of tea. "I'm thinking about it."

"Good choice. Make up for making him work while he's here on vacation."

She turned to him. "Are you going to call Melissa? Again?"

Derrick took a deep breath as he dropped the empty cup into the trash. He turned to her. "Actually Pele. Would you mind terribly if I asked your sister?"

Chapter 13

Quon sat back as he, Paul, and Phil looked at the building plans taped up on his office wall at Compound Q.

Phil laughed. "I just can't believe that anyone could forget that they owned all of this."

Paul shrugged. "Out of sight, out of mind. When the funding was cut, they locked up the map and plans in storage. Most of it was vacant land, and the facilities we're interested in are mostly underground."

"Deep under by the looks of it." Phil shook his head as he stared at the plans. "And other people built on top of it."

"And I really own it now?" Quon asked.

"It's all yours, my friend. The surface parcel you bought is the key to the rest."

"Why?" Phil asked. "Why doesn't the government want to try to get it back?"

Paul reached for his can of Coke. "Some things are best left forgotten. It was shelved and locked away for a reason. And…"

"And?" Quon asked.

"I haven't told anyone about what I've found except the two of you."

"No one?" Quon asked. "Not even the other part of *We?*"

"OK. One more person knows. But he is the one who said to keep it this way." Paul got up and walked over to the map on the wall. "We have an opportunity to create something unique here my friends. An ace up our sleeves."

"So how do you suggest we proceed with this?" Quon asked.

"We need to come up with an overall strategy. Get a manufacturing facility in place for some of your ideas. Set up a command center. We will set up some kind of cover lease agreement to get an income flow for your company ASAP."

"A Command Center?"

"Do you remember how we were able to get information during our case with Dobson?" Paul asked.

"Yes."

"Well, we need a backup facility. One that is more secure, and is--"

"Off the grid?" Phil asked.

A slight smirk crossed Paul's face as he raised and lowered his eyebrows. "One that is known only to us. At least for as long as we can keep it that way."

Quon nodded. "I have a financial person in my company already. I should bring him in. Is that OK?"

Paul nodded. "Todd Pendergast."

"You know him?"

Paul smiled. "He already has clearance to work with us."

"Does he know about this yet?" Quon asked.

"Not yet. But you should call him. Get him out here."

"I have never been here," Pele said as she looked around the dimly lit restaurant. It seemed like stepping off Oahu and onto Honshu. "It's like going from Honolulu to a quiet garden outside Tokyo." There were intricate works of art, paintings, jade, gold leaf and shell designs, as well as statues from across Japan. They depicted its long and traditional history as they lined the nooks and crannies of the walls. The secluded booths along the walls were each set up as an island unto themselves. You felt as though you were transported to a different world. A different time. Soft oriental music filled the air as servers dressed as Geisha girls further added to the ambiance of the experience.

"Do you like sushi?" Kengi asked.

"Let's just say I don't dislike it. I just don't have the opportunity to eat it often."

"Meaning?"

She looked down at her water glass. "I work a lot. I don't go out much."

"I find that hard to believe. A woman as beautiful as you?"

She continued to stare down at her glass. "The only time I have been out to dinner in the last six months, or a picnic on the beach has been with Derrick. And that was work."

"It was work?"

She looked up at him. "I mean work-related. It wasn't work going out with him."

"Are you two…?"

"I didn't mean going out with him." She shook her head. "We are just partners."

"So is he dating your sister?"

"No." She opened the menu. "What is good here?"

"I have no idea. So why don't we each get a dinner special? And three different items. We can share and sample them."

"OK. What are you going to get?"

He ran his finger down the list. "I will order the Sashimi, Ahi Vegetable Tempura, and the Broiled Sabe." He looked up at her. "And what will you order?"

"How about... the Butterfish Misoyaki, the Nigiri Sushi, and the Mini Tempura Udon?"

"And a bottle of sake?" Kengi asked.

"A bottle?"

"We took a cab."

"OK. But first I have something for you."

"A gift?"

"Not exactly." She reached into her purse and pulled out an envelope. She slid it across the table to him.

Kengi's eyebrows furrowed as he opened it. He smiled. "An invitation?"

"There is a big party this Saturday night. I know it means you staying a couple of extra nights."

"Are you going?" he asked as he closed the envelope.

She reached for her water glass and ran her finger around the top. "I thought maybe... that is if you would like to stay and go..."

"Would you do me the honor of accompanying me to this party Ms. Pele Kobayashi?"

She looked up at him. "Yes, Mr. Nakamura. I would love to accompany you to the party. But it's a Hawaiian theme."

"No problem. I bought a shirt to take home as a souvenir."

"Ask Bink if he would like more brownies," Becky said as Derrick talked on the phone.

"You're the first one out of the game again Uncle Derrick," Kattie said as she picked up his piece and removed it from the board.

Derrick looked over at Becky and Haruku. "He said he would love some if you are making them anyway."

Becky looked over at Haruku.

"I think we can whip up a batch," Haruku said.

"You heard that?" Derrick asked as he glanced over at his laptop screen. "What did you and Mildred decide about the..." He sat back in his chair. "Well look. The thing is on this side of the island. And my condo is empty. Don't spring for a couple more nights over there. Why not stay at my place?" He nodded and grinned. "Good. It's settled then. I'll meet you on Friday. Just let me know when you will be here." He paused for a moment. "Then it's settled." He hung up.

"What was all that about?" Haruku asked.

"Nothing. Just Bink and his wife getting ready to go back home."

"When do they leave?"

"It looks like Sunday afternoon now. The 1st of July."

"A couple of extra days?"

"It's paradise."

"I win!" Kattie yelled out.

"And now it's time for bed," Derrick said.

Becky looked over at her sister. "We should get a better prize than that for winning."

"So you are going to let them stay in your place?" Haruku asked.

"Why not," he said as he helped Kattie clean up the game. "It's empty. I'm here with you."

She smiled as she picked up the dishes and set them in the sink.

Kengi looked over at Pele as he sampled the Misoyaki. "Aren't you going to get that?" he asked as her purse rang softly.

She looked down at it, then across the table at him. "No. Not tonight."

Kengi nodded approvingly as he picked up another piece with his chopsticks. He held it out toward her. She leaned over as he slid it into her mouth.

The messaging service on her smartphone took the call. "Please leave a message, and I will get back to you as soon as I can."

"Hi, Pele. It's Eddie. I've got some info on that number you left me. Not sure if it means anything. Give me a call when you get the chance. Bye."

"We had fun in China town," Kattie said as Derrick tucked her in. "I am glad you could join us."

"Me too," he said as he pulled the sheets up around her. "I just wish I could have gotten there earlier."

"You weren't that late," Haruku said.

He looked over at Haruku. "Well when we finish up this car case, I'll be all cleared up at work."

"They have strange food there," Becky said.

"You told me you liked it," Haruku said as she tucked her in.

"I did. But some of it felt funny."

"That was the octopus," Derrick said. "It's a delicacy."

"It was chewy," Kattie said.

"What is a delicately?" Becky asked.

Derrick looked over at her. "It is something exquisite that people don't get to eat every day."

"I'm glad it's a delicacy," Kattie said.

"You mean you don't want it for breakfast in the morning?" Derrick asked as he tickled her. "I got some special just for you."

She squirmed and giggled. "No."

He got up and kissed them both good night. "Now you two get to sleep."

"What are we going to do tomorrow?" Becky asked as Derrick and Haruku walked over to the door.

He reached for the light switch. "Well, I have to go to work in the morning. But we will do something in the afternoon." He sat there for a moment. "Maybe late afternoon."

"Promise?" Kattie asked.

He stood there with his hand on the switch. "I can't promise tomorrow."

"Do you have more bad guys to chase?" Becky asked.

"Yes."

"Your job sounds like fun," Kattie said.

"No it doesn't," Becky said. "You don't get to do anything else."

"Can we go snorkeling again?" Kattie asked. "The day after?"

"Back with the sea turtles?" Becky added.

"We'll see." Derrick turned to Haruku.

She nodded. "We will spend the day around Waikiki. Call when you are getting off. I'll have them ready when you get home, and we'll pack a picnic somewhere."

"Can we make more brownies?" Becky asked.

"You're going to turn into a brownie," Derrick said.

"Brownies after surf lessons?" Haruku asked.

Kattie looked over at Becky. "Yes," they said together.

"OK. You two get some sleep now," Derrick said as he turned off the light.

"Good night Uncle Derrick. Aunt Haruku," they said together.

"Good night," Haruku said as Derrick closed the door.

"I'm impressed," Kengi said as he slipped his credit card into his wallet.

"About what?" Pele asked.

"You finished dinner without checking your messages."

She set her shoulders back as she sat there. "Yes. I did. If it were really important, they would have called back. And they didn't. So there."

He laughed. "I will try to remember that. Never answer the first call."

"Thank you for a wonderful dinner Kengi."

"Thank you for joining me."

Pele reached for her purse as they got up from the table.

"Perhaps someday you will come to Tokyo, and I can take you to one of our excellent restaurants there?"

She looked up into his eyes and smiled. "Perhaps."

Derrick and Haruku were sitting on the couch with the living room lights dim, looking out over the glowing lights of Waikiki.

He turned to her. "You know, there is this thing on Saturday night." He glanced down at the table and reached out to push a coaster back from the edge. "It's a big party thing that we've been asked to attend… the captain, Pele, and I…"

"Don't worry Derrick. I can watch the girls."

He turned back to her. "No. I was thinking that… I mean if you would like…"

Her eyes sparkled as she watched him.

"If I would like what Derrick?"

"Would you consider going with me Haruku?"

She tried not to smile. "You mean like the two of us… on a date?"

He gazed into her eyes. "Yes." He could feel his heart skip a beat as he leaned ever so slightly toward her. "Yes. Absolutely. I've been told it will be the social event of the year."

Suddenly she leaned back away from him. "Melissa turned you down again?"

His shoulders slumped as he reached out and took her hand. "I didn't ask her." He continued to stare into her glistening hazel eyes "I want to take you. I want to do something special with you. Something fun. This came up, and I thought of you."

"Really?" She leaned toward him ever so slightly. "I was really the first person that popped into your head?"

"Yes," he replied. "Is that so hard to believe?"

She beamed as she held his hand. "Are you sure you want to be seen with me? There might be photographers there."

"I would be honored to be photographed with you."

Chapter 14

Derrick was at his desk in the station before anyone else. His laptop was open, and he was checking the Dallas DMV database for any records of Jack Crawford. He sat back and slumped down in his chair as he clasped his hands in front of him. He sat there bouncing them off his upper lip as he stared at the screen. "Nothing."

He had gone back five years in Melissa's bank statements. The only change was when Jack's checks stopped coming in. That by itself could support her story. They split up, and he moved out. At that time, she also set up her own account. However, the joint account wasn't closed, just inactive. It had been inactive for four years. With the exception of one annual one hundred dollar deposit. Every March.

The money taken out of the joint account paid off the mortgage on the house that was in both names. The title was still in both names. Maybe she got the house. Her business loans were paid off over the next four years. The business was in her name only. On the surface, things looked in order. But why was the joint account still open? And why was the house still in both names?

Derrick pulled his cell out of his pocket. He scrolled down and dialed a number.
"Hello."
"Todd?"
"That you Derrick?"
"Sorry to wake you. I was just going to leave you a message."
"I'm always up early these days. Business is booming. How are you? What can I do for you?"
Derrick sat back. "I'm good. I've got something I'd like you to look into."
"Official HPD?"
"Could be…"

Haruku was looking through one of her sketchbooks as she sat at the dining room table waiting for the girls to get up. She reached for her tea and took a sip. She set it down and flipped through a few more pages. They were drawings she had done years ago. So long ago that it seemed like another lifetime.
"Good morning Aunt Haruku."
She looked up and closed the book. "Good morning Kattie. Did you sleep well?"
"Uh huh."
"Is your sister awake?"
"I don't know."
"Well, why don't you go check, and I'll get breakfast started."
"Then can we so surfing?"
"Yes, we can."
Kattie turned and ran off down the hall to get her sister out of bed. "It's time to get up Becky."

Derrick sat there staring at his laptop screen. If Melissa and Jack had split their assets, he couldn't find any evidence. Maybe they had stocks or bonds? Maybe he had a pension that balanced the numbers out? But why was the mortgage paid, yet the title still held jointly? He sat back and stretched his arms and shoulders. Todd could go through their taxes and figure things out. Maybe see something he was missing.

Derrick shook his head slowly as he rubbed his chin. "Hmmm." There was still one nagging question that he couldn't explain away.
"Good morning."

He looked up as Pele dropped her backpack onto her desk. "You look cheerful this morning."

"I am."

He reached out and closed an open file lying out on his desk. "Any particular reason?"

She shook her head. "What have you got there?" She glanced over at his screen. "Melissa again?"

Derrick took a deep breath. "Her husband."

"What did you find?"

He snorted. "It's what I'm not finding."

"What aren't you finding?"

"Him. Jack. There is no record of him in Dallas or anywhere else in Texas. I think I'll have Quon run him through the other states."

"Speaking of which, I ran into Quon on the way in. He was on his way out with Xin and Joyce."

Derrick looked up at her. "Why?"

"The boat is here."

"The Azami?"

"How many boats are we working?" Pele asked.

He reached over and closed the Dallas database.

She sat down. "He said to give them a couple of hours to at least get started."

"Do we have the Richardson warrant yet?"

"Should be here by 8:00."

"I can see it's going to be another busy day in paradise."

"Hi there." Derrick and Pele looked over. Kengi was coming toward them with two brown bags.

"Something smells good," Derrick said.

"And familiar," Pele added.

Kengi set them on the table and slid a chair over to the side of their desks. "A treat from Juanita and Alfonso." He opened the bags. "I didn't know what to order, but she did."

"Well thank you Kengi," Derrick said as Kengi passed a coffee to Derrick and tea for Pele. He set out coffee for himself, then three breakfast burritos.

"The boat is here," Pele said as she popped the top off her tea. "Quon is on his way over now."

"And…" Derrick took a sip of his coffee to wash down a burrito. "I did some checking on Mrs. Kagawa's phone records."

"You mean something other than…" she grinned as she nodded at his laptop.

"Yes. I had a busy morning while some of us were sleeping it away."

"What did you find?" Kengi asked then took a bite of his burrito.

"It seems there are over a dozen calls to a private detective agency over the last four months."

"Do we know what about?" Pele asked.

Derrick slid a piece of paper toward her. "No. But we will after you talk to them this afternoon. Start with the owner. Sam Goodlow. Here are the number and address."

"And where will you be?" Pele asked.

He sat back. "I--"

She nodded. "I'm on vacation. Got it." She reached for her tea. "You sure you don't want to go along. Give you a chance to mingle with the shadow forces on the island."

He sat there for a moment. "OK."

"Not all of us were sleeping late," Kengi said with a wide grin. "I have some news as well."

They turned to him. "Which is?" Pele asked.

"Mr. Etsuo Kagawa is from Kobe."

"Anything else that might shed some light on this?" Derrick asked.

"It seems he and his brother, run the three family hotels. One in Kobe. One in Tokyo and the one here."

"So?" Pele asked.

"The brothers have had more than one, how would you say it? An altercation with each other."

Derrick sat back and reached for his coffee. "Any involving the police?"

"Three. It appears that after the last one, about two years ago, the brothers reached some kind of agreement. The brother in Japan would run the hotels there, and the one here would run the Hawaii hotel."

"End of story?" Derrick asked.

"I'm still digging. But I do believe that Etsuo has spent most of the last several years here in the U.S."

Derrick took a sip and set his coffee down. "OK. First things first. Let's see what Quon finds. Was this an accident or something more? Then we can…"

"Good morning all," Captain Henderson said as he walked up to them "I see that none of you knows what it means to take the day off."

Derrick looked up with a wide grin. "I am taking the girls snorkeling this afternoon."

The captain nodded. "I just thought you might want to know." He looked around at them.

"Know what?" Pele asked.

"Mr. Kagawa died about thirty minutes ago."

"And the kids?" Derrick asked.

"No change." He glanced down at their burritos. "Do we know if this was an accident yet?"

"We should have an idea soon. Quon is over at the boatyard as we speak."

"Good. Let me know as soon as you learn something." The captain walked back toward his office.

Derrick finished his coffee. "OK boys and girls. We now have either a very tragic accident."

"Or a double homicide," Pele finished.

Chapter 15

"Well now isn't this a studious looking group," Detective Soto said as he and Officer Pope walked up to Derrick's desk. "Or they are all playing internet poker."

Derrick and the others looked up from their work. "Is that what I hope it is?" Derrick asked.

"It is. We're ready to roll. The boys just left the house for school. I've got a team watching them."

"Just what are you hoping to find at the house?" Kengi asked.

66

Derrick turned off his laptop. "Probably nothing. It's a petty operation as far as car rings go. I just want to shake them up a bit."

"You sure we've got the right perps?" Soto asked.

"I'm sure."

"You don't want to wait for the lab results to get back?" Pele asked.

Derrick shook his head. "They'll just add more support to what we already know."

She turned off her laptop as she and Kengi gathered up the loose files strewn across the desk. "Just put the fear of the Dread into them?"

Derrick grinned. "Something like that. Soto, you take the house with a couple of officers and the techs. Pope, you, and a couple of officers are with Pele and I. We'll take a tech to go through the school shop."

"What should I do?" Kengi asked.

"Why don't you come along. Adds to our overpowering presence."

"Scare the shit out of them?" Soto asked.

"I hope at least one of them."

"Is this your sketchbook?" Becky asked as Haruku cleaned up the breakfast dishes and prepared their picnic for later. She opened the book laying out on the kitchen table.

"Yes," Haruku said as she looked over at Becky. "I was just looking through some old drawings earlier."

"You are so good. These people look so real."

"You could do drawings for the police," Kattie said as she sat down next to Becky. They flipped through the pages while Haruku worked.

"Who are all these people?" Becky asked as she turned the page.

"Just people I've met over the years. Friends. People out on the beach."

"Who is this girl?" Becky asked as she turned the book so Haruku could see. "She is very pretty."

Haruku reached up and brushed her hair from her eyes as she glanced over. "That was someone I knew. A long time ago."

"Do you remember her name?" Kattie asked.

"Hope." Haruku turned back to the counter.

"Was she a student of yours?" Becky asked. "Like us?"

Haruku turned to them and let out a little sigh. "Yes. You could say that." She turned back to the counter. "I'm almost finished here. Go put on your swimsuits, and I'll put on your cream. Then we'll be all set to go."

"Is kuku coming with us today?" Becky asked.

"No. She had something else to do this morning. But we will stop by the store and pick up my mother. Now get going. I'll put this in the refrigerator, so it will be ready when Derrick gets home."

Soto knocked at the door of a small house on the edge of Kapolei. He took a deep breath of the fresh air as he scanned the area while waiting for someone to come to the door. Freshly mowed grass added to the fragrance of the morning air. Three tall queen palm trees provided a little shade. A woman in her mid-forties opened the door a crack.

"Can I help you?"

"Are you Mrs. Richardson?" Soto asked as she looked out at the four police officers fanning out around the house. Two technicians jumped out of a van parked at the end of the driveway.

"Yes. What is going on here?"

He flashed his badge as he handed her the papers. "I am Detective Soto with the Honolulu Police Department. We have a warrant to search the house and the garage."

"What?"

"Is anyone else at home?"

She held the warrant in her hand but didn't look at it. "No. My husband already left for work, and our boys are at school."

Soto, one of the officers, and the two techs pushed past her. "Where are your son's bedrooms?"

"In the back. Down the hall."

Soto nodded to the techs.

"Just what is it you are looking for?" she demanded as they began searching through drawers and closets.

"Stolen auto parts ma'am."

She snorted. "You've got to be kidding. Why would my sons have stolen auto parts?"

Derrick and the others were waiting in the principal's office when Curt and Fred entered. Derrick wanted them brought here together to knock them off balance. Then he had Pele explain that they were looking into some thefts. After that, they took Curt to another room with the vice principal, while he sat down with Fred in the principal's office. Officer Pope stood straight, tall, and formidable behind the boy.

Derrick sat down at the side of the desk. He leaned back as he stared up at the boy. "Have a seat son." He nodded to a chair by the desk. The principal sat in his own chair behind the desk.

Derrick leaned forward and put his hands down on the desk. Palms down. He sat there watching the boy for a moment. "You look like a smart boy Fred." He sat back and stared across the desk at the boy who was looking more frightened by the minute. "I'm guessing that you know why we are here."

"I don't know what you are talking about," Fred said. "We haven't done anything wrong."

He sat there for a moment as his stare bored into Fred's eyes. The boy shifted nervously in his hard wooden chair.

Derrick drew in a long, slow breath as he placed a file on the table and slowly opened it. He watched as Fred looked down at the photos of the stolen cars. Derrick pulled a few out. Slowly. One at a time he spread them out across the top of the principal's desk. Then he pulled out a couple of surveillance photos. Some with the stolen cars, some with their father's pickup truck.

"Do you know that you are old enough to be tried as an adult in this state?" Derrick asked as he continued to take photos out of the file.

"It... it wasn't my idea."

"So it was Curt's idea to get into the auto repair business?"

"We just wanted to fix our cars up."

"Then you expanded to helping friends?"

"That was his idea too. Make a little extra cash," he said.

Derrick took out the last photo. The one of the 2002 red Taurus. "And this one? Was this for a friend as well?"

Fred sat there. He was shaking. Fear filled his eyes. "A friend of a friend who heard about us."

"Kind of risky wasn't it? Someone you didn't know?"

"Curt…"

Derrick leaned forward. "Curt what?"

Fred shook his head.

He sat back again. "Your brother has already taken steps down the wrong road, Fred. Are you sure you want to follow in his footsteps?"

He sat there staring down at the photos.

"What will your parents think? What will mother think?"

Fred just sat there.

"Officers are with your mother as we speak."

He looked up at him. His eyes grew wide. His body stiff.

"We have a warrant to search your home, your locker here. Bring in your friends for questioning. We have tied specific people that go to school here with specific years and models of cars that you and your brother have stolen. Do you really want to put your family and friends through all this? They may go to jail for receiving stolen goods you know. What kind of a friend would do that?"

Fred looked down at the photos again then back up at Derrick. "What do you want?"

"A confession would be a good start," Derrick said. "But I'd also like to know why? Why go to all this trouble?"

The boy shrugged. "The excitement?"

"You'll see how exciting jail can be too. Is that what you want?" He sat back. "This doesn't have to end badly Fred. Not for you."

"What do you want to know?"

Derrick and the others were all outside the school. He was on his cell as officers loaded the boys into separate patrol cars.

"So does this mean that you finished up the car case?" Haruku asked.

"It does. I'll leave the paperwork to your sister."

"Are you coming home now?"

"Just one more stop. The Amazi is in the boathouse and forensics is going over it. I want to see if they've figured out what caused the explosion. Then I'm on vacation."

"OK. Call me when you are on your way home."

"You'll be the first one I call."

"Bye Derrick."

"Bye Haruku. Tell the girls I love them and I'll be back as soon as I can."

Derrick, Pele, and Kengi got out of his E350 and walked over to the boathouse where lab technicians were checking the Azami for clues. The HPD, the Coast Guard, and the FBI, all had investigators there to determine what happened.

Pele stepped off to the side as her phone rang. She glanced down at the number. "Eddie?"

"Hi, Pele. I left you a message last night, but I didn't hear back."

"Sorry. I, we've been busy on a case. Did you find anything?"

"I'm not sure. There are no direct calls from the number you gave me to this Lonnie guy. But, there were four calls from that number to a lieutenant in the Donatello family, followed by four calls from that number to Lonnie. Like within five minutes. Tony Minucci owns the number. I also emailed you his name. Now that can't be a coincidence."

"No. I don't think so either. Thank you, Eddie."

"Does that help?"

She looked over as Quon climbed down from the boat. "Yes, it might."

"So who is this guy making the calls from Hawaii?"

"Just a hunch at this point Eddie. I've got to go. For now, let's just keep this between us."

"OK."

"I'll talk to you later. Thanks."

"OK. If you need anything else, just holler."

"Thanks. Bye." She hung up, checked her email, and rejoined the others as Quon walked toward them.

"Any ideas yet?" Derrick asked.

"Marta was by earlier. She took the remains of the woman's body back to her lab." Quon shrugged slightly. "What was left of her anyway. Between the explosion and the fish."

"So we know it was a woman?" Pele asked.

"Yes," Quon said.

"What about the cause of the explosion that sank the boat?" Derrick asked.

"We are still working out the details," Quon began. "But this was not an accident."

Pele glanced over at Derrick. His shoulders slumped as he turned back to Quon.

"You're certain about that?" Derrick asked.

"We have found traces of C4. And from the blast area, I would say it was a shaped charge."

"And the trigger?" Derrick asked.

"We are still working on that," Quon said.

Derrick turned to Pele. "Check out that detective working for Mrs. Kagawa. See if he has any kind of background in explosives." Derrick began pacing in a small circle.

"And access?" Pele asked.

Derrick nodded as he turned to Kengi. "Could you--"

"I will do more digging on the brother," Kengi said with a slight bow.

"Two prime suspects already," Pele said. "We're good."

"Two and a half." Derrick grinned. "If the PI was working on the wife's behalf." He reached up and rubbed his chin as he thought for a moment. "Let's see if we can find any surveillance footage of the marina area, where he docked his boat. We might get lucky."

"How far back?" Pele asked.

Derrick stopped pacing and rubbed his chin. "Try to go back three or four days before the explosion."

"And just what are we looking for?"

"I don't know. Something? Someone that looks out of place?"

"Like who or what?"

Derrick stopped pacing and turned back to Quon and the other forensics people pouring over the boat. "We might get a better idea when they figure out how the bomb was detonated."

Derrick let Pele drive his Mercedes to the ME's office as he sat in the passenger seat on his cell.

"I'm sorry Haruku. This is going to take longer than I thought."

"The boat?"

He stared out the window at the passing scenery. "Yeah."

"It wasn't an accident then was it?"

He shook his head as he sat there. "No. No. It looks like murder."

Derrick pushed open the stainless steel doors. The odor of chemicals and death spilled out into the hallway.

"Hello, darling." The energetic woman with short auburn hair and deep brown eyes and blood-stained lab coat smiled as they entered.

"Hi there Marta," Derrick said as he led the way across the room to where the medical examiner was working. "Cut your hair?"

"She grinned. You noticed."

"I see all. Sometimes."

She went back to looking at a piece of a body, holding it up in her glove covered hands as she twisted it around in the light for a better view. "And who is your new man toy Pele?" Marta asked gazing over at Kengi.

"This is Kengi Nakamura," Pele said. "Inspector Kengi Nakamura. He is from Tokyo. He is helping us on this case."

She winked a flirtatious wink. "You don't say."

"So what have we got?" Derrick asked as he stepped up to the table and scanned the various parts of a body.

"I gave Connie a hand," Marta laughed. "Literally. She's trying to get some prints off it as we speak."

"Any chance of facial recognition?" Pele asked.

"If only I had a face to work with dear."

"Can you tell us anything yet?" Derrick asked.

Marta shrugged as she looked around. "Sorry, darling. Not much of a head left." Marta picked up a pelvic bone. "I can say with some certainty, that she was in her late thirties, possibly early forties. And had one, probably two children."

Derrick glanced over at Pele.

"Fits the story of the valet," Pele said.

"I've got an ID for you, Lieutenant."

Everyone turned. Connie was standing there.

"Hi, Connie. Bet you miss the classroom today," Derrick said as he glanced down at the hand in her tray.

"Professor Li said there would be days like this. But sitting in the classroom listening to him talk about it doesn't really prepare you." She looked down at the disembodied hand. "Does it?"

"So who is she?" Pele asked.

Connie looked back up at them. "According to the fingerprints in the DMV database... only one good one actually, she is Katsua Onaga."

Pele looked over at Derrick. "The mistress?"

Derrick shrugged. "OK," he began. "Let's get an address and see if the children in the hospital are hers. And try to find her husband, boyfriend, estranged husband, whatever, or any next of kin." Derrick rubbed his chin as he turned back to the table of body parts. "Let's see if we can piece together her last few days."

Quon sat in a nearly empty office on a newly completed office building in Honolulu. The smell of fresh paint filled the air. The only furniture in the room were three brown, cold, metal folding chairs. Paul walked in with two cups of coffee. He handed one to Quon.

"I can't stay long," Quon began. "I am in the middle of a big case."

Paul nodded. "And finishing up your Ph.D. You're a busy man Quon."

He looked up at Paul. "I am sorry if I have caused an inconvenience. It's not that I don't trust you, Paul."

Paul shook his head as he grinned. "To tell you the truth, I would have been disappointed if you hadn't demanded this." He took the top off his coffee. "In fact..." he sat down and took a sip. "If you hadn't, I was prepared to pull the plug on this whole deal."

The door opened. Quon looked over. "You?"

Chapter 16

Derrick pulled up in front of the station. "Call me when you come up with something new."

Pele turned to him. "Go have fun with the girls. We will do more digging and call you later."

"I've got my laptop with me. Call me after dinner, and we'll touch base."

"Or I could bring breakfast in the morning. Down in Quon's lab? Say 6 AM?"

Derrick grinned as they got out. "We can do that, but let's touch base this evening for a few minutes. Now that we know we have an official murder on our hands."

"And Goodlow?"

"Just get some background on him for now."

Pele closed the door and started up the steps of the station. She turned and waved. He nodded then pulled out into traffic.

The door closed. Paul turned to Quon. "What we discussed here remains in this room."

"But..."

"For now. That's the way it has to be." Paul finished his coffee. "Do we have a deal?"

Quon nodded. "Yes. But I do need to bring Todd in on this."

"Of course. And I want to be there when you do."

"That was fun," Kattie said as they all walked out of the water toward Kailani. She had their picnic all set up and waiting for them.

"Did you girls see anything exciting?" Kailani asked as she handed everyone a towel.

"We saw three turtles," Becky said as she let Haruku dry her off.

"And a school of Yellow Tangs," Kattie said.

"And some red and yellow war asses," Becky said as Haruku finished drying her.

"Flame Wrasses," Haruku said as she put the towels in a pile at the edge of their blanket.

"They were pretty red and yellow fish."

"So what have you girls made for lunch?" Derrick asked as he sat down with them and reached over to open the picnic basket.

"Hi Uncle Derrick. Are you finished working for today?" Kattie asked.

"Yes I am."

Haruku glanced over at him.

"For now. I hope."

"Haruku made lunch today," Becky said. "We were looking at some of her old drawings."

He smiled. "That sounds like fun."

"How did it go with the boys this morning?" Haruku asked as she handed Derrick a sandwich.

Derrick shook his head. "I think the older one is headed for hard time."

"And the younger one?"

"I think there is still hope for him."

"Why did they do it?"

"Save a few bucks, help a few friends…."

"And then the addiction?"

He nodded. "The thrill. But then Curt, the older one got greedy. And made a mistake."

"How?"

"They started to move too fast. Three cars in a few weeks. Before it was just one every month or so."

"Why take the chance?"

"A girl."

Haruku laughed. "Blaming us poor girls for all men's problems are we?"

"You beautiful women are a constant source of motivation."

"And what was the motivation this time?"

"According to Fred, Curt wanted to take his girlfriend to a fancy dinner and concert. He didn't have the money, and his father wouldn't give it to him. He told him to go out and earn it."

"And stealing a car was his answer to earning it?"

"Apparently so."

"How are those children from the boat doing?" Kattie asked as Kailani passed out bottles of water.

"Are they out of their comas yet?" Haruku asked as she helped the girls open their bottles.

Derrick grinned. "I am happy to say that they are awake now and should be fine."

"Their parents will be glad to hear that," Kattie said.

Haruku glanced over at Derrick.

He whispered. "We're still looking for other relatives."

"Was that their mother and father out on the boat with them?" Haruku asked softly.

"We think the woman was their mother."

"And their father?"

Derrick shrugged. "We don't know yet."

"Do they know what happened?" she asked.

"They still aren't talking yet."

"They are very lucky that you were there Aunt Haruku," Kattie said as she picked up her sandwich and took a bite.

Derrick glanced over at Haruku and nodded. "Yes, they are."

Pele pulled up in front of a long two-story white cinderblock apartment building in her black 328i. A few stunted palm trees and yellowing ferns dotted the landscape of browning grass around the building. She and Kengi got out and walked up the steps. She knocked on the door of apartment 106.

"I hear someone inside," Kengi said as they stood there waiting.

Pele knocked again. The door opened. Pele's eyes grew big, and her mouth dropped open as she took a step back. "Mr. Walters?"

"Yes?" He stood there in an open faded black robe as he rubbed the sleep from his eyes. "Don't I know you?"

Derrick was helping Haruku pick up the trash after their picnic when his cell rang.

Haruku glanced over at him. "They just can't live without you can they?"

"I'd better…" He reached for his cell. "Dreadlow."

"Sorry to interrupt you, Derrick. But I thought you might want to know this."

"What's that Pele?" He turned to see Haruku watching him. She was very relaxed and humming to herself as she continued cleaning things up.

"We went to Mrs. Onaga's house to see if anyone was there…"

"And?" Derrick asked.

"You will never guess who we found."

"I give up," Derrick said as he strolled around the sand in a circle.

"Mr. Walters."

Derrick stopped in his tracks. "The night manager for Mr. Kagawa?" He glanced to his right. Haruku was looking up at him. "Is he also the…"

"Yes. He is the father of the two children in the hospital. Apparently, when they got married, she wanted to keep her maiden name."

Derrick started pacing again. "He left that little detail out when we talked to him."

"Do you want me to bring him in for more questioning?" Pele asked.

"No. Not yet. Where is he now?"

"He took off to the hospital as soon as we told him what had happened."

"OK. Before we have another talk with him, let's do some background checking on him."

"Like military history, explosives…"

Derrick nodded as he paced. "Yes. We may have just uncovered a third suspect." Derrick hung up and slipped his cell into his pocket. "Who wants ice cream?"

Quon was back inside the boat with Xin, Joyce, a Coast Guard tech, and an FBI tech.

"I think I found something professor," the FBI tech said.

Quon stood up and walked over to him. He knelt down and took a closer look at what was left of a charred circuit board. "Have you seen anything like that before?"

"No Professor."

Quon looked around. "Let's see if we can find any more pieces still on the boat."

Becky and Kattie were eating their ice cream cones and watching a pair of yellowish gray and white Mejiro flit from branch to branch a large tree at the Royal Hawaiian Center.

"Where did they go?" Becky asked.

"Up there," her sister pointed to a branch above them.

"Do you think they are watching us eat our ice cream?"

"What is it?" Haruku asked as Derrick set his dish of chocolate chip mint down on the table.

"I'll be right back." He jumped up off the bench and rushed around the corner and down a hallway to the back alley.

He caught a glimpse of someone as he rounded the corner. Derrick broke into a run. A man raced down the alley and ducked in between two dumpsters. Derrick approached quietly. He waited a minute. A head peered around the corner. He grabbed the man by his shirt and yanked him out of the shadows. He slammed him back against the wall.

"Just what the hell are you up to?" Derrick asked as he yanked a camera from the man's grip.

"Nothing." The man grabbed the camera back and run away.

Derrick reached out and yanked him back. Then he reached over and ripped his hat off. "Come on Trang. You're not fooling anyone. What is your beef with Pele's sister?"

"I'm doing surveillance."

"You're stalking. There is no investigation on Haruku. You and Perkins closed that incident."

"Give me my camera back."

Derrick pulled a plastic evidence bag out of his pocket. "Always be prepared." He grinned as he slipped the camera into the bag.

Trang took a swing at him. Derrick ducked to the side.

"Chill out there Trang before you get yourself into trouble."

Trang spun around and came at Derrick with a high kick to his face. Derrick bobbed to the right. Trang winced as his foot crashed into the corner of the dumpster.

"Do you really want to add assault on a superior officer to this Trang?"

Trang threw a right at Derrick. Derrick weaved to the left and clocked him with a hard right sending him back between the dumpsters. Derrick reached down and grabbed the camera again.

"I'll have you brought up on charges Lieutenant."

Derrick slid the camera into his pocket. "Do whatever you like Sergeant." He leaned down and grabbed Trang by the shirt lifting him up off the ground. He slammed him back into the wall. "What do you think they will say when they look at the images on this camera? Following a police officer. Probably also the pictures you sent to my ex-wife as well."

Trang looked down at Derrick's pocket.

Derrick grinned. "And I'll just bet they find your fingerprints all over the memory card too." Derrick let go of Trang. "Look Sergeant. I don't know what your problem is. But..." He spun around, then grabbed him by the collar yanking him off his feet, and held him right up to his nose. "If you ever involve my family in any of your bullshit again nothing on this earth is going to stop me from ripping you into tiny little pieces." He set Trang back down on his feet and let go of his collar. "Aloha."

As he turned the corner and began walking back to the girls, he pulled his cell out of his pocket. "Hey there Bucchi. Dreadlow here."

"What can I do for you Dread?"

"This place looks like a museum more than a restaurant," Kengi said as they entered.

Pele laughed. "This place may have the most Tiki statues on the island. Except possibly a hotel I know."

"Have you come here before?"

"Once in a while. Mostly looking for people while working cases."

"Maybe we should come back sometime," Kengi said as they made their way to the bar. "You know, unofficially."

The bartender looked up at them as they sat down. Pele pulled out her badge and discreetly slid it across the bar. He didn't bother to look down at it. "I know who you are."

Kengi leaned closer to her. "I thought you said you didn't come in here much."

"Not often enough," the bartender said with a wide grin. "What can I do for you detective?"

She put her badge in her pocket. "You remember me?"

"Hottest detective on the island. What's to forget?"

She pulled a photo out of her pocket and handed it to him. "Have you seen this man in here before?"

He took it and looked at it. "Can I get you two something to drink?"

"We aren't..."

He put the photo down on the bar. "Two virgin Mai Tais coming up." He walked away.

Pele turned around and scanned the bar. Several people were sitting at the tables. A few sat at the other end of the bar.

The bartender stepped back. He set down their drinks and picked up the photo. "Now. Where were we?"

Pele reached for her drink and took a sip. "Have you ever..."

"Yeah. He comes in here. Sometimes he has dinner. Sometimes just a drink at the bar."

"Does he ever come in with anyone else?" Kengi asked.

The bartender nodded as he set the photo back down on the bar. "Usually." He grinned.

Pele pulled another photo out of her pocket and slid it across the bar. "How about her?" She took another sip of her drink as he picked it up and looked at it.

The bartender grinned ear to ear and nodded. "Oh yeah."

"Often?" Pele asked.

"Oh yeah." He put the photo down. "Sometimes with two kids. They'll sit at a table outside then. Usually on a weekend afternoon. Not the evening if you get my drift."

"Two boys?" Kengi asked. He picked up his drink and tried some. He nodded. "Good."

"Na. A boy and a girl."

"You have a name?" Pele asked.

He shook his head as he wiped down the bar. "Never asked. Bad for tips ya know."

"When is the last time you saw them?"

He stood there thinking for a moment. "I think they were in last Saturday. Maybe Sunday. I can't be sure. It was busy."

Pele picked up the photos and put them in her pocket. She got up off her stool. "Good drinks."

Kengi put a twenty down on the bar. "Keep the change."

"What change?"

Kengi pulled out a ten and dropped it onto the bar.

"Feel free to come back any time Detective," the bartender called out as he picked up the money.

Derrick came around the corner and sat back down by Haruku.

"What was that all about?" she asked.

"Nothing. Just thought I saw an old friend. From New York. You know, out on vacation maybe."

"Did you?"

"No. Why don't we take them for a walk and burn off some of this sugar?"

Pele got up from her desk and walked over to the printer. She glanced around the detective pool as she waited. Everyone was busy.

Sergeant Perkins was at his desk nearby talking on his phone. "Forget it, Hollister. You're off the case. I'm off the case. Don't call here again." He dropped his phone down in its cradle and turned back to his computer.

She turned back to the printer as Sergeant Trang got off the elevator and walked past her to his desk by Perkins. He had a big black eye.

Sergeant Perkins looked up. "What the hell happened to you, Trang?"

"Nothing." He sat down and turned on his computer.

"That looks like a whole hell of a lotta nothing there."

Trang banged away at his keyboard. "I just tried to break up a fight. That's all. Some guy got in a lucky punch."

"Maybe you should've called for backup."

Trang stared down at his computer. "Maybe if I had a partner I wouldn't have to call for backup."

Derrick was waiting at the corner of Kuhio and Seaside when a black Camaro pulled up. He glanced around, opened the door and slipped in on the passenger side. FBI Agent Carlos Bucchi pulled down his blue sunglasses and peered over the top.

"This isn't exactly my line of work you know," Bucchi said.

"Ahh. It's a gray area." Derrick bobbed his head side to side as he pulled the evidence bag out of his pocket and handed it to Bucchi. "He was working with Perkins and Hollister. So he is tied to Lynn's case. And he is taking photos with me in it. And sent them to my ex-wife…"

"You can prove this?" Bucchi asked as he reached out for the bag. He stopped just short of taking it. "What's on here?"

"That's what I want you to find out. I don't want anything to come up later saying that I compromised evidence."

"You sound pretty confident about what's on here."

"Let's call it a coply hunch."

Bucchi took a deep breath. "Karen did say we were the core team on this investigation."

"So let's do some investigating."

Bucchi shook his head slightly. "This is a bit of a stretch…"

Derrick snorted. "At the very least… let's rule it out."

Bucchi took the bag. "Process of elimination."

"That's the spirit." Derrick opened the door and got out. He bent back down. "Watch your back, my friend."

Bucchi nodded as Derick closed the door. He glanced around and pulled out into traffic. As he came to a stoplight, he pulled out his cell.

"Detective Kobayashi."

"Pele. Bucchi here. Got a question for you."

"Sure. What do you need?"

Derrick was sitting at the end of the table playing another game of mousetrap with Haruku and the girls. They were taking a break for the moment as Kattie and Becky talked to their parents. Unlike the previous couple of weeks when the girls first came to the islands, at least this time around Derrick was home in the evenings when they called.

"Are you still listening?"

"Yeah. Sorry." Derrick turned back to his computer. "The girls are on the phone with their mother."

He had his laptop on the table next to him and a video screen up with Pele on it. He reached for a fresh baked brownie. "So what else did you find out?"

"We found some footage from a couple of cameras at the marina and businesses out on the Sand Island access road. Forensics is going through them, but without something more concrete to give them it probably won't turn up much," Pele said.

"Well it's a start," Derrick said. "See if they can spot Mr. Kagawa's car coming in around the time he was placed there on Saturday. The bomb had to be planted before that."

"Oh, one more thing before I forget. I saw Trang come in before I left the station this afternoon."

Derrick sat up. "Really. Did he have anything to say?"

"No. But it looked like he was on the receiving end of a good punch. He must have been out pissing someone else off too." Pele grinned. "I overheard Perkins ask him about it. He said it was just a scuffle he got into with some guys while trying to break up a fight."

Derrick laughed. "It's not healthy jumping into places you're not wanted I guess."

"You lose again Uncle Derrick," Becky yelled out.

Derrick looked over the top of his laptop. "I've got to find a different game."

"Maybe you need to concentrate more," Pele said. "I've got an incoming call. I'll see you in the morning." The video went black.

An hour later Pele was standing in the aisle of a grocery store looking at a box of Macadamia nuts covered in chocolate.

"Hey there Bucchi." She set the box back on the shelf.

"You got it?"

She pulled out a key chain with a small USB on it and a palm tree on the top. "All set. But what do you need with Trang's case file on my sister? And why not just email it?"

"Just some background. And I don't want to tie you to this." He slipped it into his pocket. "I was just wondering if you had gotten around to removing those tracking devices on the cars for Perkins and Trang?"

She hesitated as she glanced up and down the aisle.

"Don't worry if you haven't. No one gave you a time frame."

She reached out and picked up another box of candy. "I did remove the ones on Perkins's cars."

"So the one on Trang is still operating?"

"Yes." She flipped the box over and looked at the back. "Why?"

"Can I get access to it again? I deleted it because I thought I was done with this guy."

"This have anything to do with Derrick?"

"It might."

"He still doesn't know about the devices Bucchi."

"He won't get it from me."

"OK. I'll have Quon send it to you."

"Thanks."

"Do you want to tell me what's going on?"

"I'm not sure yet."

Pele put the box back on the shelf.

"They're good," he said eyeing the box on the shelf.

"I know. But I can get them from my parent's store. For less."

"I'm sure." He turned and started down the aisle waving as he went. "Later."

"Do you live here?" Kengi walked up behind Pele as she sat working at her desk.

She looked up, blinked, then rubbed her eyes. "Sorry, Kengi. I just got caught up in a few things."

"Are you planning to leave sometime tonight?"

"I got out for a little while. Just came back to check something."

He sat down in the chair by her desk. "What is that?"

She looked at her laptop screen. "That is a tracking signal."

"Who are you tracking?"

She thought for a moment. "A person of interest."

"On the boat case?"

"No." She closed the window and turned off her computer. "Dinner?"

"Are you sure you have the time?" he asked as he stood up.

"Where shall we go tonight?" she asked as she shoved her laptop into her backpack.

"Derrick was telling me about a place called Duke's."

She slung the pack over her shoulder. "Then Duke's it is."

She glanced around the nearly empty office. She focused on the empty desks of Perkins and Trang.

"Something wrong?" Kengi asked.

She shook her head. "No. Nothing."

Chapter 17

Derrick reached for his coffee as he sat back in a dining room chair waiting for a screen refresh on his laptop.

"Would you like a refill Derrick?"

He looked up and held his cup out. "Thank you Haruku. I thought you were trying to get me to cut back."

"It's decaf. With a little nonfat chocolate milk."

He looked down at his cup as she filled it. "Really."

"Now isn't this better? An early morning swim, coffee, and you can still get some work done."

"I could get used to this."

"So could I." She turned and walked out to the kitchen gently swaying her hips as she moved. "How long will you be at work today?" she called out.

"Just a few hours," he replied as took another sip and stared at the screen.

"So if I figure seven or so I would be close?"

"You know me so well."

She walked back out into the dining room. "Yes, I do." She sat down next to him with a cup in her hand. "Are you sure you don't want me to make you some breakfast?"

"No," he said as he closed a window on the screen. "I've got to be going." He sent his laptop into sleep mode. "Anyway, I think Pele is bringing breakfast this morning. What time are you getting the girls up?"

"Another hour or so."

He leaned over to see the clock in the kitchen. "OK. If I leave now, we can get a few things done before noon." He looked over at her as he stood up slipped on his jacket. "Meet you all for lunch?"

"Becky wanted to go to Sea Life Park again."

"OK."

She got up and straightened out his tie. "I'll pack something. Now you get going, so you won't be late."

He reached out and slid his hand on her hip. He leaned in slightly then stopped himself. "I'll be home as soon as I can."

She smiled. "I'll be waiting."

Quon stared out over the beach then turned back to Todd and Paul. Paul picked up his toasted almond croissant. Todd finished his Hawaiian omelet.

"But I enjoy working at the police lab," Quon said. "Plus it gives me a perspective on what they do every day. And more important, what they need in the way of new technology."

"But you are spread so thin," Paul said.

"He's got a point," Todd said. "That's why you brought me in to handle the financial end of things. Maybe you should look at help in other areas as well."

"But I…"

"You have a gift Quon," Paul said.

"And there are only so many hours in a day," Todd added. He looked over at Paul then back at Quon. "Look, Quon. We're not saying you need to crawl into some dark hole to just think up things." He leaned forward. "Soon you will have your Ph.D. finished. That will give you some time back. Maybe you can still teach a class now and again. And…" Todd turned to Paul.

Paul nodded. "And if you build the best forensic lab in the Pacific, they will come here to you. You can hire the best people you know to do the tedious work. And you can still get your hands into it to see what is needed to solve cases and mysteries."

"Ones of your choosing," Todd added.

Quon's cell began ringing. "Quon Li." He reached for his juice. "Yes." He glanced at his watch. "Thank you. I will be there in twenty minutes."

"A break in your case?" Paul asked.

"Yes. I have to be going."

"This proves our point," Todd said. "You are spread too thin."

"I will manage," Quon said.

Quon reached for the tab, but Paul grabbed it first. "If not for yourself… then think of Fei. How much time will you have for her?"

"Or a family if you want one later," Todd added.

Paul pulled out his wallet. "Your pace today can set the tone for the rest of your life. Trust me on this Quon. I know."

"And it is hard to change," Todd added. "Take it from those of us with experience."

Quon stood up and looked at them. He took a deep breath then turned away.

"What do you think?" Paul asked as he reached for his coffee and sat back.

Todd refilled their coffee cups. "It's a lot for him to take in."

"A big change," Paul said.

"He is going from the relative comfort of employee and student, to the master of his domain."

Derrick reached for a file by his laptop. He opened it and looked at some notes he had made.

"In early again?" Pele asked as she dropped her backpack on her desk.

He glanced up then turned back to his notes. "Early in, early out. At least that's the plan."

"It hasn't worked for you yet."

"Try try again."

She set two paper bags on the crack between their desks. "Melissa?" she asked as she took out her laptop.

"Just some notes."

"Like what?"

Derrick sat back as she turned on her computer. "Well, first, she said that her husband left for a new job in Dallas. I can't find him anywhere in Texas. She said he ran off with some girlfriend, but I don't know who. The last thread I can find is his last paycheck deposited in their joint account in early March 2008. After that, there is no record of him after that. His driver's license expired in February 2009. Not renewed in Hawaii or Texas."

"Who did he work for?" Pele asked as she logged in.

"The last employer I can find was Aloha Airlines."

"They went bankrupt in early 2008."

Derrick nodded. "I can't find any record of employment or even tax filings here or Texas after that. Quon has been tied up, so Xin is running a nationwide search for me. Todd is tracking the finance trail."

"What happened to Quon?"

Derrick shrugged. "I think he's got his hands full this summer."

"Any friends of Jack here you can talk to?"

"One. A guy he worked with at Aloha Air."

"Good morning," Kengi said as he stepped up to their desks and sat down in the chair by Pele. "How are you both this morning?"

Pele glanced up. "Derrick is trying to track down the ex-husband of his girlfriend."

Kengi turned to Derrick. "This mysterious Melissa that I have yet to see?"

"That's the one," Pele said as she reached for the paper bags.

Derrick sat back. "Bink has met her."

Pele opened the bags and passed out breakfast.

"I want to transfer here," Kengi said as he opened his burrito.

"On our current real case," Pele began. "I did find out that Mr. Walters was in the army. And he served in Japan. Well, Okinawa."

"That could be useful," Derrick said.

"As a cook," Pele finished.

Derrick sat back. "Let's verify that's all he did, and not some mask for covert cover."

"Are you getting suspicious in your old age Derrick?" Kengi asked.

Derrick shook his head. "Let's just say my copness is coming back after that slap upside the head with Dobson and Mr. Jones."

Pele nodded. "Oh, that reminds me Kengi. I found five numbers Mr. Kagawa called in Japan. Do you think you could track them down?" She handed him a piece of paper with the numbers.

He took it and glanced at it before sticking it in his pocket. "OK."

"They were made after hours on his secretary's phone."

Kengi nodded. "Interesting."

Derrick's cell rang. "Dreadlow." He took a sip of his coffee. He nodded. "We'll be there in about half an hour." He hung up. "Quon says they have a theory on the bomb. He's over at the boathouse."

Haruku and the girls were walking along Kalakaua Avenue in Waikiki past her parent's store. Becky tugged at her hand. "Can we go in and get some flowers?"

Kattie looked around Haruku at her sister, "Why do you want to take flowers to the beach?"

Becky looked up at Haruku. "I want to make a stop on the way."

Haruku squeezed her hand gently as she looked down at her. "OK. But we will need a special flower." She led the girls inside so they could look at flowers.

"Good morning girls," Eito said as he looked up from stocking a shelf. "How are you enjoying your vacation?"

"I don't want to leave," Becky said.

"Is it like this all year long?" Kattie asked.

"Pretty much."

"So you don't get cold winters here?"

"No."

"Then I really don't want to leave," Becky added.

He stood up. "I think your parents would miss you."

Kattie looked down at the floor as Becky looked at the flowers. "I guess so," Kattie said.

"What are these called?" Becky asked as Haruku picked out some light yellow and white flowers.

"We call them Awapuhi-Kuahiwi, Opuhi. They are special flowers often used to make leis."

"Do you think they will like these?"

"They will love them. But you will need four."

Haruku bought the flowers, and a few minutes later, they crossed the street. They stopped by the railing around the four large stones.

"What are we doing here again?" Kattie asked.

Haruku knelt down beside Kattie and Becky. She handed the lei to Becky. "Now place one in front of each stone. Stand there for a moment and think about your wish. Do this four times."

Becky took the lei and slowly made her way around the wizard stones.

"Do you believe in these wizards?" Kattie asked as she watched her sister.

Haruku put her arm around Kattie. "The real power of the Kahuna is that they allow us to believe." Becky finished and walked back to them. "And that can help make our dreams come true."

"What did you wish for?" Kattie asked as they headed for the beach.

Becky skipped along as she held Haruku's hand. "It's a secret. Only the kahunas know."

Captain Henderson walked up to Derrick's desk.

"Mornin Captain," Derrick said as he set down his coffee.

"I've got some good news for you three," he said as he glanced over at Pele and Kengi.

"We never get enough of that," Derrick said.

"The doctor said that they see no permanent damage to the children of that boating incident. They should make a full recovery. Thanks in no small part to all of you."

"And your sister," Kengi added.

Pele grinned. "That is great news. Does their father know?"

"Yes," Captain Henderson replied. "He was called in early this morning."

"How are they?" Derrick asked. "You know, dealing with the loss of their mother?"

"That I don't know."

Derrick, Pele, and Kengi joined Quon and a few other forensics techs from the police and the FBI at the boatyard. "You've found something for us, Quon?"

"Yes. We do not have all the pieces, but there was definitely a triggering device."

"So it was a bomb?" Pele asked.

Quon nodded. "There is no doubt about it. And a very sophisticated one too."

"Military?" Derrick asked.

"Unknown. But it was creative."

"What was it?" Kengi asked.

"From what we can tell, it was two parts. One detected when the engine came on and started a timer after six hours of operation. A GPS tracker triggered the next part."

"Why would someone go to all that trouble?" Pele asked.

"Any guess about the parameters of the GPS device?" Derrick asked.

"There is not enough left to give us any more detail than that," Quon said.

Derrick rubbed his chin. "Hmmm."

"What?" Pele asked.

Derrick took a deep breath. "I'm just speculating here..."

"You have seen this before?" Kengi asked.

"Something similar. Only it had to do with altitude. This would just be the next logical step I guess."

"What is that?" Quon asked.

Derrick stared down at the charred pieces on the table. "It could be that the timer kicked off to give the boat enough time to get out away from the island."

"But how would someone know if the boat went straight out or just hugged the coast?" Kengi asked.

"That's where the GPS came in. I remember what Haruku said about the breakers. The drop off of the shelf around the islands. Perhaps the GPS triggered the explosion when the ship was out far enough so that any help would take longer to reach it and…"

Quon nodded. "… and in water too deep for an easy retrieval or rescue."

Derrick nodded. "Just a guess."

"But a damn good one," Kengi said. "It bought whoever did it a lot of time to cover their tracks."

"Yes," Pele began, "they could be out of the state by now."

Derrick looked over at the boat. "Or out of the country."

"So who could do this?" Quon asked.

Derrick paced around the table. "This leaves out the wife as the killer, but not necessarily the detective she hired."

"So she still has a motive, if not the knowledge to do it herself," Kengi said.

"A woman scorned," Derrick said. "Is not to be trifled with."

"I'm still checking out the detective," Pele said. "And if Mr. Walters had this kind of knowledge."

"I will look closer at his brother," Kengi said. "I have a contact in Kobe I can work with."

"OK," Derrick said as he stopped pacing. "We still have three primary suspects. His wife, his brother, and the jealous husband."

"Any one of whom could have hired someone to do this," Kengi said.

Derrick nodded then stopped pacing. "That assumes they would know how to find someone with this kind of knowledge."

"Shall I start to interview them again?" Pele asked.

"No." Derrick thought for a moment. "Let's do a bit more digging on these people and who they might know before we start to show our cards. See what else pops up."

"Where are you going?" Kengi asked.

Pele laughed. "He's still on vacation."

"Yes. But I've got someone to talk to about a thing before I go see the girls."

Pele and Kengi walked down one of the docks at the La Marina Sailing Club. They stopped in front of a sixty-five-foot power ketch. "Is this the slip?" Kengi asked as they approached.

"This is where Mr. Kagawa tied up his boat," Pele said. She walked up to the side of the yacht next door and pulled out her badge. "Hi there." The deckhand looked over at them. "I'm Detective Kobayashi with the HPD. And this is Inspector Nakamura."

"What can I do for you?"

She slipped her badge into her pocket and pulled out two photos. One of Mr. Kagawa, and one of his wife. "Have you seen this man or this woman?"

He studied the photos for a moment. "I've seen the guy here. He owns the Amazi." He pointed to his left. "She's usually tied up over there. They must be out on a cruise around the islands."

"And the woman," Pele asked.

He shook his head as he studied her photo. "Na. Can't say that I have." He handed her the photos.

She took them and gave him a picture of Katsua Onaga and her children.

He looked at them. He nodded. "I've seen her here a lot."

"What about the children?" Pele asked.

"Ah, once in a while." He handed the photo back.

"Do you know her name?"

"No."

"When is the last time you saw them?"

"Last Sunday."

"Do you know when they left the harbor?"

He shrugged. "Sorry. We were pulling out as they were all walking down the dock."

Pele took the photo and handed him another. "What about this man."

He took the photo. He began to nod as he studied the photo of Mr. Walters.

"You recognize him?"

He nodded again. "I've seen him."

"Do you know who he is?"

He handed the photo back. "No. But he really got into it with Kagawa about two, maybe three weeks ago."

"You saw them?" Kengi asked.

"Yes. They had quite a shouting match. Then they started pushing each other. This other guy shouted I'm going to kill you and shoved Mr. Kagawa overboard. Then he ran off."

"What did you do?" Pele asked.

"I ran over and helped him out of the water."

"Did anyone call the police?"

He shook his head. "I didn't. He said it was just a misunderstanding. Don't worry about it." He looked over at the empty slip. "Did something happen to him?"

"He's dead," Pele said. "So is the woman."

"Did you see anyone around his boat that maybe shouldn't have been?" Kengi asked.

He stood up and looked around as he thought about it. He started to shake his head. "But now that you mention it..."

"What?" Pele asked.

"I didn't see him on any of the boats. But there was this oriental guy. Kind of tall. In a black turtleneck and cap. I remember him because it was a warm morning. He was walking up the dock as I was coming down."

"Anything else suspicious?" Kengi asked.

"I don't know. Just the way he looked past me when I said good morning. Like I wasn't even there." He paused for a moment. "Oh yeah. And a white scar under his lower lip. On the left."

"Have you ever see him before or since?" Pele asked.

"Na."

"When was this?"

"Saturday morning. Around 6:00, maybe 6:30."

"Could you identify him?"

He shrugged. "I doubt it. Like I said he was pretty much covered up and I only caught a glimpse of him." He thought for a moment. "But I'll never forget his eyes. His stare."

"Why?" Kengi asked.

"It was cold. Empty." He shuddered as he spoke.

"I'd like to send someone out to try to get a rendering of what you remember. Would that be all right?" Pele asked. "I know it may not be much. But it may help."

He nodded. "I'll give it a shot if you think it helps."

"Thank you," Pele and Kengi started walking back up the dock. "Could be our guy."

"Could be a guy that someone hired," Kengi added.

"So who has that kind of expertise?"

Derrick pulled up to the flower shop and got out. He closed the door, straightened out his black Italian suit jacket then headed up to the front door. It was propped open. The fragrances of many flowers filled the air as he stepped inside. It was a good-sized shop. The store itself was in front, with two greenhouses in the back, and a garden area in between.

An older man behind the counter looked up as he approached. A young woman was busy creating a colorful masterpiece out of flowers of various shades of blue and purple.

"Can I help you?" the man behind the counter asked.

Derrick pulled out his badge. "I'm Lieutenant Dreadlow. I'm looking for Mr. Tobias."

"I'm Dick Tobias."

Derrick slipped his badge back into his pocket. "I called you earlier."

Mr. Tobias turned to the young woman. "Adrian, could you watch the counter for a few minutes please?"

She glanced over at Derrick. "Sure dad."

"We can go out back, Lieutenant. Can I get you something to drink? Juice? Water?"

"Thanks, but I'm fine."

Dick led the way to the back of the shop.

"Please, have a seat," Dick said as they sat down under the shade of a Primavera tree. There were a tree and bush nursery out behind the greenhouses he hadn't noticed on his way in.

Derrick scanned the area as he sat down. "Your own little piece of paradise back here."

"My wife started it years ago. I decided I had enough of corporate life after the airline went under so here I am."

"A great change of pace."

"So just what are you looking for Lieutenant?"

"I understand that you worked with Jack Crawford at Aloha Air."

"Yes. We were both executives at the airline."

"When was the last time you saw or talked to Mr. Crawford?"

Dick sat back and twisted the cap off his fruit flavored water. "Well… probably a couple of days after we were let go. In the grocery store."

"Do you remember anything about what he said? Did he have any plans? Opening a flower shop? Maybe helping out at an animal clinic?"

Dick laughed. "You mean his wife's clinic?"

"Could be…"

"Na. he wouldn't have gone there."

"Why is that?"

"He and his wife had split up. He was living in an apartment over in Pearl." He took a sip of his fruit flavored water. "With a girl that he met."

"Did this girl have a name?"

Dick sat there thinking as he took another sip. "Dawn... Dawn Miller."

"Did you ever meet her?"

"Once. My wife and I went out to dinner with them. The night before they canned us."

"You know anything about this Dawn or where they met?"

"As I recall, they met in Los Angeles. On one of his business trips."

"Did she work with the airline?"

Dick grinned. "She was a waitress at a coffee shop near the airport I believe."

"You wouldn't happen to remember which."

He shook his head. "Sorry."

Derrick nodded. "How was Jack that night?"

"How was he?"

Derrick shrugged. "Pissed? Depressed?"

"He was OK as I recall."

"How so?"

"We knew it was coming. He said he was going to file for a divorce, and he had a couple of offers from other airlines." Dick nodded as he took another sip. "He said he was putting this chapter of his life behind him."

Derrick glanced around again. "Looks like you did too."

He nodded. "Yep. And I never looked back."

"But Jack wanted to stay in the game?"

"To each his own."

Derrick took a deep breath savoring the sweet fragrances that came with the backyard of a nursery in paradise. "You ever hear from Jack after that?"

He shook his head. "Na. I figured he found a new life just like me. And as I said, I never looked back. Guess he didn't either."

"You ever see anyone else from the old days?"

He shrugged. "Only see some of the people I worked with once in a while at the store. Everyone has moved on. We never talk about it." He took another sip as they stood up. "I figured Jack just moved on too."

"Yeah," Derrick said. "Something like that I guess. Thank you for your time."

Now, who is Dawn Miller? Derrick thought as he walked back out to his car. And will I have better luck finding her?

Chapter 18

Detective Patterson pulled out his chair and dropped down into it. "We got anything new on that Fukuhara murder yet?"

Detective Pusch looked up from his computer. "Uh... yeah." He searched through a stack of files and notes scattered across his desk. "The neighbors said they were a friendly couple. Kept to themselves most of the time. No obvious things like infidelity or gambling debts, drugs... ah, here we go." He pulled a file from near the bottom of the stack. "Aside from the hotels he owns here in the Bay area, the guy also owned a condo building here, two condo buildings in Honolulu and one in Vancouver, as well as a hotel in each."

"A real estate mogul?"

"Guess the wife is now. Not that she seems to know much about it." Pusch closed the file. "She's back in town. Staying with friends."

"Did you talk you her yet?"

"Yeah. She's a mess. Said she has no idea who would do this."

Patterson leaned back. "See if he had any enemies or dealings that went south recently."

Pusch tossed the file onto another pile. "It's in the pipe."

Derrick raised his arms in the air and stretched way back in his chair as he glanced around the dining room table. Haruku, Kattie, and Becky were on his right. Pele and Kengi were on his left. The mousetrap game was spread out on his right, laptops, one of Quon's portable screens, and open files were spread out on his left.

Open containers of Chinese food and paper plates lay strewn across the table, as were utensils, chopsticks, and cups of green tea.

"I think we should all just get up for a moment and take a break," Haruku said.

"Good idea," Derrick added as he stood up.

"I'll just clean this up and get dessert."

"We made brownies," Becky said as she jumped off her chair.

"I thought I smelled something delicious," Derrick said as he helped gather up the dishes and empty boxes.

"I'll put on some fresh hot water," Pele offered.

Haruku glanced over at her and grinned. "Becoming domesticated are we?"

"I can boil water." She picked up the empty teapot.

"What can I help with?" Kengi asked.

"You can keep them out of trouble," Haruku said as Kattie and Becky raced out into the living room.

Derrick looked over at Haruku as she cut a pan of brownies into small squares and set them out on two large plates. "Two plates?"

"One for each end of the table." She finished and picked them up. "And you, sitting right in between."

"Bink isn't here to help me eat them tonight."

She took them out to the dining room as he put the paper plates into the trash. The hot water began to whistle, and Pele took it out into the dining room to refill the teapots. Haruku came back into the kitchen. "We need fresh tea bags."

Derrick leaned back against the counter and watched her.

"What?" she asked as she watched him watching her.

"You never cease to amaze me."

She tilted her head as she smiled. "Good." She closed the cabinet door and took the box of tea out to the other room.

"It's your turn," Becky said.

"OK." Derrick rolled the dice. "I get to build another section." He turned to Pele and Kengi.

"Why don't we recap where we are so we can come up with a plan for tomorrow?"

"I'll bring it up on the big screen," Pele said as she opened a new window.

Derrick reached for a brownie and sat back. "OK. We've got two dead people."

"A hotel owner and his mistress," Kengi said as he reached for a brownie and took a bite.

Pele was typing away at her keyboard. "We have the wife, Mrs. Kagawa, and the Goodlow Detective Agency that she hired to follow her husband."

"Then we have the brother, Gorou Kagawa that he fought with in Japan," Kengi said.

Derrick reached for his tea. "And now we also have a separated husband, Mr. Walters, whose boss, Mr. Etsuo Kagawa, was having an affair with his estranged wife, Katsua Onaga." He took a sip. "That he still lives with."

"Only to watch the kids when she's… out."

He took another sip. "Supposedly because it was best for the kids."

Pele finished typing. "Three primary suspects…"

Derrick nodded as they all looked at the screen. "All with motives." He took a bite of his brownie and chewed for a moment. "Now what we need to find are means and opportunity."

"Who could create such a device, or have access to someone who could?" Pele asked as she reached for a brownie.

Derrick and Kengi both watched as she took a bite.

"What?" she asked looking over at them.

Derrick shrugged. "You're eating a brownie?"

She finished chewing. "They are good."

He reached for another. "They are excellent."

Haruku watched them. "They are low fat. And there are more in the kitchen. We went a bit crazy this morning."

"It was fun," Becky chimed in.

"Don't tell us that," Kengi said as he picked up another.

Derrick took a bite and sat back. "OK. Here's our plan."

"Don't you mean your plan for us?" Pele asked.

He grinned. "I'll help when I can."

"So what's the plan Dread?" Kengi asked.

"OK. What do we, and by we, I mean you… have for the detective agency?" Derrick began.

"From what I've learned so far, they seem to be reputable," Pele said. "I think it's time to talk to them directly."

Derrick nodded as he sat back and rubbed his chin. "I want to find out who was working the case. And if anyone there had the knowledge to do something like this."

Pele glanced over at him. "What is it, Derrick?"

He shrugged. "We'll check out the agency. But I'd be surprised if it was them."

Pele glanced over at him. "We?"

"I'll go with you. We can do it first thing in the morning."

Pele nodded. "I'll come by the condo at seven. No point in both of us driving."

"We also have the brother," Kengi said. "I will do more checking on him and any associates he may have that might be capable of this."

Derrick nodded. "I hope you told your boss that you are working a case and not spending your vacation time on this."

"I will ask them."

Derrick made a note. "I'll send them an email just to be sure."

Pele looked over at him. "What about me? I took the day off when this whole thing started."

Derrick grinned and turned back to the screen. "I'll send the captain a note too. Then we have Mr. Walters. Not only was his wife seeing someone else, but the man was his boss."

"I'll check into his background more," Pele said. "But so far it all points to him being a cook. Pure and simple. I can go talk to him again."

"Let's wait on re-interviewing him. He may be our strongest candidate at this point. You do some more digging first. Then I want to be there when we go back to talk to him again." Derrick reached for another brownie.

"It's your turn, Uncle Derrick." Kattie handed him the dice.

He rolled and made his move to a space with Becky. "Uh oh."

"My turn," Becky said.

Pele reached for another brownie.

Derrick looked over at her.

"I took a small one." She raised it to her mouth. "How are things with the Melissa case?"

Haruku glanced over at them.

"Ahhh…" Derrick sat there lost in thought for a moment.

"Derrick," Pele said again.

"Yes. Well, Jack's checks stopped when he lost his job. No surprise there. But so did all trace of him. His driver's license wasn't renewed when it expired. He didn't show up as having filed taxes in Hawaii, Texas, or Federal. His friend said Jack told him he was filing for divorce. But I can't find any record of it. Todd is still working on trying to trace any other financial paths. His friend did give me the name of a woman, though."

"You lose again!" Becky yelled out.

"What?" Derrick turned to look at the board. "We need to find a new game."

Sergeant Trang was sitting on a worn dull cream-colored couch in his sparsely furnished condo. He reached for a beer as he watched a small color TV sitting on top of a bookshelf with no books in it.

His cell rang. He reached over to the small stand by the couch. "Yeah?"

"Hi. This is FBI Agent Jack Hollister. I would like to have a word with you."

"Don't I know you?" Trang asked as he took a drink.

"We worked together with Sergeant Perkins. Regarding the Dreadlow case."

"Oh yeah. Perkins said that case was closed."

"Officially yes. But…"

"What do you want from me?"

"I can use your help if you are interested."

Trang sat up and set his beer down. "I'm listening."

Haruku closed the door after everyone left. She had a content look on her face as she walked toward Derrick.

"What is it?" he asked.

"This past week has been almost like old times."

"Old times?"

"Pele and I haven't spent this much time together in many years."

"Maybe it's the start of something new."

She slipped her arm around his. "Thanks to you."

Chapter 19

Derrick was making a pot of coffee as Haruku walked into the kitchen. "I hope I didn't wake you," he said as he glanced over at the doorway. Her hair was still messed up from sleeping. Her black nightshirt was wrinkled, and her feet were bare.

"No. I've got a busy day today. I wanted to get up early anyway. Did you go for your early morning swim?"

"Yes," he said as he poured a cup for her. "It helps me get ready for the day."

"Maybe I can join you someday. After the girls are back home."

"That would be nice," he said as he handed her a cup of coffee. "What are your plans?"

"Picking out a dress for tomorrow night."

He closed his eyes as he reached up and slapped the side of his head. "Tomorrow night? Already?" He opened his eyes as he looked at her. "I forgot about that."

She blew across the top of her coffee as she watched him. "What are you going to wear?"

He shook his head slowly. "To be honest, I hadn't thought about it. I guess I can stop by the condo and grab a sports coat or something."

"It's a Hawaiian theme. Did you even read the invitation?"

"Only the date and time." He took a sip. "I forgot the time."

"And apparently the day of the week." She shook her head slowly. "You go to work. I'll come up with something for us."

"Picking out a dress takes all morning?"

She tilted her head and smiled. "Maybe all day."

"All day?"

"It's a big responsibility. And I have to think about you too now."

"You've got a key to my condo. You can see if there is anything there that would work."

"Aren't Bink and his wife staying there this weekend?"

"Oh yeah. You might want to knock first."

Quon put the dishes in the dishwasher.

Fei stepped up behind him and slipped her arms around him. "It has been a while since we spent the night together."

He turned and put his arms around her. "Yes, I am sorry." They kissed. He leaned back and smiled. "We have not spent much time together lately have we?"

"We've both been busy."

"I think it has been mostly my fault. But I will soon be finished with my exams."

"How much longer?"

"I have a meeting with Professor Keogh later this morning."

"Then we can celebrate!" She pressed up against him and kissed him.

Derrick was sitting at the dining room table all dressed in one of his Italian suits and ready to go. He looked up at the knock at the door.

"I'll get it," Haruku said as she got up from the table.

Derrick stared at a window on his screen.

"Who is that?"

He looked up. "Pele. Good morning." He turned to the screen. "I'm trying to find Dawn Miller. The mysterious mistress of Jack Crawford."

"What does she have to say?"

Derrick closed the window and turned off his laptop. "So far, nothing." He closed the laptop. "I can't find her either."

"Coincidence?"

"I think not." He stuffed the laptop into his backpack and slung it over his shoulder. "You ready to hit the road?"

"All set."

He turned to Haruku. "I'll see you and the girls as soon as I can."

91

"Call first," Haruku said as she reached out and adjusted his tie. "I'm not sure where we'll be when."

"Got it."

Kattie and Becky stepped out into the room and walked over to Derrick. "Aren't you two up a bit early?" he asked.

"Are you going to work now?" Becky asked as she hugged his leg.

"Yes. But I'll be back home as soon as I can."

"What are we going to do today Aunt Haruku?" Kattie looked up at her as she rubbed the sleep from her eyes.

Haruku reached down and placed a hand on each of their shoulders. "Why don't we start with breakfast and then see what happens after that?"

"I will see you all later," Derrick said. He reached toward the girls. "Bye."

"Bye Derrick," Haruku said softly.

He smiled. "I'll be back soon."

"Bye Uncle Derrick," Kattie and Becky said together.

Pele glanced back at them as she opened the door.

"What?" Derrick asked as he saw her staring at them.

She shook her head as they stepped out into the corridor. "Norman Rockwell just popped into my head for some reason."

"When does this detective agency open?" Derrick asked as Pele pulled out of the condo parking garage in her 328i.

"Eight."

He looked over at her and grinned.

"OK. Juanita's it is. It's on the way. Kind of." She stopped at a light. "The captain said that the chief was happy to hear that the mayor's wife's, sister's, daughter got her car back."

"And that we solved the case?"

She waited for an elderly couple to step up onto the sidewalk before starting across the intersection. "He didn't say."

"Ah, the priorities of the rich and powerful." He looked out at the people walking along the streets. "It's nice to know that the world is back in balance."

"We are working on a murder now. Two in fact."

"Go ahead. Burst my bubble. It's not like I'm on vacation in paradise or anything."

She glanced over at him. "You've got the next best thing." She turned left on Beretania. "Working in paradise."

"With you?"

"With me."

"Who could ask for more?"

Kengi stepped out of the shower in his hotel room. He dried himself off as he reached for his cell on the corner of the sink. "Inspector Nakamura here."

He stood there drying his hair. "Hello." He stopped and looked into the steamy mirror. "Oh." He wiped some steam off the mirror. "No. Nothing is wrong. I just... I just wasn't expecting to hear from you again."

Juanita glanced over at Derrick as she set plates down in front of him than Pele. "Breakfast out this morning?"

Pele looked up at Juanita. "He wanted to try and avoid going into the office this morning."

"Great. Thank you, Todd." Derrick hung up as he gazed down at the huevos in front of him and the Hawaiian omelet in front of Pele. "Tell Alfonso it smells fantastic."

Juanita laughed as she turned to another table. "I will."

"So how are things going with you and Kengi?" Derrick asked as he picked up his fork and cut into his huevos.

"How are things going with you and my sister?" She picked up her fork and stabbed into her omelet.

He nodded slightly. "Fine." He reached for his coffee and took a sip. "The girls love her. They are learning a lot from her. And becoming exceptional little surfers." He took another sip. "I'm not sure how Nancy will view that part. But she'll get points for language lessons." He set his coffee down. "I would have never made it through the month without her." He turned to Pele.

"He's OK."

Derrick chuckled. "I guess OK is good coming from you."

"And just what is that supposed to mean?"

"Nothing." He cut off another piece of huevos and slid into his mouth.

"He's fun. He's easy to talk to. We have things in common."

"Work?"

"Yes." She wiped some pineapple sauce from her mouth.

Derrick picked up his coffee as he turned to her. "Pele."

She turned to him. "What?"

"It's OK to have a life outside of work. In fact, we need it, or we lose our balance."

"You've been hanging out with Quon too much."

Derrick nodded. "Speaking of which, how is he doing? Is he almost finished with his Ph.D. testing or whatever yet?"

Pele shrugged. "Any day now I think."

"He's a busy guy. I don't know how he does it all."

"Look at who's talking."

Quon and Professor Keogh were sitting at a table in the university cafeteria.

"Everyone is in such a hurry these days my young friend," the professor said as he stirred his tea.

Quon glanced around. There were many students there in spite of it being the middle of summer. "I guess we all have things we want to get out of the way." Quon stared down into his tea. "When do you think I will be finished, Professor?"

"I'd say we will be finished with your review sometime in the next week or so."

Quon beamed.

"But…"

His shoulders slumped.

Professor Keogh sat back. "Factoring in the holiday, perhaps a couple of extra days… I'd say by the second week in July you should be done. But don't quote me on that."

"No sir," Quon said hardly able to contain his excitement. "Thank you, Professor." To finally have his Ph.D. was a huge milestone. Everything was happening so fast this summer.

"Don't thank me, Quon. You are the one who has done all the work."

Sam Goodlow stroked his thick salt and pepper mustache. He leaned back in his chair as he slipped his hands together behind his head and propped his feet up on the corner of his desk.

He and his partner had a small office at the end of a strip mall. The receptionist out front was also their bookkeeper, errand runner, and even helped out on stakeouts.

"Yeah. I remember her. An older Japanese woman. She wanted us to follow her husband. She thought he was cheating on her."

Derrick raised his hands with palms up as he looked at him. "Was he?"

"Big time." Sam grinned. "But you already know that don't you Lieutenant?"

Derrick just sat there as they watched each other, sizing each other up.

"Like your suit," Sam said as he admired the sharp Italian cut, and the red tie contrasting with the black jacket. He turned to Pele and smiled. "Yours too Detective. Same tailor?"

Derrick shrugged. "I tried the Magnum P.I. look myself for a while."

"Didn't take?"

"Only on weekends."

Sam looked him over again. "Well, Lieutenant. You overshot the Hawaii Five-O image."

"Maybe a little."

Sam leaned back a little more and stared up at the ceiling. "But now that the husband is dead you are looking for suspects. Suspects with motive."

"Standard operating procedure," Derrick said as they watched each other again.

"And poor Mrs. Kagawa, not having the know how to make anything more dangerous than a soufflé… you come to the next best thing."

"Logical assumption."

Sam grinned. "Personally, I can't make the soufflé or a bomb. Maybe a Molotov Cocktail." He slid his feet off the desk and bounced forward as he turned straight at them. "However, I am more than positive that my partner could." He sat back again. "If he so desired."

"And where is your partner?"

"Max is on an assignment. In LA. He has been there for the last three weeks."

"And you can prove that?" Pele asked.

"Ahh…" He shrugged nonchalantly. "It's a government thing."

"We have clearance," she said as she joined in on the stare down contest.

Sam turned to Derrick. "I'll just bet you do." He sat back again. "Well, if you feel the need, come on back with a warrant, and I'll see what I can do." He leaned back as he held his hands out palms up. "But in the interest of saving taxpayers money… it wasn't us. Trust me. There are a few lines we *might* be tempted to cross. Now and then. But murder isn't one of them."

"What do you think?" Pele asked as they got back into her 328i.

"Let's get the warrant. Just in case."

"But you don't actually think they had anything to do with it do you?"

Derrick looked back out at the building. "No. I believe they are basically on the side of good."

"She could have hired someone else."

"That's a possibility."

Pele started up the car. "Now where to?"

Derrick glanced at the time on her dash. "I can't put it off any longer. Let's go to the station. Kengi should be there. And Bink is coming by to get the key to my condo. I'm letting them stay there for the weekend. It's closer to the party than Turtle Bay."

Pele looked over at him and grinned. "First one of your cars, now your condo?"

"He's a good friend."

"If you say so."

"Really good friends are hard to find."

"Like Demetri and Vincenzio?"

"Vincenzio definitely yes. Demetri…" Derrick shrugged as he watched the people along the sidewalks. "He's an acquired taste. But yes."

Derrick walked up to his desk with a cup of coffee in his hand. Kengi was sitting at his desk and on his phone. Kengi looked up at him. "You look right at home." Derrick waved for him to stay there. Pele was at her desk. She hung up her phone as Derrick sat down in the chair beside her desk.

"You give the captain an update?" she asked.

He took a sip. "All updated."

"Did he say anything?"

"The usual. What are we doing and when will we have it solved?"

"You give your key to Bink?"

"Yep. Just in time. Mildred wanted to go shopping. Bink is going to drop her off at the mall then come back for me."

"Oh yes. You need a ride back home don't you?"

"Got it covered."

"I just got off the phone with the army," Pele began. "It seems that Mr. Walters was just a cook. He went through basic but never out in the field. He did a tour in Okinawa. Cooking his way through. And some PR work when things required it. Since he knew the language and all."

"Any friends that might know how to make a bomb?"

"Nothing obvious in his records. And he has no police record anywhere. Honorable discharge."

Derrick sat back and rubbed his chin. "So far the wife, the detective agency and Mr. Walters are sliding down on our list of viable suspects. Down but not out."

"We still may have an acquaintance of Mr. Walters that we haven't uncovered yet," Pele said. "And the wife."

Kengi hung up. "Well, that was interesting."

Derrick and Pele turned to him.

"And what would that be?" Derrick asked.

"It seems that Mr. Gorou Kagawa has a tie with the bōryokudan in Kobe."

Derrick sat back "The Yakuza?"

"One of the world's largest criminal organizations?" Pele said.

"Yes."

"What kind of tie?" Derrick asked.

Kengi sat back. "It is hard to trace. But there is a rumor that Gorou borrowed some money during the economic downturn in Japan to stave off losing the hotel in Tokyo. They were just getting it started at the same time as their expansion here in Hawaii."

"Any direct ties to the hotel here in Hawaii?" Derrick asked.

"I can't say for sure yet. I'll keep digging and see if I can come up with any names."

"It looks like the brother has moved up a notch on our list," Pele said.

"And just in time." Derrick stood up and began pacing around the desks. He stopped and turned to Pele. "Go back over the phone records of Etsuo. At the hotel, cell, home, any phone, email, etc."

"His secretary?"

"Everything we've already done. But go back further. See if we can pick up any scent of a trail."

"What am I looking for?"

"You and Kengi compare them with any known numbers in Japan that might provide a link."

"But I've already done most of that," she said.

"Then let's do it again."

Derrick swung open the garage door.

"Which one are you going to select for the party," Bink asked as the door rolled to the top. "The big red one?" He grinned as the door stopped.

"I was thinking a classic."

"Ah yes," Bink said as they stepped in and admired the choices before them. "You can't go wrong with the 280 SE. They ride like a dream. Mildred wants one."

"I'm glad she approved of your choice."

"So which one are you going to go with?"

"I was thinking the dark green."

"They are still out shopping," Derrick said as he slipped his cell back into his pocket after parking the dark green 280 SE in the condo garage. "For once it's not me holding things up."

"And you got the cars swapped out," Bink said. "How about some lunch? It just so happens that I am free this afternoon as well."

"There's Duke's across the street."

"That's no fun. We can walk there."

"You are enjoying driving this aren't you?"

"It's exciting driving on the wrong side of the street."

Derrick glanced down at the blue 280. "Tell you what. I need to stop in at the hospital and check in on the kids from the accident. We can drive over there, then drive back here and walk across the street."

"Your logic never ceases to amaze me, Derrick."

"It keeps the bad guys guessing."

Pele looked up from her computer. "How are you coming there Kengi?"

He looked over from Derrick's desk. "Slow. How about you?"

"I've got a few more calls to the numbers I've already given you. Nothing out of the ordinary yet. And I still can't get a hold of this…" She looked down at her notebook. "This number listed for a Mr. Fukuhara in San Francisco." She leaned back and stretched. "Do you think this guy's brother would hire someone to kill him?"

"It certainly wouldn't be the first time."

She picked up another list and looked at it. "I wonder if the wife knew anyone in the Yakuza?" She set it aside and picked up another list. One for the secretaries' phone. She scanned down the list of numbers and stopped.

"Find something?"

She sat there for a moment. "No. Nothing." She recognized one of the numbers. It was listed several times. And, she didn't need to write it down to remember it.

Derrick and Bink walked down the hall toward the hospital room where the children were. He looked in the window. Mr. Walters was there. He got up and came out.

"They look like they are doing better," Derrick said.

Mr. Walters turned to them. "Yes. The doctor said I should be able to take them home soon."

"How did they take the news?" Bink asked.

"Who are you?"

"Allow me to introduce Chief Inspector Whitcomb. He helped us rescue your children."

Mr. Walters held out his hand. "Thank you, Inspector."

"I am glad we were there to help out. I am sorry for your loss, though."

Mr. Walters shook his head slowly as he turned back to the children. "She is no loss. To me or the world."

"You having a rough time with her?" Derrick asked.

"She was a gold digging tramp."

"And Mr. Kagawa?" Derrick prodded.

"An arrogant ass. I'm glad they are dead." He turned to Derrick. "I suppose that makes me a suspect."

"It earns you a spot on the list."

"I didn't do it."

"And we should just take your word for it?" Bink asked.

Mr. Walters continued to look in at the children. The girl turned and waved at them. They all smiled waved back.

"I knew she would destroy herself someday. It was just a matter of time."

"So you were just waiting?" Derrick asked.

"It was the only way to get my children back." He turned to Derrick. "I wouldn't kill her because I would go to jail. And they would be alone." He turned back to them. "I knew it was just a matter of time until she brought something like this on herself."

"So who do you think did it Mr. Walters?" Bink asked.

"I don't care who did it. But... Kagawa's wife would be my guess."

Bink sat back and enjoyed the view of surfers and bikini-clad girls strutting up and down the beach. "I wonder if Mildred would ever consider moving here. A retirement home maybe?"

Derrick glanced out past the sidewalk by the restaurant. "There's something for everyone here I guess."

"Ripe for the picking?"

Derrick picked up his Mahi Mahi sandwich. "Some people seem to think so."

"No love lost there," Bink said as he looked down at his burger.

"None," Derrick added as he took a bite.

"Do you believe him?"

Derrick sat back as he finished chewing. "The anger is definitely there. And I think he is capable of killing his wife. However, I also think he's smart enough not to. And maybe he was right. Maybe her time was up. I'll have to do a little more digging around on her." He raised his sandwich to his mouth again. "And him. Just in case." He took another bite.

"He obviously knows more than what he is telling us to come to that conclusion about Mrs. Kagawa," Bink said as he raised his burger and took a bite. "Ummm."

"Or he just wants to send us down a different trail."

Bucchi was sitting in the shadows of the underground parking lot at the Ala Moana mall. Sergeant Tang's car was seven cars down the row. Haruku had parked Derrick's Jeep eight cars further down.

He grinned as he scrolled through the list Pele sent him. "You have been a busy little bad boy haven't you Sergeant Trang." He looked up as Haruku, and the girls got into the jeep. He looked around. Trang was getting into his car.

Haruku drove off. Trang drove off after her. Bucchi started up his car. "You are one tenacious little shit aren't you?" He followed Trang out of the parking garage. "But what are you looking for?"

Bucchi reached into his pocket as his cell rang. "Bucchi here."

"Hi. What's so important that you had me pulled out of a meeting with the director?"

"I thought she was joking when she said that." He laughed. "Sorry. I didn't realize you were that tight with the boys at the top. Guess that's the Special in Special Agent."

"Special Agent In Charge now."

"Got it."

"Well, now you've got me."

"OK, Norton. Special Agent In Charge. Are we still working the Lynn Dreadlow case?"

"Is there a new development?"

"I don't know. Just fishing right now. Derrick has asked me to track this guy following a friend of his. Or maybe him too. I'm not sure what he's really up to yet."

"Who is this friend of his?"

"The sister of Pele Kobayashi."

"And who is the person doing the tracking?"

"Sergeant Trang. Of the HPD."

"The one who was working with Sergeant Perkins?" she asked.

"Who was working with Agent Hollister."

"Small world isn't it?"

"Too small if you ask me."

"So what do you want from me?"

"I'd like to put a tap on his phone and email accounts."

"Give me a day to think about it."

"Take all the time you need Special Agent In Charge."

"If you weren't good at what you do I'd have you on report."

"That and the fact I'm the only one in the FBI you can trust."

"I'll get back to you."

Chapter 20

The shadows of the champagne glasses danced in the candlelight of the table as the server finished pouring. "Will that be all sir?"

"Yes. Thank you."

"And you madam?"

"I am good. Mahalo."

Kengi reached for his glass. "I know it's kind of touristy."

Pele glanced around as she reached for her glass. "A fun touristy." The room was dim and filled with couples of all ages, unaware of the soothing sound of the waves rolling up and lapping against the side of the ship. Candles everywhere flickered in the glassware and star-struck eyes as the gentle breeze filled the room with the cool ocean air.

They raised their glasses in a toast. "To the most beautiful woman I have met in Honolulu."

Pele looked at the bubbles streaming up in her glass. "You haven't gotten out much. Since you arrived, you've been stuck in an Interpol conference, and then working a crime."

"But I have been all over the island, walked the streets of Waikiki, and I am a trained observer."

"Then thank you." They clinked their glasses and drank the toast.

"And to the most interesting man I have met in a very long time."

He bowed his head slightly as he smiled.

As Pele set her glass down, she gazed out across the water. Her senses taking in all the evening offered. She saw Honolulu basking in the golden glow of the setting sun as the cruise ship slowly made its way across the bay. She breathed in the sea air and the scent of colorful bouquets that filled the room. She listened as the music of the jazz band filled the room.

Kengi stood up and extended his hand. "May I have this dance while we wait for the next course?"

She reached up and placed her hand in his. "You may." She followed him out in her light blue, floral-patterned, silk dress. She clutched her matching purse with her gun and badge in her other hand.

Derrick was walking along the beach with a dish of chocolate chip mint ice cream. Haruku had mango and French vanilla. The girls had already finished theirs and were racing the sandpipers in and out of the surf. The sun slid below the horizon as the last vestiges of the day slipped into the darkness of night.

"I can't believe that they still have so much energy," he said as he licked at a spoon full of ice cream.

"An ice cream cone for dessert and a short nap in the afternoon contributed a lot," Haruku said as she scooped a spoonful out of her bowl. She held it up to his mouth. "Here, try some of this. Expand your horizons." She slid it into his mouth then slowly pulled back as he wrapped his lips around it.

He nodded approvingly. "It's very tasty."

He scrapped a spoonful of his green chocolate chip mint and held it up for her. "Like to try some of this?"

She gazed into his eyes. "I would love to." She closed her eyes as he slid the spoon gently into her mouth. She closed her lips around it and held it for a moment in her teeth. "Ummm." He slowly pulled it out. She slowly opened her eyes. "That was very good."

"Look, Uncle Derrick," Kattie yelled out. "The fireworks are starting."

Pele leaned over the side as she rested her arms on the railing. She watched the foam from the bow and the ripples of waves rush out as the ship cut across the top of the ocean. Kengi stood silently by her side and gazed out over the water. "You were unusually quiet during dinner Kengi. Is everything OK?"

He stood there. "Yes." He gazed out over the ripples spreading out across the water.

She turned to look out over the water and lights of the shoreline glistening on the waves. She took a slow deep breath as she drank in the cool sea air. "Lost in thought?"

He glanced over at her then back out over the water. "No. Just admiring the view."

"You live on an island too. Surely this isn't new to you."

He reached out and ran his finger over the top of the railing. "Yes, it is."

"What do you mean?"

A quick popping noise drifted out from the coast. A murmur rolled through the crowd on deck as everyone turned. The fireworks display had begun.

Kengi slid his hand across Pele's back and rested on her shoulder. "It's quite a sight. I can't believe I missed it before."

"They set them off every Friday night."

"Do you watch the fireworks often?"

She took a deep breath as she watched the shoreline creep closer and closer. The dinner cruise was coming to an end. In another twenty minutes, the ship would be back at the dock and the evening would be over. Or would it? She watched him out of the corner of her eye. She took a deep breath then turned and gazed into Kengi's eyes. "I had a lovely evening tonight Kengi."

He stood there, stiff and silent for a moment. "So did I Pele." He took an ever so slight step away.

"Are you all right? A bit sea sick after that big meal?"

"I. I just have something that…"

Her smartphone went off. She glanced down at the purse in her hand. "Ignore that." It stopped. She reached out and put her hand on his. "What were you going to say Kengi?" The phone went off again.

He glanced down at the purse in her hand. "Maybe you should just get it. Might be important."

She sighed as she opened her purse and pulled out the phone. "Kobayashi." She glanced over at him then back out across the water. "OK. OK. Give me about an hour," she glanced over at Kengi. "I'm kind of in the middle of something." She hung up.

"What was that about?"

"Another case. I'm afraid that when we dock, I'll have to take you back to your hotel."

"I understand."

She slipped her arm around his. "I'm sorry Kengi. This was a wonderful evening. It really was."

He slid his hand over hers as they watched the dock grow closer. "Things are what they are. We can't always fight it."

Derrick watched as Kattie and Becky were walking slowly along the beach now. The fireworks were over, and their energy was crashing fast. And they were down to their last week in Hawaii with him. On top of that, he was back in the middle of a big case with no clear suspect yet.

"So you don't think their father killed their mother?" Haruku asked as she and Derrick followed the girls along the sandy beach back toward home.

"Huh?"

She reached out and took his hand in hers. "The children from the boat?"

"Oh. No. Not really. He had a motive. But I believe him when he said he wanted the children back. He couldn't ever get them if he were in jail."

Derrick paused as his phone rang. "Dreadlow here."

"Hi, Dread. Just wanted to let you know I was on the job."

Derrick glanced around. "That you Bucchi?"

"The one and only."

"What does on the job mean?"

"I am now officially tracking Trang to see if this leads to anything else."

"Such as?"

"This guy has been contacted by Hollister after being blown off by Perkins."

"So you think he is working with Hollister now? And it's not just about... you know..."

"You're with her now. That's cool. It's not just about her. Or Pele. Or even you. I think this guy is a loose cannon and he's after all of you. Or anyone else that gets in his sights."

"You think he's unstable or something?"

"Or something."

"I thought that Hollister was told to stop his..."

"He was. You just go about your daily routine. I'll keep an eye on our slimy friend."

Derrick hung up and slipped the phone back into his pocket. His little talk with Trang in the alley apparently went unheeded.

"That sounded serious. Is anything wrong Derrick?"

Kattie and Becky laughed and giggled as he reached out and scooped them up in his arms. "Na. Just new info on an old case."

"That was fun Uncle Derrick," Becky said. "Can we do it again?"

"I think it's time to get you two to bed."

Pele and Bucchi were sitting in his car in the alley behind her parent's Waikiki store.

"Does Derrick know all this about Trang?"

"He's the one who asked me to follow him."

"And he thought it was just Trang following my sister to find something on her?"

"That was the start of it."

"And now Trang is working with Hollister, who is supposed to be off Derrick's dead wife's case."

Bucchi reached for his steering wheel and pushed back in his seat. "You've got it."

"Why?"

"I'm working on that." He glanced over at her. "Like I told Dreadlow. You just go about your normal routine. Norton asked me to watch your backs. Again."

"All three of us?"

He grinned as he peered up over the top of his mirrored sunglasses. "I'm good."

Pele reached for the door handle. "Let's hope so."

Chapter 21

Kattie tossed her fishing line back into the water. "I have two now, and you don't have any."

"I'm waiting for a gigantic one," Becky said as she watched the water.

"So your copness has finally begun to return?" Ailani asked as he finished his apple Danish.

"I guess you could say that," Derrick said as he took a bite of his.

"Brought on by what?" Ailani took a sip. "The cases aren't that different than back in New York. Crime is crime. Murder is murder."

Derrick took a sip of his coffee as he watched the old couple out on their deck having breakfast. "The sea air?"

"New York is by the ocean."

"This is the Pacific."

Ailani nodded as he chewed slowly. He swallowed. "Maybe it was the case we the public don't know about."

"What case would that be?"

"I've been around long enough to put two and two together and come up with twenty-two." He took a sip of his coffee. "I know government math my friend."

Derrick nodded as he took another sip. "You're fishing."

"Faulty fuel line, Interpol conference, statues that don't exist, dead men? Need I go on?"

Derrick turned to him.

"I read the news. Often the story isn't in what they report. It's between the lines."

"You a conspiracy nut?"

"That's Chief Conspiracy Nut."

Derrick shook his head.

"Plus I have friends in low places."

"Now that I believe."

"And now you are suspicious of your girlfriend." Ailani took a sip of his coffee. "You sure the pendulum hasn't swung too far the other way now?"

Derrick glanced over at him again. "What? Now I see crimes where none exist? I'm paranoid or something?"

"Paranoid? No. You said it yourself that she was too good to be true."

"I've also said this is paradise." He finished his Danish.

Ailani raised his Danish to his lips then paused. "How does one recognize paradise if there is nothing to compare it with?"

"In your Yoda mood this morning?"

"Just a question." He took a bite.

"A good one I guess."

"Look at your track record with women. It is... how shall I say this?"

"It stinks?"

Ailani nodded. "That works."

Derrick opened the second bag. He pulled out his second Mocha Frappuccino Light and Danish. "A two coffee morning." He took a sip as he watched Kattie and Becky fish.

"So Haruku said getting ready for this party could take all morning?" Ailani unwrapped his apple Danish.

"It's a hair thing."

"All morning?"

"Apparently so. Maybe longer. She said she'd call when she was finished." Derrick took a bite of his Danish and chewed for a moment. "I guess these things take a while."

"It's just hair," Ailani said.

"Absolutely. It's not like this is a grand ball with the queen or something." He took a sip of coffee.

Ailani watched as Becky got a nibble. Then the line went slack. "On the other hand, it is a big social event. And you invited her."

"I guess it's an art." Derrick took another bite.

"Beauty must be a lot of work," Ailani said as he sat there.

Derrick glanced over at him as he sat there in his shorts, red Hawaiian shirt, and stringy long gray hair. "I guess you wouldn't know about things like that."

Ailani nodded to the women walking their dogs in the park. "How long do you think it takes them to get ready before coming to the park every Saturday morning?"

"The social event of the week?" Derrick drew in a long deep breath. "I'll bet longer than either of us could imagine."

They sat there in silence as they watched the women stretch and talk. Boats meandered out of the marina for a day of sailing. Derrick took another sip. It was another day in paradise.

"So what's in the backpack?" Ailani asked as he glanced over at Derrick's pack. "Kind of heavy for a Saturday morning isn't it?"

"My laptop."

"Trying to get in a little work?"

"Kind of."

"Another case?"

"Kind of."

"Well don't let me stop you."

Derrick set his coffee down and pulled out his laptop. He opened it and sat there as it came back to life. "This new technology and wireless stuff is a blessing and a curse."

"I'll bet the emperor of China said the same thing about printing when it first came out."

"Hmmm."

Ailani looked over at him as he finished his Danish. "Something you didn't expect?"

Derrick sat back and exhaled. "I half expected it. But I didn't want to."

"I always hated that feeling."

Derrick grinned. "You get a lot of that during your days in the merchant marine?"

"It had its moments." Ailani took another sip of coffee. "So what is it?"

"Ah... two people I have been trying to locate. Xin just sent me an email on state searches and Todd another on tax filings he searched."

"And?"

"They both seem to have dropped off the face of the planet at the same time. March of 2008."

"That generally means one thing."

Derrick closed his laptop and reached for his coffee. "Yeah, it does."

Chapter 22

Pele yawned as she sat at her desk in the station. There were only two other detectives in on Saturday morning. Crime never took the weekend off. But cops are people too. Kengi walked up behind her.

"Good morning."

She looked up from her computer. "Hi, Kengi. I'm sorry about last night."

"I understand." He set a large bag down on her desk. "I brought breakfast."

"You getting a taste for burritos?"

"They are quite good." He opened the bag and passed her a burrito and a large tea.

"Also, to brighten your morning... I have more information from Kobe."

"Breakfast. Tea. News on our case." Pele unwrapped her burrito and sat back. "What more can a girl ask for?"

"We have traced some of the phone calls to a man named Hirokazu Amano."

"Who is he?"

"He is a low-level soldier in an organization linked to another man named Hidehisa Domen."

"Who is?"

"A Yakuza boss in Kobe with ties to Tokyo."

"Any connection to Kagawa's brother back in Japan?" Pele asked as she reached for her tea.

"Not that I can find. Yet. But my guess is that there will be. It's hard to penetrate this organization."

She raised her cup to her mouth as she sat back. "It is a piece to a puzzle." She took a sip. "But is it our puzzle? The Yakuza have their fingers in many things. Legal and not."

"I will keep digging."

"I've got one! I've got one!" Becky yelled out.

Derrick set his coffee down and rushed over to her. "OK, now Becky. Just reel him in slowly."

"Why do you always call the fish him Uncle Derrick?"

"That is because the female fish are too smart to get caught."

Derrick and Becky looked up.

Becky grinned. "Hi, Bink. You are just in time to watch me catch a fish."

"And it... he... looks like a big one."

Derrick reached for the net. "OK now Becky, raise him out slowly."

She took a step back from the railing as she raised the pole as high as she could. Derrick reached out with the net.

"Nice catch," Ailani said.

Kattie turned to look at them. "I already have two this morning. And one is bigger."

"The morning is still young," Derrick said as he slipped the fish into the cooler.

"Try this lure," Ailani said as he helped Becky get her line ready again.

"Out for a stroll this morning?" Derrick asked as they sat down on the bench.

"Yes. Apparently, Haruku called Mildred and asked her if she'd like to get her hair done for the party tonight. I think there was something about nails involved as well."

Derrick smiled. "And you weren't invited."

"Not my cup of tea. Haruku told me where I could find you and the girls. She said I was probably late for coffee and Danish, though."

"I thought you were broadening your horizons here?"

"Not that much."

"Sorry about the coffee. We're just finishing up. But I could go make another run."

"No thank you. I had a cup of Haruku's mango tea. Quite refreshing." Bink watched Becky as she tossed her line back out. "So where is Pele in all this? Shouldn't she be there with them as well?"

Pele was standing under a palm tree near the King's Village and Guard shops. Agent Bucchi was standing on the other side pretending not to know her. To the tourists wandering in and out of the shops they didn't even exist.

"Has Derrick seen these yet?" she asked as she slipped the USB device into her pocket.

"No. I thought you might want to see them first."

"Why? What's on it?"

"Photos of Haruku, him and…"

Pele reached back and ran her hand over the butt of her gun. "The girls?"

"He gave it to me to check out. So he has an idea about what I found. But still. I didn't know how he might take it to know it's true."

"I think at some point, we're all going to have to sit down and have a talk about all of this."

"One step ahead of you. I am setting up a meeting with Karen, the DA, and the three of us for when you get back from New York. After the girls are back home and we can put things into proper perspective."

"And just what is the proper perspective?"

"Maybe I'll know more by then."

"So what time is your flight back?" Derrick asked as the girls resumed their fishing competition and the men turned back to watching the women in the park.

"Nice view from here," Bink said.

"It's paradise," Ailani said. "We expect nothing less."

"Well you certainly have the perfect spot to enjoy it in all its splendor," Bink said with a wide grin.

"You should tell Mildred you want to stay another week," Derrick said.

"Yes. Well, all good things must come to an end, my friend."

"I hope not," Ailani said as the women began their walk back toward them.

"Our flight is at 11:30. Sunday morning."

"Well we'll try to see you off," Derrick said.

"I thought we'd take a cab. I'll leave all your keys on the kitchen counter."

"Sounds fine."

Bink took a deep breath as the women walked past with their dogs.

"Hello there," the tall one closest to him said with a slight smile and a soft, low voice.

"And a lovely good morning to you," he said graciously. The women continued past without breaking her stride. "Capital spot you have here Ailani."

Derrick watched the women as they sashayed on down the sidewalk. "They ever say good morning like that to you old wise one?"

105

He peered up over the top of his sunglasses. "One told me once that there was a fish on my line." He turned back to watching Kattie and Becky. "But never in that tone of voice."

Bink grinned from ear to ear as he took a deep breath. "What an incredible trip this has been. I am going to miss paradise."

Derrick grinned. "It's not over yet. We still have that party tonight."

Pele tossed her gun and her badge onto the bed as she stepped over to her closet. She slid the door open. She stared at the line of dark pants suits, then slid the door shut, and opened the other side. Tucked up against the right side were several dresses. Mostly black or dark blue. She reached in and slid them a few inches to the left.

There were a few colorful dresses of varying lengths. Some were Hawaiian in design. She pulled out a brightly colored, sleeveless sundress and held it up in front of her as she turned to the full-length mirror off to the side. It came to just above the knee as she held it up in front of her.

She had only worn it twice. Once to a restaurant for lunch. With Derrick when he was gathering evidence in a case he failed to mention. She took a deep, slow breath. And once before. Years ago.

She shook her head and put it back.

"Oh hell. Why did I say I'd go to this?" She grabbed a purse off the shelf and stuffed her gun and badge inside. "Oh yeah. The captain said we had to go."

Twenty minutes later, she was in a shop looking at Hawaiian style dresses.

A service girl walked up to her. "Can I help you find something? Something special perhaps?"

Chapter 23

"Are we going to spend the night there?" Becky asked.

"No," Kattie said. "We didn't pack a bag or even a toothbrush. You need those things when you spend the night someplace else."

Becky nodded. "I hope I am as smart as you when I get to be seven."

"Don't worry Becky. I'll teach you."

Derrick knelt down by them. "Now you be good while you are with Ailani and Ahulani."

"Are you and Aunt Haruku going out to dinner?" Kattie asked.

"Something like that."

"And we can't go with you?" Becky asked as she twisted from side to side and put her fingers in her mouth.

"We would like to take you with us, but it is adults only."

"Are you taking a toothbrush with you too?" Becky asked.

Derrick reached out and brushed her hair back. "No. We will be home later. Probably after you are fast asleep."

"Don't worry about a thing," Ailani said. "We have a fun filled evening planned for them. And Father Bishop is downstairs waiting for us."

"And your wife?"

"Still busy."

"Uh huh." He leaned over and kissed the girls on the forehead as he stood up. "Don't tire them out too much girls."

"We won't," Kattie said.

"Was that Ailani?" Haruku asked as she strolled down the hall with a towel wrapped around her.

Derrick nodded as he closed the door. "He picked up the girls and the Cherokee while you were in the shower."

"Did he have his wife with him?"

Derrick laughed. "Father Bishop is down by the Jeep. He insists he's married. But I've never met her."

"Some people think you are dating a vet. But no one ever sees her either."

Derrick shrugged. Maybe he would have been better off if he'd never seen her either. But then, there may be two victims of murder here that someone has to find. "Your hair looks nice."

"Thank you. I thought I'd try it up tonight. Are you going to get ready now?"

"I guess I can't put it off any longer. What do you think I should wear to this thing?"

She strolled back down the hall to her room. "I've put something out on the bed for you. I hope you like it." She turned and swung her hips as she shut the door.

State Senator Richard Aneko and his wife, Police Chief Barbara Murdoch, stood up by the podium. The chief scanned the room as her husband talked to one of his staff members.

"… and you double checked the seating arrangements?" he asked.

"Yes sir," the young woman replied as she glanced down at her clipboard. "Maximum cross exposure."

"Good. They can mingle all they like before and after. But I want to make sure some of them get to meet each other. And this should take care of that."

"Yes, sir." The young woman glanced off toward the kitchen. "If there is nothing else I would like to go check on dinner."

Aneko nodded. "That's all, for now, Peggy. Mahalo."

"Are you sure that's a good idea?" Chief Murdoch asked as the young woman raced off across the room.

"Controlled chance my dear." He turned slowly as he looked around. He grinned proudly. "This should be a great evening for Hawaii."

Pele was calling a number on her phone as she pulled up in front of Kengi's hotel. "Mr. Fukuhara. It is important that I speak to you as soon as possible. Call this number. Anytime."

Kengi got in as she stopped in front of the door. "Still working?" he asked as she hung up.

"I'm still trying to get a hold of this Fukuhara guy." She pulled out of the parking area and onto the street. "Anything new on your end?"

He sat there for a moment and watched the throng of people waiting at the crosswalk.

"Kengi?" She glanced over at him. "Lost in thought again?"

He turned to her. "Huh? I haven't heard anything new from Japan yet. Have you reached that Mr. Fukuhara in San Francisco yet?"

"Nervous about tonight?"

He nodded slightly. "Maybe."

"Don't be. Trust me. We're not famous. No one will pay attention to us. No one will ever even know we are there."

"Is Pele going to the party with us?" Haruku asked as they waited for the elevator to reach the garage level.

"No. She said she was going to pick up Kengi at his hotel."

The elevator stopped, and the doors slid open.

"Are we going in your car or mine?" she asked as they stepped off the elevator.

He pulled a set of keys out of his pocket. "Mine."

She looked over at his space. "Where is your car? I think someone parked in your space."

Derrick walked up to the car and unlocked the door. "I thought we'd go in style." He opened the door to the dark green Mercedes 280 SE.

"Is this one of your cars that I've heard about?" she asked as she slid in. "It's beautiful." She ran her fingers over the soft light brown leather. "And elegant."

"A beautiful carriage for a stunningly beautiful lady," he said as he closed the door.

Her eyes sparkled as she smoothed out her dress and gazed up at him. "I love it. Thank you."

Bink handed the keys of the blue 280 SE to the valet. He opened the door and bowed slightly as he held out his hand to his wife. "Lady Westfield. We have arrived."

She reached out and took his hand. "Oh, Bink. Do you always have to put on a show?"

He beamed as she linked her arm with his. "Entrance is everything, my dear. Isn't that what you told me once when we first met?"

"That was for my father's benefit. Not a luau thing."

Bink smiled as the door opened for them.

"It's just the sensor dear."

"I know. But just imagine a well-appointed doorman there to greet you."

"Have you been drinking?"

"No. It's just been so long since we've gone to an event where there wasn't someone with their hand out for something from you." He glanced around the entrance. "That way," he said nodding to the sign. "Anyway. A party with you is like an evening in heaven dear."

"You are so full of--"

"Charm?"

"I was going to say something else." She looked over at him. "I think you've been away from work too long."

"Like Derrick said, it must be the islands." He grinned as he looked at her. "By the way Mildred. You do look smashing in that dress. So… so… colorful. And I love your hair."

"I may have to have a Hawaiian night for one of our events when we get home. What do you think?"

"It's a capital idea dear."

The valet opened the door of the car and Haruku slipped out. Derrick extended his left arm as he handed the valet the keys with his right hand.

They followed the signs into the reception area where people were gathering for dinner. A young staff, dressed in various costumes from across the South Pacific, served colorful drinks and appetizers. In the far corner, up on a stage with palm trees on either side, a large screen was cycling through scenes from around the Hawaiian Islands in HD. A band was entertaining with Hawaiian music.

They bent their heads slightly as a beautiful islander couple stepped up to them. The woman was tall dark and slender, the man, taller and muscular. They slipped leis of red, white, and yellow flowers around their necks. "Aloha," they said then stepped back for the next arriving couple.

"Aloha," Derrick and Haruku replied together.

Derrick scanned the room. "They went all out didn't they?"

"Yes," Haruku said.

"Well look at you two?"

Captain Henderson and his wife Patty were standing there admiring their choice of clothes for the occasion. Derrick was wearing a blue chevron Hawaiian shirt with black slacks. Haruku was wearing her hair up, sporting a thin gold chain with matching bracelet and earrings that accented her smooth dark skin. She was dressed in a matching blue chevron wrap around skirt that came just above the knee and a black spaghetti strap shirt.

"You see Nick," Patty began as she nodded toward them. "Some men aren't afraid to share a style with the woman they are with."

The captain nodded as he looked at Derrick and Haruku. "Is that what it is?"

"Well you two are both bright," Haruku said admiring his red shirt and her long yellow and orange tie-dye dress. "Complementary colors yet the same palm tree motif."

Captain Henderson glanced at his shirt then at her dress. "Tried to slip one past me didn't you."

"Maybe next time you will follow your Lieutenant's lead and take the next step."

"Now look at what you've done Dreadlow."

Derrick grinned. "At least I'm an influence. Hopefully for the best."

The captain took a sip of his white wine then nodded toward the doorway. "Well, they don't match Patty."

They all turned as Pele and Kengi walked toward them. Kengi had on dark brown slacks and a bright yellow Hawaiian shirt with a few blue waves on the side. Pele wore black slacks, a light blue striped spaghetti shirt, and her black running shoes with the purple stripe. Some things never changed.

"You packing under that?" Derrick whispered as he leaned close.

Pele checked out his shirt hanging loosely around his slacks. "You?"

"Never know when you might need a cop."

Captain Henderson finished his drink. "Let's go mingle with the rich and famous folks. An opportunity like this for the force comes only once in a blue moon." The three couples all drifted off in different directions.

Derrick noticed that Haruku still had her arm wrapped around his ever since they got out of the car. She felt soft and warm next to him. He glanced over into her dark brown eyes. They each squeezed a little tighter. Somehow, it felt right. Words weren't needed.

A server walked up to them. Derrick picked two drinks. He hesitated before handing a glass to Haruku.

"Are you wondering if I will be safe?"

"Well, I don't want to…"

She tilted her head down and glanced up at him. "Knock me off the wagon?"

"Something like that."

"That phase of my life is behind me, Derrick. Trust me. I can nurse a drink all night with the best of them." She raised her glass in a toast. "To an evening in paradise."

He gazed into her eyes and smiled as he raised his glass. "An evening in paradise together."

She raised her glass to her lips and took a tiny sip. "Plus… when you are almost finished with your glass, we can switch."

"I have to warn you. I've gone nearly seven hours on one glass."

"You're on."

"How is it coming?"

Paul and Phil looked up from the console they were working at.

"I didn't expect to see you here tonight," Paul said.

"Fei got called into the hospital. A patient of hers was admitted unexpectedly," Quon replied as he scanned the area. "This looks like it is coming along really well."

Paul stood up as they looked around at the new command center taking shape in the bowels of the Q. "A couple more days and we'll be up and running."

"Exactly what will *we* be running? And who will be in here running it?" Quon asked.

Paul glanced over Phil.

"I'll finish up here," Phil said. He turned back to his work as another technician entered with a cart filled with cables and HDMI interface units.

Paul nodded for Quon to follow him. They walked down the corridor. People were crawling all around the complex like busy worker bees. "I have someone coming out from Washington on Monday I want you to meet."

"Who is he?" Quon asked.

"She is a Human Resources Manager you could say."

Quon laughed. "I do not have any Human Resources to manage. Yet."

Paul raised his hand and pointed up in the air. "Yet being the operative word my friend." They walked over to the elevator. "Let's go up to your office."

Detective Patterson was turning burgers in his tiny backyard nestled between townhomes. A small table for two, three rose bushes on a trellis, and a small lemon tree in a large pot were all that fit next to his grill.

"Make mine medium rare."

Patterson looked over. "Bout time you got here. Mary come with you?"

"She's inside with Carol."

"Running late while she got ready?"

Detective Pusch shook his head. "No. I got a message just as we were leaving home. Someone left a message on Fukuhara's machine."

"Who? Why?"

"Don't know. Just said to call her."

Patterson tossed two more burgers on the grill. "Interesting."

"So I had it traced."

"Get a name?"

"Kobayashi. Pele Kobayashi. Out of Hawaii. I've got someone tracking down who she is."

"Maybe we've finally caught a break."

Chapter 24

Derrick and Haruku were the last couple to arrive at their table. He glanced around at the setting. The centerpiece was an arrangement of low cut flowers so that everyone could see and talk to each other with unobstructed views. Every detail was well thought out. From the China, to the crystal glasses, to the ornate silverware.

He nodded and smiled at everyone as they set their barely touched glasses of white wine down. He slid Haruku's chair out for her then took his. "Aloha," he said as he glanced around again at the other four couples seated at their table.

"Aloha," replied the man on his right. "I am Elmer Walsh, and this is my wife, Rosalynn." He pointed to the next couple on his right. "This is Marshall Nihipali and his wife, Murial. And on your left, we have Colonel Leong and his wife, Winona. And then across from you, we have Daisuke, dah EE soo keh… did I get that correct?" The man gave a slight nod. "Daisuke Mayeda and his wife, Akari." Elmer raised his hands triumphantly as he glanced around the table. "There. I made it. I've been taking these memory classes. They really work!"

Rosalynn turned to Derrick and Haruku "You and your wife make a lovely couple."

"Derrick Dreadlow," he replied. "And this is Haruku."

"It's nice to meet you all," Haruku said with a gracious smile.

A server set a salad in front of them, refilled the bread dishes, and filled their water glasses.

Haruku nodded. "Mahalo." The server nodded and stepped quietly away.

"Looks like you got here just in time," Elmer said as the governor stood up and made his way to the front of the room. He stepped up to the small podium.

Derrick could see Pele and Kengi a couple of tables away as they turned in their chairs to watch the opening speech.

The governor took a brief moment to look around the room. "I would like to thank you all for coming tonight. And even though this is an election year…"

The crowd laughed.

"I'm not going to make any election year speeches."

Everyone laughed again.

"But before our hosts begin serving us this marvelous dinner of which we have been teased by the aroma of so far this evening, I am going to turn the podium over to State Senator Richard Aneko, who's idea this event was." The governor leaned into the podium. "Senator Aneko has promised me not to make any long speeches either."

The crowd laughed and applauded as the governor sat down and Senator Aneko stepped up to the podium.

He beamed as excitedly as a little boy at Christmas. He waved then placed his hands on the edges of the podium "E komo mai! Welcome. And good evening everyone. I am so thrilled and honored to see you all here tonight." He paused as he scanned the room.

Derrick turned slightly in his chair for a better view. Haruku leaned close to him and whispered. "You didn't tell me there were going to be speeches."

"The price of admission I guess."

"No election speeches. This event tonight is bigger than that. Bigger than any of us." He paused for a moment as he scanned the room. "I would like to welcome all of you here tonight for what I hope will become an annual event. Our theme for tonight is 'Hawaii. Gateway to the 21st Century'." He scanned the packed room again.

"Oahu truly *is* the gathering place. We all have our reasons for coming to these beautiful islands." He smiled. "Some of us were lucky enough to be born here." He paused for a moment. "The rest of us, through some design, accident, or twist of fate, have found our way here. But no matter how we got here, we have all come here tonight with a purpose. The great state of Hawaii. Our great state of Hawaii. Is poised to be at the center of a new world as this new century unfolds. It will be an era filled with great opportunity, and great challenges. And many of us here tonight will have a say, and an influence, in our respective fields on how we respond to these opportunities and challenges." He paused as he surveyed the room. "And working together, we can make our dreams a reality."

Senator Aneko took a deep breath as he stood up tall. "Take this opportunity tonight to get to know each other, make new friends, and discover new ways in which we can work together to make our state, the one that will lead America, and the world into the future." He nodded and waved as he sat down to a loud round of applause.

"Short and sweet," Derrick said as he passed the bread to Haruku. "Just the way I like it."

"You are not a politician," Colonel Leong said.

Derrick shook his head as he set the bowl down. "Not hardly. You?"

He shook his head. "No. Never had much use for them."

Pele reached into her purse and slipped out a pair of black rimmed glasses.

"I didn't realize you wore glasses," Kengi said softly.

"Only if my eyes get tired." She blinked a couple of times then scanned the people at the table and the tables nearby.

"Are they OK?" Kengi asked as she kept reaching up to adjust them.

She stopped her fidgeting and reached for a glass of water. "I'm good. Just not used to wearing them I guess."

She watched the white-haired man at Derrick's table. He was talking to one of the servers as she leaned closer to hear something he was saying. Pele set her glass of water down and readjusted her glasses again. The girl appeared to be taking one of the man's plates away.

"So Mr. Mayeda," began Elmer as he reached for the bowl of Poi. "What is it that you do here in the great state of Hawaii?"

Derrick watched him across the table. The stern looking man with the short, pure white hair and light skin with a pinkish tinge, sat back in his chair. He was the only one at the table with a jacket on. Maybe the only person in the room other than the governor. Even Aneko had on a bright orange and yellow Hawaiian shirt.

Mr. Mayeda studied Mr. Walsh for a moment. "I am in the tourist business. And you sir?"

The quick non-committal answer followed by a faster deflection. Derrick reached for his glass of water.

"I…" he turned to his wife, "that is we… supply fresh flowers to many of the hotels here on the island. If you are in the business, perhaps we supply one of your establishments?"

Mr. Mayeda nodded slightly. "It is possible."

Elmer turned to Marshall.

"I own a large laundry. Not glamorous, I know," Mr. Nihipali said. "We take on the laundry for those hotels and companies that want to outsource that part of their business. You know, so that they can concentrate on what they do best." He laughed nervously. "Not clean up the towels and the sheets."

Elmer then turned to Colonel Leong and his wife. "And what is it that you do?"

"I'm a colonel in the air force."

"You're out of uniform," Elmer joked.

Colonel Leong smiled. "We do dress down for special occasions." He turned to his wife. "And Winona is the assistant director of the tourist council for the arts here in our great state."

"So you put on the arts festivals and things like that?" Rosalynn asked.

"I do my part. Yes," Winona replied.

Derrick had been watching Mr. Mayeda as they went around the table. There was something about him. He couldn't put his finger on it. Maybe it was his answer to Elmer. Being in the tourist business could mean a lot of things.

Haruku glanced over at Derrick as he studied Mr. Mayeda.

Mr. Mayeda broke his silence. He turned to Derrick. "And what is it that you do Mr. Dreadlow. Are you and your lovely wife in the entertainment business?"

Derrick shrugged slightly as he sat back. "Well, I have been known to tell a joke or two…"

"Even sing once in a while," Haruku added.

"But you are not an entertainer. At least not one that I am aware of," Mr. Mayeda said flatly. He spoke in a monotone and showed a poker face. It was as though he was studying everyone.

Derrick studied back. "No. I'm more in the background you could say. Keeping an eye on things."

"So are you an agent of some kind?"

Derrick smiled politely. "You could say that."

Haruku reached out and placed her hand on Derrick's arm. "He's very good at spotting people's hidden talents."

Derrick turned and placed his hand on hers. He glanced down at it. It was soft and warm. He looked into her eyes. "Thank you, dear."

Her eyes sparkled. "My pleasure darling."

Derrick turned to Winona. "Haruku here is quite the artist."

Haruku glanced down at her plate. "Not really."

"Have you ever shown any of your work?"

Haruku looked up. "Once. A long time ago. At school."

"I would love to see it sometime." She smiled at Haruku. "We're always on the lookout for good local talent. And if your husband thinks you are good, I would be interested in seeing your work sometime."

"This food is just marvelous," Rosalynn said as she cut into her slice of pork. "It is so tender."

"It's probably some old Hawaiian receipt," Elmer said with a grin.

Haruku glanced at Derrick watching Mr. Mayeda. She leaned close and whispered. "Are we undercover?"

Chapter 25

Paul glanced around Quon's spacious, and mostly empty office as they entered the room. "I love what you've done with the place, Quon."

Quon shrugged as he looked around. There were an old table and four folding chairs. A gray file cabinet sat in the corner. The third drawer from the bottom was opened slightly. The blinds were dusty and askew. A ceiling tile in the corner was pitched half in the space above the room and half down in the office. The slightest breeze and it would come crashing down on the floor.

"I've been busy with other things."

"Your Ph.D. being one of them."

Quon nodded as he gazed out the filmy window into the darkness settling across the island.

"We need to have a talk," Paul said as he motioned for Quon to take a seat at his desk.

"I work in a store," Pele said to the woman on her right.

Her eyes widened in an incredulous stare. "They invited a clerk here?"

"My family owns a chain of stores. On different islands."

"Oh." She turned back to her husband. "That explains it." He nodded.

Kengi sat there staring down at his plate.

Pele turned to Kengi. "You are awful quiet tonight."

"Just have things on my mind I guess."

"The case?" she whispered.

"Yes." He poked at his salad.

She looked up and scanned the room again. The woman on her right was talking to other people. Probably more interesting people than some girl who worked at a store. Even if her family did own it. She didn't mention she was also a detective for the Honolulu Police Department.

Bink reached for his mango tea. He turned to the man seated on his left. "You know, I've never even heard of this tea until last week. Now I can't seem to get enough of it."

"Refreshing I suppose you could say," he replied without really caring.

A middle-aged woman in blue with three strands of white pearls around her neck smiled and bounced in her chair as she went on. "It is too bad you are leaving in the morning, Lady Westfield. There is so much we would have liked to show you of our island. And the things our organization does."

"There is just so much work in the world that needs to be done," Mildred said as she reached for her wine glass. "Isn't that true dear?"

Bink turned to her and nodded. "Oh yes." He set his tea down. "So much so that one hardly knows where to begin."

"Well we are all so pleased to meet you, Lady Westfield," a young woman across the table added. "Perhaps someday our organization can do a joint project with one of yours? Maybe Africa or something. They always need help there."

"I think that would be a lovely idea," Mildred replied. "Don't you?"

Bink nodded as he scanned the room. "Yes dear." He couldn't see Derrick or anyone else he knew. But it was a big party. "Whatever you say, dear."

Paul unfolded a chair and sat down. "You know Quon." Paul reached up and ran his fingers through his hair as he took a deep breath. "You are a brilliant guy Quon. Exceptional."

Quon looked up from his seat behind his table serving as a makeshift desk. "Thank you."

"You... You have a fantastically creative mind, and an eye for detail mixed with a nose for practicality."

"There are a lot of problems in the world that need solving."

"Absolutely my friend. However… You've got to start thinking a bit like an executive too as you start to get your company off the ground."

Quon nodded as he sat down. "I suppose you are right. But I have been so busy."

Paul slid his chair closer to the table. He glanced down and ran his finger across the top picking up a line of dust as he went. He sat back in his chair. "Look. Quon. You are the brain which forms the heart of this new venture. You are its biggest asset."

Quon continued to sit there in silence as he observed Paul and pondered the situation.

Paul took a deep breath. "What I am about to say isn't a bad reflection on you." Paul ran his tongue over his teeth as he sat there thinking, speaking slowly. "You've had the foresight to hire Todd to handle the financial end. And I am getting some of your technological infrastructure in place for you." They sat there staring at each other. "And it is an opportunity I'm grateful you asked me to help with. I think you have a great future ahead and I am excited to be a part of it."

"I am glad you are too," Quon said.

"You need more help than just Todd and my people, though."

Quon looked down at his dusty table and around at his cluttered office filled with garage sale rejects.

"I know this seems like a big step Quon. That's because it is."

Quon reached out and touched the disconnected phone on the side of his desk.

"Even Bill Gates knew when it was time to move out of the garage."

"He ran his own company."

"I don't think he handled every detail beyond the core business."

Quon shrugged and nodded. "Probably not I guess."

"This is the moment to shit or get off the pot, my friend. You are at that point, where you move from a plan on paper, to a company in reality. What do you want to do?"

Quon nodded as he sat there. He drew in a deep breath and exhaled slowly. "OK, Paul. What do we do next?"

Haruku picked up her water glass and turned to Derrick. "That Mayeda keeps watching you."

Derrick reached for another helping of Chicken Adobo. "Maybe because he thinks we're talking about him."

"We are." She shivered and took a drink. "He gives me the creeps."

"There is something about him."

"Did you know that that Chicken Adobo you're eating is actually from the Philippines?" Elmer asked.

Derrick sat there for a moment. "Well, they are islands in the Pacific I guess." He took a bite. He swallowed then glanced over at Mr. Mayeda. "Good eats."

Mr. Mayeda nodded then looked away.

"Is that your brother and his wife over by the waterfall?" Derrick asked as he leaned toward Haruku.

She looked in that direction. "Yes. It is."

She leaned a little closer as everyone else talked about the fantastic food. "Do you see that older man three tables on our left?"

Derrick casually scanned the room in that direction. "The big man with the not quite as big woman next to him?"

"That is my Uncle Marcus. My father's brother."

"Really. Pele has never mentioned him."

"I'm sure she hasn't. He is like the black sheep of the family. My father and his brother haven't spoken in years."

Derrick glanced over at her.

"Even worse than me."

"Believe me Haruku. You are no black sheep." Derrick shot another glance over at them. "Is that woman his wife?"

"Kathleen. Kathleen Scarpelli. She's lost a lot of weight."

Derrick looked over at her. A Scarpelli? "Really." No, he thought. It's a long way from New Jersey.

"Oh my yes," Haruku said. "I'd guess she's lost maybe twenty or thirty pounds."

"So why would he be here?"

"He must be here because of our resorts. Well, his split of the resorts," she whispered.

"His resorts?"

"Uncle Marcus and my father had a bit of a falling out years ago. I was only a little girl back then, so I don't know why. But they split up the family businesses. He got some, and my father got some."

"Why isn't your father here?"

"Tomas is the official head now."

"And you and your sister?"

She laughed. "Neither one of us are the corporate type. We just get paid our share as family members. Tomas does the real work."

"And he's OK with that arrangement?"

"He gets a bigger share."

Derrick reached for his glass of wine and took a sip. Eito and his brother Marcus had a falling out years ago. Split up the family businesses. Marcus is married to a Scarpelli. This Mayeda guy... His coplyness was tingling in overdrive.

Paul leaned back in his chair and glanced down the empty hall. He turned back to Quon. "On the business side, I've got some contracts lined up for you. You've got your portfolio of patents."

"I do some web marketing and get some sales that way."

"Think bigger Quon."

"It feels strange."

"You are about to dive into the real world of business. We need to put a face on your company." Paul waved around the room. "People want to do business with a company they feel comfortable with. One that they have confidence in."

"Image as well as substance?"

Paul reached out and slammed his hand on the table. A cloud of dust flew up. "Exactly!"

"I also have legal counsel," Quon said.

Paul nodded. "A lawyer is a good step. But now it's time to start getting a few employees."

Quon grinned. "And a cleaning crew?"

"Be good too. But we... You... Need more than that."

Quon nodded. "This is moving faster than I anticipated."

Paul leaned forward. "You need people to do things. The things that support what you come up with in that brilliant head of yours. And you need people to make sure that those people do their jobs. Take on the daily routine of running a business."

"How do I do that?"

"What you need is an office manager. And this HR manager I have coming in."

"But how do I know who to hire?" Quon sat back in his chair. "I will need people I can trust."

Paul chuckled. "You are also going to need people with the right levels of security clearance for some of the work you will be doing here."

"Like this command center?"

"Like that." Paul sat back. "But also your intellectual capital. Your labs and manufacturing. Corporate espionage is big. And you will become a target. It's not a matter of if. But when."

Quon stared across the table at him. "And how do I do all this?"

Paul grinned. "I'll help you with all that. Trust me."

Pele continued to scan the room as they sat there having their dinner. People were talking around her, but she was lost in her own world scanning the room. Occasionally she would reach up and adjust her glasses.

Kengi leaned over. "Maybe you should wear them more often so that you get used to them?"

"Maybe."

She watched the people two tables over. Her Uncle Marcus was sitting there along with his wife, Kathleen. They hadn't spoken in fifteen years. Maybe more. She reached for her tea as she wondered who made up the guest list for this event. She took a sip then turned to Kengi. "Are you enjoying the party?"

"Yes." He looked down at his plate. "This food is quite good."

Paul stepped out into the corridor as Quon talked to Phil in the command center. He selected a number and pressed call. Paul looked around the center. It was coming along nicely. Another week and they would be up and running.

Paul turned away from the doorway. "Sir. I'm sorry to disturb you. I thought you would like to know we are moving on to the next phase." Paul turned slightly to look back at Quon. He was in an animated discussion with Phil. They looked happy and excited. Paul turned away again. "Yes sir. We are on schedule."

Chapter 26

As coffee and dessert were served, Senator Aneko marched back up to the podium. He adjusted the microphone. "I hope you are all enjoying this fantastic banquet tonight. And the company of new friends at your tables." He smiled graciously as he surveyed the room. "As we finish up this part of our evening together, our hosts at the hotel are preparing the ballroom for dancing and other rooms for more intimate discussions and networking. It is my sincerest hope that from tonight we come away with new contacts and new ideas to help us carry this beautiful... Our beautiful and majestic state, forward into the 21st century and beyond."

"Ever the consummate politician," Derrick said to Haruku as the room burst out in applause.

Senator Aneko grinned and waved for a moment at the podium while photographers captured his moment for posterity. The morning news and instant tweets probably didn't hurt either.

A few minutes later, the majority of the crowd had spilled out of the banquet room and into the corridor and adjacent rooms. Derrick glanced over at the lobby. It seemed like no one was making an exit yet. There was still fun to be had, exotic food and drink to savor. And contacts to be made.

"How is this command center going to connect to the rest of the world?" Quon asked. "Are we running cables from a nearby substation?"

Phil pointed up. "One of the cooling towers up on the roof of the main building is only half a unit. The other half is a satellite station so we can uplink and downlink to a satellite in orbit."

"Geosynchronous?"

"Yes."

"What happens if there is a satellite shut down to say, a CME?"

"A sun storm?" Paul laughed as he walked up behind them. "That's what I like about you Quon. Always one step ahead."

"So what happens?"

"We will be running a set of cables through the network of cables to a substation south of this facility."

"And the termination point?"

"I'm still negotiating that."

Derrick and Haruku strolled into the ballroom where people were standing around talking or dancing.

He turned to her. "May I have this dance?"

She gazed up at him with a sparkle in her dark eyes and moist lips. "Yes, you may."

He led the way out onto the dance floor. He slid his hand around her slender waist as she slid hers up along his back and down along his arms. Their hands touched and their fingers intertwined. "Is this what paradise feels like?"

"I hope so." She laid her head on his chest as they floated with the music.

Several dozen other couples in various degrees of closeness also enjoyed the music and the fragrances of fresh flowers that filled the ballroom.

After a fast dance, the band played another slow, close number. Haruku turned Derrick to their left. "Do you see that man standing by the punch table talking to the bartender? He's in the dark blue polo shirt and black slacks?"

"The longish gray hair, dark eyebrows."

"Stocky build."

"Who is he?"

Haruku rested her head on his chest as they danced. "That is Tony Malini. One of the three families as we call them."

"The three families? Who calls them that?"

"You haven't run across the Malini's yet?"

"Should I have?"

She shrugged slightly. "I guess they haven't been linked to any killings lately."

He pulled his head back and stared down at her.

She smiled up at him then placed her head back on his chest. "Back in the early 1900s three friends got together."

"To do what exactly?"

"Oh, let's just say make a better life for themselves. Fight the powers that had taken over the islands."

"Uh huh."

"So, there was Geno Malini, Gengi Kobayashi." She glanced up at him and grinned. "My grandfather."

"And family number three?"

"Peter, Pete, Murdoch."

"Not…"

"He was your bosses' grandfather."

"Really."

"And he was a former Chief of Police in Honolulu as well."

"So what did these *friends* do to make a better life for themselves?"

"Generally make life more difficult for others. Nothing illegal at first. Depending on your point of view. Organizing labor," she thought for a moment. "More like controlling it I guess. Then branching out into other things. More or less legal."

"And the Malinis are still active? In more or less illegal activities?"

"They and the branch of my family under Marcus. The Murdochs went straight. As far as I know." She looked up at him. "At least that's the history. I don't know what any of them are really up to these days."

"And Eito and you all?"

"Legal as far as I know."

The music stopped. Derrick took a half step back from Haruku, but they still had their arms around each other. "Your family seems nice."

"I'll take that as a compliment." She scanned around the room. "I can't help but wonder, who drew up the guest list for this party?"

Derrick looked around. "Me too. Now that you've filled me in on some of the local color."

The bandleader stepped up to the microphone. "We're just going to take a ten-minute break, and then we will be right back." He leaned over and turned on some canned music. From their latest CD no doubt.

They both saw Mr. Mayeda watching them as they left the dance floor. "What was really going on in there between you and Mr. Mayeda?" She asked.

Derrick slipped his arm around her as they walked over to a table with two large bowls of fruit juice. "Nothing gets past you does it?"

"I am an artist. I notice things."

"Right." He took a deep breath. "I don't know. There is just something about him."

"Your coply instinct?"

"Yeah."

She wrapped her arm through his as they waited in line. "Well darling, then you should be in overdrive tonight."

"I need to be going now," Quon said as he and Phil joined Paul at the doorway to the command center.

"When will you be finished with your exams?" Phil asked.

"With any luck, I will be done with everything in the next week or so."

"I am sure Fei is looking forward to that time as much as you are," Paul said.

Phil winked at him. "Maybe more."

"I will try to stop by as soon as I can," Quon said.

"You know where to find us," Paul said.

"Hi there."

Derrick and Haruku turned as they stepped off the dance floor.

"Tomas," Haruku said as her brother and his wife Mary joined them.

"You two look cozy tonight," Mary said as she gave them a quick once over.

Derrick held out his hands and shrugged. "Haruku's doing."

Mary nodded. "No doubt."

"So Tomas," Derrick began. "Are you one of these new century movers and shakers?"

He reached up and scratched his head as he looked around. "Someone seems to think so."

Mary put her arm around Tomas. "Don't be so modest dear. You work hard to bring in tourists and take care of the people that work for you." She looked at Haruku. "And your family."

Derrick reached out and gave Tomas a pat on the back. "It's good to see all your hard work hasn't gone unnoticed."

"Someone must have noticed you too," Tomas said.

"And the captain. And your other sister."

"Pele is here too?" Tomas asked.

"Along with a couple of my Interpol friends that were still here on vacation."

"That is interesting," Tomas said.

"That's what I thought. But hey, can't turn down a free party like this now can I?"

"Well enjoy it," Tomas said. He turned to his wife. "Shall we?"

She took his hand as he led her out onto the dance floor.

Derrick turned to Haruku. "Would you do me the honor of another dance?"

She slid up close to him. "I would love to."

Haruku looked up into Derrick's eyes as they held each other and danced. "Thank you for asking me here tonight."

He felt a quiet calmness as he gazed down into her dark eyes. He could feel the warmth of her breath as they drew closer. "Thank you for coming."

"I can't remember when I have enjoyed an evening so much." She laid her head on his chest as they swayed to the slow music. Her soft hair brushed against his face. He could smell the light, gentle fragrance of her perfume.

"Me either," he whispered. For a few moments, the world around them disappeared.

All too soon it seemed, the music stopped. A young man in white slacks and a bright yellow Hawaiian print shirt stepped up to them. "Mr. Dreadlow?"

"Yes," Derrick replied.

"There is someone who would like to speak to you." The young man turned to Haruku. "This won't take long ma'am."

Derrick glanced over at her and shrugged.

Haruku nodded. "Why don't I go get us some drinks?"

"OK. Fruit juice. Not spiked. I'll be back as soon as I can."

Bink and Mildred walked up behind Haruku as the young man escorted Derrick out of the room. "You know Haruku," Bink began, "The last time someone escorted Derrick out of the room we didn't see him for the rest of the night."

"Oh come now Bink," his wife chided. "Don't frighten the poor girl. Go get us some drinks while we wait."

The young man opened the door to a room on the second-floor and motioned for Derrick to step inside. He looked around as the young man left and closed the door. The room looked like one of the hotel offices. It was nicely furnished. Elegant but not opulent. Light woods and cloth chairs in a light sea blue. Perhaps it was the office of the secretary of the head manager.

"We shouldn't keep our guest waiting."

Senator Aneko nodded as the person turned in the swivel chair to gaze out the window. "We will talk again later Senator."

"Yes, Chief." Senator Aneko turned and went out the door.

Derrick turned as the door to an adjacent room opened. Senator Aneko stepped through and closed the door. "I am sorry to keep you waiting, Mr. Dreadlow."

"Just got here. Nice party. Thanks for inviting us."

"I am pleased you are enjoying it. I hope you are getting to meet a lot of people."

"I am." They each took a couple of steps and met in the middle of the room. "So. What can I do for you, Senator?"

"Your vote in the fall would be helpful." He grinned as he extended his hand.

Derrick reached out and shook it. "Could be. You make a compelling commercial."

"You've seen some of them?"

"When I'm in the gym working out."

"I hope you know that there is actual substance behind what I say."

"Let's hope."

"I will make this brief Lieutenant." He motioned to the couch by the wall.

Derrick sat down after the Senator. "Nice crowd. Did everyone show up that you invited?"

"Yes. Thank you." Aneko sat back. "I am glad you and your associates could make it as well."

Derrick smiled. "I'm not sure why we were invited. It's not like we are movers and shakers here in the islands. But thanks just the same."

There was a twinkle in the Senator's eye as he smiled. "Perhaps not movers and shakers. But you are the stabilizers."

Derrick sat there silently as he stared into the senator's eyes for any other hint of true purpose.

"I have great plans for this state."

"So I've noticed."

"It is a beautiful state. It has a promising future."

Derrick nodded. "Yes. I saw the brochures and the posters downstairs."

"As such, where things are happening, there is money to be made."

Derrick nodded again.

"And where there is money to be made… there are opportunities for some unsavory elements to try and get a piece of the action shall we say. Attempts made to carve up paradise."

"And that's where the… stabilizers come in?"

"The islands have a history of being carved up by someone for personal gain."

"The pineapple plantations?" Derrick asked. "And other early settlers?"

121

Senator Aneko sat back and nodded. "Whalers, missionaries."

"A lot of change happened back then too. Lots of opportunities."

Aneko laughed. "Have you heard the saying about the missionaries after they arrived?"

"No. Can't say that I have."

"It was said that they came to the islands to do good." He stared at Derrick unblinkingly. "And that they did good... for themselves."

"That says it all I guess."

"Indeed. The people of the islands were decimated."

"So I've heard."

"I do not want history to repeat itself."

"There aren't many real full Hawaiians left."

"True enough. But there are others that have been here for generations now. I don't want them to share in that fate."

Derrick stared back. Both still unblinking. "You and your family being among them."

Aneko snorted and blinked. "Yes. My family and I being among them. But so are a million other people. And... now you."

"I love paradise as much as the rest of you."

Aneko sprung up from the couch and walked over to the window. He gazed down on the gardens below. "You came here from an island Dreadlow."

Derrick sat back. "I'd hardly compare Manhattan with Hawaii."

Aneko turned to him. "But you have the island spirit."

"It's the sea air, the blue sky. The surf."

"The islands have a long and proud history. And some sad parts. Parts that I don't want to see repeated."

"Then you have my vote, Senator."

Aneko looked at an old photo on the wall of men standing on the beach a long time ago. It was a time before tall buildings. A time before hotels. "Long ago the islands were divided among the warring chiefs and kings of the different islands."

"Paradise seems to have come in second place."

"Not again. Not on my watch." Senator Aneko came back and sat on the couch again. "Big players are already on the islands. And more arrive every month."

Derrick stared into Aneko's eyes. "So is this a party? Or a sizing of the competition?"

Aneko sat there calmly. He nodded toward Derrick with that politician's twinkle in his eye. "It is also a show of force Lieutenant. To let them know that I know. And to let them know that I am watching."

"And by that, you mean that we are watching."

"I knew it was a good idea to invite you."

Derrick sat there thinking as he drew in a long breath. "Manhattan went through the same growing pains. I guess it's human nature."

"Everyplace worth living in does." Senator Aneko stretched his arm out across the top of the couch. "I'd like to stay one step ahead of human nature."

"You and me both."

"Yes, Lieutenant. I invited you and your associates here tonight to meet some of the players in our future. I want you to get to know them."

"Especially the unsavory ones?"

"They also get to know you."

"You're playing us off against each other?"

"I'm seeking balance." The Senator stood up.

Sensing the meeting was about to end, Derrick followed. "And for you Senator?"

He smiled. "All I'm asking of you is to uphold the laws of our state Lieutenant. Nothing more. Nothing less." He extended his hand. "I honestly believe that ultimately, we are on the same side."

Derrick reached out and shook it. "Serve and protect sir." He took a step back. "Within the law."

Senator Aneko nodded. "Then we understand each other." He stepped over to the door and reached for the knob. "Enjoy the party Lieutenant Dreadlow."

"Good luck in the election Senator Aneko."

Derrick stepped into the hallway. Aneko closed the door. He wondered how many other little chats would be going on throughout the course of the evening. And with whom? He took the stairs down to the first floor.

"What is it?" Pele asked as she and Kengi were dancing. "Your mind seems to be a million miles away." She pushed away a little as she looked up at him. "Did I say or do something to upset you?"

The music ended. "There is something I have to tell you Pele. It can't wait any longer."

"Miss me?" Derrick asked as he stepped up behind Haruku talking to Bink and Mildred.

Haruku turned to Bink. "See? He didn't vanish for the night." She slipped her arm through his.

"Must be the company," Bink said.

"So what was that about?" Haruku asked. "Or is it a secret."

Derrick shrugged as he admired her. "Just a little meet and greet."

"What is going on over there?" Mildred said nodding toward the doorway. Several other people watched as well.

They all turned. Pele slapped Kengi then stormed out of the room.

"That can't be good," Derrick said as they all stared toward the doorway.

Kengi ran out after her. "Pele…"

"What do you suppose that was all about?" Bink asked.

Derrick turned to Haruku. "Do you think maybe you should…"

"Oh no."

Mildred was shaking her head. "You don't want to go there, Derrick."

Pele's Uncle Marcus slipped off to the side and pulled his cell phone out of his pocket. "Are you still following her?" He glanced around the room. "Well go and try to pick up her trail again. She's leaving the hotel." He hung up.

Quon was sitting on the couch in Fei's living room. Fei refreshed their cups of tea.

"This sounds like a good thing Quon. These people seem to know what they're doing."

"I suppose." He reached for his cup. "I guess I never gave much thought to all the details involved with actually setting up a real company."

"It is a good thing that you and Paul met then. He sounds like he knows just what he is doing. And you have Todd and a lawyer. You are becoming a regular Fortune 500 CEO."

Quon took a sip. "Fortune 5000 maybe."

"So what is the next step?"

"I have a meeting on Tuesday with some HR, Human Resources person that is coming to Honolulu. Then we get an office manager. A security company. A cleaning and maintenance crew."

"It sounds like Paul has thought of everything."

"And I have to set up a meeting with Paul, Todd, and my lawyer."

Fei leaned over and kissed him on the cheek. "My boyfriend. The big executive."

He reached over and slipped his arm around her. "My girlfriend. The great doctor."

She nestled up against him. "We are on top of the world."

Kengi searched the hotel lobby and the various rooms where people had gathered. Pele was nowhere to be found. He jumped into the nearest cab, and they raced out of the parking lot. He kept trying to dial her phone as they weaved in and out of traffic.

When he got to her condo, he raced to the elevator. A few minutes of no answer at her door and he was down in the parking garage. Her RAV was gone. "Damn!" He slammed his hand up against the concrete pillar. "Where are you Pele?"

Haruku slipped her arms around Derrick as they stood in the kitchen. "Thank you for tonight Derrick. I enjoyed it very much."

He put his arms around her and pulled her in closer. "So did I."

She closed her eyes as she pushed up on her toes. He leaned in.

"Can I have a drink of water Uncle Derrick?"

Haruku and Derrick took a step back from each other. "Becky." Derrick stammered.

"I thought you were…" Haruku began.

Ahulani stepped out into the kitchen. "They wanted to be here and awake when you got home." She reached out for Becky and took her hand. "Come on dear. I'll get you a drink from the other room."

Becky turned back to them. "Are you going to tuck me in Uncle Derrick?"

Derrick sighed. "We'll be right there Becky."

Kengi drove out to the beach where she first took him to teach him how to surf. They never got into the water. He got back into his car and sat there. Staring out at the white crests of the waves as they rolled up onto the beach.

Crack! Crack! Crack! The sounds of semi-automatic weapons fire filled the empty range. It was still dark out. The headlights from her RAV barely made it to the other end of the range. Not that it mattered.

She ejected the clip and slipped in another one. A few dozen spent casings lay strewn about her feet. She made her stance. Raised her pistol. Flexed her shoulders and cocker her head. She emptied the clip in seconds.

Chapter 27

Derrick opened his eyes. "Ohhh," he groaned as he woke up on the couch. He sat up and raised his arms and tilted his head from side to side to get the kinks out. Opening and closing his eyes, he stood up and stretched, then proceeded out to the kitchen to start a pot of coffee.

Haruku opened her eyes. She lay there for a moment with a content look on her face. She turned in her bed and reached out. She felt around the other half of the empty bed. The blanket and the sheet on the other side were undisturbed. "Oh," she sighed as she pulled the sheet up close to her chin and closed her eyes again.

Pele opened her eyes. "Ohhh hell." The sun was streaming in. She sat up in the front seat of her RAV. She looked over at the passenger seat. Her pistol was laying there. Six boxes of shells were strewn across the seat and the floor. She reached over and picked them up. She shook them. They were all empty.

Rubbing her head, she noticed her smartphone sticking out from under the seat. She bent over and pulled it out. "Damn!" She slammed her fist into the steering wheel. The horn blasted. "Son-of-a-bitch!" She scanned the area. She was still on the shooting range. She was alone.

Pele took a deep breath. "Ohhh crap!" There was a bullet hole right through the center of her phone.

After a quick swim, workout, and shower, Derrick was sitting at the kitchen table with his coffee and his laptop. No one else was up yet, so he was getting in a little work. He was looking at the DMV records for Hawaii and Texas again. "No license, no registration." He knew there was nothing there, but he checked again anyway. Maybe he missed something before. A typo or something.

He opened a window and checked his email. There was a message from Xin. He reached for his coffee and sat back. "No record of a current license for Jack Crawford in Hawaii or Texas. Or in any other state either. And nothing for Dawn Miller either." He took a drink while he sat there thinking for a moment. He leaned forward again. "OK Jack, Where are you? Where is your girlfriend?" He stood up and paced around the table. He glanced down at the laptop. "And where is your BMW?" He sat back down.

"Do you always talk to yourself in the morning Derrick?"

He looked up. Haruku walked over to the counter toward the coffee pot. Her white nightshirt clung to her body as she moved.

"I just wish I'd talk back with the right answers."

She reached out and ran her hand across his shoulders as she passed. "I never drank this much coffee in the morning before." She laughed. "I never used to get up this early before. Well... not recently anyway."

"It's decaf. I never used to drink that before."

She poured herself a cup. She stared across the top of her cup as she blew on it. "Maybe we are good for each other?"

He smiled as he took a sip. "I enjoyed last night."

She stepped up to him as he sat there and rubbed her long soft leg against his arm. "So did I."

He sat there without moving.

"Good morning Uncle Derrick," Kattie said as she walked in and pulled out a chair.

"What are we going to do today?" Becky asked as she joined them.

"Good morning everyone." Ahulani walked out into the kitchen. "Did you all get a good night's sleep?"

Derrick sat back. "Tell you what. I'll make breakfast while you girls all get ready. Then we'll take a drive all around the island. You haven't seen it all yet." Derrick turned to Ahulani as she got a glass of water to take a pill. "Would you care to join us?"

"No thank you, Derrick. I should be getting on home. Your friends wore me out yesterday."

"We can have a picnic along the way," Kattie said.

"Or stop someplace for lunch," Derrick said.

"Yippee." Becky jumped off her chair.

"But first we have to stop by the airport," Derrick said. "Bink and his wife are going home this morning."

"We have to give him his brownies," Becky said.

"Brownies?"

"We made some for him yesterday," Kattie said.

"And we have some mango tea for him," Haruku added.

Derrick stood up. "Then you'd all better get moving, so we don't miss him."

The girls all left the room to get ready. Derrick picked up his cell and scrolled down his list. He dialed a number.

"Morning Soto. I hope I didn't wake you."

"No. I always get up early on Sunday morning. We try to have a quiet breakfast out on the lanai once a week. You know. Enjoy the islands."

"I need a favor from you."

"Personal or business?"

Derrick hesitated. "I think it will be business. So if you are busy assign it to someone else."

"What is it?"

"I need you, or someone, to watch an address. Have them call me when they are in place." Derrick closed his laptop and got up to make breakfast.

Kengi stood in line for his flight.

"This is the final boarding call for Flight 1703 to Tokyo, Japan," called out the disembodied voice of the airport intercom system.

He pulled out his boarding pass as he approached the attendant by the on-ramp.

"You have reached the phone mail for Detective Kobayashi. Please leave a message..."

He hung up and slipped his phone back into his pocket as the attendant checked his boarding pass. "Have a nice flight."

Kengi walked down the ramp and onto the plane.

Pele was standing between the two children in the hospital as their father sat on the side of his daughter's bed.

"They are improving very fast," The nurse said as she removed the IV stands from the room.

Pele looked down at them. "I guess that means you will be going home soon."

"Good," the boy said. "I don't like it in here. I want to be back in my own room."

"Can either of you tell me anything about what happened the day of the accident? Anything at all?"

"We were playing a game down in the front of the boat," the little girl said.

Her brother looked over at her then back up at Pele. "It was the master stateroom in the bow."

Pele nodded. "Did you see anything, hear anything? Anything at all?"

"Mommy was in the kitchen making lunch," the girl began. "Mr. Kagawa was up in the top driving the boat."

The boy looked up at Pele. "Mom was in the galley. She told us lunch would be ready soon Then there was a big explosion. The boat rocked. Then it tilted to one side and water came pouring in. We tried to get out but she was scared, and it was too strong." He turned to his dad. "It all happened so fast."

"It's OK," Mr. Walters said. "The main thing is that you are safe now."

"Do you know why you went out sailing that weekend? Were you going any place in particular?" Pele asked.

"Mr. Kagawa liked to go out for the day or weekend. Most of the time we'd just sail around the island," the boy said.

"So you did that a lot?"

"Almost every weekend," the boy replied.

"What about during the week?"

He shrugged. "We never went out during the week. Only on weekends."

"And not every weekend," the girl added. "Maybe once or twice a month."

"And how did Mr. Kagawa seem on this trip. Was he happy? Sad?"

The children glanced at each other.

"Worried," the boy said.

"Scared," the girls said. "He was very quiet this time."

"How was he normally when you went out?"

"He'd let me steer the boat," the boy said.

"This time he made us stay below and play games," the girl added.

"There he is!" Becky shouted as she pointed to Bink and Mildred.

"They wanted to give you this care package for your trip home," Derrick said. "Don't worry. No liquids or gels in it."

"We made brownies for you Bink," Becky said.

"And boxes of mango tea," Kattie added.

"It was so nice meeting you both," Haruku said as they all hugged.

Mildred knelt down by the girls. "Someday you'll have to get your uncle to bring you to London to visit us." She glanced up at Haruku. "All of you."

Becky turned to Derrick. "Can we Uncle Derrick?"

"That will probably be up to your mother." Derrick's cell went off. "Excuse me a second." He stepped away as they all talked while the security line inched forward.

"What's up Soto?"

"I've got Pope out there."

"Thanks."

"Just what is he looking for?"

"A 2007, silver BMW convertible. If he sees it, follow it and see where it goes. And call me."

"Is this another part of the car case?"

"No. Another case. Thanks, Soto. I've got to go." Derrick hung up.

Pele walked into the Ala Mona mall and up to one of the smartphone stalls.

"Can I interest you in a new phone today?" the young woman asked.

Pele looked around at the selection. "Yes. I was thinking about getting a new one."

Derrick pulled up to a small convenience store only a few miles east of Diamond Head. Haruku took the girls inside to use the restroom. He stepped out and dialed a number on his phone.

"Dr. Crawford."

"Hi, Melissa. How are you?"

"Derrick. I, I'm OK. How are you?"

"I'm good."

"Are the girls still with you?"

"Yes. We're out exploring the island."

"Did you take them deep sea fishing?"

"No. I don't think their mother was too keen on that idea."

"I wish I had the time to meet them. But I've been so busy. You know how it is."

"Yes. I understand completely." He watched the cars go past the store. "I was wondering if you could do me a favor."

"Sure. What?"

"I need a place to store my trailer with the motorcycle. I thought maybe you had some room in that big garage you've got."

"I thought you had a big garage?"

Derrick laughed. "Three. But I am working on a friend's truck and need the space. I don't want to leave it outside. It would only be a couple of days while we swap out the engine…"

"I don't know. It's kind of messy out there."

"I'm a guy. We're used to that."

"I suppose so. Just give me time to straighten out a few things. I'll call you when I've made some space."

"Thanks, Melissa. I really appreciate it."

As beautiful as the drive around paradise was, by the time they got to Hau'ula, Kattie and Becky were restless.

Haruku turned to the girls. "Now stop slapping each other girls."

Derrick pulled his cell out of his pocket. "Settle down there girls. Dreadlow here."

"Lieutenant Derrick Dreadlow?"

"Yes. Who is this?"

"Detective Taylor. Hollywood Division. I got a call that you were checking into a Dawn Miller."

"Yeah." Derrick glanced back up into the rearview mirror.

"Can't we get out and go swimming somewhere?" Becky said as she pouted in her seat.

"I worked that case about four years ago."

"Did you find her?" Derrick asked as he slowed around a bend in the road.

"No. The case went cold. Have you found her?"

"No. I'm working another case here in Hawaii. A man that disappeared about four years ago. Dawn's name came up."

"So how can I be of help Lieutenant?"

"Anything you can tell me about her? Friends? Family? Where she worked?"

Haruku glanced over at Derrick. He shrugged and continued driving.

"She worked at a coffee shop near the airport. Lived in Hollywood. Wanted to be an actress."

"Doesn't everyone," Derrick said. "You talk to her coworkers?"

"Yeah. Her boss had no idea where she went. Another waitress she worked with said she said something about paradise."

"Hawaii?" Derrick asked.

"Don't know. She said Dawn had all these big dreams. She thought it was just some new guy who promised he was going to take her away from the boredom of her life at the coffee shop."

"Maybe he did. Did she have any family?"

"Yeah. Hold on a sec..." Derrick slowed into another curve. The view of the water was breathtaking.

"When can we stop?" Becky asked.

"Got it. A sister. Sandy Miller."

"Got an address?"

"Yeah. Got a pencil handy?"

"No. Can you text it to me? Kind of got my hands full at the moment."

"Sure. She's in Kentucky. Or she was three years ago. She's the one who filed the missing person's report."

"Thanks."

"Let me know if you find anything Lieutenant. Maybe I can finally close up this case."

"I'll do that detective."

Quon was sitting in the university library working at his computer. He got up and walked over to the window. He pulled his cell out of his pocket and selected a number.

"Dr. Chen."

He turned and gazed out over the campus. "Hi, Fei. I miss you. How are you?"

"I miss you too. And I am tired after yesterday and last night."

"How did the surgery go?"

"It went better than expected. How are your exams coming?"

"Almost done. Would you like to have dinner tonight?"

"How about at my parent's restaurant? That way neither one of us has to think about cooking."

"Six?"

"I will see you then."

"I love you, Fei."

"I love you too Quon."

He slipped his phone into his pocket. It would be nice to spend more time with her he thought as he walked back over to his table. And how long had it been since he, Pele, and Derrick spent a Saturday morning in the park practicing their tai chi? He sat down and stared at his books and notes. Too long.

Derrick glanced up in the rearview mirror. "You go swimming every day."

"We like it," Kattie said.

Derrick glanced over at Haruku. She turned back to the girls. "How would you like to see some real Maori warriors and beautiful dancers. And men tossing sticks of fire?"

Becky turned to Kattie. They turned to Haruku. "That sounds like fun."

Derrick grinned. "The Polynesian Cultural Center?"

Haruku nodded. "It's just a few miles up the road. And we can have lunch while we're there too."

"Can we Uncle Derrick?" they yelled out together.

"The Polynesian Cultural Center it is."

Pele was sitting in her 328i as the sun set. She was restless, so she drove out and relieved Pope so he could go home to his wife. She hunkered down in her seat as a red pickup truck approached. It slowed down then turned onto the long dirt driveway. She sat up a little and reached for her camera. She pointed it toward the truck and zoomed in. The door opened, and Melissa got out and went into her house.

A few minutes later, she came out and walked over to the garage. She unlocked the door, flipped on a light, and stepped inside.

"I can't believe they are still going after an afternoon of this," Derrick said as they left the buffet at the Polynesian Center.

"They are on a sugar high after that ice cream and cake," Haruku said.

"Where are we going now?" Kattie asked.

"When do we get to see the men throwing fire at each other?" Becky asked.

"Soon," Derrick said.

Haruku knelt down in front of them and placed her hands on their shoulders. "When it gets dark there will be a big show. With stories, music, dancers…"

"And men throwing fire sticks?" Becky asked again.

"Yes," Derrick said. "And men throwing fire sticks."

"We should go now and get good seats," Haruku said.

Soon the girls were watching wide-eyed as the men with fire sticks twirled the flaming sticks into circles of fire in all directions at the base of a magnificent tropical cliff.

An hour or so later, Melissa opened the garage door and drove her car out. She closed the door and drove down the driveway.

Pele stayed back as she followed Melissa in a silver BMW east on the H-1. There were still a lot of cars on the road for a late Sunday evening. She reached up and adjusted her rearview mirror. "Brights asshole," she mumbled. The car went past her at over sixty-five. She wanted to flip on her lights and nail them, but she had something else to do. She took a deep breath to calm herself.

Derrick took the off-ramp from the H-1 to Waikiki. "Looks like they are out cold," Derrick said as he glanced back at Kattie and Becky asleep in their car seats.

"They had a long day," Haruku said as she turned and adjusted Becky's seat while she slept. "But I think they had fun."

"Something different to tell their friends when they get back to school."

Haruku sat there quietly and stared out the window.

"What is it?"

She turned to him. "What do you mean?"

"That quiet look."

She put her hands together on her lap. "Do we know each other that well already that we can read each other's moods?"

"You're an artist. I'm a cop. We're faster than most couples."

She stared straight ahead. "Couples?"

"You know." He cleared his throat. "What's on your mind?"

"Will you… I was just… I was just wondering if you might need help, or like the company when you take the girls back to New York."

He drummed his thumbs on the steering wheel for a moment. "Huh. That would have been a good idea. A great idea even."

"I shouldn't have brought it up. I'm sorry."

"No. It's just that Pele is going back with me."

She turned to him. "Pele?"

"Yeah. A couple of cases we are working on have ties back to New York. We thought we could take care of them at the same time."

She turned to face the side window. "It's OK," she said softly. "That makes sense."

Derrick's cell went off as he pulled into the condo parking lot. Haruku looked over at him. "Do they ever let you sleep?"

He shook his head as he pulled into the space and answered his phone.

"Hi, Derrick. It's me."

He glanced over at Haruku. "Pele?"

"Is she OK?" Haruku asked softly.

"I think you need to come up here?"

"Up where? What's going on? Are you all right?"

"Are we home?" Kattie asked as she woke up.

"Yes sweetheart," Haruku replied as she watched Derrick.

"I'm up off the Pali Highway."

"What are you doing up on the Pali Highway?" He glanced over at Haruku as he turned off the engine.

"Your girlfriend has just dumped her car over the side of a cliff and hitched a ride back to the city."

"Damn." Derrick pounded the top of the steering wheel. "Did she see you?"

"No. I don't think so. I wasn't expecting that. What's going on?" Pele asked.

"What is going on?" Haruku asked.

"I'm thirsty," Becky said.

Derrick turned to the girls. "OK, Pele. Call Quon. Or Xin, Joyce. Somebody, and get them up there to go over the car with a fine-tooth comb."

"What are they looking for?" Pele asked.

"Let's just see what they find. I'll be up there as soon as I can."

"What about Melissa?"

Derrick sat there for a moment. "She's probably on her way back home. Call Soto and have a twenty-four-hour tail put on her. Just in case."

"You want me to call Soto now?"

"I interrupted his Sunday breakfast this morning. It's your turn." Derrick hung up.

"What happened Derrick?" Haruku asked.

Derrick opened the door and helped Haruku get the girls out of the jeep. "Another case I'm working. I'll help you get the girls to bed then I've got to…"

"How many cases are you working while you're on vacation?"

He picked up the girls as she got out the key. "Too many. Next time I take a vacation, remind me to go someplace else."

"OK." Haruku closed the doors. "I'll take you someplace quiet."

"You're on."

"Should I make some coffee for you and Pele? Regular?"

Twenty minutes later, the girls were in bed, and Haruku handed him a thermos and two cups. He grabbed his keys and headed for the door.

"I'm really sorry Haruku. I just keep dumping my responsibilities on your lap. I guess now I know that I'd never make a very good father."

She smiled as she reached out and put her hand on his arm and rubbed it. Her touch was soft and reassuring. "It's a hard job to have to do alone."

He reached for the doorknob. "Damned near impossible I'd say."

Chapter 28

Derrick's mind raced faster than the speed limit along the Pali Highway. He took a deep breath and sat back. He didn't want to use his siren and lights on this trip. There was no body at the site. Well, not at this site. "Hmmm. Na," he said aloud. "She wouldn't have kept them in the trunk. Not all this time."

He shook his head as he stared out onto the almost empty highway in front of him. "But then what would she have done with them? Assuming she did anything. He could be wrong. Maybe."

"You tell him he owes me."

"Who was that dear?" Kali asked as she turned on the light.

Soto got up out of bed. "Kobayashi."

"What happened?"

"Dreadlow."

"You shouldn't have borrowed one of his cars."

Soto grinned as he reached for the light. "Next time I'm going for the Studebaker."

"Studebaker?"

"He's got a '56 Golden Hawk."

"Isn't that what your father gave you?"

"Before it got creamed by that cement truck."

"You're just lucky no one was in it at the time."

He turned the light off. "Go back to sleep, my love. I'll see you at breakfast."

"Looks steep down there," Derrick said as he stepped up to Pele and peered over the edge.

"We may have never found it if I hadn't watched her drive it over the edge."

"It's a long way down."

"In a couple of days, this will all be overgrown again."

"Keeps the island looking pristine."

"And hides the trash."

Derrick peered over the edge again. "Let's hope there isn't much of that going on."

"So what is this about?" Pele asked as they stood at the edge of the road watching the techs and tow crew work below. "Why would she drive her car off a cliff?"

"It's Jack's car." Derrick poured another cup of tea from the thermos Haruku made for them. "She lied," Derrick said as he took another sip.

"Melissa?"

"No. Your sister, She said she was going to make us coffee."

"She gave you two cups and one thermos. What did you think would be in it?" She shook her head as they drank their tea. "If that's his car? Where is he?"

"Good question." He took a sip.

"I stopped by the hospital to talk to the children."

"How are they doing?"

"They should be getting out of the hospital soon."

"I'm sure their father will be happy about that. Did they have anything to say?"

"Not much about the explosion. But they did say that Mr. Kagawa was behaving like he was nervous and scared." She took another sip. "Maybe he knew his wife or brother were on to him and his liaisons with Mr. Walters's wife?"

"Perhaps." Derrick took another sip.

There was some chatter on the radio of an officer standing nearby. He stepped over to them. "Lieutenant."

"Yeah."

"They found another car down there."

Derrick and Pele turned to him. "Another car?" Derrick asked.

"About twenty-five feet further down. They said it looks like it's been down there for quite a while."

Derrick took another sip. "Have them try to get the make, model, year, and VIN if they can. Let's see who dumped that one and when. Oh… and one more thing Officer."

"What's that Lieutenant?"

"Check it for bodies. The driver, passenger… trunk…"

"Yes, sir." The officer turned and walked back to his position as he sent the request by radio to the people below.

"So when are you going to tell me what is going on here?" Pele asked as she took a sip.

Derrick looked at her. "What are you doing here? I thought Pope was on this?"

"I gave him the night off."

"Couldn't sleep?"

"Why would she drive his car off the cliff? Now?" They looked down at the car a hundred feet below them.

"I may have put a little pressure on her."

"And she panicked?"

"Could be."

"So where is Jack?" Pele asked.

Derrick took a deep breath. "I think I have an idea."

"That doesn't sound good."

"I could be wrong."

"You think so?"

He shook his head slowly.

"So you think Melissa murdered her husband?"

He scratched at his chin as the tow truck driver lowered a cable down to the car. Joyce and Xin were making their way back up. "And his mistress."

Pele looked down at the work going on below. "Damn. That sucks."

"Especially for them." Derrick reached out and helped Xin and Joyce up over the edge. "Got anything useful?"

"We have prints, hair samples, and fibers if that's what you mean," Joyce said.

"How soon do you need them?" Xin asked as they took their kits and evidence bags to his car.

"Four years ago would have been great."

They looked over at him. "We will get right on it," Joyce said.

The tow truck operators and other officers joined around Derrick.

"Do you want both cars taken to the station lab?" the officer asked.

Derrick nodded. "Yeah. Let's find out what we're dealing with here."

"Yes, sir."

"Oh. One more thing everyone." Derrick looked at the men and women out with him. "We need to keep this out of the press for now. Until we go over the evidence and get a warrant."

The group broke up and went about their business.

"A warrant for her arrest?" Pele asked.

"Yes. But first, let's get a warrant to search her property. In particular, under her garage." Derrick turned. "Xin. Do you or Quon have anything that can tell me if there are bodies under a slab of cement?"

"I believe so," Xin replied.

"And second?" Pele asked.

Derrick looked out at the flashing lights. "Let's see if she made any additions at the clinic in the last few years."

"Like in 2008?" Pele asked.

"Spring."

Chapter 29

Detective Patterson walked up to his desk at the station. He looked over at Pusch. "You get in touch with that Kobayashi yet?"

"No. Just left a couple of messages." Push sat back. "Turns out she's a cop. In Honolulu."

Patterson sat down. "Really? I wonder why she's trying to get in touch with Fukuhara?"

"Coincidence?"

Patterson sat back. "Don't leave her another message yet. Let's do a little digging on her first. Find out who she works with and reports to."

Derrick was still sitting at his desk at 6:00 in the morning. And still in his khaki slacks and red Hawaiian shirt from the day before.

"I'm sorry to disturb you, Sandy. I am Lieutenant Dreadlow with the Honolulu Police Department. I got your name and number from Detective Taylor in Los Angeles."

"Have you found her? Have you found my sister?"

"No. Not yet."

"Do you know where she is?"

"I'm working another case here in Hawaii. And your sister's name has come up. I'd like to ask you a few questions. If you don't mind."

"I told the other detective everything I know. Which wasn't much."

"Did she ever talk about a man?"

"All the time. There were too many to keep track of."

"How about a man named Jack. Jack Crawford?"

"Not that I remember. No."

"Did she ever say anything about coming to Hawaii? Moving? A vacation?"

"No. I would have remembered that."

"When was the last time you talked to her?"

"Just after New Years. I called her to wish her a good year."

"So early January of 2008?"

"Yes. January 3rd. That was the last time we ever spoke." She paused. "But now that I think of it, she did leave me a message."

"What was that?"

"The usual. That she met the man of her dreams. That she was madly in love. Again."

"When was that?"

"I think in February. Maybe early. I know it was before Valentine's Day."

"OK. Thank you. I am sorry to have disturbed you."

"You will call when you find her won't you?"

Derrick sat back. "Yes. I will." He hung up.

"You never went home?"

Derrick looked up. Pele was standing there in her usual black pantsuit and black running shoes with the purple stripe.

"Long night."

Captain Henderson walked up to their desks. He looked down at Derick. "I know you're on vacation but isn't this taking it a bit far?"

"We got called out last night," Pele said. "He's been here all night following up."

Captain Henderson shook his head. "Next time you go on vacation you might want to try Fiji."

"He knows the police there," Pele said with a grin.

"Yeah, well, the chief wants to see you upstairs."

"Just me?" Pele asked.

Captain Henderson looked over at Pele. "Both of you."

"Doesn't she know I'm on vacation either?"

"Are we in trouble again?" Pele asked.

Chief Murdoch looked up as Derrick and Pele knocked on the doorjamb. "Come in. And close the door behind you."

Pele glanced over at Derrick. He shrugged.

The chief looked up at him.

"I've been working a case all night."

"And he's on vacation," Pele added.

"What can we do for you this lovely morning Chief?" Derrick asked with a grin.

She picked up a newspaper on the side of her desk. She opened it up, turned it, and dropped it on the desk in front of them.

"Good party," Derrick said. "Did you enjoy it?"

"It looks like you did." She pointed to Derrick and Haruku in a tight embrace out on the dance floor gazing into each other's eyes.

"I've got to get a copy."

The chief turned to Pele. "And perhaps you can explain this photo, Ms. Kobayashi?" The chief pointed to a picture of a wide-eyed Pele striking Inspector Nakamura in what looked like a fit of rage.

"Oh shit."

Chief Murdoch sat back and stared up at her. "Oh, shit is the best you can do?"

"I… it was…"

"Are you still attending your anger management classes?"

Derrick glanced over at her.

Pele looked down at the paper. "Once a month."

Chief Murdoch sat back. "Maybe you need to go back to once a week for a while."

Pele looked up. "Oh. I'm fine. It was just… it was personal."

"On this job, we can't afford to have the lines blurred."

"They aren't Chief. I can assure you of that."

The chief sat there staring down at the photo. "And I can't have my people making public spectacles of themselves."

Pele looked down at her hands as she twisted them together. "I'm sorry. Chief."

"This was an event for working together in the spirit of cooperation. To build a pleasant future for the people of Hawaii. Not to assault an Inspector from another country, and possibly start an international incident. Fortunately, Inspector Kagawa said it was just a misunderstanding and is not pressing charges."

"Pressing charges? Why would he?"

Chief Murdoch sat back. "Are you going to fly off the handle again detective?"

Pele took a deep breath. "No. It won't happen again."

The chief opened up her drawer and pulled out another photo. "This was taken at 1 AM out on the shooting range." She handed Pele the photo. Derrick glanced over at it. Pele was standing there firing away on the range. "We recorded the sounds of over two hundred rounds being fired."

"I'll go back to sessions once a week."

"I've warned you before." The chief sat back. "It's that or your badge."

The elevator door closed. Derrick stared up at the red digital numbers. "Anything you'd like to talk about?"

The doors opened.

"No." Pele stepped off and walked over to her desk.

Derrick headed for the breakroom to get a cup of coffee. His cell rang on the way. "Dreadlow."

"Hi, Derrick. Are you coming home sometime today?"

"I'm sorry Haruku. This case is just… Look. I'll explain it all to you later."

"OK. We're going to have breakfast then I'm taking the girls to the beach. Call me when you can."

"Thank you Haruku. I don't know what I'd do without you."

"Well, this is interesting…"

Pele looked up from her computer. "What?"

"A United ticket for a Dawn Miller to Hawaii. February 12th. 2008. LA to Honolulu." Derrick looked up. "So we *can* place her here on the island."

"Did she leave?" Pele asked.

Derrick typed away at his computer again. "She had a return ticket to… Dallas. Four weeks later. But it wasn't used. And one for Jack Crawford. Same flight. Unused."

"That would explain why she isn't in any of our databases," Pele said. "She was just passing through."

"Yes." Derrick sat back.

"I guess now the question is… Where have they been hiding?"

Derrick peered across the desk at her. "Or where have they been hidden?"

"We should have the search warrant for her garage this afternoon."

Derrick reached for his phone.

"Oahu Animal Clinic. How may I help you?"

"Hi there Julie. This is Derrick Dreadlow. Is Melissa there?"

"Oh hi. She's been practically living here this past week. Let me find her. Hold on."

He sat back and poked at his keyboard.

"Hi, Derrick. I was going to call you as soon as I got the chance. I have some space cleared out for your trailer."

"That's great Melissa. I really appreciate this. When is a good time for me to come out?"

"I'm afraid I am going to be busy all day. But I left a key for you under the third pot on the right of the porch."

"Great. Thanks."

"Bye."

Derrick hung up. "An invitation to go out. But let's make it official and wait for the warrant." He leaned forward. "Where are we on the Kagawa case?"

Pele pulled a sheet out of a file next to her laptop. "I went back a few more weeks on his phone calls. At work and his cell. His secretary's office phone."

"Anything interesting?"

"A few calls more calls to a number in San Francisco. To that man named Fukuhara. I'm still trying to get in touch with him." She looked up. "Oh shit!"

"What?"

"I left my number for him to call me back."

"So?"

"I... I changed phone plans yesterday. I have a new number now." She pulled her new smartphone out and started to call Fukuhara's number.

Derrick stood up. "I'm going for a cup of coffee. You want anything?"

"Another one?"

He looked at the three empty cups on his desk. "OK. Maybe not." He looked over at her. "Tea?"

"OK."

Quon sat across the desk from Professor Keogh. They were in his cluttered office at the university. The professor was going through some notes on his computer. "So what are your plans after you complete your Ph.D. Quon?"

Quon sat there for a moment. "I have to get through this first."

The professor nodded as he scanned the notes. "I don't see that as a problem." He typed at the keyboard for a moment. "Are you going to want to teach more classes? Or spend more time at the police lab?"

"I like doing it all."

"We've talked about burning the candle at both ends and the middle before. You can't keep it up forever Quon. Even a young man has his limits."

"So I've been told." He glanced out the window. "It's just that there is so much to learn. And both places give me new insights."

Professor Keogh turned to Quon as he sat back. "Your Ph.D. will be finished in a few days. Why don't you plan on teaching just one class this coming semester? And maybe just a few hours a day at the station. Then you can take some time to get your thoughts together and get a new perspective on things."

"I will think about it and let you know."

"I need to know by July 13th. That is if you want to teach next semester."

"Do we have anything else on the Kagawa case?" Derrick asked as he set the tea down in front of her.

She stared down at the sheet. "A couple of calls to other people. Some were to Tomas. A few weeks back."

Derrick looked up. "Your brother?"

"Yes."

"I wonder what that was about?"

Pele shrugged. "They are both in the hotel resort business. Both in the Chamber of Commerce."

Derrick sat back as he took a sip of his tea. "Speaking of which… what did you think about the party Saturday night?" He took another sip. "Before the photo incident."

She reached for her tea. "You referring to some of the guests?"

"You are a good detective." He took a sip. "So what are your thoughts?"

She reached for her tea. "There were some interesting choices in guests there." She took a sip. "Some that I wouldn't exactly want to be on my planning committee for the future of the state."

Derrick nodded. "I'd like you to call Senator Aneko's office and ask for a copy of the guest list." He leaned forward. "And a copy of the seating chart while you're at it."

She laughed. "You think he is going to give me a copy of the seating chart?"

Derrick set his tea down and turned off his computer. "Let's see." He sat back. "And see what photos you can come up with of the night."

"I already have some."

"Press release?"

She pulled her glasses out of her backpack. "Quon's special design."

He nodded. "Good."

"Are you going home now?"

"I want to have a shower, and change first. Then lunch with the girls."

"After that?"

"Let's see if the warrant is ready. And see if we can have a few minutes to chat with your brother. Maybe he can shed some light on what was bothering Kagawa."

Chapter 30

Derrick and Haruku were sitting on a beach blanket as Kattie and Becky built a castle in the sand.

"You are becoming quite the energetic little architect there Becky," Derrick said as he sat back and enjoyed watching the girls and the sunset.

"For one thing, they get some sleep," Haruku said. "You, on the other hand, haven't slept in what? Thirty-six hours?"

"Maybe closer to forty-eight."

"You fell asleep for four hours here on the beach."

He looked at his arms and legs.

"I kept moving the umbrella to keep you from being burnt to a crisp. I figured you needed the sleep."

"Pele was supposed to call me."

"She did."

"Why didn't you wake me?"

"She said the warrant was delayed. She'll have it this evening. And you have a meeting with Tomas in the morning at 8:30. What's that about?"

Derrick shrugged. "Just some Chamber of Commerce stuff."

He sat there watching the waves roll up on the beach. The sounds of the surf. The girls running and shouting as the waves chased them.

Haruku leaned closer and looked at him. He could feel her warmth. Smell the fragrance of her skin. "Are you sleeping with your eyes open?"

"Just thinking," he replied unflinching.

"About what?"

"These last few weeks." He sat up and folded his arms over his knees as his gaze remained fixed on the water moving in and out. "If this had been a parenting test, you would be an A student, and I would have flunked out. Miserably."

She turned to him and folded her legs up under her as she rested on her hand beside him. "I guess life always tests us. But you are not failing."

"I think I took too many courses this semester."

"My course load was light. So between us, it's working out."

"You ever think about having kids? Someday?"

The waves stopped. The ocean was silent. Kattie and Becky stood still as they looked out to sea. "Here they come!" Becky squealed as the next set rolled in.

"Did you and Nancy ever…"

"That was a big one," Kattie yelled up to them. "Did you see it Uncle Derrick, Aunt Haruku?"

"Yes we did," Haruku said.

"It reached out to grab you," Derrick added as they chased after the receding wave. "It wasn't just that, we were both busy and away at odd hours."

She watched him stare out over the ocean. "The risk of the job? Your job?"

"You are very perceptive."

"I'm an artist." She turned to look out over the water as it rolled in then back out again. "And Melissa?"

Derrick just shook his head as he stuck his foot out and dug his big toe into the warm sand. "I'm a fool."

"Many men are."

"But I'm a big fool."

"Pele filled me in. Do you really think she could have, killed them?"

"How could I be so blind?"

"She was busy. Career oriented. Animals can get sick at all kinds of inconvenient hours." Haruku brushed a strand of hair out of her eyes. "A match made in heaven?"

Derrick sat there. "She was safe."

Haruku pulled her head back as she looked over at him. "You thought you were two of a kind?"

He shrugged.

"You had the perfect relationship?"

He snorted as he shook his head. "Just one little flaw in that perfect relationship."

Haruku turned to the ocean. "She is probably a murderess."

"That would be it."

Haruku kept her gaze forward, but turned her head slightly toward him. "Was that the only flaw? Were you in love with her?"

He sat there for a moment. "No. There was no real--"

"Connection?"

He dug his toe into the sand again. "Every time I called her, and she was busy…" He took a deep breath. "It was OK. Maybe even a relief."

"That's definitely not love."

He snorted. "No." He looked up at the girls. "I didn't miss her. It was more of... we had been going out... I should call her and invite her..."

"An obligation?"

"Exactly."

"That's not love either."

"Now when I think of you... here with the girls..." He glanced over at her then back out across the water. "That is exciting."

Haruku smiled slightly. "So maybe you didn't love her."

"I guess if I really did... I would have looked the other way when things didn't add up. And I would feel bad about arresting her. But I didn't. And I don't."

Haruku turned to him. "I have flaws. Did you feel bad when I was arrested?"

He turned to her and smiled. "First of all, I didn't arrest you. Your sister did. And yes, I felt bad when I heard about it. I felt bad for you. It wasn't you. Not the real you."

"And you know the real me?"

He turned to her. He reached out and touched her cheek. "I suspect not everything. But we all have flaws. And secrets. And you have so much more to offer. Melissa has a major crack."

"Would you look the other way If I had done something bad?"

He took a deep breath. "I don't think you could."

"Hypothetically then?"

"I'd probably need to find another line of work."

Pele stepped out of her condo building for a walk to clear her head in the warm evening air. Kengi. Her job. Everything was a mess. She wanted to go back to the shooting range, but she decided to give that a rest. At least for a while.

She looked in a store window as she turned a corner. A van was moving slowly down the street behind her. A man in dark shorts, a Hawaiian shirt, and a dark blue baseball cap stopped to look in a window. She turned the corner and continued walking. The van turned the corner. Still behind her. The man in the dark blue cap also turned the corner. She made a left at the next street. The van went on ahead and turned right. The man on foot was behind her.

She turned right. The man hung back. But the van was parked ahead of her. She ducked into a store and quickly out another side door.

She raced down the block and then down an alley then into her parent's store.

"Well hi there Pele," her mother said. "Are you here to visit or help out?"

Pele glanced out the window. Was she being followed or was it just her imagination running wild after a stressful weekend?

"Pele?"

She turned to her mother. "Hi. I was just out for a walk and thought I'd stop in to say hi. Hi."

Kattie and Becky were asleep on the ends of the beach blanket. The sun had set. Only lovers holding hands still strolled along the water's edge.

"You've seen a lot of ugly things in your line of work Derrick. It is only natural that you question your ability to feel anything. I'm sure that given enough time most cops get jaded."

"Cold, cynical..." He took in a slow deep breath. "When that happens it's time to move on." He reached down and brushed Kattie's hair off her face as she slept there. "Maybe past the time."

"You are just frustrated, Derrick. Not jaded, or cold, or cynical."

"Frustrated?"

"You can't do it all? Everyone tries. We think we need to keep up. With everything. All the time. But no one can." She slid over and leaned against him. "We need to disconnect once in a while."

He shook his head as he laughed. "You know, over the years I've seen it all. I've arrested people, parents, for stealing to feed their children. Maybe buy them a present at Christmas. Pay a medical bill. Single mothers just trying to make ends meet working two jobs and trying to still be a good parent. I was upholding the law I told myself."

"You were."

"Yes." He exhaled slowly. "That's my job." He reached up and rubbed his chin as he sat there thinking. "But these past weeks…" He turned and stared into her eyes. "I was on the other side." He turned back to the white crests rolling gently up onto the beach as the tide went out. "Not the stealing part. But the no time part. Add to that the no money part… the being alone part…" He turned back to her. "It can't all be done. You just can't do it. Not well anyway."

"A lot of people have to. They have no choice."

"But what could they… their children accomplish if they had it even a little easier?"

"You can't take on the weight of the world Derrick."

"I know. I couldn't even take care of two little girls."

She reached out and took his hand. "You see this as negative. Failure even."

"I did fail. If it weren't for you…"

She reached up and lightly put her finger on his lips. "I see it as a policeman who is growing."

He chuckled. "Growing?"

"You have empathy, Derrick. It's what I admire most about you. And with that, you don't see people as merely lawbreakers. You see that there may be a story behind this person's actions."

He snorted. "Well, some people really are bad to the bone." He shook his head. "And it isn't my job to judge people."

"But it's in your nature. And that is a good thing. For everyone."

"People aren't all good. There is a fair share of bad ones out there."

She slid her finger gently across his cheek. "But you can tell the difference." She sat back a little. "And that is what makes you a good cop. And one that really does protect and serve."

He sat there for a moment. He squeezed her hand. "I didn't see it in time with Melissa."

"Yes, you did." She pushed her sandals off to the side. "She got away with her crime for four years until you came here. No one else saw it. You did." She leaned up next to him again. "You still know where the line is."

Together, they watched the waves roll up on the beach. She shivered slightly. He slid his arm around her shoulder and held her.

Pele glanced from the front door to the side door as she waited on her phone. "Bucchi."

"Bucchi," Pele said.

"What can I do for you?"

"I was wondering if you knew Trang's location."

"Your phone not working?"

"I had to get a new one. I still need to get with Quon to reload his app."

"He's at home. Been there all afternoon."

"He's at home? Or his car is?"

"Well, I saw him go in around four. I stayed outside for about half an hour then left."

"So he could be out walking or taking a bus?"

"We don't have a device on him. But I do have his cell. And that's still home as well."

"Thanks, Bucchi."

"What's up?"

She scanned the store again. "Probably nothing. I'll talk to you later."

She slipped her phone back into her pocket. Trang could have slipped out without his phone. She put her hand back in her pocket and felt her phone. Or he may also have a new one.

She peered through the shelves as she watched the people outside walking by. This wasn't Trang. At least not him on the street. But was he in the van? Did Hollister have someone else working with him now? Or it could be someone else entirely. But who?

She took a deep breath. Or… it could just be all in her imagination.

Chapter 31

"Are you sure about this?" Todd asked.

Quon scanned the hotel restaurant. "This is where Paul said he'd meet us."

"I mean jumping in so fast. And with these people. You don't know them."

"I have worked with them before. Well, with Paul. And he is a friend of Derrick."

Todd reached for the pot and topped off his coffee. "Look, I like Derrick. And I trust him. But he's also got a lot of connections with people in… how shall I say this…" He topped off Quon's coffee and set the pot down. "Shadowy places?"

Quon looked down at his coffee. "Yes."

Perry Ansen set his cup down, reached out for the pot, and refreshed his coffee. "I found out they did a background check on me. They even had me sign some special papers."

"How does that affect your ability as Quon's lawyer?" Todd asked.

"How does it affect your ability as his financial person?"

Todd took a sip. "It's going to be interesting."

Quon looked over at them. "Is there a problem?"

"Nothing that we can't handle," Todd said.

Perry sat back and grinned. "Don't worry Quon. We'll go through the contracts with a fine-tooth comb to protect your interests."

Quon looked up as Paul approached with a woman by his side. "With so many people looking out for me, why don't I feel in balance anymore?"

Todd leaned close and whispered. "You've got to take charge of your own destiny. We work for you. Don't forget that." He sat back and smiled as they stepped up to the table.

"Good morning. Sorry we're late." Paul turned to the woman beside him. "This is Esther Franklin."

"Good morning gentlemen."

They stood as she took her seat.

Quon waved to his right. "Ah, this is my finance person Todd Pendergast, and my attorney, Perry Ansen."

"Nice to meet you," Paul said as he reached out and shook Perry's hand. "Good to see you again Todd."

Todd nodded. "You too Paul."

They all sat back in their seats. "Aloha," Quon said as they studied each other around the table for a moment.

"Thank you," Esther said as she sat back. She was a trim woman, professionally dressed with well-coiffed white hair that made her deep blue eyes stand out.

Their server came up to the table and took their orders.

"It is great to be back in the islands," she said.

"You've been here before?" Todd asked.

"Many times."

"I apologize for the early meeting," Quon said. "But I've got to go out on a case in a little while."

She nodded. "Rule one Quon. You are the boss. Never apologize." She reached for her coffee. "It is we, who are here to help you do your job."

Quon shot a quick glance over at Todd. He nodded slightly.

Derrick stood off to the side as Joyce handed out assignments to all the techs. Several officers secured the area around Melissa's home and garage with crime scene tape.

"Quon said he would be here as soon as he can," Joyce said as the officers unlocked the garage. They slid the wide double doors open. It was filled with all kinds of old trailers, tires, construction materials, racks of feed, and stuff Derrick had no clue what it was used for.

"Is she a packrat?" Joyce asked as they stood there looking in.

Derrick looked around. "Seems so."

"OK guy's," Joyce yelled out. "We will begin by taking photos of everything then cataloging it as we remove it."

Xin, the other techs, and the officers nodded as they set about searching for clues in the disappearance of Jack Crawford and Dawn Miller.

Joyce turned to Derrick. "Do you think we're going to find bodies in here?"

"My guess is under."

"There is just one more detail," Paul said as they were about to finish their breakfast meeting.

"Yes?" Quon asked.

"There is a piece of property I think you should buy. I hear it is coming on the market for a very good price."

"We haven't even fixed up what we have?" Todd said as he set down his coffee.

"This is one of those strategic pieces we talked about," Paul said.

Todd looked over at Quon.

"Is it the one at the end of the…"

Paul nodded.

"What?" Todd asked.

Quon turned to Paul. "Will we need it in the future?"

"The very near future," Paul added.

"OK. And I think we should meet again on the ninth," Quon said. Everyone nodded.

Paul leaned over to Quon. "You, Todd, and I need to discuss the property. I also have a couple of new people for you to interview."

"And Perry?"

"If he can make it. Fine."

"All right," Quon said. "Can we do that before the other meeting?"

"I'll set it all up."

Derrick stood outside Melissa's garage as Quon, Xin, and Joyce went through it looking for anything linking to Jack or Dawn. "Thanks, Julie. Remember, this a surprise so let me know if she decides to come home."

"I think she plans on spending the night here," Julie said. "Construction. And the fireworks tomorrow. The noise scares some of the animals, so she usually stays here."

"OK. I appreciate it."

"I don't think she likes surprises. But from you, I'm sure she won't mind."

"I guess we'll find out won't we?"

Derrick hung up as Pele drove up. She parked and got out of her RAV.

"Couldn't wait to get started?" she asked as she stepped up to him with a fresh coffee she picked up on the way. She held it out to him.

"Thank you," he said as he took it.

"It's decaf."

He popped the tab on the top.

"Haruku called. She said you weren't getting much sleep lately."

"You double teaming me again?"

"Someone has to look out for you." She scanned the area. "So what do we have so far?"

He took a sip. "Xin said they found hair samples in the trunk of the BMW matching the DNA samples we procured of Jack and Dawn."

"Maybe they were packing for a trip?"

Derrick looked over at her.

"Just saying…"

"Possible, but not probable."

"Anything here in the garage or the house?"

"We haven't gone in the house yet. My guess is any evidence we find will be out here. Or under here."

"What if Melissa comes home?"

"I told Julie I was planning a surprise party and to call me if she left the clinic."

"We have a meeting with Tomas at 8:30." She glanced down at her watch. "We should leave soon."

Derrick waved at Quon to join them outside.

"Yes?"

"We've got to go to a meeting about another case Quon. How soon do you think it will be before you start scanning below the foundation?"

He turned to look in the garage. "It is a big garage. It will take us a few more hours to go through the contents and move them out. Then we can start scanning below for holes or anomalies under the foundation."

"So maybe noon or one?"

Quon stood there for a moment. "Give us until two."

Derrick turned to Pele as Quon went back inside. "Let's roll partner."

"Who's car? No point in both of us driving."

"You can drive."

Pele sped up as she turned onto the H-1 heading back to Honolulu. The early morning traffic was lighter due to the upcoming holiday. The morning sun was burning off the early morning clouds setting up another beautiful day.

She glanced over at Derrick. "The children are getting out of the hospital later today."

"Well, that's some good news. I'll bet their father is excited about that."

"Do you think we can rule him out as a suspect?"

Derrick finished his coffee. "Let's leave him on the list of possible suspects for now." He reached into his pocket as his cell went off. "Dreadlow here." He glanced over at Pele. "Hello there Kengi. How are you? You left in such a hurry we didn't get a chance to say goodbye."

"Just some family business. Nothing life-threatening, though," Kengi said. "But I do have more information on the case."

"I hope things are OK back home." He glanced over at Pele. She stared straight at the road ahead. "Hold on a second." Derrick lowered his phone and pressed a button. "OK. I've got you on speaker. What have you got for us?"

"Hello Pele," Kengi said.

"Kengi," she replied coldly.

"You were about to say Kengi?" Derrick chimed in.

"Yes. There have been several calls between Mrs. Kagawa and the brother here in Kobe during the two weeks prior to his death."

"Any reason to suspect foul play?"

"I don't know. There were also calls between Gorou Kagawa and another number I tracked down. A man named Hirokazu Amano."

"Gorou is the brother in Japan?"

"Yes."

"And this tells us what?"

"Hirokazu Amano is a suspected soldier in the Yakuza in Kobe. He also spends most of his time in Hawaii now."

"Why would Gorou Kagawa be calling him?"

"Only two possibilities I can think of."

"Which are?"

"One, Gorou Kagawa wanted a hit on his brother."

Derrick shrugged. "Possible I guess given their animosity toward each other. And the second possibility?"

"Amano was acting as an intermediary with someone higher up."

"Any idea who?"

"My guess would be the biggest Yakuza boss in Kobe. His name is Hidehisa Domen."

Derrick sat there for a moment.

"She could have asked the brother to hire someone to kill her husband. Someone out of the country," Pele said still focused on the road ahead.

"A continuation of the family feud?" Derrick asked to no one in particular.

"We know the brothers didn't get along," Pele said.

Derrick looked down at his phone. "OK Kengi, here is what I'd like you to do. Check to see if there could have been anything going on between the wife and the brother. And check their financial records to see if there may be links between the brothers and the Yakuza. In particular this Domen character. In Japan or here in Hawaii."

"Should I go question the brother himself?"

Derrick thought for a moment. "No. Not yet. Let's try to get a clearer picture of just what may be going on here first."

"I'll get right on it." Kengi hung up.

"Are you going to tell me what's going on between you two?" Derrick asked as he slipped his phone back into his pocket.

"Nothing."

"He said he had a family thing come up and he had to get back home. Did he mention anything to you?"

She continued to focus on the road ahead. "We'll be there in a few minutes. What are we going to say to Tomas?"

Chapter 32

Tomas was sitting behind the large mahogany desk in his third-floor office of the family's Grand Tiki Resort. Pele and Derrick were sitting in two dark leather chairs across from him.

"So what can you tell us about Mr. Etsuo Kagawa?" Derrick asked as Pele sat there with her notebook out and pen in hand.

"We were in the same business, hospitality," Tomas began as he sat back in his plush black leather chair. "We served together on Chamber committees from time to time." He glanced over at his sister as she made notes. "Just what is it that you're looking for?" He shifted his gaze back to Derrick.

"Your phone number is listed on the records for Mr. Kagawa during the past few weeks," Pele said.

He turned to her. "So? Like I said, we work together on various projects and events from time to time."

"Anything lately?"

Tomas shrugged as he leaned forward. "Nothing important. Why? What did he say?"

"Not much," Pele said.

"He's dead," Derrick added.

Tomas's shoulders slumped as he sank back in his chair. "My god. What happened? A heart attack or something?"

"His cruiser blew up," Pele said.

"He was murdered," Derrick added.

"Along with his mistress," Pele said. "Her two children survived, though."

"Thanks to Pele and Haruku," Derrick added.

Tomas's eyes brows furrowed as he stared at them.

"We were in the neighborhood, and they dove in to rescue them," Derrick said.

"Do you know of any reason why someone would want to kill him?" Pele asked.

Tomas sat there staring down at his desk for a moment. Derrick watched as he got up and walked over to a credenza on the right wall. He opened a door and reached in. He pulled out a dark blue notebook, then walked back to his desk and sat down. He set the book down on the desk.

Derrick shot a quick glance over at Pele. She tilted her head slightly and shrugged.

"I'm not saying this is the reason." He stared at the notebook for a moment then slid it across the desktop toward Derrick. "But it might be worth looking into."

Derrick reached out for it. "What is it?"

"I told him not to get involved with these people."

"What people?" Pele asked.

Derrick turned the notebook in front of him, but he didn't open it. "Why don't you start from the beginning, Tomas."

Tomas took a long slow breath as he sat back. "It all began about six, maybe seven months ago." He nodded at the dark blue notebook. "With that."

Derrick and Pele looked down at the notebook. "What is this?" Derrick asked.

Tomas reached up and rubbed the back of his neck as he stared down at it. "It's called the Blue Line Report."

Derrick looked at him. "A new bus route?"

Tomas shook his head. "Our future. Hawaii's future." He glanced over at a small globe on a shelf. "The future of the world actually."

"I have something back here," Joyce said as she turned to the others in the large garage.

"What is it?" Quon asked as he and Xin walked over to her. "It looks like a pink suitcase buried under all this old wood and pipes. See it down in the corner there?"

"I'll go get the camera," Xin said as he turned and took long strides across the garage.

"An odd place to keep a suitcase," Quon said.

"It looks like it's been here for quite a while too," Joyce added as Xin came back with the camera and a tripod.

"So what exactly is this Blue Line Report?" Derrick asked as he opened the notebook to the title page.

"Real estate. But basically, it's a report about climate change."

Derrick looked up at him. "You think people are killing each other over climate change?"

"Specifically, this report has to do with changes in sea level here in Hawaii."

"So?" Pele asked as she glanced over at the notebook.

Derrick opened it to the table of contents. "Why would someone kill over this?"

"I'm not saying they did," Tomas said. He leaned forward in his chair and put his arms on the desk. "But a significant change in sea level, in storm surge, translates into billions of dollars here in Hawaii of potential losses. Hundreds of billions." He sat back again. "Trillions... hundreds of trillions of dollars if you consider the worldwide implications."

Derrick and Pele sat there silently.

"Think of it this way Derrick. Beachfront property owners. Hotels and resorts on any coast. Insurance companies. Governments. Catastrophic storms... damage... and the costs of all of this..." He leaned forward again. "Even minor changes in sea level can ruin people, companies, and investments of all kinds along all coastal areas. Even upriver communities and flat low-level coastal areas. The water level. The Blue Line."

Derrick nodded. "OK. I get the concept. We had plans like this in New York City too. Large parts of Manhattan could be subject to flooding. The subway system..." he looked up at Tomas. "But what does this have to do with the murder of Mr. Kagawa?"

Tomas leaned back and opened the lower right drawer of his desk. He reached in and pulled out a map. He placed it on his desk then closed the drawer. "Maybe something. Maybe nothing."

He unfolded the map. It was a topographical map with what looked like property lines and what Derrick guessed were shorelines drawn in blue.

Tomas reached out and put his finger in a property marked in green. "Pahonu Knoll."

"It looks like the Ewa Beach area," Pele said.

"Where the action is," Derrick said.

"Right you are little sis."

"What does it have to do with Mr. Kagawa?" she asked.

"OK," Quon said as two officers helped them clear away debris. Joyce was recording every sight and sound on camera as they worked.

"I've got it," Xin said as he pulled the pink suitcase out from under the debris.

"Let's get some more evidence bags and a couple of boxes over here," Quon said as Xin set it down on a cleared area of the floor. "Joyce, you keep the camera rolling as we go through it."

Tomas took a deep breath as he sat back in his chair. "Several months ago four of us got together and bought this piece of property for future development."

Derrick looked at the topo lines of elevation. "For when the sea level rose?"

"It's rising now, Derrick."

"Go on."

"It was expensive. I wanted to wait a few years to develop it. The others, my partners, wanted to begin development now."

"You think one of your partners killed him?" Pele asked.

"Not exactly."

"What happened next?" Derrick asked.

"We bought the land right away. We knew the report would come out in a few weeks and we knew the property was for sale. We also knew that the price would shoot up after the report was released and people began to realize what it meant."

"Insider trading?" Derrick asked.

Tomas grinned. "Anyone with half a brain can see this coming and where it's going."

Derrick nodded, "Puts a whole new spin on buy low and sell high."

"Just good business sense," Pele said.

Tomas cracked a forced smile. "We thought so."

"Then what happened?" Derrick asked.

"We had an environmental impact study done. And an architect to draw up some preliminary plans, ballpark cost estimates… just to get a feel for what we were looking at."

"And what were you looking at?"

Tomas put his hands out on the table. "Ballpark… One point four."

"Million?" Pele asked. "That's not much."

Both Derrick and Tomas turned to her.

"Billion. With a capital B," Tomas said. "It was a luxury project all the way."

"And just where would you find that kind of money?" Pele asked.

Derrick sat back. "I'm guessing that you and your partners didn't have access to that kind of capital."

Tomas nodded.

"But someone did."

Tomas nodded again.

"Someone that Mr. Kagawa knew?"

Tomas nodded yet again. "I told him we could do this ourselves. Over time. Set up a separate development company, sell shares…"

"How much time?" Pele asked.

"I was thinking twenty years. Give or take."

"And he didn't want to wait that long," Derrick said.

Tomas sat back. "No."

"Then what?"

"He set up a meeting with an established development company."

"And the name of this company?" Derrick asked.

"IDC. The Ito Development Corporation."

"I've never heard of them," Pele said as she glanced over at Derrick.

Derrick shrugged.

"They are international. Based in Japan. Trying to expand into US markets. Mainly West Coast and here in Hawaii."

"So you are familiar with them?" Derrick asked.

"Only stories."

"What kind of stories?"

"Nothing concrete. Just stories. Maybe criminal ties." He shrugged.

Derrick turned to Pele.

She nodded. "I'll check them out."

"Have Kengi help from his end."

She looked at him.

"Is that going to be a problem?"

She shook her head.

Derrick pointed at the map again. "So Tomas. What's so special about this particular piece of property?"

Tomas leaned forward and pointed to the topo lines to the south and west. "You see these lines?"

"Yes," Derrick replied. "They denote a rather gentle slope to the south and west."

"Exactly. A fifty to sixty-five-foot slope over a quarter mile to be more precise." He pointed to the area on the northern half of the property. "Now up here we gain an additional thirty-five to fifty feet."

"A good spot to build your resort."

"Yes." Tomas ran his finger along the path of six blue lines. "These lines designate increases of six inches, then one, two, three, four and five-foot intervals of sea rise."

"And your beach front looks smaller and smaller, but still intact."

"Yes. And we can build a sea wall out here to help with storm surge." He paused. "At least with most. A massive storm or a tsunami would still be a problem."

"Waikiki will require scuba gear?" Derrick asked.

Tomas nodded. "And we will be the new beachfront place to be." He sat back. "At least that was the plan."

Derrick sat back. "Who were your partners?"

"Mr. Etsuo Kagawa, Mr. Daichi Watanabe, and Mr. Taka Fukuhara. He was from San Francisco. A friend of Mr. Kagawa I believe. I met him a couple of times when he flew out here on business. He owns two high-rise condos here in Hawaii, as well as some in San Francisco and Vancouver, plus a hotel in San Francisco. Maybe more. I'm not sure."

Pele glanced over at Derrick.

"Do you still have a share in this property?" Derrick asked.

"I am in the process of selling my share to Mr. Fukuhara. When I heard about the possibility of IDC coming in on the project I pulled out. So did Mr. Watanabe."

"Did he sell his share as well?"

"Yes. To Mr. Kagawa."

"When was this sale finalized?"

Tomas shrugged. "Not yet. Both Kagawa and Fukuhara were reworking their finances to close the deal. We're just waiting on confirmation."

"Who is handling the sale?"

"Cheetham Investment. Here in Honolulu."

Tomas watched as Pele made a note in her book.

"Have you had anyone from IDC contact you? Or heard from Mr. Kagawa or Fukuhara in the last week or two?"

Tomas shook his head. "No. I called Frank Bellview at Cheetham to see if the details were finalized yet. That was two weeks ago. He said they were still working on it. I haven't heard anything since then."

Derrick pulled his card out of his pocket. "If you do hear from someone. Anyone. Call your sister or me right away."

Tomas looked at him as he reached for the card. "Do you think his death has something to do with this?"

"I don't know yet. We also have a couple of other people of interest."

Derrick and Pele stepped out of the main building and walked over to her RAV.

"We need to talk to this Fukuhara ASAP," Derrick said as he stepped up to her car.

Pele pulled her keys out of her pocket. "Do you think my brother is in any danger, Derrick?"

Derrick opened his door. "I don't think so. If he were, they would have contacted him or killed him by now."

"That's reassuring. Now what?" Pele asked as she started up her RAV.

Derrick sat there for a moment. "It's not quite eleven. Quon said he wouldn't be ready to check under the garage until at least two. Let's head back to the station and do some digging on these new players and see where they fit in. If they fit in."

Chapter 33

"Did you find anything on that Cheetham Investment company yet?" Derrick asked as he dropped a couple of bags on the desk in front of Pele?

"Does Juanita deliver now?" Pele asked as she looked up from her computer.

"No. I saw Marsha getting ready to make a lunch run and asked her to stop by and pick up something for us. I hope turkey subs are OK."

"Fine." She reached over and opened the bags as Derrick unlocked the screen to his laptop. "As far as I can tell they are a reputable firm. They have been in business for over thirty years. No trouble with the law here. I called Todd, and he said they were clean as far as he knew. Though he's never personally had any dealings with them. He is checking their history." She handed Derrick a sub and water bottle "No coffee?"

"No. Cutting back."

"Do we want to go have a talk with this Bellview guy at Cheetham."

Derrick took a sip of water.

"Well?"

"Yeah. See if we can meet sometime tomorrow morning."

"Tomorrow is the fourth of July."

"Already?"

"Yes."

He sat back. "I've only got a few more days with the girls, and all hell breaks loose. Again." He raised his sub to his mouth. "Then try for the next hour or two. Tell him it's urgent." He took a bite as he pulled his cell out of his pocket. He selected the top number as he chewed and pressed call. "Hi Haruku, it's me."

She reached for her phone and dialed a number. "Yes. I would like to speak to Frank Bellview please."

"We've got clothes, cosmetics, all kinds of stuff packed for a trip in here," Xin said as Joyce panned the items spread out on a plastic sheet on the garage floor.

"OK," Quon said. "Let's get it all cataloged and bagged for transport back to the lab."

Xin opened a side pocket and pulled out an envelope.

"What is that?" Quon asked.

Joyce zoomed in as Xin pulled out some documents.

He held them up to the camera. "It looks like plane tickets. From 2008. For Jack Crawford and Dawn Miller."

Quon shook his head. "That is not good for Derrick's girlfriend." He turned to Joyce. "You didn't record that did you?"

"I have everything. Sorry." She turned off the camera. "I can rewind it a bit."

Quon shook his head. "No. Derrick wanted everything recorded. We do not want any look of evidence of tampering at this point."

"Yes, this is Lieutenant Dreadlow of the Honolulu Police."

Pele looked up from her computer.

"Yes. Detective Kobayashi is my partner. Who are you again?" Derrick motioned for her to follow him into the nearest conference room. "Can you hold on just a second?"

When they entered the room, he shut the door and set his cell down on the table. "OK. Could you repeat that please?"

"I am Detective Patterson. San Francisco Police. I understand that your partner has been trying to contact a Mr. Fukuhara here in San Francisco."

"Yes, I have," Pele blurted out.

"We've been trying to get in touch with you."

"I'm sorry. I changed phones and forgot that I left the old number with Fukuhara."

"Well, can you tell me your interest in Mr. Fukuhara?"

Derrick leaned forward. "His name came up in a case we're working here in Hawaii." Derrick glanced over at Pele. They were both wondering the same thing. He turned back to the phone. "Can you tell us how to contact him?"

"I'm afraid he is part of an investigation we are working here in San Francisco."

"A murder?" Derrick asked.

"How did you know?"

"We have the same problem here."

"When?" Detective Patterson asked.

"The attempt was made on June 24th. He died a couple of days later. But we believe the device that killed him was set up sometime before the 24th." Derrick sat back. "Your turn."

"Our man, Fukuhara was killed on the 24th. A bullet to the head. We found him a couple of days later." He paused for a moment. "You think they might be connected?"

"I think it's interesting that they were partners in a real estate deal here in the islands. And now they are both dead." Derrick leaned forward. "Have you found anything there about anything with Pahonu or Pahonu Knoll on it?"

"I don't recall it, but we were grasping in the dark. I'll have my partner go back through the evidence and see what we can find."

"And anything else that may be related to Hawaii might be useful," Derrick added.

"I'll send you what we have, and you send us what you've got."

"You got it, detective. We'll talk again soon." Derrick hung up.

He and Pele both got up and headed back to their desks. "I guess this takes the wife and the brother off the table as well as Mr. Walters," Pele said.

"Not necessarily. Just shuffles the order a bit for now. Let's keep trying to learn more about the wife and brother at least." They sat back at their desks. "We still have two brothers that divided the resort world between them. Maybe one wanted to expand into the other's territory."

"Maybe one was tired of the brother in Japan and seeking new partners?"

Derrick leaned back and stretched his arms behind him as he clasped his hands behind his head. "Real estate can be complicated. Let's talk with this Bellview guy."

Frank Bellview sat down behind his desk. "Yes, I am handling the sale of shares between four partners in the Pahonu Knoll Project."

"What is taking so long?" Derrick asked.

"Equity. Two of the partners, the ones trying to buy out the others, are leveraged to their eyeballs. We're working with their lawyers, banks, and accountants on juggling things around to make the deal happen."

"And are you getting close?"

"Yes. All we need are a few more days. We could have been finished this week if it weren't for the holiday."

"And now the deaths of the two partners," Pele added.

"Yes." Frank sat back as he shook his head. "That does throw a wrench into things."

"So what happens now?"

"Technically, the two sellers still own their shares, and the estates of the other two partners, however, they are set up, own the other shares." He took a deep breath. "This is going to be one big cluster fuck." He glanced over at Pele. "Sorry."

"I've actually heard that financial term used before," she said as she took notes.

Frank turned to Derrick. "Interestingly, we did receive an unsolicited bid about a week ago from a company. I just put it aside because we thought this deal would work out."

"Why did you set it aside?"

"For one thing, it was a lowball number. I didn't think anyone would be interested in it."

Derrick glanced over at Pele then turned back to Frank. "Who was the bid from?"

"Ah, let me see," Frank turned to his computer. "Some kind of acronym… they all begin to sound alike after a while. ICD… IDC…"

"Ito Development Corporation?" Derrick asked.

Frank looked up from his computer. "That's it. How did you know?"

"What happens now?" Pele asked.

Frank sat back. "I don't know. I'll have to talk to the sellers, the lawyers."

"And who are the sellers?"

"A family from California. They want to cash out."

"Any other buyers?" Derrick asked.

"We'd have to start the process over again. That could take a couple of months."

"And these people are in a hurry?" Pele asked.

"Yes."

"Is there a deadline for this deal?"

"August 3rd. Then we automatically go back to square one. The clients won't be happy about that."

"Why's that?" Derrick asked.

Frank sat back. "It's part of a structured domino deal between five different parties on five different properties in four different states."

"A cluster fuck?" Pele asked.

Frank nodded. "A colossal one."

Derrick handed Frank his card. "Don't do anything without calling us first."

Quon stood in the doorway as the truck backed up. All of the contents of the huge garage had been pulled out and were scattered across the field. He motioned for the truck to stop.

Xin and two of the officers stepped up to the back and opened the door. They pulled out a ramp and rolled off his underground sensing equipment.

"I finished laying out the grid on the floor," Joyce said as she tried to wipe the blue chalk off her hands.

Quon nodded. "All right everyone. We will start at the center of the grid and work our way out."

"Now what?" Pele asked as they walked out the front door.

"I think it's time to go see what Quon has found."

As they drove westward on the H-1, Pele turned to Derrick. "Do you think my brother and Mr. Watanabe are safe?"

Derrick stared out the window. "Yes."

"How can you be so sure?"

"I think something went wrong with this deal. And Kagawa and Fukuhara were involved. If they do go after your brother and the other guy, they will try to make a deal with them first. Otherwise, there is no one left to work with."

"They could go to the original sellers," she said.

Derrick bobbed his head from side to side. "Maybe. But if this whole chain falls apart, there may be no reason for the sellers to sell anymore. Maybe they will get wind of the Blue Line Report and hold out for more." He turned to her. "A lot more."

"I'll get on this IDC. See what I can learn about them."

"Good. And let's see what Kengi comes back with."

"Do you want me to stay here?" Pele asked as she pulled up near Melissa's garage.

Derrick opened the door. "Thanks. But I think our other case is more important. I've got this one. You should go back to the station and send Patterson our info. See what they've got. Maybe we can put this together and see who's behind it. And see if this IDC has anything on anyone's radar in this country. Start with the west coast and Hawaii. Maybe even Vancouver."

"Your friend Ethan with Interpol?"

"Be a good place to start. I'll talk to you later."

She nodded as he closed the door. "Bye." She drove off.

Derrick walked over to Joyce. "Anything yet?"

"We found their plane tickets in a suitcase."

They stepped into the garage. There was a big hole cut in the western edge of the slab.

"We also found an anomaly about half an hour ago," Joyce said. "We cut through the concrete with jackhammers. Now Quon and Xin are digging down into the soil."

"They look like those guys in a movie digging up a mummy," Derrick said as they stepped up closer.

"I have got something," Quon said as he reached for an air bottle and blew away the dust.

"What is it?" Derrick asked as he knelt down at the side of the hole in the concrete.

Quon brushed away a little more. Xin was working the other end of the trench.

"It looks like the top of a skull," Quon said looking up at Derrick.

"I think I've got a femur here," Xin said.

Derrick took a deep breath. It felt like a lead weight had just landed in the pit of his stomach. He had expected this. But he held out hope that he was wrong. He almost wished his coplyness hadn't returned. He turned and looked up at Joyce. "Let's get Marta out here before we go any further."

Joyce nodded and pulled out her cell. She walked over to the door as she dialed.

Derrick rubbed his eyes and ran his fingers through his hair as he lowered his head over his computer.

"Maybe you should call it a day," Haruku said as she sat down next to him at the kitchen table.

He looked up at her. "You're probably right."

"Tomorrow is a holiday."

"Crime doesn't take a holiday." He turned to his laptop. "This new case is a mess. And now it has spread to California. Maybe beyond."

"A good night's sleep will help clear your head."

He sat back. "I know that you're right. But we've got three dead people now. They are all probably connected. Maybe."

"The one could have been unexpected?"

"Collateral damage we used to call it."

"I don't know about that," she said. "But if someone plants a bomb in a place where more than one person usually gathers, that tells me maybe they didn't care who got hurt."

"Hmmm." He nodded as he thought. "So Kagawa and Fukuhara are the primary targets, his mistress was just in the wrong place at the wrong time…" He reached up and rubbed his chin. "Kagawa and Fukuhara were the last players in this Pahonu

Knoll Project…" He stood up and began pacing around the kitchen. He walked over to the coffee pot and picked up a cup.

"It's empty. You are cut off for the night."

He nodded as he set his empty cup down.

"It still could be the jilted wife or the soon to be ex-husband…" He turned to Haruku. "And some unknown assailant in San Francisco that we don't know about yet."

"Do you really believe that?"

He stood behind his chair and pushed it under the table. "At this point no. But I've got to keep our options open."

"Now what?"

He looked down at his laptop. "Now I should take a closer look at what Patterson sent." He started to pull the chair out again.

Haruku stood up and pushed it back as she lowered the screen of his laptop. It beeped as she shut it. "You need some sleep to think clearly."

He looked down at the closed laptop. "You're right. I can't see clearly. And then I've got…"

"Melissa?"

He nodded. "And your brother's life if I'm wrong about what is behind this other case."

She stood up and took his hand. "The best thing for you, and my brother, is a good night's sleep."

He looked down at the table as his cell went off. He stared at it as it vibrated across the tabletop. He reached for it. "Dreadlow here." He nodded. "OK. Thanks."

"Marta?" Haruku asked.

He nodded.

"She's still working this late too?"

He nodded as he turned slightly away.

"Jack and Dawn?"

He nodded again. "Thank you, Marta. Now go home."

"Is it?

He flipped his cell shut and set it down on the table. "Yeah."

"That means…"

"Afraid so."

She reached out and slipped her arms around him. In a daze, he pulled her in close.

"Georgio. Don't make anyone shoot you."

"I can't back down!"

In a flash, Georgio raised his gun and started firing. Four shots rang out. Three landed around Pele. Dust chips from the concrete floor flew up on her black shoes with the purple stripes.

Georgio lowered his gun to his side. He staggered. He fell forward, off the platform landing about thirty feet in front of Pele.

Derrick turned. Pele was standing there with her arms stretched out in front of her. Her gun still raised. She stood there in silence.

The image wavered and began to blur.

"No! Ian! Don't go in there!"

Pele jumped up in her bed. A cold sweat covered her skin. Her nightshirt clung to her moist skin. She got up and raced out into the living room and over to the lanai. She slid open the door and stepped out into the cool night air.

The night was filled with the sounds of a city at rest, but not asleep. The occasional car passed thirty stories below. Delivery trucks and trash trucks were making their rounds. The occasional large wave crashing on the beach echoed between the buildings.

She shivered as the breeze caressed her wet body. She wrapped her arms around herself for warmth then went back inside. She closed the screen but left the sliding door open. She wanted to hear the sounds of the city. She needed to hear the sounds of life.

Chapter 34

"Sorry to get you up early on a holiday," Derrick said as they headed west on the H-1.

"It's no problem," Pele replied. "I couldn't sleep anyway. So you sure about everything?"

"Marta confirmed it last night."

"Are you sure she's still at the clinic?"

"Yes. I've had her watched for the last couple of days."

"Are you sure you don't want Soto and I to do this?"

He looked out at the new day dawning. There wasn't a cloud in the sky. The air was calm. "No. But unfortunately, this comes with the job."

"I know." She sighed as she stared out the window. "Sometimes our jobs suck."

"Amen to that."

Derrick and Pele walked up to the front door. Officer Marsha Kendal stood behind them as another officer went around to the back. The door was locked. He knocked on the glass again.

Carrie, the other veterinarian at the clinic, peered around the corner and waved. She walked across the reception area and unlocked the door. She glanced out at the patrol car parked in the lot as they stepped in.

"Hi, Derrick. Is something wrong?"

"Good morning Carrie. Is Melissa in?" he asked as they all streamed past.

"Yes. She's up in her office."

"How is the reconstruction coming?"

"The expansion is done. We're in the finishing stages. Fixtures, trim, painting, stuff like that. Then we bring in the new equipment."

"The light at the end of the tunnel."

Carrie led them across the reception area and back into the long hallway. She pointed to the elevator down the hall. "Melissa is upstairs to the right after you get off. Shall I take you up?"

"I think we can find our way."

Carrie looked at Marsha and Pele. "Has something happened? Is Melissa OK?"

"We just need to talk to her for a minute," Pele said.

"I... I'll be back in the kennel if you need me."

"Thank you, Carrie." Derrick motioned to Marsha to take the elevator as he and Pele went up the stairs. They met at the top then proceeded down the hall.

The smell of new construction permeated the air. Drywall was waiting for paint, light fixtures were hanging down from the ceiling, and plastic sheets were lying around on the floor.

"How can they operate while this is going on?" Pele asked as they walked down the hall.

"They are renting a mobile clinic. It's out in the parking lot." He turned to Marsha and whispered. "You wait here."

She nodded and took up a position by the door.

Derrick peeked through the partially open door as he knocked.

Melissa looked up from her desk. "Derrick. Hello. Aren't you the early one?"

"I never was one to sleep in late," he replied as he and Pele entered the office. "Are you an early riser as well?"

Pele nodded as she stood slightly behind Derrick. The walls were still bare. Only a desk and two chairs were in the room. Two file cabinets stood in a corner about a foot from the freshly painted walls.

"Looks like it will be a fantastic place when it's finished," Derrick said as he stepped up to her desk.

She sat back in her chair and looked up at him. Her long reddish blond hair was tied back in a ponytail. Her deep blue eyes studied him as he stood there in his black Italian suit. "A bit overdressed for a holiday aren't we Derrick?"

"We just happened to be in the neighborhood investigating a case. I thought I'd drop by and see how you were doing." He scanned the room quickly. "You know, how the construction was coming along."

"I'm pleased to tell you we are a week ahead of schedule."

"Fire the old contractor?"

She grinned. "No. Just built a little fire under him."

Derrick nodded. "That type A personality at work."

She bit her lower lip as she looked up at him. "It never stops. My one flaw." She took a breath and leaned forward. "So what's this case that it is so important that it gets you and your partner up so early on a beautiful Fourth of July? Anything interesting?"

"You might find it interesting. We're investigating a disappearance." He noticed a quick glance in her eyes to Pele then back to him again. "It happened a few years back. Unsolved at the time." He smiled. "Actually that's not correct. No one realized it ever happened."

She sat back and smiled. Her eyes sparkled in the morning light as she chuckled. "So you are investigating a case that never happened?"

He sat down in the chair across from her desk as Pele stood behind him. "Well, there was another disappearance. A real case that happened around the same time. On the mainland."

"I see." She folded her hands on the desk. "And you think the two are related?"

"I believe so."

She took a deep breath and unclasped her hands as she sat back. "And you think that I can help somehow?" She glanced up at Pele then back at Derrick.

He nodded. "I believe so."

"And who is this missing person? Or persons?"

"His name was Jack. Jack Crawford. I believe you knew him as your husband."

She sat back and laughed. "Jack? Why I haven't seen or heard from him in years."

Derrick stared into her eyes. "I believe you."

"What happened to him?" Pele asked as she watched the woman sitting coolly, calmly, on the other side of the desk.

Melissa shrugged as she looked down at her desk momentarily. She smiled again as she looked back up at Pele. "One day he was in my life." She shrugged again. "The next he wasn't."

"What about Dawn Miller?" Derrick asked.

She turned back to Derrick. "Who is Dawn Miller?"

"Jack's new friend."

Melissa shook her head slowly as she thought. "I don't believe we ever had the pleasure of speaking."

Derrick nodded. "That could be true too."

"Then why are you here?"

He took a deep breath. He felt more numb than he thought he would. "We found them yesterday."

"Really?" Her voice cracked slightly as she rubbed her hands together on her desk. "I hope they were all right."

Derrick shook his head. "Not so much."

"And what does this have to do with me?"

"They were residing in your garage," Pele said.

Melissa forced a soft laugh. "They were living in my garage?"

"Not so much. Technically, under the garage," Derrick corrected. "And not really living."

"We found a pink suitcase, with their plane tickets in it," Pele continued. "From 2008."

"I don't know how those things got there. I mean he did live there too. Well, he kept some of his things there. Out in the garage. He moved out someplace else. I don't know where." She glanced back and forth at them. "I haven't had the chance to clean it out since he left."

"You built it after he left," Pele said.

"I, I didn't know if he was coming back. So I may have put some of his things out there. You know. For when he came back. Or called for them."

"Like his silver BMW?" Derrick asked.

"I don't know where that thing is. I thought he took it with him."

"He didn't," Pele replied.

Melissa looked up at her. "He didn't?"

Pele straightened up as she stood there. "I followed you the other night. Up the Pali Highway. Where you ran his BMW off the side of the road."

She laughed nervously. "Why would I do that?"

"I took photos if you'd like to see them. We've got the car at the station. Fingerprints. DNA."

"Oh." She stared down at her hands for a moment then she looked back up at Derrick. "He was going to leave me, Derrick. For that… that no good, airhead waitress half his age." She sat up firm and determined as she clenched her fists on the table. "He was going to destroy everything I had built. My dream that I had worked so hard for. He was just going to walk away and shatter my life." She looked up at Pele and then Derrick. "You understand Derrick. I couldn't let him do that. I just couldn't."

"So the story about the amicable split of resources wasn't true?" Derrick asked.

She took a deep breath. "That was true." She looked back down at her hands. "Well, at first."

"So why kill him? Why not just let him go off with his new girlfriend instead of putting everything you worked so hard to build in jeopardy?"

She looked down as she opened her fists and spread her hands out on the table, palms down. "When Jack lost his job, he lost everything. He had all his money tied up in company stock. I told him that was a stupid thing to do. But would he listen?" She looked up at Derick, "No. Then he said he wanted half of everything I had. The house, my business…" Her whole body shook. "Well. I couldn't let that happen. I just couldn't."

"Type A," Derrick said. There wasn't a glimmer of a tear in her eye.

"Damn straight." She took a deep breath. "Failure is not an option. Not in business. Not in marriage. Not in life."

Derrick stood up and motioned Marsha to step in. "You got that part right."

Pele read Melissa her rights as Marsha put cuffs on her and led her down the hall.

Marsha unlocked the car and opened the back door. Melissa turned back to Derrick. "My only mistake was getting involved with you."

"There might have been a couple of others," Derrick replied.

She turned as Marsha guided her into the back seat and shut the door. The other officer got in behind the wheel.

"That is one cold bitch," Pele said as they watched the patrol car drive off. "What did you ever see in her?"

Derrick shook his head as he watched the patrol car drive off. "Can I claim temporary insanity?"

Derrick glanced over at Pele as they drove along the highway. "Did you find anything on IDC yet?"

"I got with Todd. They are part of a chain of companies I think. He is untangling it. Stop by the station?"

"No. I think we can afford to take an hour off."

She sat there fidgeting. "It just seems like we should be doing more."

"I know. But we can't run 24x7, or we won't be any good to anyone. Anyway, it's not like we're not doing anything."

"We aren't."

"We're waiting. There's a difference."

"Waiting for what? The killer to send us an email?"

"Well, for starters, we've got Kengi working the angle in Japan. The brother, the wife. He's also got that composite drawing from the deckhand." Derrick shrugged. "Such as it is."

"I guess."

"Then we have Ethan in Canada going through Fukuhara's holdings in Vancouver. And I've also got Todd going through the estates of Kagawa and Fukuhara."

"Bet he loves us this holiday."

"And we've subpoenaed the financials for their businesses to see if there is anything else going on. So you see, we're very busy."

"Other people are working while we are waiting."

"I seem to recall you telling me it was delegation."

"So we're taking the rest of the day off."

"Survival of our sanity." He grinned. "Plus, I have the HPD liaison with the military asking if they have misplaced any C4 in the past few weeks. And, I have a meeting set up in the morning with a Lieutenant Carnevalli."

"Isn't he on the gang squad?"

"Yes. I'm hoping he might have some insight to share with us."

"Such as?"

"If there is one killer, he, or she, couldn't have acted alone. They needed help getting a bomb and a gun. At the very least, they didn't carry them through the airports."

She turned to him. "Are you thinking Yakuza?"

"At this point, I'm leaving my options open."

Derrick was making breakfast as Haruku set the table. Pele, still in her dark suit, was pouring juices and teas.

Haruku looked over at her with a big grin. "I am so glad you could join us for breakfast Pele."

"So am I," Kattie added as she pulled her chair out and sat down. "Did you have to shoot the perp this morning? Or did she go peaceably?"

Pele glanced over at her. "We didn't have to shoot anyone."

"How did she take it?" Haruku asked.

"I think at some level she knew it was coming," Derrick said as he cut up the omelet and slid some onto everyone's plate.

"And she didn't try to flee the islands?"

"Not in her nature to walk away."

"All that work she put into her clinic," Pele said as she sat down. "What will happen to it now? They haven't even finished the expansion have they?"

"It's a shame," Haruku said.

Derrick shook his head as he set the plates out on the table. "I have no idea what will happen."

"Will the cats and dogs be homeless now?" Kattie asked.

"They all have owners," Pele said. "They just go there when they are feeling sick."

"I'm starving," Becky said as she ran in and pulled out a chair. "What are we going to do today?"

"It's a holiday today," Derrick said as he put a stack of pancakes out on the table. "Pepper and onion omelet, with a pineapple mango salsa, and pancakes."

"Does that mean you are taking the day off?" Kattie asked.

Derrick glanced over at Haruku. "Yes, it does. At least that's the plan."

Kattie turned to Pele. "Are you taking the day off too?"

"Parts of it."

"And it's fireworks tonight," Haruku said as she set bowls of fruit in front of everyone.

"We see them every Friday night," Kattie said.

"These will be even bigger."

"Where can we see the fireworks?" Derrick asked.

"They have a fantastic display over by Ala Moana. They set them off on Magic Island."

"Is there real magic there?" Becky asked.

Haruku leaned close to her and whispered. "There is if you believe it."

"There is no such thing as magic," Kattie said forcefully.

"Yes, there is," Becky said. "I believe it, so it is true."

Ahulani and Kailani were sitting on folding chairs and reading while guarding prime beach real estate. Three large beach towels were spread wide across the warm sand. Four other towels extended the perimeter for late arrivals. Two large umbrellas were stuck in the sand between them, tilted slightly to the south to block the sun. Pele was sitting in the shade working on her laptop.

"That was awesome," Kattie yelled out as Derrick completed his best run of the morning on the gentle waves.

Haruku was standing in the water as he carried his board toward her. "You might become a surfer dude yet Derrick."

He grinned as he ran his hand over his hair. "Wow. Fulfilling my life's ambition at last."

"Get yourself a woodie and a colorful longboard to strap on top… I can see it now."

They watched as Kattie and Becky stood up and made their takeoffs. "Now they are getting good," he said as they rode up onto the beach.

"Did you see that kuku?" Becky yelled out as she and her sister ran up to the towels and dropped their boards on the sand.

"You were fantastic," Ahulani said as she handed them each a towel to dry off.

"Yes," added Kailani.

"It's time for more sunscreen girls," Haruku said as she and Derrick joined them.

As she helped dry off the girls and got out the sunscreen, Derrick grabbed a towel and sat down next to Pele. "You going to join us?"

She glanced up from her laptop. "I was just going over the police report from Detective Patterson."

"Anything useful?"

"This is my most favorite beach in the whole world," Becky said as she danced around on the blanket.

"It's really eight beaches," Pele said.

"It looks like just one to me," Kattie said as she looked up and down the tourist covered sand.

"Technically, we are at San Souci Beach. It's also a good place to snorkel."

"Can we?" Kattie asked as she turned to Derrick.

He turned to Haruku.

She smiled. "I brought the gear in that bag. Just in case."

"OK. But let's take a break first."

Kattie turned to her sister. "That means he has to do some work first."

"They know you so well," Haruku said as she put the suntan lotion away.

He turned to Pele. "Why don't you join us? You can buddy up with Kattie, and I can take photos."

"Please, Aunt Pele?" Kattie pleaded.

"Fine. But first--"

"Work," Kattie sighed as she turned back to her sister.

"Case solving," Pele said. "If you want to be a policewoman someday you'll learn that it never stops."

"That's no fun."

"We're having fun now aren't we?" Derrick asked.

She smiled a little. "I guess."

Trang peered around a Banyan tree and took a couple of photos.

Bucchi hung back and watched. As he stood there, he noticed a van driving slowly along Kalakaua Avenue. It came to a stop. A man in a dark blue baseball cap got out. He began to walk across the park as the van left. Bucchi watched as he took up a position west of Derrick and the others.

The man took out a camera and began taking pictures in their direction.

Bucchi took out his phone and snapped a few himself. "Now who the hell are you? And who are you watching?" He made a call. "Sorry to call on your day off but I need a favor." He watched as the man walked off. He noticed the van had stopped further down the street. He couldn't track Trang and the new man at the same time. But he did have a device on Trang. And he pretty much knew what he was doing. He followed the new guy. "I'm going to send you some photos. I want you to run them and see if you can identify this man." He stepped between two cars and took a photo of the back of the van. "And run these plates for me while you're at it." He scanned the area. "Thanks, Quon." He slipped his cell back into his pocket. His car was too far away to catch the van. But hopefully, Quon could tell him where to find it.

Derrick turned back to Pele. "What have you got?"

"First, that car we found below Melissa's, Jack's BMW?"

"No murder I hope."

"There was a dead engine. Blown piston. Soto tracked down the last registered owner and cited him. He's facing a big fine and recovery charges."

"I'll bet that just made that guy's day. What else?"

"An email from Patterson. They have no prints at the scene in San Francisco. No one saw or heard anything."

"He could have used a silencer."

"He sent an email to his wife, just before he died, telling her, he would be leaving in the morning to join her on vacation."

"So no indication he knew anyone else was in the house."

Pele shook her head. "The perp went out the front door. And get this. The afternoon paper was missing."

"Maybe he wanted to delay any of the neighbors noticing anything out of the ordinary."

"So how do we know it was the same person that killed Mr. Kagawa?"

"We don't." Derrick put his arms behind him on the blanket and leaned back. "It's a working hypothesis at this point. But one with a high probability."

"There is still a possibility that the wife or the brother had Kagawa killed. We don't know much about Fukuhara yet. Maybe he had his own enemies too?"

"It's possible."

"There are the two different methods for the killings. Kagawa was blown up. Fukuhara was shot."

Derrick nodded. "True."

"Why not just shoot them both if it was the same killer? Wouldn't that make more sense?"

He pushed up and leaned forward. "What if you work for a major crime organization? What if you are an assassin with a reputation to keep? Or build? What if you want to send a message that you can strike anywhere, anytime, and that no one around you is safe?" He turned to Pele. "If you cross us."

"Versatility?"

"Could be."

"What about Tomas and Watanabe?"

"It's been almost two weeks. And they were selling out."

"Trying to. The deal didn't go through."

"True. But I doubt they are in danger."

"What if they planted two other devices that didn't go off yet."

Derrick sat there for a moment then reached for Haruku's handbag. He pulled out his phone. "Hey, Captain. I hate to disturb your holiday."

Chapter 35

Derrick added two more large beach blankets to their territory as Pele and Haruku moved the folding chairs in closer. "You must have done this before."

Haruku grinned. "We grew up here remember? We know how to claim our spot early and mark it out."

"Plan ahead."

"We're going to run over to the store," Pele said as all the girls got up to leave him alone to guard the borders.

Derrick nodded as he sat there reading his eReader in the middle of their territory for the festivities.

"Hi there. We finally made it."

He turned to see Fei juggling two large bags and folding chairs while weaving her way around three children burying their older brother in the sand.

"There are one cooler and a couple of more bags," Quon said as he navigated through the crowd dragging a large blue cooler on almost useless wheels through the soft sand.

Derrick jumped up. "Let me give you a hand with that Fei."

"This is an excellent spot," Quon said as he looked around the beach.

Derrick set Fei's bags down near the edge. "I'll help you get the rest when the girls all get back Quon. Haruku and Pele said we could see fireworks from a couple of places from this spot."

"Have you been here all day?" Fei asked as she set down two plastic webbed beach chairs.

"We staked our claim early."

"And they left you guarding the spot?"

"I'm a Lieutenant. I've got to be good for something." He helped Fei unfold the chairs. "The girls all went to get dinner and bring it back."

"We brought a few items as well. I've got some things that Kattie and Becky enjoyed when we visited China Town."

"An international Fourth of July picnic," Derrick said.

"How did things go this morning?" Quon asked as they all sat down around the edges.

"As well as could be expected I guess."

"That had to be difficult," Fei added.

"I had Pele with me." He turned to Quon. "So Quon. Are you Doctor Li yet?"

"I am hoping next week. After the holiday."

"We'll have to celebrate when we get back."

"Right. You are taking the girls home in a few days."

"Will Haruku be going with you?" Fei asked.

"Pele. We have a couple of cases with ties to the area. Thought we'd do some digging around for a couple of days while we're there."

"How are you doing with that boat that blew up?" Fei asked.

"Ahhh. That reminds me. Quon, what do you know about something called the Blue Line Report?"

"An environmental study released several months ago."

"Any validity to it?"

"Absolutely." He stretched his legs out in front of him to keep a curious gull at bay. "The globe is warming on average. The sea level is rising. Some islands in the Pacific are already in real trouble."

"The melting ice sheets," Fei said.

"Not just that," Quon said. "There is also thermal expansion."

"Thermal expansion?" she asked. "What's that?"

Derrick leaned back propping himself up on his outstretched arms. "As the oceans warm up the molecules of water vibrate faster causing them to expand. And on the giant scale of an ocean, that means rising sea levels. Even without factoring in melting ice."

Quon looked over at Derrick.

"I know things."

"You are correct. And while the water takes longer to heat than land, its effects can be greater. With the oceans, it could even exceed the melting ice. Depending on how warm the air above the water gets."

"Anything else?" Derrick asked.

Quon shrugged. "Like what?"

"Do you think it could be used for predicting future investments?"

"Investments in what?" Fei asked.

Derrick looked around the beach. "Oh, I don't know. Say real estate?"

Quon sat back as he scanned the beach. "Well, depending which models you like, where we are sitting will be underwater in the next fifty to one hundred years. Sooner if things get warmer faster."

"And if they don't?"

"This is new territory," Quon said. "But a guess the wrong way could cost trillions of dollars and disrupt the world economy."

"So let's say someone was looking to buy a piece of land that could be beachfront property in the future, now might be the time to buy?"

Quon laughed. "I guess." He sat there thinking for a moment. "I suppose if you were to find a location that had a rather gentle slope over a relatively long distance… you could maximize your potential for having a great place as the seas rose. One that could factor in a range of possible levels in sea level rise."

Derrick sat there thinking. "I see."

"But you'd better factor in storm surge as well. Most people forget about that variable."

"Why the sudden interest in global warming?" Fei asked.

"I'm not sure yet. But just suppose such a piece of property existed…"

"I am certain they do," Quon said. "And they could be worth a lot of money for those looking to the future."

"Enough to kill for?" Derrick asked.

Fei laughed. "Don't you two think that's a bit extreme? I mean to kill someone for something that may be more valuable in the future?"

Derrick looked over at Quon.

Quon shrugged. "If it were in a location that was good today, and might be even better in the future… it could happen."

Her mouth dropped open. "Really?"

There was a knock at the door. Mary Kobayashi opened it.

A tall man flashed a badge. "I am Captain Leland Berry with the HPD. We have been asked to do a search of your property and vehicles ma'am."

"Why? By who?"

"A Lieutenant Dreadlow."

Mary turned to the living room. "Tomas. Could you come to the door please." Tomas came to the door. "Do you know anything about this?"

"Oh yes. I didn't think you would be here so fast. It's just a security precaution honey."

"Are we in some kind of danger Tomas?"

He smiled reassuringly. "No. Derrick just thought it might be a good idea to do some random checks."

"A random check on our family? Why would we be in danger?"

"There is no real threat. Just some holiday Homeland Security chatter regarding prominent families."

"We're hardly a prominent family."

He let the officers in. "Just a precaution dear. Nothing to worry about. The garage is through there." He pointed to a doorway down the hall. "I think it was nice of Derrick to keep us in mind. Don't you?"

"Did you get good pictures of me?" Becky asked as Derrick and the girls strolled up onto the beach after a half hour of snorkeling.

"I've got great pictures of all of you," he assured them.

"Even Aunt Pele and those yellow fish?" Kattie asked.

"Even the Longnose Butterfly fish."

"Hey there," Todd called out as they approached their growing crowd on the beach.

"Glad you could make it," Derrick said as Haruku handed him a towel.

"Got a minute for a stroll?"

"I guess. Anything in particular?"

"Pele, you might want to join us," Todd said as she wrapped herself in the large towel.

"Talk to us," Derrick said as they made their way along the surf.

"IDC."

"You found something?" Pele asked.

"The company Kagawa was working with was IDC Hawaii. It appears to be a subsidiary of Hawk Limited. Another company that is part of another holding company owned by IDC International."

Derrick watched the surf flow out around his toes. "That's a mouthful. Any names of actual people?"

"One man that I've run across before. But we've never been able to pin anything on him."

"And he is?"

"Daisuke Mayeda."

Derrick stopped in his tracks. The surf swept up and around his feet. "Daisuke Mayeda. An older man? Short white hair? Cold eyes?"

"You know him?"

"Derrick had dinner with him the other night," Pele said.

Todd's eyebrow went up. "Dinner?"

Derrick nodded. "Social event of the year."

"Ah yes." Todd grinned as he glanced over at Pele. "I think I saw some pictures in the paper about that."

"It wasn't my fault," Pele said as she wrapped the towel tighter around herself.

Marcus was sitting at the edge of a rooftop party. Guests were watching the fireworks displays across the beaches below.

A man in a blue baseball cap strolled over to him with a drink in his hand.

Marcus took a sip of his Chivas Brothers Royal Salute. "Georgio used to like to watch the fireworks from up here." He stared out over the streets and beaches below. "Any news?"

"It seems she will be going to New York City in a few days."

He took another sip as he remained focused on the view in front of him. He grinned. "Really?"

"Word is that she will be going there with her partner. To do some investigating on a case they are working on."

Marcus grinned. "Let's make sure that something finds her." He took another sip.

"Shall I continue to follow her?"

"No. But be sure that someone follows her when she gets to the Big Apple."

"That won't be a problem." The man in the cap finished his drink and headed out the door.

Bucchi leaned back against a palm tree as he spoke on his cell. "I can't say for sure Norton. It could've been Haruku, Derrick or hell... Even Pele."

"Were there other people on the beach?"

He laughed. "It's the Fourth of July. It was packed."

"Then how can you be sure the man was watching one of them?"

"Years of experience."

"OK, Bucchi. Let me know when you find out who it was."

"You want me to ask them why?"

"Let's answer the who first." She paused. "What about Trang?"

"You'd think he didn't have a day job."

"I've got a team on Hollister. Let's just play along for now."

"You got it, boss." He flipped his cell shut and disappeared into the crowd.

"Those were the best fireworks ever," Becky said. The slight scent of smoke filled the air as it drifted across the beaches.

"Thanks for inviting us," Todd said as he and his family helped Eito and the others begin their cleanup.

"Yes," Kali added as she and Soto helped with the cleanup.

Soto stepped up behind Derrick. "Nice to get a call that's not about work."

"I'm glad you all could make it," Derrick replied. "I figured I owed you for the last couple of days."

"Can we see these fireworks again next year Uncle Derrick?" Kattie asked as she jumped around Derrick and Soto.

"We will have to ask your mother and father about that."

"Can we Uncle Derrick?" Becky chimed in.

"We'll see."

Pele slipped her cell into her pocket as she stepped up to Derrick. Haruku watched as her sister leaned in close to him. "That was Captain Berry. Tomas's office, house, and vehicles are all clear."

"And Watanabe?"

"He's clear as well."

"Good." Derrick knelt down by Kattie and Becky. "I think it's time to get you two home and to bed."

"We're not tired," Becky said.

"Have you ever gone surfing at night?" Kattie asked as Pele and Haruku folded the beach towels.

"Only when there was a full moon," Haruku said.

"Can we try it?"

"I'm afraid we won't have the chance this trip," Haruku said.

"We'll be back," Becky said confidently.

"How do you know?" Kattie asked.

"I just know."

"You also have to watch for sharks," Pele said.

Becky's eyes grew large. "Sharks?"

Kattie turned to her with raised arms. "They can gulp you down in one bite."

"One bite?"

"Uh huh," Kattie teased.

"By next year I'll be bigger."

By the time they walked the few blocks back to the condo, Derrick was carrying both sleeping girls in his arms.

Haruku unlocked the door and pushed it open. Derrick stepped in and headed straight for the bedroom while Pele helped Haruku put everything in the kitchen.

"I am glad you came today," Haruku said as she led Pele back to the front door.

Pele nodded. "It was fun. Thank you for inviting me."

Derrick popped his head around the corner. "Don't forget. Carnevalli at eight." He hesitated. "Oh. Did you get that info from Aneko's office?"

"Yes."

"OK. Let's go through it at 6:30." He waved. "I'll bring breakfast." He disappeared to get the girls to bed.

"He never slows down does he?" Pele said.

Haruku reached out and gave her sister a hug. "Only when he collapses on the couch."

Chapter 36

Pele clicked on her laptop switching the image to another group of people as she and Derrick watched the screen in the second-floor police station conference room.

"Morning," Captain Henderson greeted as he stepped into the room, coffee in hand. "I trust that you're not claiming all this as vacation time."

Derrick looked up as they went through the images from the party and finished their breakfast. "Not now."

"Good." He looked over at the plastic screen as he took a sip. "Home shots from the party?"

"More like mug shots," Derrick said.

Captain Henderson took a couple more steps into the room for a closer look. "So I'm not the only one questioning the guest list?"

"Guess not."

"Where did we get the photos? Press?"

"Some from the press, and some home shots thanks to Pele."

Captain Henderson took a sip of his coffee as he stood there watching. "The more interesting ones no doubt."

"I was just curious," she said as they looked at the screen from the table where her Uncle Marcus sat.

"Who's that? I recognize the face." Captain Henderson asked as he pulled out a chair and sat down.

"Probably from a mug shot," Pele said.

"Pele's uncle. Uncle Marcus." Derrick said.

She glanced over at him.

"Haruku told me about him."

"A shadowy figure reputed to be mob connected," the captain said as he took a sip. "And on the watch list of the Chief."

"Along with all the Kobayashi," she added as she clenched her jaw.

Derrick exhaled as he nodded. "Now that explains a few things."

Captain Henderson grinned like a Cheshire cat. "Even paradise has its secrets Lieutenant." He glanced over at Derrick. "As do people everywhere I suspect."

Derrick tipped his cup then took another sip. "Makes life interesting now doesn't it?"

"Indeed." The captain looked down at the list, and the diagrams of seating arrangements spread out on the table. "And what have we here?"

"Randomness, patterns... clues perchance?" Derrick commented.

Captain Henderson poked his finger over them. "You think there was a purpose to the seating arrangements?"

Derrick set his cup down and picked up a page at random. "Bink and Lady Westfield. Just happen to be sitting with people involved in charity work."

"She's big on that?" Captain Henderson asked as he glanced at the page. He reached out and picked up another. "What about this one?"

Derrick took it. It was Pele's table. "An upper-crust family, been on the island for generations. A wannabe upper crust, and..."

"A man whose shipping company is suspected of money laundering. But can never be caught at it," Pele finished.

"Really?" Derrick asked.

Captain Henderson picked up another sheet. This one had Derrick at the table. He put it on the table between Derrick and Pele.

She brought up the same photo on the large screen.

"Ahh. Mr. Daisuke Mayeda. A rising star in society. Charity work. Chamber of Commerce. And one slimy bastard according to some."

Everyone turned.

A rather tall, lean, but muscular man was leaning against the doorjamb. The tanned skin on his shiny bald head twitched as he spoke. His close eyebrows furrowed as he stared down at the image. He reached up and ran a finger across a thin mustache and the thin line of a close-cropped beard under his chin. The diamond earring in his left ear glistened as he stepped into the room.

He bent over slightly as he pulled out a chair. A silver chain with a small silver and black Iron Cross swung off his black T-shirt and momentarily hung out of his black leather jacket. A bit much for a warm morning Derrick thought. But he showed no sign of being hot.

Derrick sat back and watched as the man sat down. "You must be Lieutenant Carnevalli."

"You said you needed my help." He glanced over at the image of Mayeda. "I can see why."

"Hello, Dan." Captain Henderson gave a slight nod.

"Captain."

"So you have had dealings with Mr. Mayeda?" Derrick asked.

Carnevalli sat there expressionless.

Captain Henderson leaned forward. "We've never been able to pin anything on this guy. He is the CEO of a company called Hawk Limited."

"Subsidiary of IDC International and holding company of IDC Hawaii."

Captain Henderson tipped his coffee cup to Derrick. "You've been doing your homework Lieutenant."

"But you know he is dirty?" Pele asked.

"I can smell it." Carnevalli turned to Derrick. "What do you have on him?"

"A scent." Derrick picked up his coffee and sat back. "A coply twinge."

The captain laughed. "Smelling and twingeing won't build a case detectives."

"I received a word of caution," Derrick said as he reached for his coffee. "While attending the social event of the year."

"From who?" Captain Henderson asked.

Derrick took a sip. "A source."

"And did this source say anything useful?"

Derrick snorted. "Not really."

"Then why do you suspect him of anything?" Pele asked.

Derrick took another sip. "I was told that the islands were in a struggle. There are people who are going to divide them up unless they are stopped."

"And we are going to stop them?" Captain Henderson asked.

"That's the hope. We are the stabilizing force. We are the balance."

Captain Henderson shook his head. "Not something we can take to the DA either."

"There is a war coming."

Carnevalli turned to Derrick. "It's already here."

"So we have front row seats to a war?" Pele asked.

"No," Derrick said. "I think we are center stage."

Captain Henderson stood up. "Well until we have something a bit more concrete folks. Let's just solve the cases we have today. With real evidence that we can take to the DA." He turned and walked out of the room.

Carnevalli sat back and looked over at Derrick and Pele. "You didn't invite me to look through family albums."

Derrick nodded. "I want to know who can make bombs on this island. C4 bombs with sophisticated electronic triggers."

"And might work with the Yakuza," Pele added.

For the first time, Carnevalli cracked an ever so slight smile.

FBI Agent Bucchi grinned as he scanned the cafeteria at the University of Hawaii. He sat back and spread his arms out as though he owned the place. "I can see why you like to teach here. And have coffee in the morning."

Two stunning coeds turned and smiled at him as they strolled past in their shorts and tank tops. A third paused for a moment. "Good morning Professor."

Quon smiled. "Hello, Chris."

"If I were you, Quon, I'd ditch the lab work and stick to teaching the young minds of tomorrow."

Quon shrugged as he glanced around at the students in the room.

"This sure beats the hell out of being stuck down in some basement."

"I have a girlfriend now."

"And I own the car of my dreams. Doesn't mean I can't look at the showroom floor." Another co-ed winked from a nearby table. He raised his coffee cup in salute then took a drink. "Reminds me of a case I did at the University of Miami a few years back."

"What was it about?"

Bucchi sat there in total bliss. "Huh? What? The case?"

"Yes."

"Oh hell, man. I don't remember. It was the experience. The rush." He winked at the girl at the table. "The atmosphere."

"I have the information you asked for," Quon said.

Bucchi set his cup down. "Yea. Right. So who are they?"

"I traced the vehicle to the B&C detective agency."

Bucchi looked over at him. "Got names?"

"Rosco Baldwin and Marvin Cantor."

"Good work."

"Who are they? What are they doing?"

"Good questions." Bucchi finished his coffee and stood up. "Good luck with your finals Professor."

"My dissertation." Quon looked up at him. "Does this have anything to do with Derrick?"

"I'll talk to you later." He pulled out his cell as he strolled out of the cafeteria like a celebrity. He could turn on the charm when he wanted, and he could lurk in the shadows when he needed. This was an occasion for charm and style. "Hey. I need you to run down anything you got on a B&C Detective Agency."

Chapter 37

Derrick and Pele looked out of place in their custom Italian suits as they sat in Carnevalli's black '68 Dodge Charger with chrome wheels and a finish that you could eat off of.

Carnevalli pulled into a strip mall just off the Nimitz Highway. There was a liquor store on one side and an Instant Loan Pawnshop on the other. A couple of other small shops rounded out the mall. A few cars were in the lot.

"How was the ride?" Derrick asked as he held the door open so Pele could crawl out of the back seat.

"Snug."

Carnevalli was silent as they walked up to the appliance repair shop by the liquor store.

Derrick leaned toward Pele. "I could sit in the back next time."

"Trust me. You wouldn't fit."

Carnevalli shoved the door open. Derrick and Pele followed.

"Well well. Lieutenant Dan." The older man peered around him and stared at Derrick and Pele. "I see you're trying to keep better company these days."

Carnevalli stepped up to the counter. He reached out for the small red dish filled with individually wrapped mints and turned it upside down. "What about you Slider? What kind of company are you keeping?"

Slider picked up the candies and put them back in the glass. "The kind who pay their bills. The kind that brings their kids in here."

"You going soft in your old age?"

Slider stood up as straight as he could. They could see he was favoring his left leg. He noticed Derrick and Pele staring at him. "Old war injury."

"Nam?" Derrick asked.

"Nicaragua. Never happened, though."

"Cut the crap Slider. Have you been a busy boy lately?" Carnevalli stepped up to the counter and leaned in as close as he could get without crawling over the top.

"I don't do that kind of stuff anymore." He glanced over at Pele. "Those days are over. I ain't got much time left. I don't want to spend it in jail."

Carnevalli stepped back a pace. "So who might be active?"

Slider shrugged. "I don't know. I keep my nose clean. Hear nothing. See nothing."

"And speak nothing." Carnevalli turned and walked out.

"Have a nice day," Pele said. She and Derrick followed him out the door.

"Wasn't he a bit hard on the old guy?" Pele asked as they walked back to the car.

Derrick took a deep breath as he pulled out his Maui Jims and slipped them on. "Nature of the beast."

The video conference screen came on. Agent Bucchi and Assistant U.S. Attorney Victoria Holt were sitting at the long conference table in the Honolulu Department of Justice Center.

"Good morning," began the blond-haired woman in a dark blue business suit on the screen. "Good to see both of you again."

"How are you, Karen?" Victoria asked.

"Busy. I didn't expect to be hearing from you two this soon."

"Any word on the Dreadlow case?" DA Holt asked as she folded her hands in front of her.

"You know the government is slow on these matters Victoria."

"Derrick's lawyer isn't."

"I'm sure Derrick understands even if his lawyer doesn't." Agent Norton turned to Bucchi. "So what do you have that is so urgent Agent Bucchi?"

He smiled. "Well, Special Agent in Charge..." He touched a key on the laptop in front of them. Two photos and bio information appeared on the right side of the screen. "These men are with the B&C Detective Agency."

"These are the people possibly following Derrick, or Haruku, or Pele?"

Bucchi nodded. "I can use a bit of help if I am to track these new players as well."

Karen grinned. "And here I thought I was working with Superman."

"Even Superman couldn't be in six places at once."

Agent Norton sat back and thought for a moment. "I've already got a team on Hollister. You on the people following Dreadlow. This is a lot of resources for a line that may not go anywhere."

Victoria leaned slightly forward. "It does beg the question though Karen. Why is there so much interest in these people? Derrick has been cleared of any involvement with his wife's activities or her death. But Hollister seems to believe otherwise for some reason. Someone did attack Haruku. It is my understanding that Derrick and Pele are still pursuing that."

"So you think there is more at play here than meets the eye?"

"Something is going on."

"Hollister is a good agent," Bucchi said. "But not that good. There is a reason, or a person egging him on behind his actions."

"OK, Bucchi. I will assign two more agents to help you. For three weeks. And I want a weekly review."

Bucchi nodded. "I'd like a warrant to search the office of this BC Agency. Just shake things up a bit. See what falls out. You know, if I've only got a couple of weeks."

"Not yet. If there is something, we don't want to spook them. What about Trang?"

"Derrick gave me a camera that he took from Trang as he was following them."

"Who's them?"

"Haruku and his goddaughters."

"What were the photos of?"

"Derrick, Haruku, and some close-up shots of the girls."

"What is he up to?"

"I don't know. But Pele also told me of photos he sent to Derrick's ex. Pictures of Haruku in, shall we say unflattering positions. His ex even flew out here to take the girls away."

"But she didn't?"

"No."

Karen sat back as she thought for a moment. "Do a background check on this Trang."

"I've already started. But he is a cop. The partner to Perkins who was helping Hollister. I think Trang is now the one helping Hollister."

"Why would Hollister be interested in Haruku?"

"I think Trang is a loose cannon."

"I'll get you authorization."

"And what if IA gets wind of it here?"

"We'll deal with that if it happens."

Chapter 38

"Dreadlow." Derrick watched the traffic out the side window as he, Pele, and Carnevalli made their way to a place in Pearl City. "Ethan. How are you? Have you come up with anything?" Derrick turned toward the back and turned on the speakerphone. "I'm in the car with Pele. Got you on speaker."

"Hi Pele."

"Hey Ethan. Do you have anything useful for us?" she asked as she leaned forward.

"I think so. This Fukuhara was known to the police here in Vancouver and has a file at Interpol as well."

"Victim or perp?"

"Victim."

"Yakuza?" Derrick asked.

"Suspected. It seems they wormed their way into his condos and hotel here through an outsourcing deal with a company called--"

"IDC?" Derrick interrupted.

"Right you are again."

"Anyone able to build a case against them?" Derrick asked.

"No. All we have are unconfirmed reports. I think intimidation was involved. And it seems to be effective."

Pele looked up at Derrick. "Anyone, anywhere?"

He nodded. "Seems to fit."

"Have you got something on them?" Ethan asked.

"We're working an angle," Derrick said.

"For what it's worth, this Fukuhara tried to stand up to them. Let's wish him luck."

Derrick shook his head as he glanced out of the car. "Too late."

"Why? What happened?"

"He was killed. Assassination style."

"These are brutal people Derrick. Watch your back. And let me know if you come up with anything we can use to crack their hold on their victims."

"Will do." Derrick hung up. He stared over at Carnevalli as he slipped his phone back into his pocket. "Don't I know you from somewhere?"

Carnevalli cracked a wide grin. "It took you long enough Dread."

"Sergeant Dan Carnevalli. You were gang back then too."

"Out of the 102nd."

"How long have you been in paradise?"

"A little over four years now. You?"

Derrick turned to Pele. "What? About five, six months?"

"The first month you were on vacation," she added.

"You like it here?" Derrick asked.

"It's OK. Warmer winters."

Pele sat back in her seat. "Is there anybody you don't know Dread?"

"The inner players of the Yakuza."

A few minutes later, they pulled up in front of an aging diner. The paint was peeling off the warped slab siding. A few of the bulbs on the marquee were missing, and grass grew through cracks in what remained of the sidewalk.

"They can still serve food here?" Pele asked as they walked up to the door.

"It's what's on the inside that counts," Derrick replied as he held the door open for them.

Three people at the counter and several sitting in the booths watched them as they entered.

"I think we're overdressed," Pele said.

"What can I get you?" the plump server in a stained white dress asked as they stepped up to the end of the counter. She pulled a stump of a pencil from the gray bun of hair stuffed under a black net.

Carnevalli scanned the kitchen area through the pass-through counter. "Gilroy in?"

"Who's askin?"

"You back there Fry!"

A man with tanned and weathered skin peered around the corner. His pale blue-gray eyes scanned them. "What the f do you want Car?"

"Got time for a friendly chat?"

"You don't know the meaning of the word friendly." He stepped around to the doorway, eyeing Derrick and Pele as he walked up behind the counter. "What do you want?"

"My friends here would like to know if you've been cooking up anything special in the back lately."

Fry turned and stared at Pele. "You look too good for the likes of this vermin." Gilroy turned to Derrick. "You late for a board meeting or something?"

Derrick pulled out his badge. "I'm Lieutenant Dreadlow. This is my partner, Detective Kobayashi. We'd like to ask you a few questions. If you've got a minute."

"He's the boss and owner," Carnevalli said as he sat down on a stool. "He's got the time."

"You want some coffee?" Gilroy asked.

"Black," Derrick replied.

"Anyone else?"

Pele and Carnevalli shook their heads.

Carnevalli poked his finger at the chrome napkin holder. "This is Gilroy Fry. A.k.a, The Cook."

"The fry cook?" Pele asked innocently.

A smirk crossed Gilroy's face as he and Carnevalli engaged in a brief but intense stare down. "Demolition and explosives training."

"What branch?" Derrick asked.

"Army. The Rangers." Gilroy turned to Derrick. "And when something is in the wind he always comes to me."

"Among others," Carnevalli added.

"And that always makes me a suspect?"

"No. But a couple of jobs off the record in Iraq and Saint Louis does."

"I did my time. I got a new life here."

Carnevalli glanced around the diner. "And how's that working out for you?"

"It's a living. An honest living."

Derrick picked up his coffee and took a sip. "We're looking for a guy who might have been looking for someone to make a bomb for him."

"What kind of bomb?"

"C4. Custom trigger."

"What kind of trigger?"

"Let's just say it wasn't an egg timer." Derrick took another sip. "Good coffee."

"Good food too. You like some?"

"We ate before coming here." Derrick set his coffee down. "Anyone come here asking for something like that?"

Gilroy's shoulders stiffened. His eyes narrowed as his gaze darted from Derrick to Carnevalli and back again. "Sorry. Can't help you."

"If I find out you've been obstructing justice, Gilroy…" Carnevalli stood up. "I'll be back. With a health inspector."

"I run a clean place Car."

Carnevalli waved as he walked out.

Derrick slipped a five spot on the counter. "Later."

Gilroy nodded as he reached out for the five and slipped it into his pocket.

"Next?" Carnevalli asked as they got back into the car.

"Let's finish this up in the morning. I've got a few other things I need to check out with Interpol first. But while I'm doing that, perhaps you can get together a list of names and photos of any gang members that either are, or are suspected outsourced soldiers for the Yakuza."

"You got it."

Derrick, Pele, and Todd were sitting in one of the conference rooms at the station. The door was closed.

"The estates of these two are interesting," Todd said.

"How so?" Derrick asked.

"The business went to Etsuo's brother. Lock, stock, and barrel."

"His wife Azami was cut out?" Pele asked.

"She keeps the house. Which is paid for. Also, she gets the furniture, the car, one point three million, and the boat."

She laughed. "So much for the boat."

Todd shrugged.

Derrick snorted. "Given what's going on with the brothers and the business she might be lucky."

"Be my guess too," Todd said.

"How much was the business worth?" Derrick asked.

Todd looked down at his notes. "Etsuo's share was down to about seventeen million. After debts."

"Out of?"

"Seventy-three million. The valuation of the hotel and the land."

"Who owns the rest?"

Todd looked over at him. "IDC."

"How did that happen?"

"Renovations, oddly set up contracts with suppliers, links back to the hotel in Japan..."

"I thought they divided the family business?" Pele said.

"The trail is a bit of a..."

"Clusterfuck?"

Todd looked up at her and grinned.

"I took a forensic business accounting class in college."

"Some class."

Derrick sat back. "Isn't that interesting? No wonder they were taking so long to get that deal done. I'll bet his Japanese partners saw an opportunity to take the whole thing."

"What about Fukuhara?" Pele asked.

"The same. But not as far along." Todd looked at his notes. "He seems to have been fighting them, trying to regain more control of his company."

"Maybe Kagawa grew a set of balls too," Derrick said. "And what does the Fukuhara family get?"

"The family keeps the house, other vacation property, cars, etc. Three-point seven million in cash, stocks, and bonds. Not in the business."

"And their share of the business itself?" Derrick asked.

"They still retain about sixty-five percent of four hundred and thirty-five million."

"Anyway to help them regain what they've lost?" Derrick asked.

"I'll go over it with your friends in Interpol as well." Todd made a note. "What about Mrs. Kagawa? Should we try to help her as well?"

"I'll ask her. But I have a feeling she may just let her brother-in-law have the business and the headaches."

"Probably just as well. From my initial talks with the financial forensics people in Tokyo, I'd say the Kagawa empire in riddled with IDC tentacles. They may be too far gone."

Derrick turned to Pele. "We should verify that your brother is clear of their influence."

"And Watanabe?" she asked.

Derrick nodded. "We want to keep these people out of paradise."

"How do we do that with Kagawa's hotel already pretty much under their control?" Todd asked.

Derrick sat back. "Good question. We may need to involve the FBI and the IRS in that."

"That will take a while."

"We've got to start somewhere."

Back at their desks, Derrick was flipping through the set of notes Todd had left them. He reached for his coffee. "It looks like after IDC gains a foothold, they get their contractors in, bleed their partners dry, then take over for a song."

Pele turned to Derrick. "Where does that leave Tomas and Watanabe?"

"And the Pahonu Knoll Project?" Derrick added.

"Yes."

"My gut guess… is they will probably be made an offer that your brother and Watanabe can't refuse." He sat back in his chair. "Unless we can turn a light on this so bright that they run and hide under the nearest rock they can find."

"How do we do that?"

"Talk with Interpol in Japan and Canada as well. Have Todd work with the FBI and the IRS to come up with a creative plan."

"It's getting late. Shouldn't you be getting back to the girls? They've only got a couple of days left here."

"Right. Let me know if you come up with anything."

"I'll take you back."

"So what's the thing with Carnevalli?" Pele asked as she pulled up outside the condo to drop Derrick off. "Why is he so…"

"Bad cop?"

"Yeah."

Derrick reached for the door handle and began to open the door, then sat back. "I never worked with him myself. But I did know of him."

"He a good cop?"

"The best at what he did."

"Which was gangs?" She put her car into park as they sat there. "What happened?"

"He was undercover. Deep. He almost single-handedly built a case against this Jamaican gang. A ruthless bunch." The door hung open a crack.

"Did he get the gang?"

Derrick nodded. "In the end. But not the way he set out to."

Derrick took a long slow breath as he stared out into space. "They tried to intimidate Dan. Make him change his story. Make evidence disappear."

"But he didn't go along with it?"

"No. Like I said. Dan's a good cop. Good to have watching your back."

"But he finally got them?"

"Sort of. But not before they brutally murdered his wife and seven-year-old son." Derrick pushed the door open.

"That's terrible." She stared over at Derrick. "What did you mean he got them sort of?"

"Dan and his team arrested some of them. Their lawyer got them all out on bail."

"Even after…"

"There wasn't any solid proof yet that the ones in jail were responsible. And the evidence they did have disappeared."

"And?"

"There was a gun battle. The gang on one side, Dan and seven officers on the other."

"And?"

"Dan and five of the other officers are still with us." Derrick slid out, leaned over, and looked at her. "Apopo." He closed the door.

"Tomorrow," she said softly as she slipped the car back into gear and drove away.

Chapter 39

Derrick and Pele were sitting in a booth having an early breakfast of ham and eggs with homemade biscuits as dawn emerged into a new day. Pele had her laptop by the end of the table and turned on.

"How was your afternoon with the girls?" she asked.

"We went snorkeling at Hanauma Bay again."

"They must like it there."

"I think Becky wants to move there and live with the sea turtles."

Gilroy, the Fry Cook, walked up to them and sat down at their booth.

"Good food," Derrick said as he picked up his coffee cup. "Got a minute for a chat?"

"I figured that's why you came back."

Derrick drank some coffee then set his cup down. "So Gilroy. Was anyone in here asking questions?"

Gilroy looked around. "Yeah. Some kid."

"A kid?" Pele asked.

"No more than twenty. Vietnamese."

Pele took a bite then turned to her laptop and punched a few keys.

"And?" Derrick asked as he took a bite.

"He came in about two, maybe three weeks ago. Acting tough. A chip on his shoulder type. Asking questions. Trying to impress me. Maybe scare me."

"You scared of him?"

"Little pissant." Gilroy grinned. "He was like something out of an old B movie. All I could do to stop from laughing in his face."

Derrick reached for his coffee. "Doesn't make him less dangerous."

Gilroy shook his head. "No."

"Was he looking for something special?"

"He gave me some specs. But I told him I didn't do that kind of work."

"What were the specs?"

"Electronic. Way over this kids head, that's for sure."

"Did he give a name?"

"It's not like people leave a business card in the bowl on the counter for this line of work."

"Would you recognize him if you saw him again?" Pele asked.

"Probably."

She turned her laptop toward him. Eight images were showing.

Gilroy shook his head. Pele went to the next page. He shook his head again. Four pages later, he leaned in close. "That's him." He pointed to the third from the left on the bottom row. He got up. "I've got orders to go."

"Thanks," Derrick said as he headed back to the kitchen.

Pele clicked on his photo. "Sebastian Luc. Nineteen. Member of the Dyong gang."

"I'm sure Dan can fill us in when we meet him in…" Derrick glanced at the clock on the wall. "Crap. Thirty minutes. We'd better finish up here, or we'll be late."

Four hours later, they pulled up in front of a small house in a stand of trees on the edge of Kane'ohe. Derrick and Pele got out of his black E350 as Carnevalli jumped out of his black Charger. They all had their hands on their guns as they surveyed the scene. There was a small house just off to the right of the dirt driveway. On the left sat a two-car garage with no doors. A pickup on blocks and an old Fiesta were on the side. At the end was a twenty by twenty, steel work shed. A radio was playing oldies from the eighties inside.

Derrick motioned for Pele to circle around back. He took the front. Carnevalli covered a side door. When they were all in position, Derrick leaned to his left and knocked on the door.

There was no reply. He knocked again.

The door opened. A tall, scruffy man with long red hair and a ragged red beard down to his chest stepped out. "What the f…" He stared down at the gun pointed up at his head.

"I'm Lieutenant Dreadlow. These are my associates, Lieutenant Carnevalli and Detective Kobayashi. We've got some questions for you."

Pele pulled out a piece of paper. "And a warrant to search the premises." She handed it to him then got on her radio to the others. "We're clear."

Three patrol cars and two forensics vans pulled in. Doors flew open, and people swarmed all over the property.

"What the hell do you think you're doing?"

Carnevalli slipped his gun into his holster, whipped out a set of cuffs, spun the man around, and slammed him into the wall. "Red Cleaver. You're under arrest for terrorism, accessory to murder, theft, receiving stolen property… should I go on?"

"I haven't done anything you f…"

"I've got traces of C4 here," a tech said.

"And these look like plans for a device of some kind," an AFT agent added.

Pele handed them to Derrick. "This looks like the trigger we found."

Carnevalli shoved a photo in front of Red's face. "You know this man?"

Red shook his head as he scowled. "I want my lawyer."

"No problem. I think we've already got enough on you. And when we find Sebastian's prints here…" Derrick smiled at Red. "Well, I'm sure you get the picture."

Derrick, Pele, and Carnevalli stood outside as the tech's swarmed all over the house and the outbuildings.

"What made you pick this guy?" Pele asked.

Carnevalli shrugged. "Instinct."

"Coply hunch?" She glanced over at Derrick.

Carnevalli nodded. "That and I went through the files of the last three probable suspects last night. Dishonorable discharge. Problems with authority. Divorced."

"Those connected?" Pele asked.

Carnevalli shrugged. "Wife ran off with some rich dentist. A couple of arrests for assault. Red seemed like a good choice."

Joyce walked up to them. "We've got prints and several tire tracks around here. Well make casts and see if any match Luc's car."

"The prints Luc's?" Derrick asked.

She nodded then went back inside.

Derrick nodded. "Good work Joyce."

"How can the army train people like this?" Pele asked as he tried to fight the officers putting him into the back of the patrol car.

Carnevalli turned to her. "You'd be surprised at who they teach. And what they teach them. It'll keep you awake at night."

Chapter 40

"How was lunch with the girls?" Pele asked as she picked him up outside the condo.

"Too short."

She pulled out onto Kuhio. "Oh. I got an email from Kengi."

"And?"

"They've got a possible match on that composite we sent them."

"Anyone interesting?"

"Itsuki Hayakawa. He is a suspected assassin for the Yakuza." She stopped for a light. "They are looking for him now for questioning."

He smiled as he watched a husband and wife trying to juggle bags, an umbrella, and three young boys toward the beach. "The pieces are falling into place."

Derrick and Pele sat across the desk from Tomas. They were in his third-floor office at the family's Grand Tiki Resort.

"So this DA has tied up the sale now?" Tomas asked as he sat back. "For how long? I have several million dollars tied up in this."

"You also have your life," Pele said.

"This investigation into underworld business dealings in the resort industry covers the west coast, Japan, and Canada as well," Derrick added.

"But we need your help," Pele continued.

"How?"

Derrick sat back. "Information. Cooperation."

"I could lose a lot."

"It doesn't mean you or Watanabe will lose your money. But it does mean that with the bright light being focused on this, no one in their right mind would try to harm you or your family now."

"So what happens? They just crawl back under the rocks and wait for another opportunity?"

"That's possible. But we are doing everything we can to stop them." Derrick shifted in his chair. "And Senator Aneko is working on a bill to try to keep companies with ties to the underworld out of the Hawaiian tourist business."

Tomas laughed. "Where there is money to be made, there are ways around governments and laws."

"You're probably right. But it's one more tool in our arsenal." Derrick stood up. "We've taken up enough of your time Tomas. Think about it."

Tomas and Pele both stood. Tomas reached out to shake his hand. "Well, I wish you and my sister lots of luck in this battle."

"We'll do our best."

Derrick and Pele were about to leave Tomas's office. Tomas reached out and pulled him aside. "Derrick. Do you have a minute?"

Derrick stopped. Pele turned.

"I guess," Derrick said. "What's up?"

Tomas glanced over at Pele.

Pele reached for the door. "I'll just wait down in the lobby."

Tomas turned and walked over to the window of his office. He stared down at the garden below.

"You have something else on the case?" Derrick asked.

"What are your intentions with my sister?" Tomas asked as he continued to stare out the window.

Derrick stood there for a moment. He glanced back at the door then back at Tomas. "I can assure you that Pele and I are just partners. Friends and partners. Nothing more."

Tomas turned to him. "I meant my other sister."

"Haruku?"

"She is my only other sister."

Derrick shrugged. "We're friends. Good friends."

"What do you think of her?"

Derrick stood there staring back at Tomas. "I like her. She's smart. A talented artist and teacher." Derrick thought for a moment. "And she's great with kids."

"And pretty?"

Derrick nodded. "I won't deny that. Yes. Very."

Tomas took a step away from the window. "I don't know what your intentions with her are…"

Derrick shifted his weight to another foot. "I don't know that…"

Tomas smiled slightly. "And I don't know what her intentions are with you."

Derrick's brow furrowed a bit as he looked at Tomas. "I'm afraid I don't understand."

Tomas took a deep breath. "Do you know the history between them?"

Derrick shook his head. "No one has mentioned anything." He snorted softly. "Although when Nancy first met them, she said there was a boy involved somewhere along the way."

Tomas nodded as he turned back to look out the window. "Yes. That's part of it."

"Part of what?"

"Haruku was a… you could say a star in high school. Top student. Athlete. Artist. And, very popular. Everything came easily to her."

Derrick watched as Tomas stared out the window. "Too easy?"

"Her first year at college was a struggle. Her grades weren't at the top. She had more competition in athletics, and there were many beautiful women from all around the world. Not just Hawaii."

"That can be a shock," Derrick said.

"Her third semester was worse."

"Is that when she dropped out?"

Tomas turned back to Derrick and motioned for him to sit down. Tomas sat down in the chair next to him. "None of this goes beyond this room."

Derrick nodded as he sat down. "OK."

"The only reason we are having this talk is because you have had an impact on my family."

Derrick wasn't sure what to make of that.

Tomas smiled. "In a good way. My father likes you. Respects you. He doesn't do that easily with anyone. And I do too." He leaned forward. "But, there are some things you should know." He paused for a moment. "At least as far as what I know." He glanced over at Derrick and smiled again. "Who knows what goes on inside a girl's head?"

Derrick laughed and shrugged. "Not me."

Tomas took a deep breath as he sat back. "Anyway. Back around 2001, a kid, well, young man, came to work in our Waikiki store. He seemed like a nice guy. Hard working at first. Good with people. And good with Pele."

Derrick's eyes opened wide. "Good with Pele?"

Tomas shook his head. "Not in a bad way. She was the nerd/cop type as soon as she was born I think. And feisty. She was smart. Started college early." He shook his head. "I'm getting off track. Well, she took this to mean that he..."

"A schoolgirl crush?"

Tomas nodded. "Her first real shot."

"That can leave a lasting impression."

"Yes." Tomas put his arm up on the back of his chair as he turned to glance out the window for a moment. "To make a long story short..." He turned back to Derrick. "Steve began dating Haruku. She was his age."

"And this didn't go over well with Pele."

"Their relationship has never been as close as it was since. Before Steve, they did everything together."

"And after?"

Tomas raised his hands and shrugged. "Less and less. Then nothing." He shook his head as he stared down at the floor. "Then Haruku left for a surfing competition in Tahiti."

"After Haruku's friend died?"

"You know the story?"

Derrick shrugged. "Just that piece."

"Pele was going to go with them to try and patch things up."

"And this Steve went along instead?"

"Yes. But everything in their lives was changing. Falling apart. Haruku dropped out early. She was doing badly."

"Her friend had just died. She probably wasn't able to get back up on the horse," Derrick offered.

"Maybe." Tomas looked back up at Derrick. "But she didn't come back home. She disappeared."

"Did she run off with Steve?"

Tomas shrugged. "We assume so."

"How long was she gone?"

"Almost ten years."

"Did you try to find her?"

"My father said she needed to find herself again. And to do that she needed space."

"You agree with that?"

"We all respected his wish."

Pele stepped over by a waterfall in the lobby. Tall palm trees bordered it, and the bottom of the pool was lined with rocks and colorful flowers floating on top. Giant orange, yellow, and white fish swam around above dozens of quarters, dimes, and coins from other countries.

Her cell went off as she stood there watching the fish swim. "Kobayashi."

"Hi Pele."

"Captain. What can I do for you?"

"It's more like what I've done for you and Derrick."

"What?"

"I've just met with Lieutenant Carnevalli. We have officers and his unit scouring the island for Luc and any members of the Dyong gang."

"Do you think they are still on the island?"

"We've alerted the other islands, as well as the west coast, and Interpol. We believe they are still here. It's their home turf. We've got eyes on the airports, ships, freighters, even patrols on the marinas. We'll catch these people."

"And what about Derrick and I?"

"Just go about your digging to build a case. And tell Derrick to spend some time with his goddaughters while he can."

"OK. Thanks." She scanned the lobby as she hung up. "Not much chance they'd be here."

"And Pele has a bit of a temper," Tomas continued.

"She can certainly take care of herself," Derrick said with a grin as he thought back to when they arrested this huge Samoan guy when he first came to the islands.

"It almost got her fired from the force." Tomas turned back to Derrick. "She has to go to counseling."

"Yeah. I know." Derrick thought back to the time when she took on Sergeants Trang and Perkins down in the parking garage. It was a good thing no one said anything about that.

"You've seen it?" Tomas asked.

Derrick shrugged. "It was justified." He snorted, "And after that photo in the paper…"

Tomas smiled. "The entire island knows."

"Do you think I fell into the middle of a sisterly feud?"

Tomas shrugged.

Derrick set back. "I've never… I don't think I've ever given either…"

Tomas sat up in his chair. "What do you think of Haruku? Honestly."

Derrick sat there for a moment. "I think she is fantastic. A lifesaver for me this past month."

Tomas leaned forward. "Are you in love with her?"

Derrick sat there in silence again as he thought about her. The first time they met. The time he helped Pele get her out of the bar. As she sat at her kitchen table playing games with Kattie and Becky. He looked up at Tomas. "She is a very…"

Tomas sat back. "She is in love with you."

Derrick didn't know how to respond to that. He did have the feeling there was more to his relationship with her than just the girls. "Well, that wasn't my intention going into this…"

"But now?"

"Well…"

"Look, Derrick." Tomas hesitated as he fished for words. "I'm not saying that this would be a bad thing. Or that I'm even against it." He smiled briefly as he stared down at the floor. "I think my parents might even be relieved." He looked back up at Derrick. "You know. If this should develop into…" He paused again. "Haruku was a mess when she first came back home. But since she met you her life has completely turned around."

Derrick forced a smile. "That's me. A source for good."

Tomas sat back. "What happens when the girls go home?"

Derrick sat there in silence.

"What happens when you two don't have an outside reason to see each other every day?"

Derrick continued to sit there in silence.

Pele glanced over at the elevators as she tried to stroll casually around the lobby. The doors to one of the elevators opened. A family of tourists stepped out.

"Are you implying that your sister is… unstable?"

Tomas looked over at him. "Which one?"

"Maybe I should go up and see what's keeping him." She started making her way over toward the elevators half talking to herself out loud. "No. Tomas wanted to talk to him alone." She turned around and walked back over to the waterfall. "But why?" Was there something more to this case that Tomas didn't want to worry her about?

Derrick stood in the hallway outside Tomas's office.

"Kattie and Becky leave for home in a couple of days?" Tomas asked.

"Yes. Early Sunday morning."

"And I promised to teach you how to cook a pig for a luau someday."

"That you did," Derrick said.

"How about Saturday? I'll pick you up at Haruku's place Thursday afternoon."

"Tomas. This is Friday afternoon."

He shook his head. "Wow. This week has just raced by hasn't it?"

"Too late for the pig?"

Tomas grinned as he slapped Derrick on the back. "No. We'll select a pig now and get it ready. Start getting the pit ready this afternoon and then begin the cooking early tomorrow morning. But we've got to go get one now."

"Right now?"

"I'll call my father, and he'll meet us." Tomas looked at Derrick and pointed to his suit. "You might want to change first."

"But the girls…"

"Haruku knows the routine. She'll get them ready in the morning and bring them to the house after we get started." Tomas glanced down at his watch. "Now, I think you've got a partner waiting down in the lobby."

"Yes. Thanks, Tomas."

Tomas reached out and shook Derrick's hand. "I'll meet you down in the lobby in about ten minutes."

Derrick nodded. "Ten minutes it is."

Pele was just about to step on an elevator as Derrick stepped out of another. She turned and stepped back out when she saw him. "There you are. What happened?"

"Ah. Tomas is going to teach me how to prepare a luau for the girls Saturday."

"That's tomorrow. And you don't have a pig."

"I know. We're going to meet with your father in a few minutes and go get one."

"Now?" She grinned. "Dressed in that?"

"Tomas said the same thing. How hard is it to pick up a pig?"

Chapter 41

Fei raised her glass as she looked around the table in a back room of the family restaurant. Her parents, her brother Xin, and a girl he brought as a date, Orianna Suen, all raised their glasses as well.

"To finishing your exams," she said smiling at Quon.

Quon reached for his glass. "I am so glad that part is over. Now comes the waiting for the review."

"The light at the end of the tunnel," Fei said. "We will have a bigger party with all your friends when you actually get your Ph.D."

They clinked their glasses and drank a toast. Quon smiled as he glanced around the room. The red walls were covered with paintings of mountain scenes and ancient cities. The room was filled with people laughing and smiling as they conversed in Chinese and English or both. Servers brought out the first course of a magnificent multi-course dinner and began serving. There were already plates of egg rolls, bowls of white and brown rice, and pots of green tea. He didn't know how many courses they had prepared. And if he drank much more of this family brew, he wouldn't be able to keep track.

"This is an ancient family receipt for Baijiu," Fei's father said as he refilled everyone's glass.

"We call it white wine," Fei said with a grin.

"I have never had a wine like this," Quon said. "My grandmother gave me something similar when I graduated high school. She called it shaojiu. However, I do not remember it being this strong."

"It is basically the same thing," Fei said. "Just a little local variation."

It was a busy, noisy Friday evening at Duke's as Derrick reached for a Poke roll. "Tomas and Pele both warned me to change, but they didn't tell me why."

"I hope you went home and changed first," Haruku said as she gave the girls some Huli Huli chicken rolls.

"I did."

"These are really good," Kattie said as she took a big bite out of one.

"How was I to know that they got the pig from this farmer's pig pen? And then butchered it right there!"

"I am sure Tomas wanted to surprise you."

"He did. Mahalo Steve," Derrick continued as their server brought their dinners.

"If you need anything else, Derrick, just let me know."

"There is." Derrick pulled a camera out of his pocket and handed it to Steve. "If you could just snap a quick photo or two."

"My pleasure." He reached for the camera and took several shots from different angles then handed it back to Derrick.

"Mahalo," Derrick said as he set it down.

Steve nodded and stepped over to a nearby table.

"Do you know him?" Becky asked as she reached for one of her fries.

"Yes. We usually chat when I come in here."

Becky put a fry in her mouth then turned to look out over the ocean. "I wish we didn't have to leave so soon Uncle Derrick. I like it here."

"I wish you didn't either Becky. But your parents want to spend time with you too. Before you both start school."

"I want to go to school here." She reached for another fry. "Aunt Haruku can teach us."

"I don't know what your mother would think about that," Haruku said.

Derrick reached for his glass of iced tea. He sat back and took it all in. It was a moment to remember from his first summer in paradise. He watched the girls eating and talking. The month had gone by so fast. The chatter of the other guests, the clanking of dishes and silverware, all drifted away. The air was filled with the smells of the ocean mixed with tropical flowers, French Fries, and barbecue sauce. The sound of the waves as they rolled gently up on the beach while the sun set. And the sight of lovers of all ages as they strolled along the beach hand in hand.

"What do you think Uncle Derrick?"

"Huh?" He turned to Kattie.

"Do you think that mommy and daddy would let us come again next year?"

"We can ask when we get back to New York."

Becky picked up her burger with both hands. "What are we going to do tomorrow Uncle Derrick?" She tried to wrap her mouth around it for a big bite.

Derrick glanced over at Haruku.

Haruku leaned over to her. "We have a special day planned for you."

Becky pulled her burger back. "What is it?"

"A surprise," Derrick said.

A single ceiling light was on in the dining room casting a shadow into the living room and the entrance to the kitchen. Pele sat at the table reassembling her Walther P99 with a blindfold on and a stopwatch off to the side.

She slipped the last piece in place and reached for the stopwatch as she ripped off the blindfold. She nodded, satisfied with her time. Laying everything aside, she turned to her laptop. She rolled her finger gently across the trackpad and selected a directory.

A window came up. 'Decryption Password Required.' She entered a password. There was one file in the directory. Ian. She selected it. Photos of a young man in his mid-twenties appeared. He had short dark wavy hair and a smooth tan. Dark eyes and a brilliant white smile. She reached up and gently touched the screen.

She flipped through the photos. Most were of him in various poses at different places around the island. A few were taken by strangers of the two of them together. Sometimes in silly poses and making faces at the camera. She paused at one where she was wearing her yellow sundress, and he was in shorts and a yellow Hawaiian shirt.

She took a deep breath, then reached out and closed the file. A window came up. 'Resume decryption?'

She selected 'Yes.'

Another window came up. 'Enter Password.'

She entered her password then turned off the computer.

Chapter 42

"Did you get it started OK?" Haruku asked as Derrick entered the kitchen.

"I can't believe that I got up at two in the morning to start cooking a pig in a large pit. And that your father and Tomas started the fire at midnight."

"How big is it?"

"One hundred and eighty pounds."

"So it should be ready by mid-afternoon."

Derrick nodded. "And all the banana and ti leaves."

"And don't forget the lava rocks."

Derrick walked over to the counter and poured a cup of coffee. "It never occurred to me how much work goes into preparing a pig for a luau."

"You are learning our secret ways."

Derrick took a sip. "Your father has quite the oven in the backyard."

"He and Tomas built it many years ago. They have to work on it from time to time too."

"Sees a lot of use does it?"

"Seven or eight times a year."

"Good morning Uncle Derrick. Good morning Aunt Haruku," Kattie and Becky shouted as they ran into the kitchen.

"You two are up early," Derrick said as he turned to them.

"We didn't want to waste a minute of time," Becky said as they pulled out their chairs.

"What are we going to do this morning?" Kattie asked.

"Yes," Becky said. "We want our surprise."

"First things first," Derrick said. "Are either of you hungry?"

"I'm starving," Becky said.

"What would you like?"

"Your world-famous huevos," Kattie said.

Derrick set his coffee down. "I don't know that they are *world* famous."

Kattie sat there for a moment. "You've made them in New York."

"Yes."

"And now you make them here in Hawaii."

"True."

"Bink likes them, and he is from England."

"And Kengi is from Japan," Becky added.

Haruku reached out and put her arm around Derrick as she slipped a paper chef's hat on his head. "I think that makes you world famous."

"You look funny," Becky said as the girls laughed and pointed at the hat on his head.

"So, I hear you arrested your latest amour for murder."

"You hear all don't you?" Derrick said as he watched Kattie and Becky fishing at the railing.

"So what's your record now?"

Derrick looked over at the women in the park walking their dogs. "My life a scorecard now?"

"Wife number one. Left you because you were a cop and you got shot."

Derrick shrugged.

"Wife number two... married you because you were a cop. But she got in over her head with some dangerous guys and got herself murdered." Ailani took a sip of his coffee. "How am I doing so far?"

Derrick took a bite of his Danish.

"Your last girlfriend," he paused for a moment. "Well before Haruku. You arrested for murdering her husband and his mistress."

Derrick took a sip of his coffee.

Ailani took a sip of his. "Am I missing any?"

"You have anyone except your wife?"

"Childhood sweethearts. Been together almost our entire lives." He took a bite of his Danish.

They sat there in silence for a moment as the women from the park walked past in front of them with their dogs. They smiled as they passed. Derrick and Ailani raised their cups in salute and smiled back.

Ailani took a sip of his coffee. "What about you? Any high school sweetheart that got away?"

Derrick raised his Danish to his mouth. "Good Danish today." He popped it into his mouth.

"I see." Ailani finished his.

"Gotta go my friend. Last day of shopping and a pig to check on." He stood up. "Then something special for the girls."

"You're going shopping?"

"Haruku is taking the girls on one last trip to the mall."

"And the pig?"

"Tonight's luau. Bring your wife if you'd like."

Derrick turned as a horn honked behind them. Haruku was sitting there in the jeep. "Come on girls."

"We're ready."

"Got to be going, my friend. See you at the luau?"

Ailani nodded. "I'll be there. And I'll Bring Father Bishop along. Never know when you might need a good tenor."

"Time to get going for a little shopping and then your surprise," Derrick said as he cleaned up the empty coffee cups and trash on the bench. "Unless you would rather stay here and fish all day."

"What is our surprise?" Becky asked as they walked over to Ailani and handed him their poles.

"If I tell you it won't be a surprise."

Becky squealed as she was dragged along the surface of the large pool.

"This is so cool Uncle Derrick," Kattie said as he floated nearby with his video camera taping the experience. "The kids at school will never believe this."

"Well, you'll have the evidence."

"My turn," Kattie yelled out as Becky let go and the dolphin swam up to her and began chattering excitedly.

"This was a great idea," Haruku said to him as she swam up to him. "But now the girls will really never want to go home."

He looked over at her. "You don't think this was too much do you?"

She smiled as she reached out and touched his arm. "It's perfect Derrick."

Chapter 43

Haruku and the girls stepped out on the lanai of her parent's home just as Eito, Tomas, Derrick, and Quon were getting ready to lift the pig out of the ground.

"We made it in time!" Kattie shouted as they raced over to watch.

"This is the trickiest part," Eito said as they began removing the plastic sheeting and then the ti and banana leaves.

"That smells so good," Becky said as they stood there with Ahulani and Haruku. Haruku was taking pictures of the girls and the men working in the background so they could show their friends back home.

"OK everyone," Tomas said, as they got ready to lift it out of the pit. "We don't want to drop it after all this work."

Kailani kept everyone back as Eito and Tomas grabbed one end of the pole, while Derrick and Quon took the other. They carefully made their way over to a long table set up just for the pigs they used.

Tomas stepped over to Derrick and slapped him on the back. "We'll make a Hawaiian out of you yet Derrick."

Derrick was leaning up against a post out on the lanai watching Kattie and Becky playing in the pool with Haruku.

"They grow up so fast," Eito said as he stepped next to him.

"Especially when you're not there to see them every day."

"This trip ended well. Maybe Nancy will let them come back again next summer."

Derrick watched as Kattie tossed a ball through a hoop and splashed back into the water. "I guess one can only hope." He turned to Eito. "How did you and your wife manage to raise three great children while building a family empire?"

Eito laughed. "First, I just expanded on what my father had turned over to me. Second, we had lots of help from my wife's family."

"I see."

It was just after 1:00 when the rest of the guests began arriving. Ailani and Father Bishop, Todd and his family, followed by Soto and Kali, along with their grandchildren. The captain and his wife were also early arrivals. Ahulani and Kailani had all kinds of food, fruits, and drinks spread out across two picnic tables. Not counting the table for the pig.

Derrick climbed out of the pool after a game of basketball with the girls, Soto and his grandchildren, and Todd's children. Quon and Fei were still in playing.

Mary stepped over by Tomas as he carved slices off the pig. "How did he do for his first luau?" she asked glancing over at Derrick.

Tomas nodded. "He did great. Jumped right in."

"Do you think he will get in the way?" She took a sip of her drink.

"Of our plans?" he took a sip and handed the glass back to his wife as he carved a few more slices. "No. He might even be an unwitting asset."

"Between your sisters?"

"Am I ever going to see this wife of yours?" Derrick asked as he sat down on the edge of the pool next to Ailani and dried himself off.

"I never got to meet that girlfriend you said you had."

"I can get you a mug shot if you like."

He laughed. "She's watching the kids of a friend of hers over in Hilo this weekend."

"Sure she is."

"So how's your latest case coming?"

"Pretty sure it was a Yakuza hit. We got the guy that made the bomb. Now we just need to get the hired help and tie them all to someone higher."

"A lot of pieces."

Derrick shrugged. "Collect enough pieces, it eventually comes together."

"Let's hope so."

"We'll get there."

"I have every confidence in you."

Pele stepped out of the house and scanned the backyard. She saw Derrick and Quon over by the large bowl of juice filling several cups.

"I'm glad you could join us," Derrick said as he handed her a cup.

"I was at the station."

"Anything new?"

"Kengi called. They tracked Hayakawa to a house outside of Tokyo."

"Who is he?" Quon asked as he picked up two cups. One for himself and one for Fei.

"The man we think might be the assassin that killed Kagawa and Fukuhara."

Derrick raised his cup in salute. "One small step for police kind."

She raised her cup slightly and took a sip. "One small step is right. He was killed in a nasty gunfight with police. The house burned down."

"Did they recover the body?" Quon asked.

"Yeah. They are IDing it now."

"And they are sure it was our man?" Derrick asked.

"They seem to think so."

"Seem to think so isn't quite good enough," Derrick said. "Stay on it."

She nodded.

"But we have the evidence to tie him with the Yakuza?" Quon asked.

She shook her head. "No concrete evidence linking him. But they did verify that he flew to Honolulu on the date in question and then on to San Francisco. He used aliases, but we were able to get positive IDs from ticket personnel and flight attendants."

Derrick stared down into his cup. "Well, at least we know what we know."

"Not enough to nail these higher up guys though is it?" she asked.

He shook his head. "No. Not yet. We still need Luc. And whatever we can get from San Francisco."

Derrick, Ailani, and Father Bishop were standing by the edge of the pool. Kattie and Becky were treading water below them. "I caught the most fish this summer," Kattie said.

"I caught the biggest didn't I Father Bishop?" Becky said.

"I believe you did."

Haruku walked up to them. "Ready to jump in again?"

"Come back in Uncle Derrick." Kattie and Becky swam up to the edge and reached out for his legs.

"You going to miss them?"

Derrick looked up at her. "The bad guys?"

"No." She nodded over at Kattie and Becky.

"Oh. Them." He grinned. "Yeah. I am."

"Giving any thought to going back to New York?" she asked. Ailani and Father Bishop turned to him waiting for him to say something.

Derrick took in a long slow breath as he looked around. The sky was azure blue and unblemished by any clouds. The palm tree fronds swayed in a gentle onshore breeze. Pele, Quon, and Fei were off talking and laughing. Eito was carving more pieces of the pig. Soto and Kali were talking with Todd and his wife. Tomas's kids were in the pool swimming with Soto's grandkids.

"Home is here on this island now."

"Good." Haruku reached out and pulled at his hand. "Are you going to come in and join us?"

"Come in Uncle Derrick!" Becky yelled out.

Derrick turned to Ailani. "Gotta go."

Haruku dove in yanking Derrick along beside her landing in a huge splash that flew out covering Ailani and Father Bishop.

"That looked like fun," Kattie yelled out. "Can you do that again?"

Eito stepped over next to Kailani. They watched Derrick and Haruku playing with the girls and the other kids.

Kailani turned and looked up at her husband. "She looks happier than I have seen her in such a long time."

He slipped his arm over her shoulder and smiled. "A very long time."

"Maybe the demons that haunted her are gone."

"It's time for bed," Haruku said as they all piled into the condo.

"It's our last night. We don't want to sleep," Kattie said as she stamped her foot on the floor and made little fists.

"It's late, and you have a very busy day tomorrow."

Kattie and Becky stepped up to Derrick and Haruku. "We have decided that we want to live here with you two."

Derrick laughed. "I think your mom and dad might have something to say about that."

"Why don't we go back here for a minute," Haruku said as she reached down and took Kattie and Becky by the hand. She turned to Derrick. "You too Derrick."

She led them down the hallway to her bedroom.

"Where are we going?" Becky asked.

"I have a surprise for each of you."

"Another surprise?" Kattie asked.

"I like surprises," Becky said.

"Me too," Kattie said as they entered the room.

Haruku turned to Derrick. "What about you?"

"It depends."

"On what? If you like it or not?"

"What kind of a surprise it is."

"If you know what it might be, then it isn't a surprise now is it?"

"That's what you told us," Becky said.

Haruku sat them all down on the side of the bed and walked over to her closet. She slid the door open, then pulled out three thin one foot by one foot boxes. She handed one to each of them.

"What is it?" Kattie asked.

"Open it and find out dear."

Kattie and Becky watched as Derrick flipped open the top of the box then they followed. At the same time, they all pulled out the objects and stared at them.

"These are incredible," Derrick said. "Thank you Haruku."

"Yes. It's beautiful," Kattie said.

"They are so real like," Becky added.

"I hope you like them," Haruku said standing there shifting from side to side as she rubbed her hands.

"What's not to like?" Derrick said as he glanced up at her then back again. "It's better than any photograph."

They all sat there admiring the pencil sketches of the three of them, with the palm covered island, and a mountain in the background. "We are each in the middle of our own," Kattie added as she glanced over at the others.

"But where are you?" Becky asked.

"You should be in it," Kattie said.

"Oh no. It's a family…"

Derrick looked up at her. "You belong in the center."

"Yes Aunt Haruku," Becky said.

Her eyes watered as she shook her head. "No."

Derrick held it up to look at it. The girls followed his example. "Next time."

"Yes," Kattie and Becky said in unison as they all looked up at Haruku.

Haruku wiped away a tear. "Now it's time for you to get to bed. You've got a long day ahead tomorrow."

"Are you coming back to New York with us?" Becky asked.

Haruku sat down on the bed between them and put her arms around them. "No. I have to stay here and take care of a few things."

"Awww." Becky moaned as she threw her arms around Haruku. "I'll miss you."

"We both will," Kattie added as they threw their arms around her. She looked up at Derrick as her eyes filled up again.

"My sister will be going back with you. She and your Uncle Derrick have some official police work to do while they are there."

"Will you come and visit us?" Kattie asked.

Haruku looked up at Derrick.

Derrick knelt down in front of them. "We'll see what the future brings." He took their hands. "But for now, the future says that you two get ready for bed."

Haruku stood up as they jumped up and ran out of the room with their sketches.

Derrick turned to her and put his arms around her shoulders. "This is going to be hard isn't it?"

She took a deep breath as she tried to smile. "We should go make sure they…"

He stepped back. "Right."

Chapter 44

Derrick glanced at the red light of the alarm clock as he reached for his cell on the nightstand. It flashed 02:17 AM. "Dreadlow."

"Hey, Derrick."

"Pele?"

"Carnevalli just called me. They've got a line on Luc. The captain has SWAT mobilizing and other units on their way. I'll meet you down in the garage in five."

"On my way." Derrick jumped out of bed and reached for the nearest clothes he could find. A pair of pants with a lot of pockets and a dark blue Hawaiian shirt. He stumbled around as he unlocked a small metal lockbox. He opened it and grabbed his Glock, four clips, then strapped his Smith & Wesson to his ankle. He stuffed his badge, a small wooden box, and a box of .357 shells in his pockets. He paused. Then grabbed two more clips for the Glock. He looked down. The box was empty.

Haruku stepped out of her bedroom in her nightshirt. He stopped and stared for a moment. "What is it, Derrick?"

Even with her hair all mussed up, she looked beautiful standing there. "Pele called. They think they've found our primary suspect in the bomb making here on the island."

"Don't forget about your plane…"

"This should be quick. I'll be back soon."

She stepped up to him and slid her hands up his chest. "Be careful Derrick."

He smiled as he placed a hand on her waist. "I will." He turned and started back down the hall. He stopped and turned back to her. "Just in case I'm running a little late for some reason…"

"I'll have the girls ready. Don't worry. You just watch out for yourself. And my sister."

"I've got your vest on the back seat," Pele said as he jumped in the open door. "You might want to suit up. Just in case."

"And Quon's ear device?"

"Already on." She pointed to her right ear as she one-handedly squealed out of the garage with lights flashing.

Derrick fitted on the earpiece. "So where is Luc?"

"He was last seen leaving a bar in Pearl City. One of Carnevalli's men is tracking him. Officers and SWAT are hanging back to see where he goes."

"They think he may be going to meet the others?"

"Let's hope so. We could nail them all at once and wrap this case up before our plane leaves."

"We should be so lucky."

She slowed down, then raced through a red light jumping onto the H-1 going west to Pearl City. She glanced over at his bulging pockets. "Ready for a fight?"

He looked down at the backpack by her side. "You?"

"Here…" she tossed him a small portable police radio. She had one clipped to her belt and in her other ear. He strapped his on. He could hear the chatter as he slipped the plug into his ear.

"This is Max. He's exiting the H-1 at Kalihi Street."

"Stay with him," Carnevalli warned.

Pele reached over and flipped a switch. She glanced over at Derrick. "This is a whoopee moment if there ever was one."

He grinned as the siren blared. She weaved effortlessly around cars and trucks along the highway. Not that early Sunday mornings were particularly crowded.

"Max again. He's crossing under the Nimitz Highway. It looks like we're heading into an industrial section of Kaliawa."

"Stay on him," Carnevalli said. "The Calvary is right behind you."

"This is Dreadlow and Kobayashi here. We're right behind you Dan."

"Got it," Carnevalli replied. "We'll set up a command post as soon as he lands."

Pele flipped off the siren as they approached the Nimitz Highway. "It's just up ahead," she said as the flashing lights reflected in buildings a few blocks ahead.

"So much for the element of surprise," Derrick said as they drew closer.

Derrick and Pele jumped out. He scanned the area. The neighborhood was a mishmash of businesses, warehouses, apartments, and duplex rentals. The businesses were cinder block. The warehouses a thin corrugated steel. The homes were cinder block, with a few wood frame. Most of the buildings were two-story. There were also a fair share of single story, and the occasional three-story building dropped into the mix. A few scraggly trees for landscaping were dispersed around, though it was hard to make out in this light if they were still alive.

"Where are they?" Derrick asked as he and Pele ran up to Carnevalli.

"He went into that apartment across the street." He pointed to a two-story structure halfway down the block.

"What's around it?"

"Businesses. And a warehouse complex behind it."

Derrick took a deep breath as he looked around. "It's a sure bet he knows we're here by now."

Another car pulled up at the scene along with five more patrol cars and two SWAT vans. Captain Henderson got out and walked over to them.

"I didn't expect to see you out here," Derrick said.

"I'm just here to observe and support. It's still your operation Dread."

Derrick nodded as Pele brought a 3D map of the area up on her laptop. Then she hooked up Quon's large plastic screen.

"That's kind of cool," Carnevalli said as he watched.

"We're here," she said as she marked the spot with her finger. A red X appeared.

"OK." Derrick studied the map for a moment. "Carnevalli, I want you and your men to concentrate on the apartment. Captain, if you could set up a perimeter around…" he ran his finger across the screen. A red line appeared.

"The new version has touch and drawing capabilities too," Pele said.

Derrick nodded as he continued to draw a circle. "… around here."

"And us?" Pele asked.

"We'll take a few men and set up back here between the warehouses and the apartment."

"You think he's going to make a break for it?" Carnevalli asked.

"I'd bet on it. If he hasn't already." Derrick looked over at the apartment. "Do we know if the rest of the gang is in the area?"

Carnevalli shook his head.

"OK people. Positions." Derrick turned to Carnevalli. "You and your team take a few SWAT people and go in. My guess is that you'll flush him out if he isn't already out."

Two officers, the SWAT commander, and two SWAT team members joined Derrick and Pele as they made their way around the back of the apartment to the warehouses. The rest were with the captain to set up the perimeter.

Derrick scanned the area as they went. There was an alley between the apartment and the wall around the warehouses. He noticed a dumpster pushed up against the wall. He motioned for everyone to stop. He pointed up at the barbwire fence along the top of the wall.

"It's been cut," the commander of the SWAT team said.

Derrick nodded. "My guess is that he's already left the apartment."

"Now what?" Pele asked as they looked around.

Derrick turned to the two officers. "You two stay down behind that dumpster. Watch the alley. Make sure they don't backtrack."

They nodded and took up their position.

"You got bolt cutters with you?" Derrick asked the SWAT commander.

He nodded as one of his men pulled out a long pair.

"The rest of you follow me."

They made their way back along the wall to a gate. "We go in through here." Derrick got on his police radio. "This is Dreadlow. I've got reason to believe that Luc has already fled to the warehouses behind the apartment. But be careful. He may have left men behind to cover his escape."

"Captain Henderson here. We've got a perimeter set up. If he's in there, he's not getting out."

"Good. Carn. I want you to go in and make sure the complex is clear. Then we move on to plan B."

"What's plan B?" Pele asked.

"Search the warehouses. It's now *our* plan A."

There were two rows of sheet metal buildings with a thirty-foot alley between. Twelve units on each side. Every other building was two stories. One two-thirds of the way down the far row was three stories. And it looked like it had windows at the top. There appeared to be a three-story building on the close side down toward the end of the alley as well.

"Looks clear," the woman on the SWAT team wearing night vision gear said as she surveyed the buildings.

Derrick continued his scan. There were dumpsters and a pickup truck, along with two three-quarter ton vans scattered along the row of buildings. Not in any particular order. One parked here and there. The mercury vapor lights filled the scene with an eerie orange glow that drowned out all but the brightest stars. The salt breeze from the nearby ocean filled the air. At this quiet time of the morning, he could make out the occasional lapping of the waves against the piers.

"It's awful quiet," Pele whispered as she gazed at the seemingly empty buildings.

"Too quiet." Derrick turned to the SWAT commander as he spoke softly on the police radio. "We're going to make our way down the left side and check the buildings. One of you with us, the other two provide cover if we need it."

The commander nodded. "Shelby."

"Yes sir," he replied.

"You're with Dreadlow." He turned to the woman. "Kowalski."

"Yes sir," she replied.

"You're with me. Keep an eye out with that gear. Let me know the second you see anything move."

"Yes sir," she replied.

Derrick reached for his radio again. "OK, everyone. Showtime. We're going to start with the row of warehouses on the east side. When the apartment is secure come on out and join us." Derrick looked around at the people near him. He reached for the radio again. "Let's do it!"

Carnevalli and his men entered the apartment. The SWAT team went in first. There were four units. He looked at the names on the unit mailboxes. "Damn!" Luc wasn't on any of them. Everyone looked at him. "There's four units and eight of us. One SWAT guy and one of my team. We hit them all at once. Pair up." He reached out and grabbed the closest SWAT member. "You're with me kid."

Captain Henderson positioned several SWAT members to the back and the sides around the warehouses and three more of his own officers to support the apartment. He also sent two SWAT members to join the officers in the alley behind the apartment. Just in case. He slipped on his vest and joined his men taking up a position where he could go either way if needed.

Derrick, Pele, and Shelby slowly made their way to the door of the first unit. It was locked from the outside. Derrick crouched low to look under the first van. There was no sign of anyone hiding on the other side. He motioned for them to proceed to the next building.
The SWAT commander watched their progress as Kowalski kept scanning the rooftops and windows.

Carnevalli looked around as his fingers counted down. He nodded. Three. Two. One. Four doors crashed open as eight men and women raced in guns drawn. "Police!" Echoed throughout the hallway.

Derrick and his team slid up to the door of the third warehouse. He and Pele stood on either side as Shelby scanned the surrounding buildings. Derrick tried the door. It was also locked. He looked around. "OK. This next one has windows. And there is a van on this side of the door and a dumpster on the other. I'll check out the van and dumpster first. Pele, you keep an eye on the windows. Shelby the other buildings."
They nodded as he slid along the wall toward the door. Every muscle tensed for action. Every nerve ready to spring. Was Luc back here somewhere? Was he alone? Was he already gone?

"Clear!"
"Clear!"
"Clear!"
"Clear!" echoed through the upper and lower landings of the apartment building. HPD officers were left to the aftermath of scared residents as Carnevalli, his men, and the SWAT team exited the rear of the building to join Derrick.

Derrick slipped up to the back of the dumpster after checking out the van. As he made his way to the other side, a shot rang out. It ricocheted off the top of the dumpster. Another shot bounced off the wall just inches in front of him. Four more rapid-fire shots rang out. He looked around but couldn't see anyone. "Shots fired," he yelled into the police radio. "You see anything Pele?" he asked her over their ear devices.

"Nothing Derrick. Where did the shots come from?"

"Shelby. You see anything?" Derrick looked back. He couldn't see him. "Shelby. Where are you?"

"I see him!" Pele said. "Officer down!" she called out over the police radio. "Shots fired. Officer down in the alley behind the apartments."

Derrick took a quick look around. It looked clear. He ran from the cover of the dumpster and dove behind the van to join Pele. Three shots chased him as he landed on his stomach. Pele fired two shots up at the third-story window across the alley.

"We see him," the SWAT Commander called out.

Derrick quickly spotted Shelby. He looked back at him as he tried to crawl back. Two shots landed between them and Shelby.

"Those bastards are using him as bait," Pele yelled out as she popped up and fired off three more rounds.

Two shots came from the third-floor window and two more from somewhere in one of the buildings across from them.

Derrick reached up for his police radio. "They are multiple people in multiple buildings. Numbers unknown. Positions unknown. They've got us pinned down, and Shelby is being used as bait."

"Can you determine Shelby's position?" Captain Henderson asked.

"About ten feet from us. Exposed. He is hit in the leg. I can't tell how bad."

"OK. We've got an APC on the way and police snipers moving into positions along the fence between the warehouses and the other end of the street. But we don't have the high ground."

"ETA on the APC?"

"Twenty to thirty minutes."

"Copy that." Derrick glanced over at Pele.

"We can't let him just lay out there."

"No." Derrick looked around for options. "He may not have that long if he's hit badly." He reached for his police radio again. "Commander."

"Yeah Dread."

"Can you have Kowalski cover the third-floor window?"

"What do you have in mind?"

"You and Pele cover the other buildings. Lay down fire while I go grab Shelby."

"Two of us can't cover the entire side when we don't even know where the shots are coming from?"

"Carn here. I'm at the back of that first dumpster behind you Dread. The three of us can fire at any window to give you maybe thirty seconds cover. We divide the street into thirds. I'll take this end, Pele you the far end. Commander, the center. That enough for you Dread?"

"It's going to have to be. Wait for my signal." Derrick turned to Pele. He handed her his Glock. "Fresh clip."

She nodded and slipped out her clip and put in a fresh one. Taking a gun in both hands, she stepped to the corner of the van.

Derrick looked out at Shelby and gave a slight wave.

Shelby gave a nod.

"Now!" Derrick shouted as he charged out toward the fallen officer.

Pele popped out with both guns blazing as Carnevalli, and the SWAT Commander sprayed the opposite side of the street and Kowalski laid down fire at the third-floor window.

Derrick felt the surge of adrenaline as he raced out to Shelby. He grabbed him by his jacket as the young man clutched at his rifle. They both dove back behind the van as return fire blew out the windows and tires on the other side.

A roar of gunfire erupted from several officers shooting from the wall behind the apartment as well as Captain Henderson and his men from the other end of the street.

Pele set down her empty guns to tend to Shelby as Derrick slipped in two new clips. He reached for his radio. "Anyone have any idea how many of them there are?"

The SWAT commander came back. "I'd say at least five positions with at least one person at each."

"There are eight known members of this gang," Carnevalli added. "He may also have new recruits."

"Just peachy," Derrick said as he reached for Shelby's AR15.

"It's got a laser on it," Shelby said looking up as Pele patched his leg.

"You'll live," Pele said as she picked up her Glock. She ran her hand over the van where the shots fired at them penetrated the other side and left indentations just inches from them. "Damn."

Derrick got down on his stomach, inched his way to the edge of the van, and scanned the buildings across the street. "This isn't going to work." He shimmied back then crouched down as he looked over at Shelby. "Can you move Shelby?"

"Yeah."

"Then I want you and Pele to get back to the first dumpster with Carnevalli."

"What about you?" Pele asked.

"We can't stay here."

"Why not?"

Derrick sniffed the air and pointed to the ground. The fuel tank had been hit. "We're sitting next to a bomb. Another couple of shots and we're all gonna be toast."

Derrick relayed his plan to the others as Pele got Shelby ready to run.

Pele put a fresh clip in her Glock then pulled her Walther P99 out of her pack. She took a deep breath. She could feel the adrenaline pumping through her body. Her hands and fingers limber. Her legs ready to fly like the wind. Her vision in perfect acuity with the orange pale over the street. She turned to Shelby. "You ready?"

Shelby nodded.

"Go!" Derrick yelled out. All hell broke out along the street again as Derrick raced for the dumpster and Pele led Shelby back. Rifle in his left hand Derrick fired at any open door or window that he could see with his Glock in the right hand. He dove behind the dumpster to catch his breath. He could feel his heart pounding. He peered around the corner. A muzzle flashed from the other side, third door down. He raised his Glock and emptied his clip into the doorway. The firing from there stopped. He didn't take the time to wonder why. He loaded another clip then holstered it as he picked up the rifle again.

As Derrick yelled go, Pele pushed Shelby out in front of her. He ran as best he could in spite of the pain. That or being shot was a strong motivation. Acting as a shield, she turned, firing both guns as they ran toward Carnevalli. Carnevalli stepped out from behind the dumpster to draw fire and blasted away as they ran toward him.

They all ducked behind the dumpster as asphalt, paint chips, and chunks of cinder block flew around them. Sparks flew off the steel walls like fireflies.

Pele slid her thumbs over both guns dropping clips on the ground and just as nimbly reloaded.

Before anyone could say a word, she dashed out firing at the doors and windows as she ran back toward Derrick.

Carnevalli leaned around the corner as Shelby crawled toward him. They both began laying down cover fire for Pele.

She dove and shot at the lock on the sliding steel door behind Derrick then pushed it open.

Derrick sat behind the dumpster watching the third-floor window. A figure appeared and began firing at Carnevalli and Shelby. Derrick lined up his shot and fired one round. The figure slumped forward, fell out the window, and rolled down off the roof.

The van behind him exploded into a billowing ball of flame and black smoke, illuminating the entire alley. The shock wave knocked him to the ground. He quickly rebounded in time to see another figure across the street taking aim at Carnevalli. He aimed and fired two rounds. The figure fell backward out of view. Their shot went up into the air.

"Back here Derrick!" Pele yelled out as the fireball died down.

Derrick turned and ran back to Pele as the flames died down. The van was a smoldering hulk of metal. The acrid smelling smoke of burnt tires, polyester seats, and whatever was stored in the back of that van, drifted up and toward the apartment building.

"I think you got two of them," she said as they ducked behind the steel walls of the unit and reloaded.

"Maybe three," he said. "But we're still pinned down."

"Captain. When is that APC getting here?" Derrick asked as he checked his ammo supply. "I've got four shots in the AR 15 and three fresh clips for the Glock. And seven rounds for my Smith & Wesson."

"I don't think that's going to be much use here," Pele said.

"How are you?"

She looked in her pack. "Four clips for the Glock. Six for the P99."

"It's here." the captain came back. "But we've just been told that there may be people in one of the buildings. A homeless family is staying in it. A friend let them use it until they get back on their feet. We're trying to get confirmation before we go charging in."

"Which one?" Derrick asked.

"We're trying to get that information now."

"I hope they aren't hostages," Pele said as she looked over at Derrick.

"Don't shoot. Don't shoot me please."

"Oh crap," Derrick said as he turned to peer out the doorway. A seven-year-old boy was walking down toward the apartments waving his arms up in the air as he went. "Don't shoot me. Please."

Derrick watched as Carnevalli waved the boy over to his position. "Come on now son. You'll be fine. Just walk this way."

"They have my family. They are going to shoot them."

Carnevalli lunged out, grabbed the boy and pulled him around the corner.

Derrick reached up for his radio mic. "Talk to me, Carn."

After a brief pause, Carnevalli came back on. "The kid says his mother and father, as well as two sisters, are still in there. He said his father was hit during the gunfire. He said his mother had stopped the bleeding for now, but he looks bad."

"OK, everyone. This is Captain Henderson. We now have a hostage situation. I have called in a hostage negotiator, so I want everyone to stay calm and remain in their current positions while we reassess the situation."

Derrick peered around the corner of the doorway.

"What can you see?" Pele asked.

"No movement." He sat there thinking. He reached up and rubbed his chin.

"You got an idea?"

He got up and walked around the inside of the building they were in. There were a couple of dim nightlights and a lot of shadows.

Pele got up and joined him. "What are we looking for."

He walked back over to the doorway and scanned the other side of the street. "These warehouses and businesses are all separated by a wall. At least one. Probably two. One for each unit."

"So?" she asked as she looked around. "We can't work our way into another building through the wall. We're trapped like they are."

He grinned. "Yes. They are trapped and separated."

"What are you getting at?"

He reached for his mic. "Carn."

"Yeah Dread."

"Ask this kid how many of the bad guys were in with them?"

Derrick glanced out across the street and down two units from where the boy had emerged.

"He said two. But they were talking on their cell phones to others."

Derrick nodded. "OK. We've got to try to keep them separated in their own units." Derrick turned to Pele. "Call Quon and see if he has some new toy he's been working on that can let us see who is on the other side of that wall."

She nodded as he reached for his mic again. "Captain."

"Yeah?"

"Can you get a team started cutting on the back of the unit we are in and the second unit down from us?"

"OK. You have a plan?"

"I have a plan for a plan."

Pele turned to Derrick. "He said he just happened to have a prototype for a neutron scanner that can penetrate steel up to an inch thick. We won't be able to tell who is who, but we can tell how many people are in there and their mass. I guess he means height and weight."

"Can he bring it here?"

"He's already on his way."

Derrick, Pele, and everyone else sat around as the clock slowly ticked off an hour that seemed like a lifetime. There was no word from the gang members. They still didn't even know if Luc was in there.

Derrick turned as he heard a cutting torch at the back of the building. Fifteen minutes later Captain Henderson entered.

"Hi there. What have you got? And why are Quon and Paul here?"

Derrick's eyes widened. "Paul Covington?"

"Yeah."

"I don't know."

"There's also something else you don't know. We believe that there is another sniper on this side of the street in an identical three-story building on the other side."

"I think Derrick took out one, maybe two snipers on the other side," Pele said.

"Can you get one of our snipers in place to cover it?" Derrick asked.

"Already done." He walked up to the doorway and peered outside. "They are just finishing cutting through in the other building. Quon is probably setting up now."

"Have someone take up a position in here. Pele and I are going to go to the other building."

"I'm coming with you."

"What brings you back to the islands?" Derrick said as he walked up behind Quon, Xin, and Paul.

Paul turned around and shook his hand. "I was just passing through and stopped by to see how my young friend in crime fighting was doing. And to see if you were free for dinner tonight. By the way, Paula sends her love."

"We're just about ready," Xin said as he walked past with a screwdriver.

"How did you end up here at this time of morning?" Derrick waved his hands around at the chaos.

"Jet lag. Couldn't sleep. I caught this on my scanner."

"Jet lag? That never bothered you before."

"I'm getting too old for this shit Dread."

As Quon set up his equipment, Derrick pulled Carnevalli aside. He turned so that the others couldn't hear what he was saying. "Didn't you say there was a rumor that you heard about linking Mayeda to gang activity?"

Carnevalli looked around. "We haven't been able to substantiate--"

"I think this might be a good time to bring him down to the station and ask him a few questions."

Carnevalli nodded slowly. "Come to think of it, it might have been one of these guys who let it slip."

"Only one way to know for sure."

"You know he won't talk."

"I don't care. I just want him to listen."

"And in an hour he'll have an army of lawyers at our front door."

Derrick grinned. "We were just checking leads in a critical hostage situation. Time was of the essence."

"You got it Dread." He pointed to one of his men. "Max. You're with me. The rest of you help Dreadlow."

Captain Henderson, Derrick, and Paul were looking over the plans for the buildings along this back street.

Derrick ran his finger over some lines on the plans. "There are dividing walls and barbed wire fences in between each street of warehouses."

"That will help with containment," Paul said.

Captain Henderson pointed to several spots on the plan. "I've got teams in all these positions to cut them off if they try to make a run for it."

"How is the hostage negotiator doing?" Derrick asked.

"He finally made a connection with them. We also showed the boy some photos. Luc and one of his gang are the ones in the building with the hostages. They want a million dollars and a plane with enough fuel to take them to Vietnam. Luc also said that in an hour they would begin killing the hostages if their demands aren't met."

"Of course they will," Derrick said as he studied the plans.

Pele joined them. "What about the boy's father?"

Captain Henderson shook his head. "They won't release him."

"What else do you know about them?" Paul asked.

"There are two in the building with the hostages," Derrick said. "And from the observations I've pulled together from the teams during the firefight, they occupy five other buildings in addition to the one with the hostages."

"I guess that helps a little," Pele said.

Derrick began pacing around the table. "OK. There are eight known gang members. I think I took out two, maybe three."

"There are no other confirmed hits," Captain Henderson added.

"OK." Derrick nodded as he thought for a moment. "Two are with the hostages."

"There is a new one in the third-floor of the building on the other side," Captain Henderson said. "And the one up in the third-floor window on this side of the street."

"That's four," Pele said. "And the one in the window down the street that you may have hit."

"So that's four buildings with possibly five people," Paul said.

"That leaves us with these two buildings, one two doors to the left of the hostages and one three doors to the right. With three people."

"If there are just eight known gang members," Derrick said as he stopped and stared down at the plans.

"They have at least a couple new recruits," Pele said.

"I put them at ten to twelve members tonight." Derrick turned to the captain. "Tell the negotiator we need to know how many people Luc has so he can get the right size plane and fuel capacity."

Captain Henderson smiled. "Interesting play."

As the captain contacted the negotiator, Derrick put his finger down on the building with the hostages. "This building is the key."

"It's got the hostages and Luc," Pele said.

"We take these two guys out, and the others have nothing left to bargain with," Paul added.

Quon stepped up to them. "Even with my new device, we can't tell who is who."

"But we can see size and position?" Derrick asked.

"And some extremity movement," Quon said.

"That may be enough."

Chapter 45

"What is the meaning of this?" Mr. Mayeda protested as the police escorted him from his house.

"What should I do?" his son asked as he ran down the steps after them.

"Call my lawyers." Mayeda turned to Carnevalli. "You will regret this intrusion Lieutenant."

"Bring it on old man." Carnevalli shoved him into the back of the patrol car.

Derrick turned to Captain Henderson. "I want two high power rifles with rounds capable of cutting through this steel and hitting their target."

"I can get that. But that is going to be some pretty fancy shooting. Who will be doing the firing?"

Derrick turned to Paul.

Paul nodded.

Derrick turned back to Captain Henderson. "We will."

Paul stepped away as his cell rang. "Hi, Chief." He glanced around as everyone worked. "Yeah." He turned away again. "I think we've got a good field test here."

Derrick, Paul, Pele, and Quon were studying the images on the video monitor.

"Judging by the information from the boy," Quon began. "I would say that these two are his sisters. This one is the biggest, but he seems to be lying down and hasn't moved since we began."

"Must be the injured father," Derrick said.

"And this one sitting next to him must be his wife," Pele added.

"That leaves these two by the opposite wall as our targets," Paul said.

Captain Henderson walked in with two officers behind him. They set two cases down on the table.

Derrick opened the first one. He nodded. It was a modified Heckler & Koch PSG1.

Pele glanced over at him as he reached in and picked it up.

Paul opened the other box and took out the rifle. They both held them up and felt their balance.

"These are..." began Captain Henderson.

"Beautiful," Paul said as he held it up and checked the sighting.

"I'll assume that means they are acceptable?"

"You may," Paul said. He turned to Derrick. "I'll take the one in front? You the one in the back?"

"Feeling a bit rusty are we?"

"The APC is parked just around the corner," Captain Henderson said. "Just outside the alley."

Quon reached into his toolbox and pulled out three small wooden boxes. He handed one to Captain Henderson, one to Paul, and opened one for himself.

"What are these?" The captain asked as he opened the box.

"Special communication sets," Pele said pointing to her ear. "Derrick and I have them so we can talk to each other off the regular channels."

"We might need that ability at this point," Quon said.

"Good thinking," Derrick said. "Captain why don't you go out with the negotiator. Let us know the moment by moment status of the situation. We'll monitor their movement from in here while you get a feel for how things are going from there."

Captain Henderson nodded and left the building to join the hostage negotiator.

"Derrick. Can you hear me?"

"Loud and clear Captain."

"I'm with the negotiator now."

"How is the negotiator doing?" Derrick asked.

"He thinks these guys are scared and unstable. And way in over their heads. They also said they have twenty-five men."

Derrick snorted. "Bull."

"Yeah. But scared, proud, and having something to prove..."

"That makes them dangerous," Paul said.

"Very," the captain added.

Pele turned to him then back at Derrick. "You two have experience with this too?"

"We're versatile," Derrick said as he walked back over to Quon's monitor. "But shooting is a last resort." He stared at the screen. "Luc is our link between the bomb and Mayeda. If we lose him..."

"What about the hostages?" Pele asked.

"I don't think we have a choice," Paul said. "Their deadline is approaching, so it's now or never."

Derrick nodded and walked back to the table. "OK. Here's what we're going to do. If we have to."

The SWAT Commander got six of his men into the APC just around the corner and out of sight from the gang on the street. Captain Henderson positioned two police snipers for clear shots into each of the third-floor windows. Other officers were posted along the walls behind the apartment building and the end of the street. Everyone was instructed to remain quiet and out of sight until Derrick and Paul had completed their parts. If it came to that.

Everyone would wait for Pele's signal to move in.

Carnevalli and Max sat across the table from Mayeda and two of his lawyers.

"You can't hold our client here. This is harassment, and you know it," the gray-haired lawyer on his left said.

Carnevalli sat back. "We aren't charging Mr. Mayeda with anything, sir. We're just asking him a few questions. I'm sure that as a concerned, upstanding citizen he would like to do everything possible to assist us in this situation and save innocent lives."

Mayeda scowled at Carnevalli. "I do not know these people you speak of."

Carnevalli shrugged. "Maybe not personally. But people you know, know them. And one of them said they know you."

"And I knew people that knew people that once met Saddam Hussain. You going to turn me over to Homeland Security for that?" the younger lawyer that appeared fresh out of college demanded as he slammed his hands on the table.

Carnevalli snorted. "I'll check with the NSA and get back to you on that."

The kid lawyer sat back. His eyes wide and his mouth open.

Mr. Mayeda sat there quietly as he and Carnevalli studied each other intently.

All the lights were out in their building now. Technicians had cut small windows into the upper walls looking out onto the street and the building across the street. Derrick and Paul were stretched out on platforms up in the rafters. They each had a pair of glasses with a small monitor screen with a tracking grid that Quon and Xin had rigged up to help them acquire their targets. And, they had a clear view of the buildings across the alley.

Derrick took a slow deep breath as he adjusted his sight on the little monitor. It took a little getting used to, but he and Paul adapted quickly. He knew they would only get one shot at this. If they missed... he didn't let the rest of that thought enter his mind.

"We've got movement in there," Derrick said as he watched his monitor keeping his mark on his target. "What's happening Captain?"

"We've got three minutes to their deadline," Pele announced.

"They say we are stalling and that they are going to kill a hostage," Captain Henderson announced over Quon's system.

"One of them is crossing the room," Derrick said.

"Hold on a second. Let me try to talk to the negotiator."

The images were fuzzy, and you couldn't make out details, But they could see on the monitors that someone had crossed the room. The image they pegged as the wife and mother jumped or was yanked up from her position by the image they identified as the father. The two forms merged but Derrick kept his mark on what was the head of one of the hostage takers. From the police reports, this would have been Luc. Or possibly a newbie. He was betting on Luc.

"It looks like one of the perps just grabbed one of the hostages," Pele said.

"Things don't look good in there Captain," Derrick said. "Talk to us."

"The hostage takers are just yelling right now I think they are losing it..."

"They look agitated," Derrick said calmly.

"My target is starting to pace," Paul added.

"Paul," Derrick said calmly.

"I'm with you Dread."

"Dread. I think it's going south," Captain Henderson said.

The big image on Derrick's glasses separated. One seemed to fall to the ground. Derrick stayed focused on the one standing. "Two... one..."

What could be an arm from the larger image extended out from the image, and pointed to the one now on the floor.

"Now!" Pele yelled into the police radio.

One thunderous shot rang out as Derrick and Paul fired together.

The Armored Personnel Carrier roared around the corner. Police popped up along north and south walls and trained their guns on all of the doors and windows.

Another shot was fired from somewhere by someone. Then all hell broke loose out there.

A couple of officers fell back from their positions.

"We're taking heavy fire from two other buildings!" Captain Henderson yelled through Quon's special system.

"We've got them," Derrick replied. "You ready Paul?"

"One step ahead of you."

Derrick and Paul began firing through the steel walls as Quon aimed his scanner from one building to the next.

The police snipers quickly silenced the lone shooter in the third-story window on their side of the street, and then the other.

The APC ran up to the door of the building where the hostages were located. The SWAT team opened a door and blasted the lock on the door. The commander glanced over at the bodies on the floor. A clean shot through the head of each. "All clear," he called back as his men checked the hostages and the rest of the building. "The two perps are down. The family is safe. We're evacuating them to the APC."

"Copy that," Captain Henderson replied. "Now let's clean up the rest of this mess."

"Lower your weapons. You have nowhere to run to," the negotiator yelled out on his bullhorn trying to get the other gang members to surrender. But his calls were met with gunfire.

Fifteen minutes later, the street was silent.

Carnevalli slipped his phone back into his pocket.

"I demand to know who is supplying you with these slanderous accusations against my client," the older lawyer said as he placed his hands out on the table palms down and stared at Carnevalli.

Carnevalli nodded to the officer standing by the door. "Let them go."

"You have nothing on my client. No one to claim he had any knowledge of this horrific action."

"Not anymore," Carnevalli said as he stared deep into Mayeda's eyes. "They are all dead."

With no expression on his stone cold face, Mayeda stood up and left the room as his lawyers followed.

"I guess we got them all," Xin said as they watched the body bags being removed from the buildings.

"We saved the hostages," Quon said.

"What about our people?" Derrick asked.

"Four officers and Shelby. Nothing serious, fortunately." Captain Henderson added as he stepped up to them. He turned to Derrick "It was an ugly situation with no way out. You did the best you could."

"We won," Xin said softly.

Derrick shook his head slowly. "We got some pawns here, and maybe a knight in Tokyo. But the kings and the bishops got clean away."

Captain Henderson took in a slow deep breath as he watched the cleanup. "That may be true Lieutenant." He turned back to Derrick. "But now some of these kings and bishops have names."

"And we know where they live," Pele added.

Derrick stepped away from everyone and stood silently.

Paul stepped up to Pele and Captain Henderson. "What's wrong with Derrick?" she asked as they watched him standing there alone.

"His worst nightmare," Paul said softly. "With Derrick, shooting is always the option of last resort."

"He didn't have a choice," Pele said. "It was them or those innocent people."

"Command decisions can be tough," Captain Henderson said. He turned to Paul. "And I'm guessing he's had to make his fair share over the years."

"More," Paul said almost in a whisper. "More."

"A tragic waste of young lives," Captain Henderson added.

"I don't think I could have waited that long to fire," Pele said as she watched Derrick.

Paul started to turn away. "He knows when the final second has arrived." He shouldered the Heckler. "And when it's time to take the shot."

Derrick scanned the scene as officers, SWAT team members, forensic teams, and paramedics scurried all over the street. It looked like a war had been fought on this back alley. He took a deep breath as he glanced up at the clear blue sky. The sun peeked over the top of a nearby palm tree. A new day was dawning. Derrick reached up and slapped his forehead. "Oh crap!"

Pele glanced over at him. "Our plane left thirty-five minutes ago."

Other Works:

I hope that you have enjoyed this book. If you have, a ranking or review on Amazon or Goodreads is greatly appreciated.

Thank you for your support,

Julien

You can find a complete list and links to my other works at:
www.julienrapp.com

The Derrick Dreadlow Series:

1. Oahu: The Gathering Place
2. We Can't Choose Our Families
3. When Luck Runs Out
4. The Dobson Affair
5. Murder On The Blue Line
6. Death In The Glow of Kilauea
7. The Night Marchers
8. Whispers From The Dead
9. Blood In The Water
10. The Curse of The Esmerelda
11. Sanctuary

New adventures are in the works.